## "You can't le

Rhett told Dixie.

"I don't want to."

Rhett let his breath out audibly and turned away from her, punching his hands into his pockets. To keep from tearing his hair? he wondered. Or from touching her again...?

Because he wanted to—oh, how he wanted to. It was all he'd been able to think about.

"The children," Dixie said in a constricted voice.

Rhett nodded without turning. "It would be hard on them if you left."

*And on me,* he added to himself. *Especially on me...*

Dear Reader,

What a lineup we have for you this month. As always, we're starting out with a bang with our Heartbreakers title, Linda Turner's *The Loner*. This tale of a burned-out ex-DEA agent and the alluring journalist who is about to uncover *all* his secrets is one you won't want to miss.

Justine Davis's *The Morning Side of Dawn* is a book readers have been asking for ever since hero Dar Cordell made his first appearance. Whether or not you've met Dar before, you'll be moved beyond words by this story of the power of love to change lives. Maura Seger's *Man Without a Memory* is a terrific amnesia book, with a hero who will enter your heart and never leave. Veteran author Marcia Evanick makes her Intimate Moments debut with *By the Light of the Moon*, a novel that proves that though things are not always what they seem, you can never doubt the truth of love. *Man of Steel* is the soul-stirring finale of Kathleen Creighton's Into the Heartland trilogy. I promise, you'll be sorry to say goodbye to the Browns. Finally, welcome new author Christa Conan, whose *All I Need* will be all *you* need to finish off another month of perfect reading.

As always, enjoy!

Yours,

**Leslie Wainger**
Senior Editor and Editorial Coordinator

# KATHLEEN CREIGHTON

## MAN OF STEEL

Published by Silhouette Books
**America's Publisher of Contemporary Romance**

SILHOUETTE BOOKS

ISBN 0-373-07677-0

MAN OF STEEL

**Books by Kathleen Creighton**

Silhouette Intimate Moments

*Demon Lover* #84
*Double Dealings* #157
*Gypsy Dancer* #196
*In Defense of Love* #216
*Rogue's Valley* #240
*Tiger Dawn* #289
*Love and Other Surprises* #322
*Wolf and the Angel* #417
*A Wanted Man* #547
*Eyewitness* #616
*One Good Man* #639
*Man of Steel* #677

*Into the Heartland

Silhouette Desire

*The Heart Mender* #584
*In from the Cold* #654

Silhouette Books

*Silhouette Christmas Stories* 1990
"The Mysterious Gift"

---

## KATHLEEN CREIGHTON

has roots deep in the California soil, but has recently relocated to South Carolina. As a child, she enjoyed listening to old-timers' tales, and her fascination with the past only deepened as she grew older. Today, she says she is interested in everything—art, music, gardening, zoology, anthropology and history, but people are at the top of her list. She also has a lifelong passion for writing, and now combines her two loves in romance novels.

In loving memory of Nancy...

A good many people in the state of Iowa made it possible for me to write this book. They all prefer to remain anonymous, in spite of the fact that I *promised* not to blame any of my mistakes on them. Special mention must be made, however, of the young man in the attorney general's office in Des Moines, who informed me, just in the nick of time, that Iowa doesn't have district attorneys. My heartfelt thanks!

# Prologue

*Somewhere on the outskirts
of Dallas, Texas*

The hotel room was dark, the only light a pale streak seeping through the almost closed bathroom door. Dixie focused on it and forced herself to listen to the voice on the other end of the line. The voice was crusty, but not unkind, as it spoke aloud the words her exhausted brain had been repeating over and over in an endless litany of anguish.

*Peter Grant is dead.*

"And," the voice continued, "I'm afraid that, as far as the *Times* is concerned, so is the story. I'm sorry, Ms...."

"Parish." She had to force the word past a choking band of grief. "Dixie Parish."

"Ms. Parish." The voice softened almost to a sigh. "Peter's death has upset us all. It's a tragic loss, not just to the world of photojournalism, you understand, but a personal one for me as well. If there was anything, even the tiniest shred of evidence to suggest that the fire was anything but a tragic accident, I'd be on it in a minute. But as it is..."

"It wasn't an accident!"

Another sigh drifted down the line. "The police are satisfied it
was, Ms. Parish. Apparently there was a gas leak. The house had
been empty for months, all that time he was down there in Nicaragua. The gas built up... he comes home, walks in, flips a switch
and a tiny little electrical spark sets it off. Whamo." There was a
pause before the gruff coda. "For what it's worth, I don't think he
suffered."

Dixie stood very still with her eyes closed, hugging the receiver
against her cheek and fighting overwhelming waves of pain. Finally, drawing a long, silent breath and using the pressure of it to
control her voice, she asked the question she was almost certain she
already knew the answer to. "His film. All the pictures he took in
Nicaragua. He must have had it with him. Was it—"

"There wasn't a thing left, from what I've been told. What the
explosion didn't destroy the fire took care of. Nobody's more sorry
about that than I am. Because without any hard evidence to back
up your story, this paper is sure as hell not going to print it. Ac-
cuse a U.S. government agency of mass murder? I'd have to be
crazy."

"A *massacre*," Dixie cried, forgetting her vow to be logical and
unemotional, her voice thick with remembered horror. "Of innocent women and children. Old people. *Babies*. I was there, dammit. I saw it. Peter and I—we both *saw* it. Someone has to know,
don't you understand? They can't be allowed to get away with
this!"

"I understand better than you think I do." The voice on the
telephone spoke gently once more. "But without Peter's pictures
there's nothing to give credence to your story. And I just can't—"

"But...what if..." she interrupted, and then her breath caught,
locking the rest in her throat. She darted quick looks into the motel room's shadowy corners like a hunted animal, her skin prickled with a rash of goose bumps. There it was again. The sense—no,
the *certainty*—that someone was nearby, listening. The very air
around her seemed to hum with the intensity of the listener's focus.

"I'll call you back," she whispered urgently into the funnel of
her cupped hand, and dropped the receiver into its cradle as if it
had suddenly grown red-hot.

She stood for a moment, mechanically rubbing her sweat-damp
palm on the front of her slacks. Then slowly, slowly she slipped the
hand into her pocket and closed her fingers around a small metal
cylinder. It was already warm from the heat of her body. She drew

it forth and held it up, stared at it in the dim, gray light, light that robbed it of its familiar yellow orange color. Ironically, it occurred to her, the color of flames.

Her lips drew back, baring her teeth in silent, helpless anguish as she pressed her fist against her newly rounded belly, her body curling instinctively and protectively around the tiny life stirring there. Then she drew one sobbing breath and jammed the roll of film back into her pocket.

She lurched for the door, snatching up her purse and jacket from the foot of the bed on the way. Through the two-inch crack allowed by the security chain she could see that a light rain had begun to fall. It gave the sparsely set streetlights gold-dust halos and ran in multicolored ribbons down the concrete drive in front of the motel marquee. The few vehicles in the parking lot looked lonely and abandoned. No one passed by on the usually busy four-lane highway.

She paused for a moment to steady herself—she knew her shakes and light-headedness were from fear and grief as much as lack of food and sleep—then closed the door, unhooked the chain and opened it again. On the sheltered walkway outside she shrugged her jacket over her shoulders and once more surveyed the parking lot and the street beyond. A panel truck with a telephone company logo on its side was parked in front of the motel across the street, the usual warning cones set out fore and aft. It looked as dark and deserted as the street.

Finally, pulling her jacket collar up around her ears and clutching it tightly under her chin with one hand, she stepped out onto the glistening pavement.

She crossed the parking lot quickly, then the grassy verge that separated it from the street. There were no sidewalks here, so far out on the edge of the city, only a low concrete curb and a gutter that was already beginning to flood and overlap the grassy verge in spots. The street had probably once been a major highway, before the nearby interstate had supplanted it; now the motels and gas stations and fast-food restaurants that lined it like gaudy beads on a string catered mostly to bleary-eyed travelers and the occasional trucker looking for a shower and a bed that didn't vibrate.

Two blocks away on the opposite side of the street Dixie could see the lights of a twenty-four-hour diner, one of a nationwide chain. There was certain to be an indoor pay phone there, she was sure. She jammed her hands into the pockets of her jacket, hunched her shoulders against the chill of the rain and began to walk toward the light.

One or two cars passed her going slowly, causing her pulse to quicken and her scalp to prickle, wetting her with their muddy spray. An eighteen-wheeler plowed toward her on the other side of the street, shifting gears. Somewhere behind her an engine roared suddenly to life. She glanced nervously over her shoulder but saw only the telephone company truck making a slow U-turn across all four traffic lanes. As she watched, it started down the street toward her, its headlights stabbing through the rain, its windshield glistening black, opaque as onyx.

For some reason, as the panel truck accelerated, so did Dixie's heartbeat. She quickened her step, but lost her balance and wobbled a little on the narrow curbing before stepping briefly into the flowing gutter, thoroughly wetting her shoe. Another quick, panicky look back told her the panel truck was still coming, but no longer picking up speed. It came slowly . . . just keeping pace with her.

Keeping pace with *her*.

At that realization, blind, numbing terror seized her. In the very next instant, adrenaline exploded through her body and instinct took charge.

Just ahead she could see where the treacherous grass and curb were broken by the driveway of a fast-food restaurant, closed at that hour. The moment she felt the solid asphalt under her feet she began to run.

As she did, she heard the roar of a powerful engine and half turned, automatically throwing her arms up across her face. It was a futile defense against the headlights that lashed at her from out of the darkness and rain.

That was the last thing she remembered.

# *Chapter 1*

Everett Charleton Brown, attorney at law, junior partner in the old and prestigious firm of Starbuck, Cline and Brown, coughed, cleared his throat and solemnly intoned, "What I am about to tell you may be difficult for you to understand . . ."

Ah, hell. He sounded as if he were making a summation before a jury. And looked like it, too. He drew a deep breath and tried his best to relax his facial muscles.

"Ethan, Lolly, I'm afraid I have some bad news."

The face that gazed back at him from the bathroom mirror grimaced in exasperation. No good. He should probably avoid using negative words like *afraid* and *bad*.

*Objection. Leading, your honor.*

Anger interrupted his rehearsal, welling up inside him like an erupting geyser. Dammit, how was he supposed to explain this lunacy *without* employing negatives?

He gripped the edge of the sink and watched his lips twist and his eyes narrow with a wholly unfamiliar rage—something disconcertingly primitive in nature. It seemed to demand of him some sort of violent physical action, so he brought his closed fist down hard on the marble countertop. *Damn* Elaine, anyway! How could she have done such a heartless, such an idiotic thing? Had she completely lost her mind?

*Easy does it, counselor... get a grip on yourself. Don't let them see you're upset.*

He coughed and tried once more, this time cutting out the negatives. "Children, I have some news."

News? Oh, brother.

*Flash! Dateline—Des Moines: Wife Of Candidate For State Attorney General Runs Off With Director Of Children's Museum!*

His shoulders sagged and he turned from the mirror, his anger tempered now by a creeping despair. What in heaven's name was he supposed to say to them? In a way, he wished he were facing a jury—it would be a lot easier.

*Ladies and gentlemen, what we have here is a clear-cut case of abandonment. Elaine Singleton Brown has herself admitted, ladies and gentlemen, that she deserted her husband and children, but claims she did so because she fell in love. The facts, however...*

The facts. The facts were so preposterous he still couldn't believe them himself, although it had now been two days since he'd arrived home from work to find his house empty and Elaine's letter propped on the mantelpiece. Two days during which the contents of that letter had become permanently etched on his memory without one word of it penetrating to the level of his understanding.

"Dear Rhett," it began, conventionally enough. Typed single-spaced on her expensive personalized vellum stationery, the kind she usually used for polite hand-written notes in response to social invitations.

There is simply no easy way to do this. I have chosen this way in order to avoid an unpleasant scene—call me a coward, I guess.

You may not have noticed, but I haven't exactly been happy for some time now. I didn't know why, I only knew that something important seemed to be missing in my life. But something has happened, something incredible. Suddenly it all makes sense, at least for me.

I didn't plan for this to happen, Rhett—please understand that. The fact is, I've met someone. And... I've fallen in love with him. And the unbelievable part of it is, he feels the same way about me. You've met him, I believe—Dr. Sherrell, the director of the Children's Museum. Robert and I have been working together on this benefit ball—the museum fund-raiser? You know about that, or... then again, perhaps you don't.

In any case, we've decided that we want to—no, must—be together. I know this is sudden. But life is short, Rhett. I deserve to be happy. So do you. Please forgive me.

Sincerely, Elaine

*Sincerely?* Well... that did sound like her, actually.

Rhett made a rude sound of sheer disbelief. That his wife had actually left him was unthinkable enough, but to expect him to believe she'd done so for *love*—no, that he simply couldn't swallow.

And that last part. "Life's too short, I deserve to be happy"? What was that crap? Why shouldn't she be happy, when they were on the brink of achieving everything they'd worked so hard for, everything they'd ever dreamed of?

What could have come over her, to leave everything she'd worked and planned and nagged him for over the years? She'd had it all—the requisite two perfect children, one of each, of course; this house, an elegant English Tudor in the woodsy, old money neighborhood "south of Grand"; financial security and all that went with it; the social status....

Some sort of mental breakdown, he decided. Yes, of course, that must be it. Midlife crisis. Like him, she was about to turn forty, and he seemed to recall reading that forty was a critical age for a woman.

But... fall in love? *Elaine?* Nonsense.

After sixteen years of being married to her, he figured he ought to know.

The crunch of tires on brick drew him to the windows before the bleakness of that thought had time to register fully on his consciousness.

That would be Deirdre, no doubt, bringing Ethan and Lolly home. As Elaine had explained in a hastily hand-written postscript to her letter, she'd arranged for the children to spend the weekend with her older sister. To make things easier, she'd said, "for all concerned."

Yeah, right. Easier for her, that was all she cared about. One thing hadn't changed—Elaine was still the most selfish person he'd ever known.

"I haven't told them anything," the postscript continued, at least as he remembered it. "Do as you think best—you're so much better with words than I am. Please tell them that I love them and that I'll be back for them as soon as I'm settled."

As always when he recalled that line, the seething anger gave way to a cold, hollow feeling in the pit of his stomach. *Over my dead body.*

Now, peering through the wavy, leaded glass windowpane he looked down upon the roof of a pale gray Cadillac, watching as it slowly circled the flower beds and came to a halt beside the brick-paved path that led around the side of the house to the kitchen door. The wheels of the Cadillac had barely stopped turning when three of its doors flew outward simultaneously, reminding him of a broken umbrella popping open lopsidedly at the touch of a button.

His daughter emerged first—erupted, more like, obviously in a temper—and made for the house without a backward glance, her straight blond hair lifting at the sides and fluttering like streamers in the breeze of her own making. When her aunt—elegantly dressed, as always, with hair currently the color of a newly minted penny—climbed out of the driver's seat and called to her, she turned reluctantly and waited, hip-shot and impatient.

His sister-in-law's voice drifted up to Rhett, rendered small and distant by the house's thick walls and double-glass windows. "Lauren—Lauren, dear...don't forget your suitcase—"

Meanwhile, Ethan had popped out of the car like a bird hopping down off a stump, perky and full of himself. Rhett had to smile as his son's voice, too, floated upward. He was singing—chanting, actually—his six-year-old's voice breathy with mischief.

"Lolly-pop, Lolly-pop, oh Lolly-lolly-lolly..."

"Shut *up*, Ethan!"

"Lolly-pop, lolly-pop..."

"*Stop it!*"

Deirdre had the trunk open and was pulling out an assortment of overnighters and backpacks and setting them on the brick driveway. Ethan was making his way to the back of the car in a series of hops and skips, the peculiar rhythm of which suggested to Rhett, even though he could no longer hear it, that his son was still singing the forbidden ditty just under his breath.

It was a supposition proven right a moment later when Lolly, going to collect her own suitcase, socked her brother smartly in the arm.

"Ow!" yelled Ethan, loudly enough to make sure somebody in authority heard it. "Quit hitting me!"

"Quit singing that stupid song, then. I'm *sick* of it!"

"Children—Lauren, *please*—"

"It's not either stupid! Uncle Bobo said it used to be on the radio."

"So? It's still stupid. And if you don't quit singing it I'm going to punch your stupid *face* in!"

Deirdre had closed the trunk and now stood gazing up at the house, one hand planted above her eyes like a sun visor. Rhett could see her lips moving, in the manner of one importuning a saint. Since just about the last thing he felt like doing right then was dealing with a member of his wife's family, he stepped back away from the windows and didn't respond. A few moments later he heard a car door slam, the roar of a powerful but well-muffled engine, and then the diminishing crunch of tires.

Downstairs a door opened and closed with studied care; even quarreling, Ethan and Lolly knew better than to slam, in case their mother happened to be suffering one of her ubiquitous headaches.

The future Attorney General of the State of Iowa closed his eyes, counting pulse beats in his hollow stomach. Then he took a deep, fortifying breath and went to intercept his offspring.

He found them in the kitchen, in the process of unloading their gear onto the immaculate black surface of the kitchen counter—somewhat less immaculate than usual, he noticed with a belated sense of guilt; apparently he'd forgotten to wipe up after the sandwich he'd made himself for lunch. Forbidden crumbs dotted the polished granite, along with a few shreds of wilted lettuce and a small, irregular puddle of tomato juice.

"Hi, Dad."

"Hi, Dad."

His children greeted him with breathless innocence, the blandness of their facial expressions belied by telltale patches of color in Lolly's cheeks and a wicked sparkle in Ethan's chocolate brown eyes.

"Hi," said Rhett. Suddenly he didn't know quite what to do with his hands. After a moment he tucked them in his pockets. "Have a good time at your Aunt Dee's?"

Lolly shrugged. "It was okay."

"We had a great time," said Ethan. "We went to Adventureland. I got to ride on a roller coaster. Not the Tornado, though. I'm still too little."

"He had to sit on a bench with Bobo," Lolly said scornfully. "Aunt Dee and I went. It was great."

"I get to go *next* year," cried Ethan, stung.

Rhett frowned. "Who the devil is Bobo?"

"Aunt Dee's new boyfriend. He calls Lolly 'Lolly-pop,' and he taught me this neat song—"

Lolly rolled her eyes. "His name is *Beau,* stupid. He's Aunt Dee's new *beau.* He's her new beau, Beau—get it? *Bobo?*" She made a sound replete with derision. "He only told us that about a hundred times."

"Oh, brother," said Rhett.

"*Really,* Lolly agreed, in that dry way she'd adopted lately that made her sound so grown-up.

Hearing it, Rhett's stomach performed an unexpected twist-and-drop maneuver that he recognized instantly as dread. Lauren, his daughter...nine years old already. How had she gotten so *tall,* all of a sudden? Overnight, it seemed, she'd lost that baby roundness, even the scruffy, snaggly-toothed little girl look. The gaps in her smile were all filled in; in another couple of years there'd be braces. Oh, sure, right now she was still slender as a stick, all arms and long, gangly legs, but sometime soon there would be bras to worry about, and...boys.

Adolescent girls needed their mothers.

*Over my dead body.*

"Where's Mom?" asked Ethan, right on cue, hopping on one foot across the black-and-white floor tiles in the manner of someone playing a game of hopscotch.

"Uh...your mother isn't here," mumbled Rhett, hedging. He thought, *I'm a craven coward.* "Actually, that's—"

"Where is she? It's dinnertime. I'm hungry."

"Hungry?" Rhett frowned. "Didn't your Aunt Dee feed you?"

"Lunch. But that was a long time ago. I'm hungry again *now*."

*Hungry.* Children needed food.

Don't panic, Rhett told himself sternly. You can handle this. It's not as though you've never cooked before.

Yeah, but probably not since college. And never for two growing children. Plus, Elaine was so particular about what they ate—the whole family, for that matter. In order to keep herself in single-digit sizes, his wife had run a strict low-fat, high-fiber kitchen. He had to hand it to her, though. How she'd managed to produce edible meals without the use of sugar, salt or red meat he didn't know, and it wasn't a feat he'd even try to duplicate.

What in the hell was he going to do?

He pulled one hand from a pocket and raked it through his hair, thinking frantically. *Turkey.* He was pretty sure he hadn't eaten the last of it. "I'll make us some sandwiches," he offered with a certain sense of relief. *So far, so good.* "You go on upstairs and unpack your things, and I'll bring you a tray."

And first thing tomorrow morning he was calling the employment agency.

"Where is Mom? Is she at a meeting?" Lolly wanted to know.

Rhett threw her a quick, desperate look. "No—no, she's not at a meeting. She's...look, I'll explain in a minute, okay? Right now..."

"When is she coming home?" Lolly's features had acquired an unchildlike stillness; her slate-colored eyes seemed wary.

*Damn,* thought Rhett. His daughter always had been an uncommonly intuitive child.

Once more he drove his fingers into his hair, something he only did in moments of extreme agitation. His head was whirling, his stomach in knots. He was losing control of the situation; he could feel it. Time to call a recess, get himself in hand.

Drawing a long breath, he made himself dole out words in evenly measured tones. "I said I'd explain later. Right now I want you to take your things upstairs. Okay? I'm going to fix you something to eat. Go on—I'll bring it up."

"Is Mom sick?" Ethan was sliding along the far side of the cooking island, doing his best impression of a cruising crocodile, his round dark eyes just showing over the edge of the countertop.

"What? No! What gave you that idea? No, she's not sick."

Ethan's eyes grew larger as his voice got smaller. "Then why isn't she here?"

"Look, she's just…" Damn. This wasn't going at all the way he'd planned. In another minute, at the rate he was going, he'd have the whole room in hysterics.

Realizing he was about to wreak more havoc on his already ruined hair, Rhett jammed his hand back in his pocket and once more forced himself to speak slowly and deliberately. "I told you we'd talk about it *later.* I don't want any more arguments, okay? Take your things upstairs *now.*"

"Come on, Ethan." Lolly abruptly hooked an arm through the straps of her backpack and dragged it off the countertop. "Let's go, okay?"

"But I want—"

"Let's go, pea-brain—*now.*"

Spoken like her mother's true daughter, Rhett thought wryly. He had to admire the kid's leadership ability, if not her vocabulary. He'd gladly forgive her that small lapse, though, for giving him the time—just the few moments—he needed to pull himself together.

Lolly rolled her eyes heavenward as she waited for Ethan to climb the stairs ahead of her. She was asking for patience; her brother was moving like a stupid snail, hanging onto the banister and dragging his feet, hauling himself up one step at a time, like he weighed forty thousand pounds, or something.

Ordinarily, she'd probably have yelled at him and said something like, "Get out of my way, pea-brain."

But this time she didn't. The big baby already looked like he was going to start crying any minute, and she wasn't quite sure what she'd do if that happened. She had a strange sort of feeling herself, like the cold, hollow feeling she got sometimes when she was wa-a-ay up high and forgot not to look down.

At the top of the stairs she grabbed Ethan by the arm and dragged him with her along the landing and into her bedroom, which, since normally she'd punch him if he even *thought* about setting a foot in her room, surprised him so much he forgot about crying.

"What—" he started to say.

Lolly hissed for silence, then closed the door and paused for a moment with her hand on the knob, listening. Satisfied, she threw her suitcase and backpack onto her bed and herself onto the window seat, leaving Ethan standing all by himself in the middle of the rug.

"Lolly..."

"Shut up—I need to think."

Ethan came over and dropped to his knees beside the window seat and propped his elbows on it. "Think about what?"

"Mom and Dad, of course. You know what? I bet anything they're getting a divorce. That's why Mom's not here and Dad's acting so weird."

"What's a... a 'vorce?"

Lolly pulled her knees up and wrapped her arms around them. "That's when your mom and dad split up, dummy. Like... you know, they don't live together anymore." Lolly knew all about divorces.

But she had the cold feeling in her stomach again, so she tossed her hair back and acted like she didn't really care. "It's no big deal—my friend Jennifer's parents got a divorce. So did my friend Megan's. Only I think it was their dad that left. Anyhow, Jennifer's mom cried a lot...." She had to stop and swallow hard. Ethan was staring at her, so she looked out the window for a minute.

Ethan said, "You mean, Mommy's not going to live with us anymore?" He sounded scared, which was the way Lolly felt, only she wasn't about to let him know that. She'd never let anybody know she was scared—*never*.

She shrugged. "Who knows? Maybe. I bet that's what Dad wants to talk to us about. You just wait and see. I'll bet you."

"How... how do you know?"

"I just do, that's all." Now she understood all those looks she'd seen passing back and forth between Aunt Dee and dumb old Bobo, and the way they'd stop talking all of a sudden whenever she and Ethan came into the room. She *hated* when grown-ups did that. What did they think she was, *stupid?*

"But... who'll take care of us?"

"Dad'll probably hire somebody. Who cares? Anyway, I don't need anybody to take care of me. I can take care of myself." She stared steadfastly out the window, already seeing herself as elegant hostess, with her hair done up in a French twist, just like Mom's, serving dainty sandwiches with the crusts cut off to her father's guests while they all exclaimed about how remarkable she was.

*Can you believe it? Only nine years old, and I understand she
runs this big house all by herself—and cooks, too. Why, I hear
she even made that gorgeous cocktail dress she's wearing...*

She began to feel quite superior and noble.

Ethan was starting to look as if he might cry any minute,
though, so she tossed her head in an offhand way and said,
"Actually, it's kind of cool for the kids. Usually their parents
start being really, really nice to them. And they buy them stuff."

That did the trick. Ethan's eyes got big and round. "What
kind of stuff?"

Lolly shrugged. "Anything you want. Megan's dad bought
her brother a go-cart. And Megan got a new Nintendo, and she
didn't even ask for it."

"Why did they do that? Was it their birthday?"

"No, stupid, just because." Lolly frowned impatiently; she
was getting an idea, the best idea she'd ever had, and she
needed time to let it take shape in her head.

Hitching herself off the window seat, she crossed to the door
and listened for a moment with her ear against the panels. Then
she tossed her hair back and explained with a shrug, "I guess
because they don't want the kids to feel bad. Look—it's happening already. I bet anything that's why Mom let us spend the
weekend at Aunt Dee's. And we got to go to Adventureland,
didn't we? And we get to have supper on a tray. We usually only
get to have supper on a tray when we're sick." She elbowed
Ethan out of the way and scrambled back onto the window
seat, thinking hard.

Ethan laid his head down on his arms and made a kind of
sniffling noise. "Does that mean we aren't going to see Mom
ever ever again?"

Lolly threw him a withering look. "'Course not, dummy. It's
not like she *died* or something. She'll probably come and get us
and take us away to live with her."

Ethan's head popped up like a jack-in-the-box. "But I don't
want to leave here."

"I don't want to leave here either, but we'll probably have to
anyway. Kids don't get to say where they want to live. The parents decide. And sometimes they fight over it, and then...I
think they have to go to court, or something."

Ethan lowered his forehead onto his arms. His voice sounded
muffled. "I want to stay here. And I want my mommy to stay
here, too."

"Well," said Lolly, shrugging again, "maybe she will. Maybe Dad will wind up leaving, who knows?"

"I want Dad to live here, too. I want us all to live here, just like we do now."

"Yeah, well we can't," Lolly said in a hard voice. "Not if Mom and Dad get a divorce. That's what divorce *means*. Anyway, we'll probably wind up living part of the time with Mom and part of the time with Dad. That's what my friend Jennifer does. She lives most of the time with her mom and stays with her dad summers, and Christmas, and stuff. *That's* when they start being really nice to you and giving you presents."

"I don't want any presents," said Ethan, sniffling again.

"Well, I do," said Lolly. "I already know what I'm going to ask Dad for, too. If they *are* getting a divorce. I'm going to ask him if I can get a horse."

"A *horse?*" Ethan's eyes got big again.

"Yeah—shh—be quiet. I think I hear Dad. Ethan, I'm warning you, if you say one word about this, I'll punch your lights out."

But Ethan's voice was a whisper. "You mean, a real one? Like Rose Ellen's?"

"No, stupid, not like Rose Ellen's. Rose Ellen's horse is old and fat. You saw the pictures Aunt Lucy sent us. I want . . . a black one, with a flowing mane and tail. A racehorse—like the Black Stallion."

There was a light knock on the door. Ethan jumped up and ran to open it, but Lolly stayed where she was, savoring the daydream. She was imagining herself riding like the wind on the back of her beautiful black horse, with the horse's silky mane whipping her face, its tail and her own blond hair streaming out behind them. . . .

It would come to no one else but her, but would let her feed it treats from her hand, and stand absolutely still while she mounted, and she'd ride bareback without holding on, just like the boy in the movie.

She'd ride and ride and ride . . . because that way she could forget about the awful, sick feeling in her stomach.

Rhett's sister's voice rippled across the telephone wires on a ribbon of laughter. "You want me to find you a *what?*"

He mopped moisture from his face with one end of the towel that was looped around his neck. "You heard me, Lucy. A horse. If possible, a black one. Not too big, gentle enough for kids to ride. Oh—and not too expensive. I'm not talking Thoroughbred, here, okay? Just a nice, gentle . . . horse."

There was a suspicious pause and then: "Rhett, what are you doing?" When Lucy didn't get an answer to that question she demanded, "What in heaven's name are you going to do with a horse? You live in downtown Des Moines!"

"Yeah, in a house with a backyard that happens to butt up against acres and acres of wooded parkland, which you'd know if you'd ever been to visit. There are bridle paths all through the park and a boarding stable nearby, for your additional information. Do you think I'd consider getting a horse if I hadn't considered where I'd put it?" He closed his eyes, fought down habitual irritation and said dryly, "I haven't lost my mind yet, Lucy."

"Well, small wonder if you had, after what that woman did," his sister snapped with typical absence of either logic or tact, before she, too, moderated her tone with unaccustomed concern. "How *are* you doing, Rhett?"

"I'm doing okay."

"You sound out of breath."

"I've been out jogging. Just got back."

"In this heat? What are you trying to do, kill yourself? You're not getting any younger, you know. Oh boy—it's the Big Four-O for you this year, isn't it? In December. I almost forgot."

Rhett grimaced and rubbed a hand across his stomach, the muscles of which he'd unconsciously tightened. He knew deep down that he needn't have; his waist was as lean and his belly as firm and flat as it had ever been—maybe more so, thanks to his wife's insistence that he share her fat-free diet and regular exercise. He knew he had no reason to be ashamed of his body. And he intended to keep it that way.

"Helps to keep to the old routine as much as possible," he said mildly.

"Yeah, I guess." And then she added, with that same unspoken sympathy, "How are the kids?"

He pushed his fingers against his forehead, rubbing at the ridges of his frown. He wasn't quite sure he knew how to take this new, albeit kinder and gentler Lucy.

"They're okay, I guess. Ethan seems to be taking it the hardest, which is only natural, since he's so young. And Lauren...well, she thinks it's all up to her, now. She tries to mother him, bosses him around, which he doesn't take very well. He, uh...seems to have regressed a little bit, but the doctor tells me that's pretty normal, under these circumstances. I'm sure things will be better once everything's settled. He's always a lot worse after he talks to his mother on the phone. Right now I'm just trying to keep things as normal as possible for them, but it isn't easy."

"Hey, big brother, don't try to be Superman. Even we women find it a *little* challenging to manage a career, a house and a couple of kids all alone."

"I'm not, believe me," said Rhett, even smiling a little in wry appreciation of the sarcasm. The past few weeks had been a somewhat humbling experience for him. "I've been trying to find a good live-in, actually." So far without much success. For some reason, none of the people the agency had sent over had lasted more than a few days.

Lucy snorted, but didn't elaborate.

Before he could ask her what *that* meant, Rhett found himself momentarily distracted by sounds of a disturbance coming from somewhere in the front part of the house. He frowned. "I, uh...have high hopes for this latest one, though. Doesn't speak much English, but she seems like a nice girl. Name's Marta—I think she's from Romania. I figure she's probably had it rough enough, she can put up with—oh, Lord, *now* what?"

"Rhett?"

"Yeah. I'm here. I just thought—seems to be all okay now, though. Go ahead."

"I was just wondering, you said Elaine's talked to the kids. Have *you* heard from her?"

"Oh, sure." He paused to clear his throat, then laughed carefully. "Actually, I just got the papers a couple of days ago. She's done it—she's actually filed for divorce."

He heard the rush of an exhalation, and then an almost belligerent, "I'm sorry Rhett. But...well, I can't help but feel it's for the best."

"Yeah, well, I know you've never exactly been fond of Elaine."

"To put it mildly."

Rhett winced as the kitchen door slammed, vibrating the windows in his study. "Look, Lucy, if you don't mind, I really don't want to get into this right now."

"I'm sorry," Lucy murmured, sounding genuinely contrite. "Is it going to be messy?"

"Messy? No...no, I don't think so." Again, ominous noises from elsewhere in the house were tugging at his attention. Slamming doors, running footsteps, agitated voices. What in the world was going on out there?

He covered the mouthpiece with his hand and yelled, "Marta? Lolly?" Receiving no answer from either party, he spoke once more into the phone. "I'm probably going to have to buy out Elaine's half of the house. Which won't be easy, but I can swing that. She's not asking for alimony—apparently she plans on marrying this guy, Sheffield, or whatever, right away. Of course she wants the kids, but she hasn't a snowball's chance in hell of getting them. Listen, Luce—"

"Oh God, Rhett, I hope not. Are you *sure?*"

"Absolutely. Listen, I'm going to have to go, okay? Tell you more later. All hell seems to be breaking loose here."

"Oh—oh, sure. Is everything—"

"Talk to you later—oh! Almost forgot. About that horse thing. Do what you can, okay? I'd really appreciate it. Say hi to Gwen and everybody for me. Gotta go—*bye!*"

He slammed down the receiver just as Marta, his latest nanny, hurtled through the door of his study like a woman escaping by the skin of her teeth from a pack of wild dogs. Her face was flushed and damp with what might have been either sweat or tears, and she had, unmistakably, a suitcase in her hand.

Rhett groaned and lowered his forehead into his hands.

# Chapter 2

Lucinda Rosewood Brown Lanagan sat with one hand resting on the telephone, gazing out the windows and tapping a forefinger against thoughtfully pursed lips.

She was upstairs in the big front bedroom she shared with her husband Mike, who was currently off in Chicago working on the series of crusading columns that would appear three times a week in the *Chicagoan*, and, by way of syndication, in a couple of hundred other major newspapers nationwide.

The windows looked down on the front lawn, on the gravel drive that curved around the house to the left, on the tiny gingerbread cottage that had replaced the original bunkhouse after it had been flattened by half of the huge oak tree that had once stood in the front yard. And on the evergreen windbreak and Gwen's chicken yard, and beyond that the maze of hog shelters and livestock yards that ran down the gentle slope to the big, old-fashioned barn. From one of those yards, down near the barn, she watched a cloud of dust rise and swirl as it caught the brisk prairie wind.

"Yes," she murmured to herself, smiling.

Moving briskly herself now, Lucy went to poke her head through the door of the bedroom just across the hall. Her son Eric was still napping, sprawled on his back with his knees out in that complete and utter abandon only very, very young children enjoy. Wisps of dark hair curled damply on his forehead; his cheeks were flushed, that perfect, velvety rose pink.

Lucy caught her lower lip between her teeth and backed hurriedly out of her son's room before she let go of the breath she'd been holding. It bumped unevenly over the shoals of unexpected emotions, and she laughed softly in acknowledgment and acceptance of them. *Who'd have thought it? Who'd have guessed motherhood would betray me for such a softie?*

Well, Mike, of course; he'd probably known all along.

She was still smiling as she skipped down the stairs, calling to Gwen that she was going down to the barn for a bit and to please keep an ear out for Eric.

On the back porch steps she paused to drive her fingers into the sides of her straight, chin-length brown hair, and lifted them as an offering to the wind. The wind took them gladly and skirled on across the fields, across the endless waves of undulating green, turning up the silvery undersides of the soybean leaves and stirring the ripening corn tassels so that they shimmered like sunlight sparkling on the sea. Lucy closed her eyes and inhaled deeply, filling her lungs with the sweet, warm smell of August.

*How lucky I am,* she thought, by no means for the first time. *How could I possibly be any happier than I am right now?*

The answer came to her on the wind, along with the smell of dust and manure and the clatter of hoofbeats from down by the barn: *If all the people I love most could just be as happy as I am....*

Soon, she promised herself as she slipped her hands into the back pockets of her overalls and started down the hill. It was already happening to Earl, thanks to his new wife, Chris—and maybe Providence. With the help of her skillful therapy, his broken legs had healed so that he walked with only a slight limp now. And Earl had confided to Lucy that it was Chris's suggestion that had made him decide to go after his teaching credential. Earl—a *teacher.* Who'd a'thought it? And a daddy, too! Because, thanks to Earl's patience and love, Chris was also healing, and now beautifully, glowingly pregnant.

And now, it seemed, there might even be hope for Rhett.

Sometimes, Lucy thought, Providence just needs a little nudge.

She found Rosie perched on the top rail of the stockyard fence. She gave her daughter's small, dusty bottom a gentle swat by way of a greeting and climbed up beside her. "Hi, babe, how's it going?"

"Mommy!" Rosie spun, giggling, to give her a hug, then instantly scrunched up her shoulders and laid a chiding finger across her own lips. "Shh—be quiet. Rocky's getting a saddle on right now, see? Watch...."

Lucy murmured, "Oh, boy, already?" then joined her daughter in awed silence as they watched the battle of wills that was being waged out in the middle of the dusty corral.

A yearling colt, a sleek dapple gray, almost black on his muzzle and legs, stood wild-eyed and trembling as he pulled back hard against the tug of the rope tied to a metal ring in his halter. With a good firm hold on the other end of the rope and appearing relaxed and completely in control of the situation was the trainer—tall and lanky, slim-hipped as a rodeo bronc rider, with long legs made even longer by high-heeled cowboy boots, and a sweat-stained Stetson firmly seated and tilted slightly downward in front.

Lucy watched with tensely held breath as the trainer moved closer to the colt, murmuring soothing nothings in a calm, musical voice with unmistakable touches of Texas in it. "Easy, big boy...easy now. Tha-at's my boy, good ol' Rocky...."

As far as Lucy could see, Rocky didn't appear to be buying a word of it. His eyes were rolled back, fastened on the huge, ungainly object that was balanced against the trainer's hip.

"O...kay, Rocky, you be good now—" Suddenly, with one heave and only the smallest grunt of effort, the trainer swung the saddle up and plunked it neatly atop the heavy blanket that was already settled across the colt's withers.

Rocky's hindquarters buckled slightly; he sidestepped, then stood rock still, apparently bewildered by the unaccustomed weight on his back. Still murmuring assurances, the trainer stepped up beside him and began to stroke his neck and withers, reaching under the blanket to run a gentling hand across his side.

Little by little the colt's trembling subsided. He switched his tail and stepped nervously first one way and then the other, trying to escape the infernal thing clinging to his back. Again the trainer soothed and gentled him. The colt tossed his head,

then turned and butted the trainer's hip, but more in play than
reproach.

The trainer chuckled, a husky, infectious sound, pulled some
pieces of carrot from a hip pocket and offered them to the colt,
then turned to the audience on the fence and grinned.

"You make it look so easy," Lucy called with a wry shake of
her head, while Rosie clapped her hands and yelled "Ya-ay!
Way to go, Rocky!"

"Aw, Rocky's just a big ol' sweetheart," the trainer drawled,
sweeping off the Stetson to mop away sweat with a forearm. A
braid as thick and long as that same forearm tumbled down and
bumped against a tanned and freckled shoulder. A braid so
dark—as was the profusion of curls that had escaped from it—
that it looked almost black, except at times like this when the
sun betrayed its deep auburn secrets.

The trainer flipped the braid impatiently back over her
shoulder and started leading the colt—who was now too busy
munching carrots to worry much about the saddle on his
back—toward the fence. She was smiling her usual wide, ready
smile, Lucy noted with satisfaction, the kind that crinkled up
the corners of her eyes. She had very black eyebrows and lashes
and the bluest eyes Lucy had ever seen, chips stolen from the
august sky, all the more startling for being so darkly fringed.
Irish eyes, Mike called them. Eyes, he'd said, that looked as if
they'd been put in place by an artisan with soot on his fingers.

What the heck—Mike was a writer, after all.

As Lucy watched the horse trainer walk toward her, she felt
more and more pleased with her idea. The woman's step was
long, lithe and unpretentious. Her breasts, revealed—but not
blatantly—by the loose-fitting yellow tank top she wore, were
small and neat. Yes, thought Lucy with a sigh of satisfaction,
she's perfect. The exact opposite of Elaine in every way...

Except for being so tall, she silently amended as she jumped
down from the fence and went to meet the woman she'd hired
to train the colt born the preceding summer to her daughter's
mare, Belle. But for some reason this particular woman's height
had never bothered her. Maybe because, unlike Elaine, she
never used it as a vantage point for looking down her nose at
people.

"Dixie," she said innocently, tilting her gaze upward and
catching back a secret smile. "Are you doing anything impor-

tant the next few days? Because I have a big, big favor to ask of you..."

Dixie Parish ducked her head to peer through the bug-spattered windows of her Chevy pickup at the crenellated towers of what appeared to be a smallish medieval castle.

"I don't know, Toto," she murmured, half to herself and half to the unseen passenger in the dusty beige horse trailer rumbling along behind her. "This doesn't look a whole lot like Kansas to me. Or Texas, either."

It looked like what she remembered of Beverly Hills, actually. Or that movie star's house—what was her name?—on the Hudson River in upstate New York.

The castle slid past and disappeared from view behind a screen of towering oaks and shrubbery, to be supplanted by an elegant redbrick colonial with white columns two stories high.

"Holy cow...." Dixie uttered a low whistle, unabashedly gawking. She was thinking that it was some neighborhood Lucy's brother lived in, just about as far from the corn and livestock country he'd come from as Oz was from good old Aunty Em's. She wondered if maybe it was at least part of the explanation for why Lucy and this particular brother—Rhett, she'd called him—didn't seem to have much to do with one another. If life-styles were any indication, the two must be as different as night and day.

She glanced in the rearview mirror. "Almost there, darlin'," she promised her passenger, hoping it was true. This sure didn't look much like horse country to her. Closest thing to agriculture she could see were the gardeners putt-putting around among the trees on little riding mowers. The air was full of the genteel whirr of their motors and the soft shushing of sprinklers and smelled of flowers and just-cut grass. Dixie had to smile to herself, thinking about what one of those gardeners would do if he came upon a pile of fresh horse manure in the middle of one of those manicured green lawns.

Thinking about that, she broke into a cackle of laughter, because it was actually a pretty good analogy for her own presence in the neighborhood, which she hoped wasn't violating some kind of vehicle or noise ordinance. Except for hers, every car she'd seen so far seemed to be either a Volvo, BMW or some shiny new variety of four-by-four. Even the gardeners' pickup trucks were shiny. Dixie's sky blue Chevy wasn't shiny even when it was clean, and right now it was road-grimy and sporting a few dents, not to mention a pretty good scrape on one fender where she'd misjudged a corral gatepost.

Ah, well, she wasn't going to apologize for it, or for her trailer, either. Both had seen many and many a mile, a large proportion of them on hard Texas corduroy. And as far as she was concerned, they were good for a few more yet.

She braked gently, slowing to walking speed while she studied numbers on mailboxes and gateposts. At last she muttered, "Ah...here we are," and nosed the Chevy into a driveway paved with red brick. Once more she couldn't help but grin as the trailer rumbled and rattled over the uneven surface. At least, she thought, they'd hear her coming.

The house was brick, too, an English Tudor, charmingly asymmetrical with leaded windows and narrow chimney pots showing above a steeply pitched roof. There were flowers, lots of them—red geraniums around the entry, zinnias and marigolds in the sunny places, impatiens and primroses brightening up the shade beneath towering old trees just showing touches of fall color.

Nice and homey, Dixie thought to herself, obscurely pleased; maybe Lucy and this brother would turn out to be not so different after all.

She followed the half-circle drive past the front door of the house and parked in the shade of an oak whose leaves were beginning to turn rusty around the edges. She sat for a moment before she set the emergency brake and turned off the motor, expecting the doors of the house to burst open and children to come running the way they usually did, excited and eager to get a look at their new horse.

"Lordy, darlin', I sure do hope somebody's home," she said to the rearview mirror when the peace and quiet remained undisturbed, then altered her focus in the mirror slightly and breathed, "Oh, brother!" in dismay and exasperation. Her hair was a mess; she'd been driving with both windows wide open, due to the fact that the Chevy's air-conditioning system had long ago given up the ghost.

There wasn't much she could do about it, though—and to be truthful, the wind wasn't all to blame. Her hair did pretty much as it pleased, which was why she usually wore a hat of some kind. Now, though, in deference to the neighborhood, she snatched up a bandanna handkerchief from the seat beside her, tied it around her head and knotted it under her braid. Then she opened the door and swung her legs out from under the steering wheel. Even after ten years they still tended to stiffen up during long trips—or a hard ride—so she indulged in a few quick stretches before going to check on her passenger.

"Yeah...we'll have you out of there pretty soon," she crooned in response to the horse's impatient whicker, reaching through the front window of the trailer to give his forelock a scratch. "Hang in there, sweetheart."

Summer was taking its sweet time about making its exit this year, it seemed. It was past mid-September, but even in the shade the late-afternoon heat was fierce; in the sun it was like a deadweight bearing down on her shoulders. Walking the short distance back up the drive to the front door had her sweating like a...well, like a horse. A fine impression she was going to make on Lucy's big brother, Dixie thought.

But, as with her Chevy and trailer, the thought amused rather than concerned her; people either took her as she was or they didn't, that was up to them, and she didn't waste time worrying about something she couldn't control.

As she raised her hand to the doorbell she heard voices coming from somewhere inside the house, a man's voice and a child's. Not a happy child, by the sound of it, but at least, thank God, somebody was home. She pushed the button and listened to the music of chimes echoing through the house.

After a short wait the door opened. Her heart gave a queer little bump, half recognition and half surprise. Rhett Brown sure didn't look much like his picture.

"Yes, can I help you?" He frowned at her from the doorway, blocking it with his body.

The frown she recognized; it was the body that took her by surprise. The photo she'd seen on Lucy's mantelpiece had been a wedding portrait, with the bride virginally smiling, the groom gazing earnestly into the camera...younger, of course, but with his brow furrowed just this way. Encased in his tuxedo jacket and starched white shirt, he'd looked appropriately full of himself, considering the occasion, but a bit wooden and stiff, too, like a department store mannequin or a model for *GQ*.

Right now he was wearing a lawyer's gray pinstriped suit and a white shirt, but it didn't look a bit starched. The top button was undone, his hair was mussed and falling across his forehead, and his tie was loosened and slightly askew. She hadn't been prepared for someone quite so... *vital.*

"Mr. Brown—hi, I'm Dixie." She smiled and stuck out her hand. The frown only deepened. She took a breath. "Dixie Parish? Oh boy, I hope Lucy called. She was supposed to tell you I was coming."

"Lucy." His eyes were still narrowed slightly in confusion, but he took her hand anyway. "I don't..."

He had a nice handshake, she observed, firm and warm and all-enveloping; it was going to be a great asset to him if, as Lucy'd told her, he was bent on a career in politics.

"I have your horse," she said kindly, taking pity on him.

"My—oh, Lord. Yes—I'm sorry." He let go of her hand and used his to make a swipe at his hair, which, judging from the state of it, was something he'd done quite a few times already. "Lucy did call. But she didn't... uh, I wasn't..." He glanced past her, located her truck and the horse trailer in the driveway and let out a gusty breath. "Come in, please. Just let me..."

"No, that's okay. If you'll just tell me where you want me to put him, I'd rather get him unloaded as soon as possible, if you don't mind. It's been a long trip in this heat, and I don't like leaving him out there in that trailer any longer than I have to."

"Oh—sure. Right." He threw a quick, distracted look over his shoulder. Somewhere in the distance the unhappy voice Dixie had heard before was yelling, "I can't help it, so *stop crying.* Da-ad! If we don't go *right now* there's not going to be enough *time* to make anything...."

Beyond Rhett's shoulder Dixie could see a child—a girl about ten years old, reed-slender, with straight blond hair blunt cut just above the shoulders—come lurching around a corner into the entry hall. She checked abruptly when she saw that her father wasn't alone, threw Dixie a hostile look and then advanced with more decorum, speaking in a singsong voice through clenched teeth the way kids do when they importune a parent in company.

"Dad, we have to go to the store *now.* And Ethan's crying about his stupid costume again. He says he's not even going to go. Can't you come and *do* something?"

Her father muttered something under his breath, then exhaled sharply and said, "Yeah, I will. In a minute, Lauren, this is, uh, Dixie. She's brought you something." His frown relaxed and his voice softened, and Dixie, watching, felt something inside her own chest give an odd little bump. "Maybe you'd like to go say hello to your new horse."

It was as if someone had turned a powerful flood lamp full on the child's face. She sucked in air and for an instant went white and still . . . and then her face began to glow and her eyes to shine, and Dixie realized suddenly that when she wasn't in a temper, the girl was extraordinarily beautiful.

Her voice lost its nagging edge and became the breathless whisper of an excited child. "My horse? He's *here?* Where? Can I see him? Oh, *boy*. . ."

Dixie managed to get out of the way just in time. Her father managed a rueful smile. "Sorry about that. She's been taught better manners."

Dixie shrugged and said easily, "She's just excited. Don't worry about it." She watched the girl run headlong down the driveway, her steps slowing almost as if in apprehension as she approached the rear of the horse trailer. A few feet short of it she stopped dead, then whirled, a pirouette as graceful as any ballerina's.

"You got a black one! Just like I asked for!"

Dixie nodded and waved, then chuckled to herself as Lauren scampered around to the front of the trailer and disappeared from sight. When she looked back at the child's father she found him watching her with an odd, quizzical expression on his face.

"Ah . . . hmm," he said with a small start, and what seemed rather endearingly like embarrassment. He made that distracted gesture with his hand again but caught himself before he could do more damage to his hair and instead waved it vaguely toward the back of the house. "Do you mind if I . . . ? I just need to take care of . . . something. Be right with you—just take a minute."

"Oh, no problem. Go right ahead." Dixie smiled and leaned a shoulder against the doorframe. "Looks like you've kind of got your hands full. Sorry if I've come at a bad time."

"What?" He'd taken a step or two away from her, but now he paused and turned back, frowning again. "No—no, I was expecting you, that's not—well, not *you*, exactly." He smiled suddenly, altering his rather austere features in a way that was almost magical, and once again Dixie felt that queer little bump in her chest. She put it down to surprise. "My sister—Lucy didn't tell me *who* was bringing the horse, specifically. She just said it would be delivered sometime this afternoon. To tell you the truth, you aren't quite what I . . . well . . ."

"No," said Dixie, grinning. "I reckon not."

"Lucy's idea of a joke, I imagine." His smile quirked slightly and disappeared as he glanced again toward the door at the end of the hall. "But that's not why things are so chaotic around here right now." He drew an exasperated breath and let it out, muttering softly. Then he said, "My kids just informed me that it's Parents' Back-to-School Night tonight. *Tonight.*"

"Uh-oh," said Dixie in sympathy, although she'd had no personal experience with such things.

"Yeah. Lolly—that's Lauren, my daughter—tells me she brought the notice home last week, but—ah, hell. Anyway, she's supposed to bring cookies or something for a bake sale, and Ethan—my son—is upset because he says he doesn't know his songs, and he's supposed to have some sort of costume, and . . . God knows what else."

He waved abstractedly at her and continued on down the hall, talking to her over his shoulder. "I'm not quite sure *what* I'm doing right now, frankly. My wife always used to handle things like this. Anyway, it's not your problem, so just give me a minute to calm my son down, and then I'll be right with you, okay?" He paused and turned to deliver the last part of that with his hand flat on the panel of a swinging door, then pushed through it and disappeared.

"No problem," Dixie murmured, giving her head a bemused shake as she skipped down the steps to the driveway.

Rhett Brown wasn't exactly what *she'd* expected, either.

She found Lauren standing on the tongue of the trailer, leaning over as far as she could to stroke the horse's bony black nose through a side window.

"I'm naming her Star," she said in a rapt voice, without looking up. "Because she's got a star on her forehead."

"Well, Star's a nice name," said Dixie judiciously. "For a boy or a girl, actually. This horse happens to be a boy."

Lauren caught her breath with an audible gasp and gave Dixie a look of wide-eyed wonder. "Like the Black Stallion?"

Dixie coughed. "Well, not exactly." She didn't feel quite prepared to explain gelding to a ten-year-old, so she changed the subject. "You know how to ride?"

"I'm going to have lessons." Lauren gave her head an arrogant toss and turned back to the horse, thrusting out a hand to pat his nose. The horse jerked his head back with a loud snort, startling her so much she almost fell off her perch.

"Okay, first lesson," said Dixie. "You don't touch his muzzle all of a sudden like that. That's a real sensitive place—that's what he uses to check things out, see? Think about it—how'd you like it if somebody reached out and touched *your* nose . . . like *that?*"

"Hey!" said Lauren, rearing back with an outraged scowl.

Dixie chuckled. "Right—see? So what you do is, you hold out your hand and let him come and check you out. Horses are naturally curious. He wants to know what that funny-looking pink thing is, and whether it's got any treats in it."

"But I don't have anything," cried Lauren, dismayed.

"Hold on a sec." Dixie went around to the passenger's side of the pickup, opened the door and got her Stetson from the seat. Then she climbed into the back of the Chevy and scooped two generous handfuls of grain into it from the sack she always brought along when she moved an animal that wasn't used to the trailer.

"There you go," she said, rejoining Lauren. "Stick your hand in there and take a good handful . . . that's right. Okay, now hold it out with your palm flat, like this. That's so he doesn't mistake your fingers for snacks—horses aren't very bright."

Lauren threw Dixie a look of outrage at that, but it was almost instantly supplanted by one of surprise, and then by a giggle of pure delight. She sucked in a breath and held it, concentrating with all her strength on keeping her hand still while the horse snuffled and nuzzled and nibbled at it, until every last morsel of the grain was gone. Then she let the breath go in a rush and scrubbed her hand on her fanny, her slender body almost quivering with excitement. "Oh, boy, does that feel *weird!*"

"He likes to be scratched under here, too," said Dixie, hiding a smile as she showed her the spot just below the jawbones. "And up here, see? Around the forelock."

She watched while Lauren fed the horse the rest of the grain, just to make sure no minor appendages were lost in the process, then dumped the last few kernels out of her Stetson and left the two of them to get acquainted while she went back to the house to see what was keeping the kid's father. She'd begun to notice thunderheads piling up above the treetops, and was becoming more and more concerned about getting the animal out of that trailer and exercised and bedded down before they were hit by a cloudburst. Horses could spook easily during thunderstorms.

The front door was still standing wide open, bleeding air-conditioning into the muggy outdoors. Feeling a little guilty about that, Dixie stepped inside and pulled the door shut after her, calling tentatively as she did so. "Mr. Brown...uh...Rhett?"

There was no answer except for a small child's voice, high and quavery with distress, arguing unintelligibly somewhere in the distance. She followed the sound down the hall to the swinging door and pushed it inward as the tearful words leapt forth to meet her.

"But I *can't* go! The other kids will laugh at me. I don't want to, I don't *want* to!"

The door had opened wide into a kitchen of gleaming black and white. Everything Dixie saw seemed polished to a mirror shine—cabinets finished with white high-gloss enamel, black countertop and appliances she was sure she could see herself in, a floor done in black-and-white tile, like a giant chessboard—and in her opinion was about as warm and homey as an architect's drawing. Which made the room's two flushed, disheveled and totally human occupants seem downright Norman Rockwellian by contrast. And all the more compelling.

Rhett was sitting on a black and chrome kitchen chair facing the doorway, holding a small boy—who stood rigid as a little tin soldier—by the arms, tucked between his knees. He didn't appear to mind the interruption, but threw Dixie a bleak and helpless glare over the top of the boy's tousled white-blond head.

"Hi, sorry to barge right in," she said with a smile that was half apology, half sympathy. "Anything I can do to help?"

Rhett let his breath out in a hiss. "Ah, God, I don't know. It's this costume thing." He nodded his head toward the boy, who turned to give her a sorrowful look over his shoulder. He had just about the biggest, roundest brown eyes Dixie had ever seen, and right now they were magnified even further by a shimmering glaze of tears. Her heart turned an unexpected flip-flop.

"He's supposed to dress like a farmer," his father went on, with a disgusted-sounding snort. "I can't think of a thing—not a thing! Which is really ironic, because I grew up on a farm. My dad wore overalls most of the time. Overalls and those blue...what do you call 'em, those blue cotton work shirts, you know? And I seem to remember he always had a great big bandanna handkerchief in his back pocket. But good grief, I'm a lawyer, for God's sake. I don't have anything like that *here*. Not even so much as a . . . a . . ." He stopped short, staring at Dixie.

But the same thought had just struck her, too. Pulling off the red bandanna she'd tied around her windblown curls, she crossed the checkerboard floor and dropped to one knee beside the sniffling child.

"Hey, guy..." She turned him gently, her voice bumpy with sympathetic laughter—and other emotions she tried hard to ignore. "What's all this cryin' and carryin' on for, huh? Look what ol' Dixie's got for you, right here. Hold that a minute..." She slapped her Stetson once against her leg to shake out the last of the grain dust and then plunked it on the little boy's head. He gave a small gasp of surprise and reached up to clutch at the hat's brim as it slipped down over his eyes and bumped the bridge of his nose.

"Whoops," said Dixie, and tipped the Stetson onto the back of his head. "There, that's better. Now then . . ." She knotted the bandanna loosely around his neck and held up her hands in the triumphant manner of a rodeo calf roper completing his tie-down. "There—instant farmer. What'd I tell you? Nothin' to cry about."

"Really?" The boy's voice was hushed with hope. His eyes darted to his father's, seeking confirmation.

Rhett nodded. His face was dusky, flushed beneath a genteel tan. "You look..." he began in a gravelly voice, then cleared his throat and finished it. "You look great, son. Just like a farmer." He glanced at Dixie and seemed to pull himself together. "Uh . . . Ethan, what do you say?"

"Thank you," whispered Ethan dutifully, turning his big brown eyes back to Dixie. But she could see that they were still round and worried.

"Hey, pardner," she said, tugging at the bandanna where it looped below his chin. "You still got troubles?" Ethan looked shyly down, catching back a sigh. "Hey, come on—tell ol' Dixie. I'll bet we can fix it."

Ethan scrunched up his shoulders and pulled in his chin and disappeared turtlelike into the bandanna. From within it his voice emerged timorously. "What about my clothes?"

"Blue jeans," said Dixie decisively after a moment's thought. "You've got those, haven't you?" Ethan nodded slowly. "And a plaid shirt?"

He shook his head. "I don't think so."

"Oh, well, shoot, that's okay—I probably do. It'll be a little big, but what the heck." Something occurred to her. She looked up at Rhett with laughter in her eyes and found him watching her with that same thoughtful, almost measuring look she'd surprised him with once before. Something about it made her heartbeat speed up.

"You know what?" she said to Ethan in a conspiratorial murmur. "Your dad's a lawyer, right? I'll bet . . . that *somewhere* back in his closet he's got a pair of suspenders. What do you think?"

At that Rhett leaned back in his chair with a startled snort, very much as the horse had done when Lauren had tried to pet him. He began to laugh quietly and rather ruefully, as if laughing wasn't something he'd had much practice at lately. "I might," he said in a wondering tone. "You know that? I just might. I'll look. Later, though. Right now . . ." He brought his hands down on his knees, briskly and with purpose.

Dixie got to her feet, too, and discovered that Ethan's hand had somehow found its way into hers. Again her heart performed impossible acrobatics. A small ache settled into her throat.

"What about my songs?" he said, his eyes seeking hers first this time, bravely trusting. "I don't know all the words. Would you help me learn my songs?"

"Ethan—"

"Sure, I'll help you learn your songs," said Dixie, giving his hand a squeeze. "I'll try, anyway. I know lots of songs. What are they?"

"Umm . . . 'Old MacDonald Had A Farm' . . ."

"Oh good—I know that one. What else?"

"And . . . 'A farmer in a bell.' "

Dixie frowned. " 'A Farmer . . . oh!' " Light dawned. She chuckled. " 'Farmer In The Dell'—yeah, I know that one, too. Okay, what else?"

"And...um..." His brow furrowed under the brim of the oversize Stetson as he searched for it. "'There was this farmer and he had a dog...'"

"'And Bingo was his name-oh,'" sang Dixie, and laughed as Ethan's face lit up. "Hey, we're in luck. No sweat. We'll have those learned in no time. Tell you what—if it's okay with your dad, maybe you could come with me while I unload the horse, and we can practice on the way. What do you think?" The last she directed to Rhett, who was studying her once more, she saw, with that considering frown.

"What? Oh, well...sure, I guess so. If you're sure you don't mind." He lifted his hand as if he meant to drive it through his hair, but changed his mind and sort of clamped it on the back of his neck instead. There was a lot of tension there, Dixie noticed; the guy looked as if he needed a good neck rub—way too uptight for his own good. "Look, I don't like to impose on you like this. It's really not your problem."

Dixie brushed that aside with an airy wave of her hand. "What problem? Heck, I've got to unload the horse, right? Farmer Brown here and I are going to sing up a storm while we do it, is all. But no more crying, or the deal's off—right, guy?" She looked sternly at Ethan and squeezed his hand.

He gazed solemnly back at her. "Right."

"See?" Smiling, she brought her eyes back to the boy's father and shrugged. "No problem at all. You just show me where I'm supposed to put the horse and we're in business. You coming along, or shall I follow you?"

"Actually, you know..." Rhett shot out his wrist and gave his watch a cursory glance, muttering something under his breath. "Ah, darn—I don't even think there's going to be enough time..."

"For what?" Dixie asked. He was looking distracted again, and more tense than ever.

"Oh...nothing. It's just...like I said, Lolly's apparently supposed to bring some sort of homemade...something—cookies, I guess—for the bake sale table tonight. And I told her we'd run to the store and pick up a mix or whatever, but I don't see how there's going to be time to bake something along with everything else. Never mind—forget it. It's not your—"

Dixie held up one hand like a traffic cop. "Now, just hold it right there. What time are you supposed to be going to this thing?"

"Uh . . . six-thirty, I believe."

"Well, shoot, there's still plenty of time. What is it now, four-thirty? Just throw together some of those Rice Krispies things—they don't take any baking. Just cool 'em a bit in the fridge and you're all set."

"Rice . . . Krispies things?" Rhett was looking at her as if she'd said something in a foreign language.

"Yeah, you know—with marshmallows? Throw in a bag of M&M's and I guarantee they'll go like hotcakes."

"Marshmallows," Rhett mumbled, looking dazed. "I'll have to go to the store."

"Yeah, why don't you do that? The kids and I'll take care of the horse. Oh—you're going to need lots of butter, too. Better make sure you have enough."

"Butter," whispered Rhett.

Dixie gave him a sharp look. "Hmm . . . maybe I'd better make a list. You got something I can write it down on?"

"Uh . . ." After patting himself in the general vicinity of assorted pockets, he produced a business card and a pen and handed them to her.

She scribbled a hurried list using her thigh for a writing table and returned both the pen and the card.

"Lolly knows the way to the stable," Rhett told her as he tucked them away in his shirt pocket. "They're expecting you over there, so you shouldn't have any trouble." He glanced up at her, his brown eyes suddenly intent. "Listen, I can't thank you enough for your help. I mean it. I don't know what I'd—"

"No sweat," said Dixie, putting an end to that in a hurry. She couldn't have explained why it made her uncomfortable, but it did. "See you in a little bit." She took Ethan's hand.

She was going through the swinging door when a breathy, muffled sound made her turn and look a question back at Rhett.

"Oh, brother, I just realized," he said in a strangled voice. "Farmer Brown. He actually *is*, isn't he?" He grinned suddenly, and again the change in him seemed to Dixie like a miracle. Tension and years fell away like a discarded chrysalis, until he seemed almost to vibrate with life force and energy.

*Whoo-ee.* Charisma, that's what it is, she thought as she gulped air and swallowed against an unexpected dryness in her mouth. *Now* she could see his sister Lucy in him, and his younger brother Wood, too. All those Browns had it, it seemed—in abundance.

She laughed with him and went on down the hall, shaking her head and laughing inwardly as well, at her own silly schoolgirl response.

Rhett stood where he was for a moment, watching the swinging door whump softly back and forth before settling into place. Then he slowly took the business card Dixie had given him from his shirt pocket and stared at it. Without his reading glasses it was only a blur, but he knew what it said. *Rice Krispies. Butter. Marshmallows. Chocolate candies.*

Wow. Elaine would have seven kinds of fits if she knew.

Rice Krispies bars...he remembered them from his childhood. He even remembered *making* them. Watching the marshmallows melt to a sticky goo, stirring in the rice cereal and listening to it pop and sizzle. He even remembered one Christmas when Mom had added a few drops of green food coloring and some cinnamon red hots....

Wow. He'd forgotten all about that. Until now.

Smiling to himself, he tucked the business card back in his pocket and went to fetch his wallet and car keys. It occurred to him as he did so, that for the first time in longer than he cared to remember, he felt carefree enough to laugh out loud.

# Chapter 3

The trip to the supermarket took longer than Rhett expected. For one thing it was rush hour. The aisles were clogged with people on their way home from work stopping to pick up something quick and easy for dinner. Not to mention the frazzled housewives with toddlers in tow trying to make a grocery run and still beat their husbands home. So lines were long and tempers were short. Plus, he had some trouble locating the marshmallows. He finally had to give up and ask a woman with more kids than groceries in her cart where they were.

Even so, he was surprised to see the Chevy pickup and empty horse trailer already back in his driveway, once again parked under the oak tree, though this late in the day and the way it was clouding up, there wasn't any real need for the shade.

It gave him an odd feeling to think about Dixie being in his house with his kids, in his absence. Which might have been natural enough, given the fact that she was a complete stranger, but he didn't think it had anything to do with that. She was, after all, a friend of Lucy's, and even though he'd never gotten along particularly well with his sister, he did trust her judgment.

Besides, it wasn't alarm or concern he felt, or even the vaguest uneasiness. Just . . . a strangeness, characterized by heightened senses and a slight acceleration in his heart rate. Funny, too—those symptoms reminded him of something, but he couldn't think what it was.

Since he knew he'd be using the BMW again in an hour or so, he left it parked near the front door and carried his grocery bags around to the kitchen by way of the brick-paved walk. He was just passing through the arched breezeway that connected the house and garage, noticing how red the Virginia creeper had gotten all of a sudden and thinking that fall was just around the corner, when he heard something, something so out of place and unexpected it stopped him in his tracks.

Someone was playing an acoustic guitar. Someone inside his house. And doing so, moreover, with a considerable amount of skill and delicacy of touch.

Of course, he knew who it was. Just Dixie, obviously, helping Ethan learn his songs as she'd promised she would. She just hadn't bothered to mention that she played the guitar like a pro.

But in spite of that logic, that certainty, he stood there in the creeper-festooned archway with a grocery bag clutched in the crook of each arm while a wave of nostalgia rolled over him, all but swamping him in half-forgotten emotions. Because somewhere deep inside him there was a small boy who half believed that if he looked through the kitchen window he'd see someone else's head bending low over that guitar, familiar soft brown curls gleaming in a warm yellow light, blue eyes twinkling gently at him as she sang "…Hi-ho the derry-o, the farmer in the dell."

The voice drifted out to him on the heavy, humid air, as light, clear and easy as cool water running over mossy stones.

"Okay, now you sing with me…" The guitar accompanied the spoken words with a lilting background riff. "Ready? Come on, Lolly, you sing too. Ready, go. 'The farmer takes a wife, The farmer takes a wife, Hi-ho the derry-o, The farmer takes a wife.'

"Hey, that's great! Bravo, Ethan. Okay, what comes next?" The guitar played softly on, as effortlessly as summer raindrops pattering onto the surface of a pond.

"Um…wife takes a *child!*"

"Ya-ay—that's right! Come on, now, *sing!*"

During the course of the next verse, Rhett covered the remainder of the distance to his kitchen door. He was faintly surprised at the way his heart was pounding and aware of a lingering weakness in his knees as he hunkered down so he could reach the doorknob. He turned it and nudged the door open with an elbow.

"Dad!" yelled Ethan in delighted greeting. Both children came running to take the grocery bags from him.

But he was looking beyond them to where Dixie sat on Elaine's elegant and expensive polished granite countertop with her stockinged feet dangling over the side, like Tom Sawyer on a fishing pier. Her dark hair stood out around her face in a wild profusion of corkscrew curls and her cheeks still held the warm, rosy residue of music and laughter. It occurred to him that not even his mother's ghost could have looked more alien than she did in that setting.

She winked at him and played a chord, then stifled it with her hand and quipped, "By George, I think he's got it," but with an accent more Texas than upper-class British.

"So I heard," Rhett responded dryly. "Horse all settled in? That didn't take long."

"Oh, well, we'd have spent more time if we'd had it to spend," said Dixie cheerfully as she set the guitar to one side and hopped off the countertop. "But . . . we let him walk the kinks out and then bedded him down. He'll keep until tomorrow."

"I fed and brushed him," Lolly said with studied indifference, without looking up from the assortment of boxes and bags she was pulling from the paper grocery sacks. She tossed back her hair in that arrogant way she'd adopted lately and added, "I named him Star."

Rhett said dutifully, "Hmm . . . nice name."

And then, for some reason, he found that he didn't know what to say next, which was not an affliction he normally suffered.

He frowned at Dixie and cleared his throat. "Well. I guess I, uh . . . owe you . . ." He broke off, then, because Ethan was tugging at the edge of his jacket. He transferred the frown to him and said impatiently, "What is it, son?"

"You promised you'd look for sis . . . s-spenders."

Rhett let his breath out in a rush. "Yeah, I guess I did." It registered then for the first time that his son was wearing a yellow plaid shirt big enough to hold two or three of him. It was made of cotton flannel, soft and worn, the colors muted by many washings, the kind of shirt he used to throw on over a

T-shirt before he went out to do chores on chilly autumn mornings.

He touched Ethan's arm where the rolled-up sleeve bunched around his elbow but was looking at Dixie as he said, "Nice shirt."

Ethan peered down, puffing out his chest so he could see it better. "Yeah. Dixie gave it to me. Now I just need 'spenders and I'll look like a real farmer, huh Dad? 'Cept I don't have any cowboy boots." His expression became wistful.

Rhett ruffled his hair. "That's okay. Most farmers don't wear cowboy boots, anyway. My dad—you know, your grandpa?—mostly wore big rubber boots over his regular work shoes. Hey, that's an idea—maybe you could wear your galoshes, if they still fit you. Why don't you go and see if you can find them. Okay? I'll come up in a minute to look for those suspenders."

"Oh-*kay!*" Ethan went running off, hitting the swinging door with a *thump* on his way out, the way he always did.

Watching him, Rhett felt his throat tighten up. He looked at Dixie as he attempted to clear it. "I...don't know how to thank you enough."

She shrugged in that breezy, offhand manner he was beginning to recognize as her signature. "Shoot, it's an old shirt—he's welcome to it."

"I don't just mean the shirt."

"He's a terrific little kid," she said softly, but with an unmistakable air of dismissal. He noticed that her usually easy smile had become strained.

He would have pursued it in spite of that. For reasons he couldn't begin to analyze, it had become important to him to explain how much her kindness and generosity meant to him—or, more accurately, to the children. It frustrated him to be doing such a poor job of it when words were, in a way, the tools of his trade. Still, he'd no doubt have gone on clumsily trying if Lolly hadn't chosen that moment to intervene.

"What's *this?*" she demanded in a loud, bossy voice. "What are these for?" She was standing with a hand on one hip, holding out the bag of M&M's he'd bought. Her mouth was a tight little button of disapproval—a perfect replica of her mother's, Rhett thought with an inner sigh of regret.

Unfazed, Dixie laughed and went to take the candy from her. "Those are for the cookies, sugar, what did you think? Speaking of which, I reckon we'd better be getting started, don't you?'' She waved at Rhett with a shooing motion. ''You go on and help Ethan with his clothes. Leave the kitchen to us womenfolk.'' She winked at Lolly, who rolled her eyes as if she were saying, ''Oh, *brother!*'' to herself. Rhett could almost hear her.

As he was leaving the kitchen through the swinging door he heard his daughter say, ''We're not allowed to eat sweets—they're not good for you,'' in that haughty and disdainful tone he knew so well.

He paused on the other side of the door to wait for Dixie's response. It came on a husky little cackle of laughter.

''You're not supposed to eat 'em, sugar. Just *mix* 'em. Okay? Here, you start counting out the marshmallows....''

He smiled to himself and went on up the stairs.

The house seemed very quiet when he came back down half an hour or so later. Not an empty kind of quiet, but the peaceful kind, which, come to think of it, he hadn't been enjoying much of lately. He found, to his utter amazement, that he was whistling ''Farmer In The Dell'' very softly under his breath in time to his lighthearted tread on the stairs.

He was feeling relatively pleased with himself, and much more in control of the situation in general. It had only taken him a few minutes to find the suspenders, lo and behold, still there on a tie rack in the back of his closet. They were leftovers from his early years as an up-and-coming junior partner in one of the most prestigious law firms in Des Moines, when he'd still been self-conscious about trying to look the part. It amazed him that they'd escaped Elaine's ruthless culling of his wardrobe all these years; if he remembered correctly, she'd always hated those suspenders.

After that he'd helped Ethan locate last winter's galoshes and supervised the kid through a quick shower, then had opted for one himself, along with a fast once-over with the electric shaver. He was damned if he was going to make his first public appearance since the divorce—at least among members of his and Elaine's former social circle—in a wrinkled shirt and five o'clock shadow.

He could just hear the gossip: ''Guess who I saw the other night?'' ''Yes, and did you see how he's let himself go to pot since his wife left him for another man? He must really be broken up....''

In Lolly's words, *Oh brother.*

At any rate, at the moment, judging by the sounds coming from her bathroom, Lolly was in the shower. And with Ethan in his room struggling to tuck a couple of extra feet of shirttail into his jeans, Rhett figured to have a few uninterrupted moments with Dixie. He still had to pay her for the horse, of course, but more important—to him, anyway—he wanted to take another shot at thanking her properly, now that he had himself in hand again. Funny, he'd thought it was only his children who could put him at such a loss for words.

He found Dixie in the kitchen, just snapping the latches on an old, scuffed black leather guitar case, which she'd laid out on the glass and chrome table next to her black Stetson and red bandanna handkerchief. Together they made a weirdly artistic, incongruous but oddly compelling arrangement, Rhett thought, like a still life by Salvador Dali.

She looked up when she saw him, pushing a frizz of curls away from her face with the back of her hand, smiling her ready smile. "Hi. Everybody okay up there?"

"Yeah, great." He went to stand beside her and picked up the Stetson, turned it over in his hands and placed it back on the table. "I found the suspenders," he said, and added with a little half smile, "Just out of curiosity, how did you know?"

The light arpeggio of her laughter delighted his ears. "You mean, how did I know you'd most likely have a pair?" Her smile turned enigmatic. "Oh, just a lucky guess." She set the guitar case on the floor.

Rhett pulled back a chair and sat in it. He took out his checkbook and a pen, quickly filled in the date and scrawled his name at the bottom of a check, then frowned at it. "What do I owe you? For the horse, I mean. Have you got a bill for me, or . . ."

Dixie said "Oh!" and pulled a folded slip of paper out of a hip pocket. "There you go. I've itemized it, including transportation. Oh—and I threw in the halter and lead. I wasn't sure if you had any tack yet."

Somewhat belatedly, Rhett took out his glasses, put them on and peered at the amount on the paper. It seemed to him more than fair. He wrote it on the check, then paused, not looking up, exasperated with himself for having to ask. "Uh . . . would you mind telling me your last name again? I'm sorry. I'm afraid I was a . . . little distracted before."

He heard nothing but understanding in her soft chuckle. "No problem. It's Parish. With one *R.*"

"Parish...ah, yes, I remember." He printed it neatly on the pay to line, then sat for a moment gazing at it. He looked down at the guitar, which was sitting on the floor near his feet, then back at the check. Finally he shook his head and looked up at Dixie, feeling a slight vibration in his chest the way he did when he knew he was about to ask a question that was sure to be objected to—and probably sustained. "You're not, by any chance...you aren't related to *the* Parish family, are you? You know, the folk singers—Maude and Jed...Marilee...Tom..."

"Oh, my goodness," said Dixie, laughing faintly.

"I'm sorry—I just thought, the way you play..."

"No—no, it's okay, I'm just surprised, is all." She shook her head, her usually wide-open smile wryly askew. "Not too many people make the connection."

"Then you..." His breath was suspended, barely believing it.

She lifted a shoulder, as much an apology, he thought, as an affirmation. "Tom's my uncle. Marilee's my mom. Maude and Jed are my grandparents."

"Oh, wow," murmured Rhett, for once not bothered at all by the realization that he must sound like a starstruck teenager.

Dixie tilted her head, regarding him with curiosity and something else he couldn't identify. "Excuse me, but how in the world did you know? I mean, folk music isn't exactly in its heyday, and anyway—forgive me—you just don't seem like the type to me."

He smiled sardonically, wondering what type he *did* seem like to her. Since he wasn't sure he wanted to know, he didn't ask, but instead explained gently, in a voice that had thickened unexpectedly with the pain of an old grief, "My mother was...something of a folk singer herself. She sang Parish songs to me in my crib." He paused, not so much for her exclamation of surprise and appreciation as to allow himself a quick breath and a soft chuckle to help him through the memory. "Yeah...the Parish Family, the Seegers, Bob Dylan and Woody Guthrie...all of them. Taught me to play the guitar as soon as my fingers were strong enough to hold down the strings. Piano, too.

"When I was older, we sang together a lot—church, community gatherings, things like that. Later on my little brother Earl joined us, until I went away to college. Then there was just the two of them, I guess. Until...she died." He coughed, stopping himself abruptly. "So—why didn't you..." He waved a hand frowning fiercely. "...You know, go into the family business?"

Dixie picked up the check he'd left lying on the table, folded it once and slipped it into a pocket, doing it all with deliberate care, it seemed to him, in order to avoid looking at him. When she had the check tucked away, she leaned her backside against the countertop, folded her arms on her chest and gazed for a moment at the darkening windows.

"Try to understand," she said at last, her voice dry with irony and almost no traces of Texas. "I was raised in the free-wheelin' sixties. My parents were...well, I guess you could say I was the child of children, in a way. Flower children, you know? Peace, love and the age of Aquarius... As a little girl I danced naked in the rain and the mud at Woodstock, for heaven's sake! Don't get me wrong, it was the most wonderful childhood—music and laughter and no rules at all."

She laughed, bringing her gaze back to Rhett with a shrug. "Then...I grew into a teenager. I wanted like the dickens to rebel like any other teenager, only I didn't have anything to rebel *against,* you know what I mean? The only thing I could think of that would really shake up my family was *not* to become a folksinger."

Rhett chuckled appreciatively. He studied her for a moment. "So...you raise horses instead. Seems like kind of a stretch. How'd you get into it?"

"My family has a ranch in Texas—I run it for them." Her lashes dropped, closing off her normally expressive face to him as completely as if she'd drawn a blind.

He might have wondered more about that if it had not occurred to him just then, and not for the first time, that she had the most incredible eyes...light, vivid blue, deep-set and fringed with thick black lashes. By far her best feature, he thought judiciously, her jaw being too square and her mouth too wide, in his opinion, for real beauty. And my God, that hair. Wild as a Texas stampede. It was no wonder she liked to wear a hat....

"I'd appreciate it if you could send back my Stetson when you're done with it," she said, making him start slightly with guilt for his critical thoughts. "You can send it to your sister's, I guess. Don't bother about the shirt, though; it's an old one. I just take it along with me for those early mornings, you know? When there's a damp chill in the air, but it's not cold enough for a jacket."

"Yeah," said Rhett with a faint smile, "I remember those mornings."

"Kinda thought you might." She was studying him with that same enigmatic look he'd seen before. For some reason it made eye contact with her both unnerving and difficult to break.

"So," he heard himself mumble, "you're taking off, now, are you?"

She shrugged. "Well, yeah, it's time I was headin' on back. And y'all have a meeting to get to." She didn't really quite say "Y'all," Rhett noticed, but something that was a little softer and gentler on the ears. "So…" She stuck out her hand and he took it, noticing how strong and hard it was, for a woman's, feeling the scratchy ridges of rope calluses against his palm. "I hope you enjoy your horse. I think he'll be a nice one for the kids."

Rhett nodded somberly, and for some reason found that it was as hard to let go of her hand as her eyes. After another awkward moment he mentally shook himself and said, "I hope you won't leave without telling them goodbye. I know they'll want to thank you. Especially Ethan. He's…been going through kind of a rough time lately."

"I know." Dixie gently extricated her hand from his and bent to pick up the guitar case, effectively breaking the eye contact as well. "Lucy told me about his mom." She reached out as if to take the Stetson from the tabletop, then grinned and said, "Oops—force of habit." She laughed, and Rhett laughed with her. "Well, I guess I'd better…"

"Here, I'll get that for you." He jumped forward to put his palm flat on the swinging door just as she did the same. They laughed at that, too.

Then there was a little silence, during which Rhett found himself staring again at the curls that floated free around her face, realizing that they were almost on a level with his eyes. He hadn't noticed before that she was such a tall woman. Taller even than Elaine…

Footsteps thumped calamitously on the stairs. Dixie laughed and said, "Oops, it sounds like—" just as Rhett let out a breath in a relieved gust and said, "That must be—" They looked at each other and both jumped back away from the swinging door just in time.

There was a loud *thump,* and the door flew inward to deliver a flushed and tousled Ethan. He was scowling in frustration and holding on to the dangling ends of a pair of striped suspenders, the other ends of which he'd managed to clip crookedly to the front of his jeans.

"Dad! Will you help me with these? I can't . . ." He stopped short, the impatient tone and expression both vanishing as he took in the guitar case slung over Dixie's shoulder. In a stricken voice he said, "Are you leaving?" and lifted his round, liquid eyes to her face.

She dropped instantly to his level, balancing on the balls of her feet as she took the now forgotten suspenders from his hands. "Have to, sugar. It's time for y'all to leave, too." Rhett wasn't surprised at the huskiness in her voice; he knew the potency of that particular act of his son's only too well.

Dixie turned Ethan around and drew the ends of the suspenders over his shoulders. "Time for you to go sing those songs we practiced, big guy." She tied the suspenders in a knot to shorten them and clipped them to the back of his jeans. "You haven't forgotten what I taught you, have you? Because I'm really counting on you."

Ethan said nothing. His head wilted, his chin coming to rest on the buttoned front of the yellow plaid shirt. From where Rhett stood the back of his son's neck seemed pale and incredibly vulnerable. He felt his own breathing stumble slightly when Dixie put her strong, callused hand on that frail stalk and gently shook it.

"Hey, sugar, you hear what I said? I'm countin' on you to go down to that school tonight and sing out nice and loud and pretty, just like I know . . ." Rhett was as unprepared as she undoubtedly was when Ethan suddenly squirmed between her hands, threw his arms around her neck and burrowed his face into the rampant masses of her hair.

Rhett actually felt as though his chest had contracted. There was a break in his own breathing just as he heard Dixie give a tiny, barely audible gasp. Then her eyes flashed upward, seeking his with a look so dark and fierce he thought for an instant it must be anger, until he saw how gently her arms enfolded his

son's small quaking body. How tenderly her hands stroked his
silky, still-damp hair.

"Hey, fella, what's the matter?" she murmured in a voice so
at odds with the anguish on her face it seemed not to be coming from her at all. "I thought we had a deal. No more tears,
remember?"

Ethan's head bobbed an affirmative against her shoulder.

Unable to stand by and watch that strangely poignant scene
any longer, Rhett put out a hand to touch his son. A slight
movement of Dixie's head stopped him. So instead he drew his
hand back and stuck it in his pocket. His fingers curled involuntarily into a fist with the effort it cost him not to intervene,
as he silently watched Dixie take Ethan by the shoulders and
put him away from her so that her fingers could cup his quivering chin. Gently but firmly lift it.

"Okay, so what's this, huh? What are these?" Smiling now,
she brushed a knuckle across one tear-damp cheek. "Hey,
you've got a great farmer outfit, you've got your songs down
pat. So what's the trouble? Come on, tell ol' Dixie, now."

Rhett's own breathing was almost forgotten as he listened to
Dixie coax and cajole and console his youngest child. So caught
up was he in the suspense of the moment that he dismissed the
terrible intensity with which her eyes had clung to his only a
moment ago. He must have imagined it, he told himself as he
watched her face take on the sunshine glow of her easy smile.
Imagined it was pain he'd seen in those eyes . . .

He had to admire her patience. Ethan resisted, but finally he
scrubbed his fists into his eyes and mumbled something Rhett
couldn't quite hear.

Dixie pulled his hands away from his face and said, "What
was that? Tell me again, sugar."

"I *said*, I thought you were going to be there. I wanted you
to hear me sing. Aren't you going to come?"

Rhett stifled a snort of surprise. Dixie threw him a helpless
look, for once speechless herself, it seemed.

"Can't you come with us? Ple-ease?"

"Son—"

Dixie ruffled Ethan's hair and stood up. "Of course I'd like
to hear you sing, sugar, you know I would. But tonight's supposed to be special. It's supposed to be for your *parents*."

"But my mommy's not coming," Ethan said in a small voice.

It struck Rhett suddenly how very small and bereft his son
looked, standing there between two tall, omnipotent adults. His
throat tightened with the now familiar recurring geyser of his

anger. *How could you, Elaine? How could you just abandon him like you did?*

"Well, I know, but your daddy'll be there," Dixie pointed out, not looking at Rhett.

Ethan fixed her with his most intractable gaze. "I want you to come, too."

She drew a breath and opened her mouth, but only a faint, frustrated laugh came out. Now she did look at Rhett, helplessly, and shrugged as if to say, "He's your son—what do I do now?"

Rhett did the only thing he could do. He caved in. Which was pretty much the way he'd been handling things involving his children for the last two months.

He drove a hand through his hair, exhaled slowly and said to Dixie in an undertone, "Would you mind terribly? Is there some place you need to be?"

"Well, no...I guess not," she murmured back, while Ethan watched avidly, missing nothing. "I was just going to head on back to Sioux City while there's still some daylight left. But my goodness, y'all don't want—"

"I have no objections," Rhett cut in. Truthfully, there were one or two he could think of right off the bat. "I just don't want you to feel pressured into changing your plans. Are you sure you wouldn't mind?"

"My goodness, no, I don't mind!" Dixie said with a laugh, raising her voice and bending down to include Ethan in the conversation once more. "I'd be tickled to death to come and hear you sing, sugar, if you really want me to. Now—now that that's all taken care of, where's your hat? Oh, there it is..." She plucked it from the table and placed it ceremoniously on his head. "There you go, Farmer Brown—knock 'em dead."

A giggle came from under the Stetson. Using both hands, Ethan raised it far enough so he could see and smiled impishly up at her, not a tear in sight, of course, now that he had his way. He went hopping happily off across the kitchen, singing "Old MacDonald had a farm, E-I-E-I-O!" at the top of his lungs.

Rhett watched him, frowning and jingling his keys in his trousers pocket, wondering when he was going to feel that he had his life under control again. Belatedly aware that Dixie had spoken, he transferred the frown to her and said, "I'm sorry, what was that?"

The look in her eyes seemed wary. "I said, do you want to give me directions, or shall I just follow you?"

"Oh—no need to do that. Why don't you just ride with us? Parking's always at a premium at these things, and you've got the trailer..."

While he was saying that, Lolly came through the swinging door with so little momentum he had to suspect she'd been standing on the other side of it for a while, listening. She did like to eavesdrop, he knew. Which may have helped account for the high color in her cheeks as, self-consciously refraining from looking at anyone else in the room, she marched straight to the refrigerator, took out a pan full of Rice Krispies bars and carried it to the counter.

"Need a hand, sugar?" asked Dixie.

"No, thank you, I can take care of it myself," said Lolly politely, her voice about as warm as what Rhett could see of her profile, which looked like something that belonged on a coin.

Dixie gave Rhett a shrug and a bright smile, although her eyes still had that strange reserve he'd noticed a moment ago. "Well, okay, then. Just give me a minute to wash my face and run a comb through my hair...maybe see if I can find a clean shirt, okay? I'll try not to hold you up..."

"Take your time," murmured Rhett to the flapping door. He couldn't imagine a comb and a clean shirt making that much difference, anyway; no matter what she did, Dixie Parish was going to stick out tonight like a sore thumb. God, he dreaded this. What were people going to think when he showed up at Parents' Night with a strange woman in tow, barely two months after his wife's abdication? Probably that he'd given her cause, he thought with a moody snort.

"So," said Lolly casually, not looking up from the Rice Krispies bars she was arranging with geometrical precision in a rectangular plastic container. "She's coming with us?"

"Yes, she is," said Rhett firmly. "Ethan invited her. That okay with you?"

"Sure." She lifted an indifferent shoulder.

Rhett sighed inwardly and went to get his jacket. But as he was leaving the room, just out of the corner of his eye he saw his daughter pause to lick marshmallow off her fingers, then look around guiltily to see whether anyone had caught her at it.

There was just something about a school building at night, Dixie thought. Something different—about the smell, the feel, the echoing hallways filled with harsh, artificial light and subdued, almost furtive footsteps. Something exciting, even suspenseful in a fun, giddy kind of way, like playing hide-and-seek outdoors after dark when you were a child.

She wondered if that could be the reason for the little knot of tension under her ribs, the quiver of butterflies in her stomach.

She said something of the sort to Rhett—except for the part about the butterflies—as they sat together in his BMW, having just dropped Ethan and Lolly off in the loading zone near the main entrance. Since they were late, the plan was for Lolly to take her brother to his classroom first, deliver the Rice Krispies bars to the bake sale table in the cafeteria while they found a place to park, then meet them at the front door. But for some reason, Rhett didn't appear to be in any hurry to carry out his part of the agenda. He gave a noncommittal grunt in response to Dixie's comment, then went on sitting there staring morosely through the windshield and drumming his fingers on the leather-covered steering wheel.

Dixie watched him for a moment, then drawled, "If you don't mind my saying so, you don't seem exactly thrilled to be here tonight."

He threw her a dark look. "No, *thrilled* is not the word I'd choose to describe how I feel about it." He put the car in gear and rolled away from the white painted curb, and a streetlight briefly revealed a sardonic twist of a smile. "I think I've probably looked forward to oral surgery with more enthusiasm."

"Mind if I ask why?"

For a while she thought maybe he did mind, because he didn't say anything as he drove slowly along the street, scanning the unbroken line of cars for a space big enough to squeeze a full-size BMW into. He turned down the first residential side street they came to and pulled in behind a station wagon and shut off the motor.

Since it didn't seem to trouble him that two feet or so of the BMW's rear end were in someone's driveway, Dixie didn't mention it.

She was about to open the door when Rhett abruptly cleared his throat and said, "It's got nothing to do with the kids. Or you. It's just that I—or at any rate, my private affairs—happen to be the current hot topic of gossip among most of the people who'll be there tonight. I guess Lucy's probably told you..."

"Yes, she did—about you and your wife separating, and you getting a divorce, you mean? That's not such a big deal these days, is it? I mean, not as far as gossip goes, anyway."

His chuckle was dry and humorless. "Yeah, well, you see, my wife left me for another man—quite suddenly, as a matter of fact. That makes it a little more interesting."

"I see," said Dixie. Then all at once she *did* see. Laughter bubbled up and burst out of her before she could stop it. "Oh, my Lord. And now you're about to show up at Parents' Night with *me* in tow. I guess that's going to make it a *lot* more interesting, isn't it? Rhett, you should have said something. I'd never have come if I'd—"

"I told you, it's not you." He pulled the keys from the ignition with restrained violence, opened the door and got out. Dixie did the same, and waited while Rhett locked the car, set the security system and pocketed the keys. "Trust me," he said savagely, "it would have been no better if I'd come alone. And I'm *damned* if I'll disappoint my son because of what a bunch of people I don't even like very much might think."

Maybe not, thought Dixie, but you're sure not happy about it, are you?

It seemed to her he cared quite a bit about what people thought—even the ones he didn't like very much. Which was really a shame, she thought as he took her elbow and guided her with grim courtesy across the dark street. Because she'd have dearly loved to share with him the deliciously wicked idea that had just come to her. Since she was here and nothing could be done about it, what fun it would be to play this thing to the hilt—to *really* give the gossips something they could sink their teeth into!

She stole a sideways look at the man beside her as she matched her step to his long, hurrying stride, and then, with an effort, controlled her smile and gave a small, inner sigh of regret. This, obviously, was the Rhett Brown his sister Lucy had told her about, the one she'd referred to as a stuffed shirt. *So* handsome and distinguished...so stiff and serious. So...a term from her childhood came to mind: *Uptight.*

Too bad. She doubted very much he'd see the humor in this situation.

# Chapter 4

Lolly was waiting for her father in the front hallway near the main entrance doors, like he'd told her to. However, she'd chosen a spot far enough back from the doors so that she could see everyone coming up the steps without peeking through the glass like some dumb little kid watching out for her daddy. Also, she'd taken care to adopt a pose—shoulders leaning against the wall, arms folded on her chest and one leg across the other—which she thought made her look totally nonchalant.

*Nonchalant.* She'd just learned that word, and she liked it a lot because it meant feeling really cool and calm, and it seemed like most of the time lately she felt anything but.

Right now, for instance. Her insides were jumping all over the place. She wished she was dead. Well, not really, of course, but she did wish she was someplace else, like at the stables with Star, or at home in her room playing Nintendo, or even reading a book. Any place but *here.* She wished it was still summer, and that Ethan wasn't such a crybaby, and that her parents weren't getting a divorce.

Most of all, though, she wished Dixie hadn't made her bring those stupid Rice Krispies things with the M&Ms in them for the bake sale.

It had been *so* embarrassing. The lady in charge had said, "Oh, look, how *cute!*" when she'd seen what Lolly had brought. She'd said it loudly enough for everyone in the whole room to hear, too, in a syrupy sweet voice that made Lolly feel really, really dumb.

Especially when she'd gotten a good look at that table. It was all covered with white lace paper doilies and loaded down with the most gorgeous cakes and pies and cheesecakes and chocolate fudge brownies and some really neat cupcakes decorated with flowers made out of pink icing. Her Rice Krispies things were *dumb*. They looked like something a kid would make.

It was all Dixie's fault that tonight was turning out to be so awful, Lolly decided. Even though she'd been really nice, showing her how to take care of Star, and everything, and it was pretty cool the way she played the guitar and got Ethan to stop crying...

But Lolly still didn't see why Ethan had to ask her to come here with them—to *Parents'* Night, of all things! Dixie was nice, but she wasn't Mom. It felt weird, having her here—kind of embarrassing, actually. What was she going to tell people if they asked her who that woman was with her dad?

She heard voices and footsteps outside. Leaning just far enough away from the wall to look out, but still being nonchalant about it, she saw some people she didn't know hurrying up the steps, a man and a woman, looking worried because they were late. The man had on a suit, like Dad's, and the woman was wearing high heels and sort of a flowery dress with a white collar, and her hair was short and blond and just a little bit curly. The man smiled at Lolly as he held the door open for his wife. They went past her and on down the wide hallway, the woman's heels clicking on the shiny linoleum floor.

Lolly sighed and looked outside again, and this time she could see her dad and Dixie coming, way down the sidewalk. They were almost running, it looked like, Dixie taking great big long steps in her jeans and cowboy boots in order to keep up with Dad. Lolly tried to imagine Mom, or the lady in the flowery dress walking like Dixie. But she couldn't. Because, of course, like the lady in the flowery dress, Mom would be wearing high heels, and nobody could walk like that in high heels.

Thinking about her mother made Lolly's throat feel tight and achy. She tried to remember what Mom had worn last year...oh yeah—that cream-and-black knit dress with the gold buttons with little anchors on them, and earrings to match. And black pumps. Mom had easily been the most beautiful, elegant person there, as always. Mom and Dad had always looked so great—like movie stars, almost. Lolly had felt proud, seeing them together. Proud that they were *her* parents.

Not that Dixie didn't look nice, too, she had to admit as she watched her come up the steps beside her dad. She'd brushed her hair so it was nice and smooth and coiled her braid up on the back of her head, and she had on a white shirt made out of some kind of silky material. It had long, flowing sleeves, like a pirate's, which Lolly thought looked very romantic. And she had this really neat belt made out of silver, with turquoise blue stones in it, and earrings to match. Lolly really liked those earrings. They were long and dangly, and the blue stones in them exactly matched Dixie's eyes.

Mom would never wear earrings like that, she thought, swallowing hard to make the ache in her throat go away. Not in a million years.

She resumed her pose of nonchalance just in time.

She resents my being here, Dixie thought, watching Lolly's set, unhappy face as she and Rhett pushed through the wide double doors together. Dixie didn't blame her. Poor kid was probably missing her mom, feeling protective of her dad...maybe even a little bit jealous. Dixie wished she could reassure the child, somehow, find a way to let her know she had nothing to fear—from *her*, anyway.

Just for a moment, she allowed herself to acknowledge the sadness she usually kept buried, like a keepsake from a lost loved one lying hidden at the bottom of a drawer.

Poor little girl, she thought, laying her own memories carefully away once more. This divorce must be hard on her. Dixie thought of her own parents, of their deep love and abiding friendship, and the way they spoke to each other across a stage or a shared microphone with only their eyes. Then she thought of the child she'd gotten acquainted with that afternoon, so excited about learning how to feed and brush a horse for the very first time. A child that was suddenly having to grow up too fast...too fast.

"Hi, pun'kin," Rhett said, frowning and out of breath. "Sorry it took us so long."

Lolly made a face and said crossly, "Yeah, well, you're late, that's why. You've already missed the PTC meeting, and you're going to miss Ethan's program, too, if you don't hurry *up*."

"PTC." Rhett snapped his fingers and stopped in front of the membership drive table that was set up where the two main hallways crossed. "Don't I need to sign up, or..."

Color rose in Lolly's cheeks. She gave a put-upon sigh. "Da-ad, you already did that. I brought the envelope home last week, don't you remember?" She took hold of her father's hand and tugged on it. "Come *on*, we're going to miss Ethan's program."

Lolly was sure they would have, too, if she hadn't made them almost run. Even so, when they got to Ethan's classroom, the kids were already lined up in front, getting ready to sing. As always, Ethan was in the front row, because he was one of the littlest.

Naturally, all the chairs in the room were taken, so they had to stand along the wall in the back, in front of a bulletin board that was decorated with the kids' pictures stuck on autumn leaves made out of different colored construction paper. Lolly remembered the teacher had done that for Parents' Night when she was in first grade, too. Next month it would change to Halloween pumpkins.

Ethan saw them come in, and of *course* he had to wave. Which was okay—everybody expected you to wave at your parents when you were in first grade.

But then—oh no. Lolly wanted to die. Dixie was *waving back*. And not just a little wave, like, "Hi," either. A great *big* wave, with her hand way up high in the air, like she was trying to flag down a bus or something.

Lolly looked at her dad to see if he was going to say anything, but he just kept looking straight ahead like he hadn't even noticed. So all she could do was scrunch back against the wall and hope nobody would think that those weird people were with *her*.

Just then, though, the teacher, Mrs. Tatum, sat down at the piano and played a chord, and Ethan and all the little kids went, "Hmm." They started singing "There was a farmer had a dog, and Bingo was his name-oh!" at the top of their lungs, and after a while Lolly forgot that she was embarrassed. She thought those little first-graders were actually pretty cute, and she was sure that Ethan's farmer outfit was one of the best, even if he *was* her stupid brother. Dixie's big black cowboy hat kept falling down over his eyes and she could tell that even the other kids' parents thought he looked adorable.

After the "Bingo" song, they did "Old MacDonald Had A Farm." Everybody got mixed up on the animals, and then they started to giggle, and pretty soon all the parents were laughing, too. When they finished, everyone yelled, "E-I-E-I-O!" really loud, and the parents all clapped and cheered, so Lolly didn't mind so much when Dixie did it, even though she was louder than anyone else.

But then there was a lot of shuffling around and whispering while several of the kids, including Ethan, got out of line and ducked around behind everyone else. Then Mrs. Tatum played another chord and all the little first-graders went "Hmm," while one of the tallest boys from the back row came out and stood by himself in front of everybody. Lolly felt sorry for the kid. His face was bright red, and he looked very embarrassed.

Meanwhile, the first-graders were singing, "The farmer in the dell, the farmer in the dell, Hi-ho the derry-oh, the farmer in the dell."

When they got to the part about "the farmer takes a wife," a girl came out from behind the other kids wearing a pioneer dress and a big white sunbonnet. She went to stand beside the tall boy and tried to take his hand, which Lolly could tell he didn't want her to do. But the girl made him hold her hand anyway, and his face got even redder.

Next, for "The wife takes a child," a little kid came riding out on a tricycle, licking a great huge lollipop, the coiled up kind you can buy at amusement parks. All the parents laughed at that.

Then came "The child takes a nurse." Lolly had never been able to understand that one, because why would a child need a nurse unless it was very sick? And if the child was very sick, then that would make it a very sad song, so why were they singing, "Hi-ho the derry-oh," like everything was merry and bright? It was a dumb song, if you asked her.

But anyway, after the nurse came the dog, the cat and the rat, and they were pretty cute. The dog was another kid, of course, dressed up in a costume that looked like those sleeper pajamas with feet in them, and sort of a beanie thing on his head with big floppy ears attached to the sides, and a painted-on nose like a black triangle. And the cat was just a black cat costume that kids wear for Halloween. The rat's outfit looked a lot like the cat's, except it was gray with a big pink tummy, and had little round ears instead of pointy ones.

"*. . . The rat takes the cheese, the rat takes the cheese. . .*"

There was some more shuffling, and then, out from behind the rows of kids came a great big yellow cardboard cheese, the kind with holes in it. Most of the holes were just painted on, but one was cut out so the kid holding the cardboard could look through it.

When Lolly saw the face in the hole she gave a little gasp and looked up at her father to see if he'd noticed that the "cheese" was Ethan. It was hard to tell—he was just sort of smiling, the way parents do at times like that—but before she could point it out to him, she realized that it had suddenly gotten very quiet, and that, for the moment, nobody was singing.

When she looked back toward the front of the room, she saw that the other kids—the farmer and his wife and child and all the animals—had gotten back in their rows, and that now Ethan was standing there in front of everybody, all by himself.

*Oh, no.* Lolly felt her heart begin to beat faster.

Mrs. Tatum played the chord again. Through the hole in the cheese Lolly saw Ethan's mouth open. And then she heard his high squeaky voice, all by itself.

"*The cheese stands alone, the cheese stands alone. . .*"

Lolly clapped her hand over her mouth to hold back a squeal of amazement. She couldn't believe it. Scaredy-cat crybaby *Ethan* standing up in front of everybody, singing a solo? She'd die if she had to do that—she'd just *die.*

*. . . Hi-ho the derry-oh, the cheese stands alone. . .*

Again, Lolly looked up at her father's face, searching it for some kind of hint about what he was thinking, what he was feeling. Because it was such a surprise, Ethan being so brave, and because everything felt so different and weird, she wasn't sure anymore what *she* was supposed to think or feel—about *anything.*

But her father's face didn't tell her anything. It seemed odd—sort of stiff, like a wax statue—and looking at it made her feel even more confused than before.

"*Hi-ho the derry-oh. . . the cheese. . . stands. . . alone!*

As the whole class joined Ethan for a repeat of the last chorus, Rhett drew a shaken breath, trying to ease the tension in his chest and throat. *His son.* Shy, timid little Ethan. What in the world had gotten into the kid? Who'd have ever thought he'd have it in him to do such a thing? Rhett had never felt so proud in all his life.

The song had ended with a crashing chord on the piano. He huffed out the breath he'd been unconsciously holding and began to clap enthusiastically along with everyone else. When a loud whistle from very nearby suddenly pierced the patter of applause like a lightning bolt through a summer shower, he winced involuntarily. Then, maybe because he was still in such a stage of shock and euphoria over his son's accomplishment, he began, in spite of himself, to grin.

"Yay *Ethan!* Bravo! Way to go!" Dixie was yelling and waving her fists in the air as if it were the World Series and Ethan had just hit a ninth-inning home run.

Rhett stole a sideways glance at her just in time to see her put both little fingers into her mouth, so he was more or less prepared for the next ear-splitting whistle. Lolly, however, cringed back against his side and made a face that seemed to indicate she was suffering acute pain. Rhett put his arm around his daughter's shoulders and gave her a little squeeze of sympathy.

By this time, Ethan was wriggling his way through the crowd of standing parents, valiantly holding on with both hands to his oversize Stetson.

"Did you see me?" he cried as he broke free at last and came to a breathless halt a few feet away from them. "Did you see me, Dad? Dixie, I did it! I did just what you told me to, and it *worked.*"

Stunned, Rhett turned to Dixie, mouthing the words, "You *knew?*"

But she was already down on one knee, gathering Ethan into a huge, laughing hug, sweeping off his hat in the process, and all Rhett could do was stand and watch them in a state of bemusement that seemed almost surreal.

Realizing that some sort of response was required of him, he said gruffly, "Good job, son," and then, knowing how stiff it sounded, he reached out to ruffle Ethan's already tousled and sweat-damp hair. But his eyes followed Dixie as she put his son gently away from her and rose, brushing at the knees of her jeans.

"What did you tell him?" he asked her in a wondering tone when she was standing beside him once more.

The throaty cackle of her laughter burst like sparks through the chatter of voices in the crowded room. "Oh—nothing, really. A little performer's trick my mama taught me. I just told him to look over everybody's heads and think of the happiest place he could possibly think of, and imagine that he was there."

"A happy place..." Rhett tilted his son's head back and gave it a gentle shake. "So, what did you think of, son?"

"Disneyland!" yelled Ethan, with a gleeful little hop.

"Figures," Rhett muttered, laughing. "His favorite place in the world."

"Dad," Lolly broke in in a sullen, whiny voice, "can we *go?* I want to show you my room now."

He looked down at his daughter, his euphoria fading like a rainbow when the sun goes. He hesitated, guilt over not officially checking in with his son's teacher doing battle with a strong desire to escape while he still could.

Right now, all the parents he knew were still occupied with their own kids, busy searching for that certain art masterpiece on the wall, being dragged off to check out the hamster cage. In another few minutes, though, they were going to start finding excuses to come over and talk to him. He'd already intercepted several avidly curious glances. While acknowledging the quickly produced smiles and false little waves of greeting from across the room with nods of his own—and some grimly bared teeth—he'd been mentally rehearsing what he was going to say if he had to introduce Dixie.

*"Oh, yes—this is... Dixie. A... (cough) friend of the family."*

Uh-huh. Right.

Self-preservation won, hands down. "Yeah, pun'kin," he said with an exhalation of sheer relief, "we can go now, I guess."

Once he was safely out of the room, though, with Lolly towing him through the crowded hallways like a barge through river shoals, and a humid breeze cooling the claustrophobic sweat on his brow, he began to feel mean-spirited and small. As he listened to the sounds of the two people dawdling along behind him—his son's happy chatter, little gusts of laughter from Dixie—he was suddenly beset by a whole host of unfamiliar emotions, the most easily identifiable of which was shame. After everything Dixie had done for him, and for his children ... and he was worried about what people were going to think?

But maybe that was because *he* didn't know what to think. Dixie just wasn't like anyone he'd ever met before. She was loud and brash, casual as bare feet. She was also warm and generous, spontaneous and kind—which, he realized, were all perfect antonyms for the words he'd have used to describe Elaine. Dixie was funny and affectionate, a natural with kids and animals. She was sunshine and fresh air blowing through a dark, stuffy house.

*His* house ...

Rhett wasn't aware that he'd stopped walking until Lolly yanked on his arm, scolding, "Come *on*, Dad, this isn't the one. My room's down *there*."

"I was thinking," Dixie murmured, coming up so close beside him he caught the smallest whiff of her scent, something elusive, but vaguely familiar. Soap, he thought. Ivory soap. "Maybe y'all might like to have some time alone, just the two of you?"

And then, before he could say anything one way or the other, she announced in a louder voice, "Hey, Ethan and I are going to go have some punch, check out the bake sale, okay?"

"Oh—yeah, sure." Rhett gave Lolly a quick, puzzled glance. He'd have sworn he'd heard her start to say something, but her expression was merely aloof—and belied by the impatience in her folded arms and tapping foot. "We'll meet you there, then."

"Great!" Dixie gave Ethan's hand a squeeze. "Come on, let's go get a cookie, big guy."

"Wait—do you know where it is? The cafeteria ..."

They were already turning to go, but she looked back, briefly, and waved that aside. "Oh, shoot, we'll find it. Farmer Brown, here, he knows—don't you?" She thumped the brim of the Stetson, knocking it over Ethan's eyes.

"Hey!" he shouted, laughing, and ran to catch up with her, holding onto the hat with both hands.

Rhett watched them walk away, Dixie with the fingers of one hand casually tucked in the back pocket of her snug-fitting jeans, Ethan skipping to keep up with her long, loose-jointed stride. He watched and felt something dormant within him quicken and stir.

"*Da-ad ...*"

"Coming," he said with a guilty start, allowing himself to be taken once more in tow.

But as he followed his daughter into her warm and bustling classroom, he was still thinking about Dixie. Not about the neat, firm shape of her bottom, or the way her hips moved with a natural, completely unselfconscious sway when she walked—certainly not about the little jolt of lust he'd just felt, taking notice of those things for the first time.

No... of course not.

At the moment he was thinking about how good she'd been for Ethan, thinking about the way the little guy had blossomed today, just being with her. Thinking that she'd be good for Lolly, too, that maybe she could even get the kid to unbend a bit and be a child again, if she had the chance. Thinking...

*She'd be good for my kids... good for my kids.*

Lolly was sure she was going to die—just *die*—if she had to go back to the cafeteria. She knew she never wanted to see that bake sale table or that horrible lady with the loud, syrupy voice again as long as she lived.

She could just imagine it—all the gorgeous cakes and pies would already be sold, and there would be her stupid Rice Krispies things, sitting all by themselves in the middle of the lace paper doilies, the only thing left on the whole table. And people would keep coming over, wanting to buy something, and the loud-voiced lady would bellow, "I'm sorry, but all we have left are these little things here, with the M&M's in them. Aren't they *cute?*" And the people would just say, "Humph," and walk away.

It was so humiliating. And all Dixie's fault. All right, so Ethan shouldn't have asked her to come, but she didn't have to say yes.

Lolly could tell that her dad wished Dixie hadn't come, too. She'd never seen him so quiet, and besides that, he'd actually told a lie. She'd heard him. Just now, when some people he and her mom knew—the Georges, who had a kid in the same grade as Lolly, but in a different class, thank goodness—stopped to talk to him, when they asked where Ethan was, her dad said he'd gone to the cafeteria with "a friend." Maybe that wasn't *exactly* a lie, but it wasn't really the truth, either, because it sounded like her dad meant another kid—that kind of friend. And Lolly could tell by the way her dad said it, sort of mumbling, that he was embarrassed.

"Well—got to go . . . see what my son's up to," said her dad now, in a loud, fake friendly voice, steering Lolly with a hand on the back of her neck, which she hated. "Nice seeing you two. G'night, now . . ."

Lolly thought his teeth looked as if they were clenched together.

She waited until they were out of sight of the Georges, then wiggled resentfully away from her dad's hand. "I don't see why I have to come with you to get Ethan," she grumbled. "Why can't I just wait for you by the front door?"

"Come on," said her father, like he was forcing himself to be in a good mood. "Don't you want to see how your Rice Krispies bars are selling?"

*No!* Lolly wanted to shout. Don't you understand *anything?*

She couldn't understand why her father was being so awful and mean. It had to be Dixie's fault.

Ethan and Dixie were waiting for them outside the cafeteria. Through the big open doors Lolly could see a lot of people standing around inside drinking coffee and punch out of foam plastic cups, and all their loud talking was like a rushing river of noise pouring out into the hallway. She cringed back away from the doors, trying hard not to catch a glimpse of the dreaded bake sale table through the milling crowds of people.

"Sorry to keep you waiting," her dad said to Dixie in a low voice. He was smiling a funny, crooked smile. "Ran into some people I know."

"Oh—I'm so sorry," Dixie said in the same soft voice, as if she and Dad were talking about something private. "How'd it go?"

Lolly's dad shrugged. Dixie smiled and held out two cups. "I didn't know if you drink coffee or not, so I got some punch, just to be on the safe side. Take your pick."

"Is the coffee unleaded?"

Dixie shook her head. "Regular."

"In that case, better make it punch."

"Want some?" Ethan asked Lolly, offering her the cup of punch he'd been holding in one hand while he licked chocolate frosting off the fingers of the other. "This is yours—I already had some."

"I can tell," said Lolly in a superior voice. "You have a big pink mustache. And there's chocolate all over your face." She shuddered—the cup she'd just taken from him had frosting all over it, too—and whispered loudly enough for her father to hear, "You're not even supposed to be eating that, and you know it. Sugar's bad for you. So is chocolate."

Ethan shrugged, not looking the least bit ashamed of himself. "I know, but Dixie said I 'served a treat. Anyway, I wanted a Rice Krispies bar, only they were all gone, so I hadda get a cupcake instead." He stuck out his lip in sort of a halfhearted pout, which disappeared when he popped another finger into his mouth.

But Lolly had suddenly lost interest in Ethan's gross eating habits. She couldn't believe her ears. For a moment she didn't say anything—it was like hearing somebody say something in a foreign language. Then she shook her head and stammered, "Th-they're gone? My Rice Krispies bars? They're *gone?*" She looked up at Dixie, feeling as if her breath had gotten trapped inside her chest. "Really?"

"'Fraid so," said Dixie. "The ladies said they were the first thing to go—went like hotcakes. They said they wished we'd brought some more. Sorry, sugar—looks like we missed out."

But she noticed that Lolly didn't look disappointed so much as dumbfounded. Poor little thing, she thought, trying to remember what it had felt like to be nine.

"Well, darn," said Rhett, snapping his fingers. "I was kind of hoping for one of those Rice Krispies things myself. We used to make them when I was a kid. Oh, well—maybe we can—"

"It's okay," Lolly interrupted in a breathless rush, "I saved some. I put some on a plate—they're at home, in the refrigerator."

"Now, that was smart thinking, sugar!" And it just came naturally to Dixie to put an arm around Lolly's shoulders and give her a quick little squeeze. When she did, although she couldn't be certain, she thought she caught a glimpse of the smile, the one that transformed the little girl's habitually sullen face into something of throat-catching beauty.

After that, Dixie noticed that Lolly seemed to be sticking to her side like glue, and that she kept giving her strange, sideways looks that were half puzzled, half wary.

Finally, as they were going down the front steps together, Lolly tugged on Dixie's sleeve and said something in a low voice that she couldn't quite catch. Dixie paused, leaned down and said, "What hon?"

"I said, I like your earrings."

Dixie gave a little bark of surprised laughter. "Why, thank you, sugar."

But for her, the biggest surprise wasn't what Lolly had said about the earrings, although that was considerable. What really caught her off guard was the flood of emotions that filled her throat with aching pressure and her eyes with the sting of tears, and made her thankful for the darkness.

"Well, that's it—he never even stirred," Rhett announced as he pushed through the swinging door into the kitchen. Then he checked in midstride and muttered, "Oh—sorry..." The room was in semidarkness, the only illumination coming from the small lights outside the door.

"Didn't mean to startle you," Dixie said softly.

He could see her now, standing at the window, one shoulder leaning against the casement, the pale silk of her blouse picking up a kind of corona from the outside light, like moonlight gilding the edges of a cloud. Her face was turned toward him and therefore in shadow, but when she spoke again he could hear traces of her smile—and a certain irony—in her voice.

"This room just seems friendlier in the dark."

Although Rhett probably agreed with her in his heart, it still felt vaguely disloyal to Elaine to say so out loud, so he gave only a noncommittal huff of laughter. He crossed shadow-dappled tile to the refrigerator, opened it and shuffled, frowning, through its contents. "Where did Lolly put those Rice Krispies... oh, yeah, here they are..."

"Little rascal." Dixie's chuckle was a warming sound in the grayness of the room. "I can't believe she actually saved some of those things, can you? After making such a fuss about the sugar, and all?"

"Lolly likes to pretend she's all grown up," Rhett said dryly. "Every now and then she forgets."

He paused with a Rice Krispies bar in his hand, trying to decide whether he ought to compound his dietary sins by having a glass of milk along with it. Then he remembered that he hadn't had any dinner that evening and decided that fact could even justify another Rice Krispies bar.

Sure, why not? Cereal and milk—sounded like good nutrition to him.

In the end he took the whole plate of Rice Krispies bars and the carton of non-fat milk out of the refrigerator and nudged the door shut with his elbow. "Want some of these?" he asked Dixie as he set the plate and carton on the counter.

He heard a faint rustling as she straightened and held up her wrist, tilted so she could see her watch by the light coming through the window. "No, thanks. I think it's time I was taking off. I'd take some coffee, though, if you have it."

"Just decaf, I'm afraid. Sorry."

She made a small, dismissive gesture. "That's okay. I'll pick some up when I stop for gas." But she didn't move away from the window. She watched, apparently transfixed, as lightning flickered, briefly changing her normally vivid features to pale blue porcelain.

Rhett poured himself a glass of milk, helped himself to two big cookie bars and went to join her at the window. "Hmm . . . I'd forgotten how good these things are," he mumbled through a mouthful of Rice Krispies and marshmallow. "The M&M's really add something, don't they? That was a stroke of genius, by the way. Did I remember to thank you?"

"Just another little trick I learned from my mama," Dixie drawled. "And no thanks are necessary. I was glad I could help."

"You did—more than you could possibly know." He swallowed milk, which did nothing to dissolve the knot that had formed unexpectedly in his chest. He tried a deep breath, which seemed to help more. "You're sure you won't have one?"

She shook her head, and the outside light caught briefly on the dark curls that had already worked free of the fastener at the nape of her neck to float around her temples. "I really do need to be going. Is Lolly—I suppose she's already in bed?"

Rhett coughed and reined in his wandering thoughts. "I think so. Did she at least say thank you for the horse?"

"She did . . ." And now he could definitely hear the smile in her voice " . . . in her own way."

There was a prolonged pause, a curiously vibrant silence, until a rolling grumble of thunder seemed to set things in motion, again, like the introductory bars of a dance.

Dixie folded her arms across her chest and rubbed at her upper arms, as if she'd felt a chill. And all of Rhett's nerves and muscles twitched with a sudden, almost overwhelming impulse; he thought the only thing that kept him from putting his arms around her at that moment might have been the glass of milk in his hand.

He placed the glass carefully on the table, which took him a step further away from her, a step closer to sanity. "Storm's coming in," he said, his voice muffled and airless.

"I know. I've been standin' here watching it. What kind of tree is that, by the way? That real big one? That's a great tree—a good climbing tree. It'd make a fantastic tree house, wouldn't it?"

Rhett leaned forward to look past her at the wind-lashed darkness, just as lightning turned his backyard into a flickering silent movie. There was a loud *crrack!* and in the microsecond of suspense before the *boom* that followed, he heard a soft gasp. Not of fear, but of pleasure. *Excitement.*

"It's an elm, I think," he heart himself say above the dying echoes of thunder. Maybe that's all it is, he thought. Her mood, the storm—he was picking it up from them. That's why he felt like this . . . keyed up, as if he were vibrating inside. He hadn't felt like this since he was a kid. Not even then, not that he remembered.

He cleared his throat. "Are you sure you ought to be taking off in this?"

"I've driven in worse." Her tone was dry as she turned at last from the window. "Storms don't bother me. If it gets too bad, I'll just pull off into a truck stop and wait it out." She moved quickly through the kitchen, pushed open the swinging door.

Rhett followed her into the lighted hallway, feeling oddly jangled, his legs unreliable, as if he'd just experienced some sort of trauma.

She'd reached the front door when he called to her, "Dixie..." Just her name, because he had no idea what else he had to say to her. Except . . . he had the feeling there must be something else, and that it was terribly important.

She settled the strap of her guitar case over her shoulder and picked up her small overnight bag before turning to look at him. She was smiling her brilliant smile, everything about her warm and vibrant after the gray darkness of the kitchen . . . the silver screen turned suddenly to living color.

"Well—y'all enjoy that horse, now, okay? And tell the kids I'm sorry I didn't get to say goodbye." She took her Stetson from the hall table. Then she paused and just looked at it for a moment, and her smile seemed to waver. "Tell Ethan..." She ducked her head and set the hat firmly onto it, and when she looked at Rhett again her smile was back in its place as well. "Well, just give him a great big hug from me, okay?"

She turned abruptly, groping for the door.

Rhett's heart lurched into his throat. *She's leaving!* He was bewildered by his own sense of dismay at that thought. No—more than dismay—of *panic*. As if something absolutely vital to him was slipping out of his grasp.

"Why don't you give him one yourself?" He hardly recognized the strangled sound of his own voice.

She'd paused with her hand on the doorknob, her smile gentle. "What, you mean wake him up? Oh, now, Rhett, I don't—"

"I mean..." He drew a great breath and threw consequences to the winds. "Tell him tomorrow."

"Tomorrow? But—"

"I mean, I'd like you to stay."

# *Chapter 5*

There was a moment of utter stillness, much like the vacuum that precedes a thunderclap. Then Dixie muttered, "I beg your pardon?" Well, okay, so it was a stock response. It served its purpose, which was only to buy her some time while the shock wore off.

It was simply the last thing she'd ever have expected to hear Rhett Brown say.

"Look," he was saying now, as though he hadn't even heard her, "I know this is sudden. *God...*" He stopped there and drove his fingers through his hair.

And with that one fierce gesture, banished the last vestiges of the stuffy lawyer whose company she'd been keeping most of the evening.

It was a transformation that had probably begun when he'd taken off his jacket and loosened his tie, after he'd carried Ethan upstairs to bed. Now, with his shirtsleeves rolled half-way to the elbow and his dark hair biker-wild, he looked...well, the word *vital* had crossed Dixie's mind once before, but now another, more dangerous, came in its stead. What he was, she decided, was...*virile*. In a very fundamental, male animal way—like a stallion, or a stag with a full rack of antlers.

Put in more up-to-date terms, he looked sexy.

Oh yes, breathtakingly so—in a very literal sense; she didn't think she could have uttered a word just then if her life depended on it.

Fortunately, Rhett didn't seem to expect her to. He'd turned away from her, in fact, and was pacing in the confines of the entry hall, made crowded and tiny by his sheer vitality. And talking more as if to himself than to her. "Frankly, this amazes me, too. I never thought I was capable of doing something this... unexpected."

*Unexpected?* That, thought Dixie, was the word for it. And for her, the most unexpected part of it was how she could find someone who'd just made such a crude proposition so very attractive.

Amazing, too, the power of suggestion. Surprising images came flashing through her mind, awakening feelings she'd buried long ago. *Another lifetime. Another Dixie...*

"But actually," Rhett was saying, his tone still as bemused and wondering as she felt, "it's something I've been thinking about all evening. You're exactly what I've been looking for, the answer to a prayer." He stopped pacing, finally, to fetch up in front of her, wearing an expression she could only think of as entreating. "So... I hope you'll at least consider my offer before you turn me down. I... of course, I'd make it worth your while."

At that, Dixie's breath did leave her—audibly. Along with the gasp she managed to deliver the word, *"What?"*

"What?" Rhett echoed in a puzzled tone.

Dixie tried and finally produced more words, if only in a whisper. "Did... did you just... offer to *pay* me?"

"Well, of course I'd pay you," he said impatiently, looking even more puzzled than before. "I would hardly expect you to do it out of the goodness of your heart. Tonight was one thing, but—"

"Hold on—hold it right there a minute." Dixie dropped her guitar and dusty overnight bag onto the polished parquet and held up her hand like a cop stopping traffic. "Would you..." She gulped, cleared her throat and began again. There was, clearly, no way out of this now except to go forward. "I'm sorry, but I'm gonna have to ask you a very embarrassing question. Did you... did I, or did I not, just hear you ask me to spend the night with you?"

Now it was Rhett's turn to huff out air as if someone had punched him in the breadbasket. "*What?* No! My God, no—nothing like that." He groaned, braced a hand on the doorframe and leaned his forehead against his arm. After a moment there came a muffled, "God...I'm not doing this very well, am I?"

"That depends," said Dixie warily, pleased that her inner flutterings weren't evident in her voice. "What, exactly, is it that you're tryin' to do?" Her Texas accent had a way of taking over when she was agitated.

Rhett straightened, huffed out a breath and ran a smoothing, calming hand over his hair. Then he folded his arms across his chest, as if, she thought, he were clutching something—his dignity, perhaps—for dear life. "What I'm doing," he said frowning at her, "is offering you a job."

"Uh-huh," said Dixie, "that part I got. Doin' what, exactly?"

"Ah...well, I..." The frown deepened, going from dignified to perplexed. "I'm not sure what you call it. Nanny...or maybe housekeeper—the agency's sent me both. In any case, nobody they've sent me seems to be quite what I'm looking for. And nobody's lasted more than a week—" his lips twisted with wry humor "—not counting the lady I fired when I found her passed out on the rug in my study with a bottle of cognac clutched to her bosom. I'd been wondering why she seemed so contented."

He paused to clear his throat, but Dixie had already seen clearly where he was trying so hard to go. Seen, and veered away from, like a horse refusing a fence.

The substance of her voice seemed to stick in her throat. She whispered, "You want me to look after your kids."

"Look—as I said, I know it's sudden." Rhett leaned toward her earnestly, selling the idea, now that it had finally been introduced, with a politician's fervor. "But the fact is, I've never seen the children take to anyone the way they did to you—Ethan, especially. It's been hard for him, you know, his mother leaving him the way she did. And Lolly..." He made a wordless but eloquent sound. "She's managed to rout every candidate the agency's sent over, usually in a matter of hours. Sometimes in tears. But she seems to tolerate you." He said it in a musing tone.

Dixie snorted, but he didn't seem to notice.

"And you—you must just be a natural, I guess. For somebody with none of your own, you do seem to know kids. And God knows..." He let it trail off there and turned away from her, at the same time forgetting his dignity long enough to drag that much too masculine, all too human, I'm-at-my-wit's-end hand through his hair.

Playing me, Dixie thought in sudden, unreasoning anger. The way a fisherman plays a fish he's hooked. Letting out the line a bit... reeling it in a little more.

"I wouldn't even ask it," he said softly, still turned slightly, not looking at her, "if I weren't just about at my wit's end. I know you have a life... responsibilities of your own. You told me you manage a ranch, raise horses. But I also know you've been doing some horse training for my sister for the past few weeks, so you must have someone who can look after things for you while you're away." He looked at her then, with raised eyebrows, waiting for her confirmation.

Dixie's anger evaporated as quickly as it had come. She thought longingly of the vast blue skies of Texas, of the sprawling wilderness of scrub juniper and twisting arroyos, the horse barns and emerald pastures shaded with weeping willows and kept lush with ticking sprinklers, the spread her entire family referred to fondly as The Tipsy Pee—the brand being a capital *P* set at a slight backward angle.

Someone to look after things? She smiled slightly and thought of Piu, who had set her on her first horse, and Carmen, who had clucked over the bruises from her first fall. They'd been her second set of parents—and the ranch's true managers.

Her lips curved wryly. She nodded.

"So..." Rhett let his breath out, earnest once more. "It wouldn't be for long—just until I can work out something permanent. Just to... I don't know, get them over the roughest part of the adjustment. You understand?"

What else could she do, when he appealed to her like that? She nodded.

Unexpectedly, Rhett laughed. "God, you must think I've lost my mind, asking someone I've barely met to take care of my children for me." His smile betrayed more irony than amusement. "Well... the fact is, my sister and I don't always see eye-to-eye on things, but Lucy does have a knack for seeing through people. It's pretty hard to fool her. If she trusts you, that's good enough for me.

"Look—I can see this has come at you from out of left field. If you don't want to stay tonight, I'll understand. You probably have unfinished business with my sister, too—I understand that. But at least think about it, okay? Maybe you can give me a call in a day or two? As I said, I'll make it worth your while."

He radiates charm like a furnace, Dixie thought bleakly. Oozes it from every pore.

Once more she nodded, even though her face felt stiff, her jaw was cramped, her throat locked up tight. Without a word she picked up her guitar and duffel bag. Rhett reached past her to open the door, admitting a booming crack of thunder. Outside, rain was pelting down on the brick steps, already running in rivers down the curving brick driveway.

Dixie was glad of the rain, grateful for the thunder. They made prolonged goodbyes impossible, and made it seem a natural thing for her to sprint hell-for-leather for her truck, not at all as though she were fleeing in terror of unseen demons.

But safe in the cab of her Chevy pickup, with the rain drumming on the roof and dripping off the brim of her Stetson and onto her nose, she found that she was shivering.

Shivering...with what? Cold? She probably was soaking wet, but for some reason wasn't aware of feeling anything—physically—at all. Her emotions were in much too much turmoil.

Anger, then? Oh, she wanted very much to be angry with Rhett, but found that she couldn't be. How could she blame him? He was just a father, concerned about his kids. How could he know what his words would do to her?

*For somebody with none of your own, you do seem to know kids.*

For a few moments she was angry with herself, reproaching herself bitterly for having stayed, pounding on the steering wheel with the heel of her hand. Why hadn't she just done what she'd come to do, unloaded the damn horse and gotten the hell out of there? *Oh God...I shouldn't have let myself get involved!*

But then Ethan's face flashed before her as if on a movie screen, larger than life, all trembling chin and huge chocolate drop eyes. Something in her chest contracted sharply; her heart actually *hurt.*

No, she couldn't blame herself, either. How could she not have responded to the appeal—the *need*—in those eyes?

But I can't possibly stay, she told herself, almost in panic. And in that moment, she at last recognized her driving emotion as fear.

*They aren't mine. It would only be a temporary thing—that's what he said. And then I'd have to leave them. And that would hurt too much. Oh, Peter...*

Oh, but she'd learned long ago how to keep herself from hurting.

So, she drew a long, deep breath and released it slowly, first easing the ache and the tension inside. Then she turned the ignition key, nursed the pickup's cranky engine to a steady roar and drove carefully down the brick-paved driveway into the rain.

The windshield wipers thumped steadily, though without much effect, as she crept past the colonial mansion, the medieval castle, the towering trees lashing in the wind. Then through the wavering, shimmering lights of shopping centers and traffic signals and onto the interstate, where the big rigs plowed by in unimpeded procession, towing their great billowing plumes of spray.

Dixie eased her Chevy and empty horse trailer into a slot behind a Roadway rig going approximately the speed limit and stayed there until she was well out of the city. The rain slackened, the traffic dwindled until it seemed to be just her and the eighteen-wheelers, like some latter day wagon train pushing doggedly westward.

At the first truck stop beyond the lights of town the Roadway pulled off, and so did she.

She filled up at the passenger car pumps first, taking time out of habit to check the oil—the Chevy was old, and had a tendency to use a little. Then she parked and went into the store to pay for the gas. As she was stomping and shaking water droplets from her Stetson, she realized, suddenly, that she was hungry. And, yes, now she *was* chilled—her silk shirt was soaked and sticking to her back like a clammy second skin.

The truckers' section of the restaurant was fairly crowded at that hour, with drivers waiting out the storm, but she was able to find an empty booth with a phone near the back. When the waitress appeared with a menu, Dixie waved it away and ordered bacon and eggs over easy, and coffee. While she waited for the coffee to arrive she took out her wallet and searched through it for her telephone calling card and the small piece of paper on which she'd written Lucy's number.

The waitress—whose name, according to the name embroidered on her uniform pocket, was Donna—was back almost instantly with the coffee. Dixie thanked her, creamed and sugared the coffee to her taste, then picked up the phone and began to punch in numbers.

"Hi," she said to the rather alarmed sounding person who answered on the third ring, "it's me, Dixie. Sorry to call so late."

"Oh—God." The voice sounded disgusted—no, irritated. Fortunately Dixie knew it was just Lucy's way. "No, that's okay, I just thought something had happened to Mike. He's in Chicago—I never feel right when he's in the city, can you blame me? Are you okay? Where are you?"

"I'm fine. I just wanted to let you know I'm not going to try to drive back tonight. I got kind of a late start, and we've had some rain. Right now I'm in a truck stop just west of Des Moines, but what I'll probably do is get a motel and start back in the morning. I didn't want you to worry."

"Oh, sure—that's fine. I'm glad you called, though." There was a pause, and then, in a tone that managed to convey both trepidation and complete innocence of all responsibility, Lucy asked, "So, how did you get along with Rhett?"

Dixie picked up her coffee, blew on it and took a careful swallow. "Fine, I guess. He offered me a job." She gave a soft, incredulous huff of laughter; the words sounded ludicrous, spoken out loud like that.

There was a much longer pause before Lucy said, with very un-Lucylike reserve, "Really? Doing what?"

"Oh . . . you know. Taking care of the kids. Sort of a nanny, I guess you'd call it."

"Ugh," said Lucy.

Dixie nearly scalded her mouth getting rid of coffee so she could protest, "No—no, the kids are great. Really."

"Hmm. Okay, so what did you tell him?"

She began massaging her temples with the thumb and middle finger of one hand. "I told him I'd think about it." The waitress materialized suddenly with her bacon and eggs. Dixie looked up with a distracted frown and said into the phone, "It's not as though I need a job."

The waitress snorted and said, "Lucky you," as she slapped a ticket down on the table and departed.

On the telephone, Lucy murmured, "No, I suppose not."

"And there's the colt, too. I'd really like to spend more time—"

"Oh, don't worry about that. Rosie and I can work with him, if you tell us what to do. If that's all—"

"It isn't," said Dixie shortly.

Lucy sighed. "I *know*, Rhett can be a real pain in the you-know-what. I know *I* sure wouldn't want to work for him."

Dixie closed her eyes, rubbing again at her temples. She was suddenly overwhelmed with tiredness, and another of those unexpected waves of homesickness. "It's not him. Really, it isn't. It's ... personal stuff, Lucy. For one thing ..." A spark of irritation flared within her, straightening her spine and sharpening her voice. "I just don't know if I want to be a substitute mother to someone else's kids. Plus, I haven't been home in months. Dammit, I miss my ranch. I miss my own life."

"Yeah, I understand." Lucy's tone was unusually soothing. "So ... it sounds like you've made up your mind. Why didn't you just tell him no?"

Dixie gave a gusty sigh. "Hon, I wish it was that simple. Those kids ..."

*They need me.*

"Oh boy, I'll bet you're sorry I got you into this," said Lucy, sounding noticeably un-sorry. There was a chuckle and an interested pause. "What *are* you going to do?"

"I don't know," Dixie whispered, staring down at her rapidly congealing eggs. "I wish ..." Her voice broke. She caught a quick breath. "Listen, I'll let you know, okay? Gotta go now. See you ... bye."

"Bye—take care."

But the line had gone dead.

Lucy cradled the receiver and turned to Gwen, who was up late, too, rolling out pie crusts on the kitchen table. "It's working," she said in a hushed and gleeful tone. "I really think it's working."

"What *I* think," Gwen remarked, arching one eyebrow, "is that you'd better be careful where you meddle."

"Me? I'm not meddling, I'm just helping out Providence, is all." Gwen's laughter was a musical grace note. "No, it's true." Lucy filched a scrap of pie crust dough and studied it thoughtfully. "If you ask me, this has the hand of Providence written all over it. Why else would Rhett call me up and ask about a horse out of the clear blue sky, just at the precise time when Dixie happened to be here training Rosie's colt?"

Gwen said nothing, but the clack of the rolling pin had its own eloquence.

"I know you believe in Providence," Lucy insisted, nibbling pie crust. "You always said that was what brought Mike Lanagan, a city slicker reporter on the lam from the mob, to my doorstep on the morning after my hired hand quit and my best sow farrowed in the mud.

"And look at Earl—he says he thinks maybe the reason he didn't die in that crash with Mom and Dad, and *then* survived the truck crash in Bosnia on top of that, was because there was something important he had to do. And that something was to be there just when Chris needed him to save her when that lunatic ex-husband of hers tried to kill her." She nodded wisely and brushed flour onto the front of her overalls. "Providence—it worked for me and for Earl, and now it's Rhett's turn. You'll see."

"Maybe," said Gwen, her musical voice pitched low and in a distinctly minor key. "But it's been my experience that if you leave things alone they generally work out the way they're supposed to. And that includes Providence." She stopped and held up the rolling pin like a giant exclamation point. "Helping's one thing—pushing's another. Chances are, you'll wind up pushing something where it's not meant to go. And then..." *slap* went the rolling pin onto the dough "...somebody's bound to get hurt."

The lightning came fitfully now; the thunder still mumbled and grumbled to itself like a disappointed panhandler, but far away to the east. In the relative quiet Rhett could hear the rain drip-dripping from the eaves onto the flagstone patio outside the double French doors of his office.

Office, den, study—whatever at any particular moment he chose to call the one room in the house Elaine and her decorator hadn't reached with their art nouveau revival phase. It was a room that still wore its mahogany paneling, multipaned windows and fat leather furniture like comfortable old shoes. It was a place where he could kick his own shoes off, if he felt like it. The one place in the world where he could let himself relax.

Though tonight, admittedly, he hadn't been able to do much of that. Although it was late, he was still sitting at his desk ostensibly going over the transcripts of a trial that had ended earlier that week in a hung jury. In actuality, he seemed to be spending most of his time staring at the room's reflection in the French doors—a view that was being intermittently overlaid by dramatic glimpses of his backyard in flickering blue white and silvery gray—letting his mind wander.

That tree . . . he was sure it *was* an elm . . . she was right when she'd said it would make a great climbing tree. . . .

He'd never built a tree house. He remembered that his brother had asked him to help build one once. He couldn't remember now, why he hadn't. Probably he'd been too busy— being class president, captain of the debate team, getting straight A's . . .

Not with girls, though; he hadn't really done that much dating in high school. In college, either, come to think of it. Not that he'd been a monk, just too busy . . . always too busy. Until the time had come when he'd needed a wife, and then . . . there'd been Elaine . . .

*God . . . did she really think I'd asked her to stay with me . . . sleep with me . . . for money?*

Not Elaine, of course—Dixie. His brain had done one of those lightning quick hops across several subjects—probably in a logical progression, if he took the time to unravel it—to arrive finally at a destination so far removed from his original train of thought it seemed a complete non sequitur. From his marriage to Elaine to Dixie standing in his front hallway saying in thunderstruck tones, "Did I, or did I not, just hear you ask me to spend the night with you?"

If nothing else, that rather embarrassing incident had demonstrated to him the sheer power of suggestion. By no means for the first time since she'd walked out his door tonight, disquieting visions of Dixie rose like steam before him, visions conjured from memory rather than imagination, images he hadn't realized at the time were being recorded with so much clarity and sensual detail.

The way that tight little bottom of hers moved in those snug-fitting jeans—amazing how hips so slim could look so sexy. The way the lightning flashes had backlit the silk blouse she was wearing, throwing her upper body into voluptuous silhouette. The sudden impulse he'd had to take her in his arms. . . .

It seemed to him suddenly that it had become much too warm in the room; heat was spreading like a slug of neat whiskey through his belly. His skin burned, and not, he knew, from embarrassment.

Funny—he hadn't thought he'd miss sex as much as he had; it had never been a very important part of his relationship with Elaine. But for some reason, now that it was no longer readily available to him he found that he seemed to spend an inordinate amount of time thinking about it, whether he wanted to or not. An extremely annoying state, he considered it, for a man of his age and stature. Disgustingly adolescent. He'd even had to resort, from time to time, to that repellent cliché, the cold shower.

And obviously, this was going to be one of those times, he acknowledged with chagrin as he took off his glasses and tossed them onto his blotter, pulled off his loosened tie and unbuttoned his shirt and pulled the tails free of his slacks. High time he was getting to bed anyway, and just as well it would be alone—he had to be in court early tomorrow.

It occurred to him, too, as he leaned across the stack of transcripts to turn off the desk lamp, that it was just as well Dixie hadn't taken him up on his offer; having her around all the time would have been murder on his self-control.

He made sure the French doors were locked, took a detour through the kitchen to check that door as well, and set the security system on Remote. He was on his way down the hall to lock up the front and turn off the lights when the doorbell rang. Since it was near midnight, it startled him badly.

His first thought, which made his back teeth clamp together in annoyance, was that it was Elaine, come either to plead with him or do battle over the terms of his countersuit—she'd just about had time to get the papers he'd sent her.

But then he paused to peer through the wavy leaded glass of the sidelight beside the front door, and what he saw caused him to swear emphatically under his breath, venting emotions he couldn't have named, but that definitely were not anger.

He lunged for the door and threw it wide open. "Dixie— what in the—"

"I'm sorry to bother you so late." Her voice sounded oddly stifled. "I wouldn't have, but I saw the lights . . ."

"No—no, it's okay, I was up." *What in the world?* He started to lift his hand to his brow, stopped himself and touched her elbow with it instead. "Are you okay? What happened? Something wrong with your car..." He broke off, muttering. She was hugging herself, shivering; he could feel the vibrations in his own bones. "My God, you're wet...freezing. Come on, get in here." He stood back, holding the door for her.

She stayed where she was, her eyes riveted on his chest, and said in a flat voice, "You were getting ready for bed."

Rhett glanced down at himself. "As a matter of fact, I was," he admitted as he yanked the two halves of his shirt together and began a clumsy effort to button them. His lack of poise irritated him. She did have a way of knocking him off-balance. "It doesn't matter—tell me why you're here. And for God's sake, come in. Can I get you something hot to drink? Tea...hot chocolate..."

She was smiling slightly as she stepped across the threshold, but it didn't look right. "No—nothing, thanks. I had some coffee a while ago."

He watched as she lifted both hands to smooth back her hair, a vaguely self-conscious gesture that he was sure wasn't like her. He noticed that she hadn't been wearing her cowboy hat; the frizz of curls that had escaped the twist at the back of her head was spangled with water droplets that glittered in the yellow glow of the entry chandelier like tiny gold sequins. He saw her smile flicker like the retreating lightning, then die completely.

She cleared her throat. "That...job you mentioned. I've thought about it...."

Rhett's heart lurched, his attention zapped into sharp focus. "Yes? And...?"

"Okay, well, I have a few questions to ask." She said it gruffly, almost with belligerence, with her head high and her forehead puckered in a frown, while at the same time she was hugging herself in what he imagined must be an effort to stop herself from shivering. It was a strange contradiction, that mix of fierceness and vulnerability. Strangely affecting.

"Shoot," said Rhett, then came to his senses. "No, wait...here, come in here." He took her elbow and ushered her down the hall, through the kitchen and into his office.

He left his unexpected guest shivering in the middle of the room while he turned on the desk lamp. "We might as well be comfortable...and there's less chance we'll wake the children. Now, let me see if I..." Still talking, half to himself, he dove into a closet where he made hasty efforts to restore his clothing to a degree of propriety. Then he yanked the smoking jacket Elaine had bought him one long-ago Christmas from its hanger, paused, counted slowly to five, and exited the closet with his shirttails and most of his dignity in place.

"Put this on," he said curtly, handing the jacket to Dixie. "It's fairly warm." And it would cover that damned blouse, which kept sticking to her in tantalizing patches.

He went around behind his desk, picked up his glasses and put them on. Thus armed and protected, he cleared his throat and intoned, "All right...fire away."

I'm glad Lucy isn't here to see this jacket, Dixie thought as she slipped gratefully into it and pulled it around her. Burgundy velvet with satin lapels...heavens. Such a garment would have confirmed all Lucy's worst opinions about her brother.

Apparently he doesn't wear it much, though, she thought. It doesn't smell like him.

But how would she know what he smelled like? She found herself thrusting her hands into the jacket's deep pockets and scowling to hide the fact that she was suddenly, vaguely and unaccountably, flustered.

Anyway, she knew what he was up to, putting himself behind his desk like that, and she wasn't about to let him get away with such a blatant power play. It even amused her. She was used to holding her own in the dusty man's world of horse auctions and livestock shows. Plus, she never had been one to react well to intimidation.

Going briskly around to the far side of the desk, she moved aside a pile of bound transcripts and sat on the edge of it. And was pleased to see a little pleat of annoyance appear between Rhett's elegantly sculpted brows.

"You don't know me very well," she told him somberly.

"That's true." Rhett coughed, glanced behind him, pulled up his chair and sat. "But as I said before..."

"You trust Lucy's judgment, and I'm good with kids—I know. The thing is, I'm not sure that's good enough for *me*."

Rhett leaned back in his chair and regarded her with a scowl of puzzlement. "I don't know what you mean."

"I think...you and I are very different." A corner of his mouth quirked upward, whether in irony or amusement she couldn't tell. But he didn't say anything, and after a moment she took a breath and went ahead with it. "They say that what people fight about more than anything, besides money, is the kids."

The smile vanished. He said austerely, "Among married couples, that's probably true. That hardly applies to this situation."

"Uh-huh," said Dixie dryly. "That's what I thought." She hopped off the desk, shrugged out of the burgundy velvet jacket and laid it on top of the pile of transcripts.

"Wait a minute!" Rhett's chair twanged loudly as it sprang upright and creaked as he left it. He came around his desk to put a delaying hand on her arm. "What did I say? It's true, isn't it? We're *not* a married couple. I'd be—"

"You'd be my boss," Dixie said softly, finishing it for him, "and I'd have to follow your rules."

"Well . . ." He drew back, looking nonplussed, blustering a little. "I don't like to think of it that way, but . . . Well, of course. I'm their father. Naturally, when it comes to my kids, I'd have to have the last word."

Dixie cocked her head and studied him for a moment, then asked, "You and your wife ever fight about the kids?"

Rhett folded his arms and looked self-righteous. "No—no, as a matter of fact, we didn't. There was no reason to. She ran the house and took care of the kids—and did a pretty good job of it, I might add."

"Uh-huh." Dixie turned once more to the door.

"Wait! Now, wait just a darn minute—what in the hell's that supposed to mean?"

"Nothing," Dixie said calmly, "except, I don't think I'm the one to come in here and step into your wife's shoes." She smiled slightly as Rhett jerked back from her, looking appalled. She shook her head to forestall his sputtered protest. "I didn't mean that quite the way it sounded. I just meant that my ways of doing things are a whole lot different from hers—from yours, too, I reckon, since you say you agreed with her."

"Okay, okay." He held up his hands like a schoolmaster trying to restore order. "First of all . . . geez, the *last* thing I want is for somebody to step into my wife's shoes—in any way."

He pivoted away from her, shoving his hand back through his hair in that distracted way he had. The familiar gesture made Dixie smile; she liked him a whole lot better flustered than pompous.

She barely had time to erase the smile before Rhett suddenly whirled and pinioned her with an accusing finger, a maneuver she was sure he'd practiced on many a reluctant witness. "And by the way, just what are these differences you keep going on about? I didn't see you doing anything tonight—" he glanced at the clock above the fireplace and amended "—last night— that I'd object to."

"Oh yeah?" Dixie snapped back. "Not even the sugar?"

"The *what?*"

"The sugar." She did not say it patiently; she was beginning to feel a little warm under the collar herself. "Lolly kept going on about, she's not allowed to have this, she's not allowed to have that... I saw enough of what's in your cupboards and fridge to get a pretty good idea of the way y'all eat—"

"Oh, for pete's sake!" Rhett threw up his hands and spun away in exasperation. "We're concerned about what the kids eat, sure. What do you want to do, fill 'em up with junk food and sweets?"

"Of course not," Dixie snapped. "I just think a little common sense is in order. Y'all have too doggone many rules."

"Rules?" shouted Rhett. "What are you talking about? Kids need rules. They need discipline—"

"They need space, flexibility, a chance to use their own brains. How are they ever going to learn to think for themselves, if you make all the decisions?"

"Make all the—they're just *kids,* for God's sake!"

"Oh yeah?" Dixie's hands were on her hips, her chin in the air. "Well, for your information, studies have shown that, if left to choose for themselves, even toddlers will eat a balanced diet. Did you know that?"

Rhett wasn't impressed. His snort was derisive. "I suppose you'd have my kids running wild—like Lucy's, completely undisciplined—"

"Your niece, Rosie," said Dixie coldly, "is a perfectly lovely child. Happy, self-confident, spontaneous, loving—which you'd know, if you'd ever been out there to visit."

"Oh, now wait just a minute. My family—"

"I'm sorry," Dixie gasped, and held up a hand. "That was out of line. I'm truly sorry." She took a deep, calming breath, and after a moment added dryly, "Anyhow, if nothing else, I think I've proved my point."

To her surprise, Rhett began to laugh. "Yeah, I guess for a couple of people who aren't married, that was a pretty good imitation."

Dixie nodded, trying hard to smile herself. "But you see what I mean—why I don't think it would work out, me taking care of your kids. We're just too damn different." To her bewilderment, there was a lump in her throat. A cold desolation around her heart.

Rhett studied her somberly for a long moment. Then he took off his glasses, rubbed a hand over his eyes and said on a tired sounding exhalation, "Maybe...maybe not. I don't see why we can't find some room here for compromise."

"That's something else you don't know about me," said Dixie gently, her smile wavering as the lump in her throat became an ache. "I've never been much good at compromising."

There was another silence. She could see him struggling with it, knew he was hating to give it up as much as she did. Even so, it surprised her when he said abruptly, "Okay, suppose I agree to give you a free hand in the kitchen?"

She caught her lower lip between her teeth, holding back a gust of startled laughter. It sounded like a plea bargain. "You'd do that?"

He shrugged, then relaxed, letting his own smile come slowly. "Well, I guess if I'm going to entrust you with my children, I'd better trust your judgment, hadn't I?"

The laughter she'd been containing burst forth on a single note, much like a snort. "I guess!"

"Well, then? What do you think? Can we at least give it a try?"

"A try..." Her stomach felt tight, aflutter with emotions, most of which she couldn't name. One of which was hope. "Maybe..."

"A trial period. That way we'd both have a chance to see if we can...get along."

"A trial period," Dixie murmured. "Okay...I guess I could do that."

He let go of a breath that sounded as if he'd been holding it for a good long while and said, "Okay...okay. Deal?"

She looked down at his hand and slowly extended hers to meet it...felt it being swallowed up in his wonderfully warm, all-enveloping politician's handshake. What an amazing thing that handshake was. She could feel the warmth of it spread from that small contact point throughout her whole body. "Deal," she whispered.

"Thank God, that's settled," said Rhett briskly, and released her hand—along with whatever spell he'd had her under. "Now—you can stay tonight, can't you?"

*Charisma,* she thought, still dazed. She nodded. "If you have a place to put me."

"We—I have a guest room—will that do?"

Her laugh was husky with residual effects of the emotional battles she'd just fought, with the tiredness that had suddenly overtaken her. "Beats a bedroll on the floor of my trailer. I just need to get my bag..."

"I'll get it. Why don't you go on up? It's the first door on the right, top of the stairs. Is your truck unlocked?" His voice was kind, now that things were going his way, his manner solicitous.

"Yes... thanks."

They were moving together through the silent house, a curiously intimate thing to be doing, Dixie thought, in the dark and chill of the wee hours. Beside her Rhett was a warm, curiously reassuring presence... not like the stallion, a little wild and frightening, but somehow even larger than he'd seemed before. And neither the pompous, slightly stuffy lawyer that irritated Lucy so, nor the distracted father, so appealing in his vulnerability.

A strong man, Dixie realized. A very capable man. A man comfortable in his own shoes, and absolutely certain of the path he'd set them on.

Suddenly she was remembering his handshake, remembering the warmth that had flooded through her from that point of contact.... More than remembering—she was feeling that same warmth now, and more... a hollow fluttering in her stomach, a frightening weakening in her knees. A certain yearning...

Oh God, she thought. Oh God.

## Chapter 6

Rhett woke with a vague feeling of disorientation. A sense that something had changed. And because most of the recent changes in his life had been of the catastrophic variety, his body went rigid and still while his mind searched for reasons. Then all at once he relaxed into his pillow with a burgeoning smile.

*Ah, yes.* What was different this morning, he realized, was that he wasn't worried. He'd woken up worried every morning for weeks, now. Gone to bed worried. Eaten his meals worried—ulcers, he'd been convinced, only a handful of antacids away. But, hallelujah, now his troubles were over. Everything was gong to be all right.

Dixie was here.

As pleased with things as if it had been Mary Poppins herself asleep in his guestroom, he threw back the covers and sat up, stretched a good, long stretch while he searched for his slippers with his feet. Without success. It hadn't been cold enough yet for slippers. But there definitely was a chill in the air this morning, he discovered as he padded barefooted into the bathroom. Whatever else it might have done, last night's storm seemed to have finally blown away the lingering remnants of summer. Which was fine with him. Fall was one of his favorite times of the year. He always got a little bit nostalgic and sentimental when the leaves turned.

While he waited for the water to run hot, he gave his countenance its usual cursory spot-check in the mirror. Some remote part of his mind recorded the fact that he'd be needing a haircut soon, but most of it was busy with more important things.

The day ahead, of course. Pretrial meetings with witnesses . . . the state's attorney . . . the trial itself, unless the prosecution decided to opt for a deal.

The meeting he had scheduled for lunch recess with Newt Hendricks and the rest of the campaign strategy team . . . now, *that* he didn't like to think about. Rhett knew very well that Attorney General Rossen's decision to back his candidacy for the office when she stepped down at the end of this term was based on two things: One, his youthful, squeaky-clean image and unblemished background; and two, his father-in-law's connections to the party's political "old guard." Both had been seriously compromised by this damned divorce. No doubt damage control was going to be at the top of everybody's agenda.

What else? Back to the children, of course. No more worries there, but . . . what was he going to tell them about Dixie?

His eyebrows dipped; his razor, methodically plowing tan furrows in snow-white lather, stopped and slowly lowered. He gave a preparatory cough, and for good measure, cleared his throat. Then he announced to his reflection, in the best Mister Rogers impression he could come up with on the spur of the moment, "Children, I have some good news for you."

Not bad. A little formal, though. Making too big a deal out of it, perhaps? Okay, try a more casual approach.

"Hey, kids—guess what? I've found you a new nanny."

*Ouch.* He winced as if he'd cut himself shaving, which he hadn't. It was the word *nanny* that pained him. It didn't seem right, not as applied to Dixie, but he couldn't put his finger on exactly why.

He knew he didn't need to explain anything to Ethan. His son was going to be tickled pink. He'd accept Dixie's presence without question. Lolly, however, was another story. Oh, sure, she'd seemed to get along with Dixie fairly well last night—why not, when the woman had just delivered her precious horse, her heart's desire? *And* could be counted on afterward to disappear safely into the sunset, never to be seen again. Dixie sticking around, invading territory Lolly had lately taken to considering her own preserve—that was another story.

One good thing, he reminded himself as he patted his face dry and turned on the shower, he had this morning to prepare the children for their new nanny—oh, how he hated that word. Kendra, his cleaning lady's teenaged daughter, had been stopping by to help fix the kids' lunches and take them to the bus stop, so he'd told Dixie to sleep in and take the time while the children were in school to settle in and acquaint herself with the household. Maybe do some grocery shopping, he'd suggested, since she'd expressed so much dissatisfaction with what she'd found in his cupboards.

Shopping. That reminded him—she'd need some money for groceries.

*Money.* For the first time it occurred to him that, in all of last night's ... discussion—he refused to think of it as an argument—over the terms of this "trial" arrangement, neither he nor Dixie had thought to mention her salary. He wondered what in the world *that* meant.

No time to ponder it now, however; he had too much on his mind, too many things to do. Starting with talking to the kids.

But when he stopped in his study to pick up his briefcase and psych himself up for that task, he discovered that his agenda might have to be rewritten.

He could hear voices coming from the kitchen. One voice in particular, one that was impossible to mistake for any other. One that wasn't soft and cultured and oh, so perfectly modulated, as Elaine's had been, pitched just right for gracious formal dinners and reception lines and the occasional Junior League luncheon speech.

God, no. This was a voice as bright and brassy as a Texas sky, merry as a yodel, a voice that could swoop from one end of an impossible range to the other with the grace of a steel guitar. Dixie's voice.

For some reason, hearing it unexpectedly like that made something inside his chest go *bump,* the way it did in court when he heard a witness utter the lie that would hang him during cross-examination. What it was was *anticipation.* Excitement, pure and simple.

He'd been all set to sail briskly into the kitchen the way he did every weekday morning as he collected goodbye kisses and his usual high-fiber, low-fat nutrition bar breakfast before dashing off to work. Instead, something made him pause in what had once been the butler's pantry, open the door a stealthy crack, and unabashedly eavesdrop.

"What *is* it?" That was Ethan's voice—excited and curious.

Then Dixie, sounding like somebody with delicious secrets. "What does it look like?"

"A circle . . . and then another circle . . ."

"Look again . . . if we add one more circle . . ."

"Those are *ears!*" shrieked Ethan.

Intrigued beyond caution, Rhett pushed the door open a little more. Now he could see Dixie at the cooking island, with Ethan standing beside her on one of Elaine's expensive black lacquered chairs. His son was wearing an apron tied around his neck like a bib, clutching a plate in both hands and avidly watching something apparently wondrous that was taking place on the griddle.

"Right you are!" crowed Dixie. Then her voice dropped, became suspenseful as she brandished a pancake turner. "Okay, now this is the hard part . . . we have to turn the whole mess over at the same time, right? Careful . . . careful . . . *There* you go!"

There was a gasp from Ethan, then a cheer. "Yay . . . you *did* it! *Now* tell me what it is, Dixie, please?"

Rhett could see Dixie's long black braid snake and dance down the middle of her back as she shook her head. "Uh-uh— you tell me. Come on, now—these are the ears . . ."

"What are you doing?" That was Lolly, looking cranky and suspicious, but unable to keep a note of curiosity from creeping into her voice nonetheless. Rhett had been so intent on the drama at the cooking island that he hadn't heard her come in.

"Mickey Mouse!" yelled Ethan, doing a little jig on the chair's glossy black seat. "You made Mickey Mouse—hey, Lolly, look what Dixie made for me. See? It's Mickey Mouse— here's his ears . . ."

"We're supposed to have cereal for breakfast," Lolly bossily informed everyone. But she kept coming, Rhett noticed, until she was close enough to see what was on the griddle. To show she wasn't impressed, she hunched her shoulders and looked sideways at Dixie. "So how come you're here? Did you spend the night or something?"

"Or something," Dixie murmured placidly.

"I have a loose tooth," said Ethan. "So Dixie's makin' me pancakes. Look, isn't it *neat?*"

"Just like they make 'em at Disneyland," Dixie declared, sounding a trifle smug. "Here—give me your plate."

"Really?" Ethan watched, awestruck, as Dixie slid something floppy and oddly shaped onto his plate.

"Guaranteed. Okay, put that down here, now. See...we put a little applesauce on it...then two banana slices for eyes...a prune for the nose..."

"Unh-uh, no prunes—my loose tooth, remember?"

"Gotcha. Okay, another banana slice for the nose. You'll just have to pretend it's black. Then...half a pineapple slice for the smile and...voilà!"

"Wow! Thanks..." Ethan snatched up his plate and ran to the table with it, full tilt. Which was something his mother would never have allowed. Rhett could almost hear her cool, cultured voice saying, "*Walk,* young man." And Ethan, eyes downcast, mumbling, "Yes, ma'am..."

But Dixie didn't say a word about it—didn't seem to notice. "How 'bout you?" she said casually to Lolly as she devoted her attention to scrubbing the griddle clean with a paper towel. "Would you like a pancake?"

The corners of Lolly's mouth turned downward. "Mickey Mouse? No thanks, I think I'll just have cereal."

Dixie shrugged and picked up the bowl of pancake batter. "Suit yourself. I think I'm gonna make me a..." She let it trail off and began to drizzle batter onto the griddle with a spoon while Lolly stayed to watch in unwilling fascination.

"It's a flower," said Lolly after a moment, so determined not to be excited that her voice had almost no intonation at all.

Dixie's voice was a golden purr of satisfaction. "Uh-huh...sunflower, actually..."

Lolly watched a few minutes longer, then tilted her head warily toward Dixie and asked, "Can you make a horse?"

"Oh, brother," said Dixie, shooting her a look Rhett couldn't see from where he was standing, "you don't want much, do you?"

"Well, can you?"

"I don't know. Let's see..."

Rhett watched the two heads come together, bent in avid concentration over the hot griddle, one midnight black and curly, the other sunshine golden and straight as a horse's mane. Night and day. In more ways than one.

Impossible, a voice inside him said, answering a question he didn't even know he'd asked. *Impossible.*

"Well," said Dixie after a moment, "what do you think? Is that a horse?"

Rhett could see his daughter's mouth purse up and quirk sideways in an expression that meant she was doubtful but willing to be convinced. "It's kind of funny looking."

"It's a horse," Dixie said firmly, "and a damn—oops—darn fine one, too. Okay, hurry up, gimme your plate... *there* you go. Want some applesauce on it?"

"Yes, please..." And then Lolly said almost wistfully, "You know what'd be neat? If we had something to put on the mane and tail... you know, so it'd look like hair?"

Dixie scratched her chin. "Hmm...I think I saw some shredded wheat—would that do?"

Lolly actually laughed. "Shredded wheat on pancakes? *Yuck.*"

"Guess what?" Ethan said with his mouth full, waving a forkful of pancakes. "Dixie's gonna stay with us and be our new mommy—I mean nanny. Isn't that *great?*"

Having already taken one step toward the table with her plate in her hands, Lolly whirled back to Dixie to demand in breathless outrage, *"You?"*

"Can we have pancakes *every* morning, Dixie, huh, can we?"

"I told my dad, we don't need a nanny." Lolly's eyes narrowed dangerously.

Uh-oh, thought Rhett. Fun time's over—that's my cue.

But before he could push through the door and charge to the rescue, he heard the husky ripple of Dixie's laughter, like a broken chord played softly on a guitar.

"Well, of course *you* don't, sugar," she murmured, turning slightly to exclude an oblivious Ethan, who was too busy licking his plate to notice the feminine conspiracy she was creating with subtle voice tones and body language. "But your brother...he's still pretty little, you know."

"I can take care of him. We don't need a nanny. We don't need *anybody.*" Lolly's shoulders were tensed, her face flushed and furious.

Watching her, Rhett swore he could feel his own heart breaking in two, which was only to be expected, he supposed, when it was constantly being torn between anguish and anger.

But again, before he could intervene, something made him stop and listen instead, his ears straining to catch Dixie's murmured reply.

"Sugar...your daddy knows what a super job you've been doing, looking after your little brother like you have. But he knows what a big job it is, too, and that's why he thought, you know, now that you have your horse to take care of..." She'd been bending down, bringing her dark curls once more into that startling conjunction with pale silk. Now she straightened and laid a gentle hand on Lolly's stiff, wary shoulder. "Well...that's okay, I understand. I'm sure you dad will, too. Maybe he can arrange something with the people at the stables."

At that, Lolly snapped to attention like a horse hearing a whinny in the distance. "What do you mean?"

Dixie's shrug was elaborately casual. "Oh, well, you know— he'll have to hire somebody to ride Star every day, give him his exercise ..."

"But Star's *my* horse. I want to do that! You said—Dad said I could."

Dixie picked up her plate and made for the table, her words trailing behind her like smoke from a locomotive. "I know, sugar, but I don't really see how you'd have the time, do you? I mean, with school, and homework, and helping Ethan with his homework, and looking after him, and everything...horses take up an awful lot of time, you know. But that's okay—I'll tell your dad you've decided you'd rather take care of your brother instead. I really do admire you for that, you know? Taking on such a big responsibility..."

There in the butler's pantry, Rhett could feel delight and admiration welling up inside him, threatening to bust loose in unbridled chortles and snorts of laughter. Which would have felt awfully damn good—it had been a long time since he'd laughed like that. Under the circumstances, though, he thought he'd better make his presence known in a more circumspect manner.

He couldn't stop himself, though, from grinning from ear to ear as he pushed open the door and strode across the kitchen, briefcase in hand.

"Hi, kids . . . good morning, Dixie. Hmm . . . what's that I smell?"

Ethan hopped off his chair and ran to meet him. "Hi, Dad—guess what? We're havin' pancakes! And I have a loose tooth . . . wanna see?"

Rhett dutifully inspected his son's tooth and dropped a kiss onto the top of Lolly's averted head, noticing as he did so that she was being conspicuously silent.

"Can I get you some pancakes?" Dixie asked, starting to get up from her chair.

He waved her back to it as he turned to the cupboard. "No, thanks—I usually have a couple of these nutri-whatever bars. I see you've spoiled my surprise, though. Kids, did Dixie tell you? She's—"

"Uh . . ." Dixie coughed and interrupted, "I'm afraid there's been . . ."

From the corner of his eye, Rhett caught the sudden, sharp movement of Lolly's head. Then Dixie's whispered, "Sugar, are you sure?" And Lolly's rapid nod. Dixie carefully cleared her throat and murmured, "Why, yes, I guess I did. Sorry 'bout that." Her laughter didn't sound a bit sorry—for spoiling the surprise, or anything else.

Rhett thought that if he could figure out a way to bottle that laugh, it might just replace orange juice and coffee as a morning perker-upper.

Just then there was a knock at the kitchen door—Kendra, fidgety and fifteen, bobbing and leaning this way and that to grin and wave at them through the divided glass windowpanes. Ethan ran to let her in, and then there were introductions to be made, and the usual squabbles over the kids' lunches—a shade more subdued than usual, Rhett noticed. The presence of an unexpected stranger was apparently having a dampening effect on Kendra.

Ethan had to display his loose tooth one more time, naturally, then used it as an excuse to reject anything Kendra tried to put in his Power Rangers lunch box that was even remotely nutritious. He did finally agree to Dixie's inspired offering—a peanut butter and banana sandwich—and thanked her by throwing his arms around her neck and noisily kissing her cheek before dashing off to catch up with Kendra, who was bawling impatient threats from the front hallway.

In the quiet that followed the *shussh* of the swinging door, Lolly, who'd been dawdling uncharacteristically over her own plain brown paper lunch bag, threw Dixie a look and murmured, "Dad? Can—may I go and see Star after school?"

"You'll have to take that up with Dixie," said Rhett briskly, catching her eye over Lolly's head as he tried out the words. Smiling at her. No—smiling was too tame a description of what he was doing. *Beaming*, that was it. He could almost feel his chest inflating like a hot air balloon, feel himself filling up with a wonderfully warm, rosy sense of well-being. Yes sir, everything was going to be all right now. Dixie would see to that.

It didn't occur to him until much later that there'd been no answering smile from Dixie. Not even a glimmer.

"You bet, sugar," was her only response to Lolly's questioning look. Then she briefly touched a cheek that was flushed with a mixture of resentment and hope, pushed open the door and held it. "Better run—you'll miss your bus." Her voice was husky, but Rhett thought nothing of that, either. Or if he did, put it down to the normal scratchiness of morning.

He was running late. He kissed Lolly briskly and sent her on her way, then remembered again that Dixie was going to need money if she was going to do any grocery shopping that day.

"Why don't you stop by my office later?" he suggested, pausing in the doorway to think about it. "I've got a lunch meeting . . . tell you what, though, I'll stop by the ATM on my way in and get you some cash and leave it with my secretary—how'd that be? You can call the office—it's a one-button dial. Leanne will give you directions."

"That's fine," said Dixie. "I'll do that."

"Well . . . okay then. I have to go—have to be in court. . . ." He frowned, suddenly feeling vaguely remiss, as if there were something more he ought to say or do. Suddenly feeling strange about going off and leaving her there. Suddenly wishing he didn't have to.

The abrupt flip-flop in his mood shook him profoundly, leaving him with the sensation in his stomach much like that of a hot air balloon plummeting to earth. He muttered, "Uh...if you have any problems . . ."

"I won't," said Dixie, "and if I do, I'll call. Don't worry..." a smile was flickering at the corners of her mouth ". . . so far, so good." He couldn't see her eyes—they seemed to be in shadow. He heard her catch a quick breath. "Bye, now—good luck in court."

"Oh—yeah. Thanks." Air whooshed from his lungs in sheer relief; the balloon stopped its precipitous descent and began to float skyward once more. He smiled and touched his temple with a forefinger. "I mean it—thanks for everything. Make yourself at home . . . see you later. Have fun . . ."

There was more—he couldn't understand why it was so hard to walk out his own front door. But finally he did, closed it firmly behind him and strode briskly to his car, smiling and pleased with himself, looking forward to, even excited about the day ahead of him for the first time in weeks.

Excited about the prospect of coming home at night for the first time in . . . much, much longer.

*So far, so good . . .*

Thank God, thought Dixie as she listened to the diminishing echo of Rhett's footsteps, the tidy *chunk* of his car door, the cough and growl of its well-tuned engine. *Thank God . . .*

Thank God he was gone, thank God they were all gone, thank God she was alone. She didn't have to hold it in any longer, guard her voice and her expression, shutter her eyes.

Oh, but there'd been moments when she hadn't though she'd be able to stand it, when she'd thought surely they must hear the panic leaking into her laughter, see the anguish behind her smile.

Oh God, she thought . . . prayed. I thought I could do this. I thought enough time had passed, I thought I'd healed enough.

But from the moment when that little boy had thrown his arms around her neck and kissed her cheek and whispered in her ear, "Bye . . . I love you, Dixie," she'd realized that she hadn't really healed at all. The hole in her heart, it seemed, was permanent. All she'd managed to do in ten years was cover it with a patch.

It had been a mistake to come back here last night, she knew that now. A mistake to agree to stay, even on a trial basis. Because now she was well and truly trapped. I can't possibly leave, she thought, hollow and desolate inside . . . especially in the vicinity of her heart. *He needs me. They all need me.*

But everything in her wanted to break and run, back to the ranch, to the protective isolation of West Texas, the insulating emptiness of the plains, the great healing vastness of sky. As she'd run so many times before when she'd felt her hard-won peace threatened. When she'd felt her pulses quicken and her hormones whisper, *Now . . . maybe now . . . yes, it's time.*

Always before, her heart had cried a resounding *No!* It would not risk such pain again—another wound like the one it had already suffered would surely be mortal. She wouldn't survive it.

And so she had run.

But this time she couldn't run. A little boy needed her. So did his sister, even if she didn't know it. And his father . . . yes, his father needed her, too, although she wasn't quite sure how she felt about that. In any case, she couldn't possibly turn her back on them now, even at the risk of her own sanity.

So, instead of running she went back down the hall to the kitchen and did the breakfast dishes. Swept the floor and polished fingerprints off all the glossy black surfaces. Long ago she'd discovered the therapeutic value of housework. It required a degree of concentration, but no great expenditure of mental or emotional energy—the mind could be both occupied and empty at the same time. It gave her a sense of purpose and of accomplishment. She could vent to her heart's content—blow off steam, do battle with demon dust and emerge victorious, turn disorder into order. Very satisfying, in a way. Better than meditating, or Scotch, both of which she'd turned to at various times in the past.

Once the kitchen had been restored to its pristine and sterile state, she took stock of the cupboards and refrigerator and made out a shopping list. Then, since it was still too early to go downtown to Rhett's office, she set out to thoroughly explore his house.

She began in the living room, which she'd caught glimpses of through the wide arched doorways off the entry. It was a beautiful room, she had to admit, even though its stark, modern style didn't in the least match the house's Tudor exterior. It was all done in ivory—walls, carpet, fireplace and furniture—with a few accents in black, graceful, curving sculptures, mostly, in a style Dixie had heard named but couldn't quite recall. There was one huge print of a flower in black and white, with just a touch of seashell, over the fireplace, covered in glass but unframed. It reminded Dixie of a Georgia O'Keeffe—

maybe it *was* an O'Keeffe, for all she knew. She wasn't much of an authority on twentieth-century art.

What struck her, though, was that for all its elegance and beauty, for a living room, it showed very little evidence that any living was being done there. And no sign whatsoever that a child had ever sat on one of its fat, puffy sofas, or set a foot on its soft, thick carpets.

In fact, that pretty much summed up the entire house, as far as Dixie could see. Try as she might, she couldn't imagine a child running through its rooms and hallways, curled up in a cozy corner with a book, sprawled on the floor with a pile of Lego. Only in their own individual rooms was there any concrete evidence of the children's existence in the house. And those seemed to her almost unnaturally tidy. For some reason, they made her feel sad.

She avoided Rhett's bedroom and study, both out of respect for his privacy, and because the thought of being in his personal space disturbed her profoundly. It reminded her of last night, of those moments with him alone in the silent, sleeping house . . . the terrifying intimacy of it. Panic bumped beneath her ribs.

To escape it, and the indefinable sadness as well, she went outside to explore the backyard. It was one of those achingly lovely mornings—crisp and cool, but with the promise of warmth in the sun's hazy shimmer. It felt like fall at last. Last night's storm had brought down the first leaves. They littered the lawn and blended their colors with the late-blooming annuals in the flowerbeds, clumped in the rain gutters and lay sodden on the walkways. Here and there one tumbled, rustling like a living thing, out of a tree. A squirrel bounded gracefully among them, searching for something worth carrying home. There was a hint, just a hint, of wood smoke in the air.

What a nice, big yard it was, bordered along the back by woods and screened from the neighbors on either side by shrubs and trees. A great yard for kids, Dixie thought, although here as in the house, there was very little sign that any children lived there. No swing set or sandbox or playhouse corrupted the graceful flow of flower beds and curving brick walkways. No soccer balls littered the lawns, no toy tractors burrowed in the soft dirt beneath the hedges. Only a pair of child-size bicycles parked neatly on the covered patio just outside Rhett's study doors betrayed their owners' presence in that household.

Sad, thought Dixie. Poor little kids.

The tree she'd asked Rhett about—it was an elm, she was almost certain. And she'd been right about it being perfect for a
tree house. Yes...the floor beams would go there...and
there...and there. She could see it taking shape in her mind's
eye. What a marvelous tree it was. A truly magnificent tree. A
tree a kid could feel like a king in. Feel safe in, and invincible,
and free. A tree to climb, and hide, and play make-believe in.
To read in on lazy summer afternoons. To sit in and dream ...

What a shame, she thought, to waste it.

"It's not all necessarily a bad thing, this divorce," Newt
Hendricks said as he planted his hand on the door to keep it
from closing and waited for Rhett to follow him off the elevator. Rhett did so with a skeptical snort. "Sure—long as you're
the injured party. The sympathy factor, you know. Single father, trying to raise two cute little kids... We can play that up.
You just have to make damn sure you *stay* the injured party, if
you know what I mean. No hint—I mean, not a smidgen—of
hanky-panky between now and the election, even if you *are*
technically single. Nothing that'd lead anybody to suggest your
wife might've had reason to do what she did."

Grimly, Rhett assured his chief campaign strategist that
hanky-panky was the farthest thing from his mind.

"Yeah, well...can't be too careful," Madeline Hite, the
party chairman put in. "The way it is now, anything's fair
game. After that last election, I didn't think it could get any
dirtier, but I don't know..."

"You can go on in," Rhett interrupted, angling across the
reception area that served the law offices of Starbuck, Cline and
Brown. "We'll use the conference room. Be with you in just a
minute. I want to let Leanne know I'm back."

He opened the door to his suite of offices and nearly ran over
Dixie.

"Oh!" they both said together. And then, "I didn't—" And
then they both laughed.

"What are you doing here?" Dixie asked, glancing over his
shoulder to smile tentatively at Newt and Madeline. "I thought
you had a meeting." She was dressed for town, Rhett noticed,
in a green tweed blazer with leather Western-style yokes over a
burgundy turtleneck. And jeans and cowboy boots, of course.

He'd forgotten how tall she was. In those boots she could almost look him in the eye. And those eyes ... that was something else he'd forgotten.

He coughed and frowned, acutely conscious of the two avidly silent people behind him. "Court's in recess. We decided to meet here instead of downtown. Uh ... did you get everything you needed?"

Her smile didn't waver, but he could see uncertainty flicker in those vivid eyes. A faint flush was blooming in her cheeks as she backed away from him. "Oh—yes, sure did, thanks. Well—guess I better run. See you later, Rhett. Bye, now..." She nodded and murmured a polite greeting to Newt and Madeline, then turned and crossed the reception area in her long-legged stride.

She'd looped her thick black braid into a coil, Rhett saw as she walked away from him, and secured it with a wide leather barrette of some sort. The effect was ... unexpectedly elegant.

Someone—Madeline—coughed. Newt said, "Who the hell was *that?*"

"What? Oh ... guess I should have introduced you." Rhett made a throw-away gesture with his hand; Newt's narrow stare was making him feel guilty as sin, for no reason whatsoever. "That's Dixie."

*"Dixie?"*

"She's the kids' new, uh, nanny. Just hired her yesterday, as a matter of fact."

"Live-in?" Newt growled.

"Of course, live-in," said Rhett, trying to keep exasperation under control. "How else is she supposed to look after the kids?"

"Oh, God," said Madeline.

"For God's sake, she's a friend of ... a family friend, that's all. She's just helping out until I can get somebody permanent. You know what a devil of a time I've been having, trying to find somebody...."

"You couldn't have found a friend of the family who's old and ugly, I suppose." Madeline's idea of witticism.

"How well do you know this girl?" Newt had his head lowered in a way that reminded Rhett of a bull getting ready to charge. He paused, then asked, "You sure she's got her green card?"

"She's from Texas, for God's sake!"

"That's a joke, son," Newt growled, not smiling. "About knowing who she is, though—she somebody you can trust? She's not going to turn up a few years down the road and sell some cockamamie story to the tabloids, is she?"

"Oh, for—"

"He's right," said Madeline. "Can't be too careful, not the way things are these days. You checked her out before you hired her, though, I'm sure. You mind if we take a look at her résumé? Just so we don't have any more surprises?"

"Well, actually..." Rhett stopped himself just short of driving his fingers into his hair. He swore under his breath, then let it out in a rush. "No, I didn't check her out, as a matter of fact, and I don't have a copy of her résumé. Look, dammit, she's a friend of my sister. She trains horses. I don't think..."

Newt and Madeline looked at each other. Newt clapped Rhett on the shoulder and said in a fatherly tone, "Look, son, I'm just as sure as you are that she's okay, but like Madeline says, you can't be too careful. Why don't you let me look into her background a little, just to be on the safe side? She's lookin' after your kids, you'd want to know if there was anything...well, you know. And if she checks out fine, no harm done. What d'ya say?"

"Fine, be my guest, if it'll make you feel better," Rhett growled, giving in with an ungracious shrug, unable to come up with a reason why Newt's suggestion should irritate him so. "Just...keep it quiet, though, okay? I don't want her..."

"Well, now, don't worry about that, son." Newt was beaming like a politician on the campaign trail, now that he had his way. "If she's as spotless as you say she is, she'll never even know."

For some reason, that didn't make Rhett feel any better.

# Chapter 7

Dixie suspected something was wrong the minute Ethan stepped off the bus. As she watched him walk toward her, she knew it.

For one thing, he *walked*. Ethan—who never walked anywhere unless tethered securely to an adult hand. Walked, moreover, with footsteps dragging and his head drooping like a wilted sunflower.

"What's the matter, sugar?" she asked as soon as he was within arm's reach, laying a sympathetic hand on his head.

And as she braced herself for the devastating impact of those chocolate eyes, inside her chest she felt her heart tremble like a fledgling sparrow. It had been protected for so long...how could it stand this battering, day after day? *How?*

"He lost his tooth today at school," explained Lolly as she joined them, giving her backpack a hitch. "That's all. He's just being a crybaby."

"Am not either!"

"Hey, that's great—congratulations!" Dixie cupped Ethan's chin in her hand and gently lifted it. "Let's see—gimme a big ol' jack-o'-lantern grin."

He obliged by stretching his lips wide to show the gap

in the middle of his bottom row of teeth. Such a tiny little tooth, Dixie thought. His first baby tooth...

"Well, now," Dixie said heartily, grabbing for a breath under the cover of ruffling his hair, "I guess you'll have to put it under your pillow for the Tooth Fairy tonight, won't you?"

Ethan's only response to that was a soulful gaze, complete with shimmering eyes and quivering chin.

Lolly snorted. "No, he won't—I told you, he *lost* it."

"What?" Dixie dropped to one knee in front of Ethan, just in time to catch a spilling tear with her thumb. "Aw, sugar, what happened?"

"I dropped it in the sink in the boy's baffroom. I was washing it, and it just...slipped. And down it went." He gave a prolonged sniff, lifted his shoulders and spread his hands wide in the universal gesture that said it more eloquently than words. *Gone.*

"I tried to tell him it doesn't matter," said Lolly disgustedly. "It's just a stupid tooth."

Dixie brushed a few more tears from Ethan's cheeks and gathered him in for a quick hug. "Lolly's right, honey, it doesn't matter. These things happen. We'll just write the Tooth Fairy a little note and explain it, that's all. She'll understand."

"You mean, *he'll* understand, don't you?" Lolly hefted her backpack once more and set off for home, making it clear she'd had about enough of such foolishness.

Dixie grabbed Ethan's hand and hurried to catch up. "What do you mean, he? Whoever heard of a tooth fairy that's a he?"

Lolly threw her one of her superior looks. "It's just Dad, for heaven's sake. There's no such thing as a tooth fairy, everybody knows that."

"Is that a fact?" murmured Dixie.

"Of course it is." Lolly lifted a shoulder. "Actually, I don't bother with that pillow stuff—it's silly, anyway. It's just for babies."

"So, what *do* you do when you lose a tooth?" Dixie inquired.

Ethan sniffed and muttered to himself, "Am *not* a baby."

Lolly gave another shrug. "I usually just tell Dad, and he puts a dollar or something in my bank. It's no big deal."

"Hmm. I suppose you don't believe in Santa Claus, either?"

Lolly just gave another one of her patented snorts.

Poor kid, Dixie thought, remembering her own magical, marvelous growing-up years. Remembering cookies left on her grandmother's hearth rug on Christmas Eve, and the few telltale crumbs that always remained on the plate the next morning. And the mysterious substance that had once appeared in her baby doll's diaper—only years later had she learned it was the homemade apricot jam that had been simmering nearby in a pot on her grandmother's stove at the time. Remembering an exquisite letter in fairy script found one memorable morning under her pillow, a personal missive from the Tooth Fairy...

"You know something?" she announced to Ethan as Lolly was turning into the brick-paved driveway, making sure it was loud enough for her to hear, too. "*I* believe in Santa Claus."

"You do?"

"Yeah," said Dixie firmly, "I do. And you know what else?" Ethan turned the full force of his chocolate drop eyes on her in breathless expectation. Dixie lowered her voice to a conspirator's whisper. "I think we ought to leave the Tooth Fairy a note tonight and see what happens. What do you say?"

Ethan gave a little hiccup of excitement and clamped a hand over his mouth to contain it while he whispered back, "Okay."

Dixie felt her chest swell with emotions she didn't want, feelings she'd never expected to feel. "All right, now—scoot. Go change your clothes. Then come and have a snack before we head for the stables..." The last part was a shout, called to the little boy's back as he ran full tilt down the brick path and disappeared through the creeper-draped archway.

She paused, then, right there in the driveway, and lifted her face to the friendly autumn sun, shaking with silent laughter. Rueful laughter, grateful laughter, like that which follows a catastrophe somehow miraculously survived. How long am I going to feel like this? she wondered. So weak...so shaky...so terribly, terribly vulnerable. When will I get used to having my heart ripped from its hiding place and exposed, after all these years? And how in the world do I protect it now?

"Hi," Rhett said in answer to the light knock on the door of his study. "Come on in."

The door opened part way and Dixie's head came poking through the crack. "Sorry...I didn't want to disturb you."

"You're not." She was, but not in any way he could explain to her.

It was evening—late. The children had been asleep for hours, and he'd thought Dixie must have gone to bed as well. He'd been sitting in the silence staring at the trial transcripts, but hadn't been able to keep his mind on them to save his life—or more accurately, he supposed, his client's life.

He knew Janice Rubens, the state's attorney on the case, very well. He knew today's recess had only been a delaying tactic, and that most likely she'd be coming at him with a deal in the morning. He had decisions to make. Depending on how good a deal it was, he probably should advise the client to take it—but on the other hand, the way it stood now, he had a damn good chance of winning a full acquittal. And if the trial did continue, there was the matter of whether or not to put the client on the stand.

But tonight, all he could think about was Dixie. And with none of this morning's sense of self-congratulation, either. He kept thinking about the meeting with Newt and Madeline this afternoon. Feeling vaguely uneasy about it. And vaguely guilty for feeling uneasy, as if he'd somehow betrayed a friend.

Was I crazy to do this? he wondered now as he watched Dixie slip through the door into his private sanctum, invading his physical space as gracefully and subtly as she'd invaded his thoughts. It had seemed so right, at the time, but now...

"Are you sure?" She was smiling, but so uncertainly he realized he must be frowning at her.

He took off his glasses and tossed them onto the transcript pages, then leaned back in his chair, letting out his breath slowly and silently. Willing himself to relax. "Yeah, I'm sure. I was just going over some things for tomorrow." He paused, forcing a smile. "You're up awfully late. Everything okay?"

"What? Oh—yeah, everything's fine."

"That was a nice dinner, by the way."

"Thanks." Her smile settled in more comfortably, making it all the way to her eyes. "I figured chicken's pretty safe."

Rhett chuckled. "Yeah, we eat a lot of it around here." Then, for a moment, there was silence, which for some reason so unnerved him he coughed just to fill it, and sat up abruptly and reached for his glasses just to have something to do with his hands.

"You know," he said, deepening his voice, striving for at least the illusion of the poise and maturity that had deserted him so inexplicably, "I don't expect you to cook for me. Not the way you did tonight. I'm usually pretty late getting home, anyway—too late for the kids. I can always fix myself something later." He hesitated, then added in an informative tone, "Their dinnertime is six o'clock sharp, by the way."

"Six o'clock...sharp," murmured Dixie. "I see." Her tone was placid, but something kindled in her eyes, like a coal glowing in a breath of wind.

*Now what?* Rhett thought, opening his mouth to challenge that look. And then he stopped. He didn't want to argue with her again—not tonight. In any event he could see her mind wasn't really on dinnertimes, his or the kids' or anyone else's. She seemed distracted, fidgety, and he could have sworn she was hiding something behind her back.

"Can I help with something?" he asked at last, frankly curious.

As if he'd found the right power switch, she suddenly let out a breath and came to his desk in two long strides, long curling tendrils of hair floating around her face in the breeze of her own making. "Oh—God, I hope so. What I need is a really, really fine-point pen. You don't happen to have one, do you?"

He felt her forward advance like a strong gust of wind. It took his breath away, pushed him back in his chair, made him glad of the desk between them. And sorry. She had so much energy, so much *fire.* And as with fire, he both craved her warmth...and feared it. He knew what it could do to him if he let himself get too close.

"Well, let's see," he muttered, and dove into his desk drawer, searched until he came up with a fine-point drafting pencil, a relic of Elaine's college days, probably; she'd taken some design courses way back then, as he recalled. He offered it to Dixie. "Will this do?"

"Oh, great—thanks." She took the pencil from him and stepped closer to the desk, shifting aside some papers to make room in the circle of light from his lamp.

And now he could see what it was she'd kept hidden behind her back. It was just a piece of paper, no bigger than a large postage stamp, with the edges cut in tiny scallops. He watched in unwilling fascination as she positioned it carefully under the lamp, leaned over it and began, with exquisite care and concentration, to write on it in script so tiny he couldn't see it at all without his glasses.

"What you need," he heard himself say after a moment, "is a magnifying glass."

She shot him a look, wide-eyed and eager. "Do you have one?"

As a matter of fact, he did. He had one in his briefcase, useful for examining photographs and the minute particles that evidence so often consists of. He got it out and handed it to her.

Instead of taking it, she glanced up at him and murmured, "Could you hold it for me?"

"Uh...sure." He had to get out of his chair and come around his desk to do it. Had to stand beside her, lean over her, so close he could feel that fearsome heat, smell the sweet, clean scent of her hair, feel it tickle his cheek and his chin. Oh God, he thought, please don't let my hand shake.

He was sweating. His heart was pounding. He couldn't breathe. He was drowning in her heat, her scent, her nearness.

He wanted her.

He thought, this is insane. I'm in the middle of a divorce. About to begin an election campaign. What am I doing with this woman in my house?

He couldn't even *think* like this.

With a supreme effort of will, he blinked, bringing his hand, the magnifying glass and the tiny scrap of paper into focus. He blinked again and said, "Good Lord. What in the world are you doing?"

"Writing a letter," said Dixie, barely moving her lips, her whole body tense with concentration. "From the Tooth Fairy."

Rhett gave a bark of sheer amazement, which earned him a severe glare and a stern, *"Hold still."*

"The *Tooth Fairy?"* Why was he whispering? In a normal voice he demanded, "What for? Ethan doesn't believe in that stuff."

"That's why." Dixie straightened, arched her back and rotated her head as if stretching out kinks, then bent once more over the magnifying glass. "I want to prove to him that there is a Tooth Fairy."

"Okay...now wait a minute." Rhett gave his head an incredulous shake. "*You* are writing a letter from the Tooth Fairy in order to prove the existence of said Tooth Fairy. Don't you sense a bit of a contradiction, here?"

"Not at all." She added no arguments, no explanations, as if she'd just stated a fact so obvious it needed no explanation. "There—all done." She moved back a little to give him a better look. "What do you think?"

The truth? He thought it was exquisite. What he couldn't understand was why a letter written by a grown woman posing as an imaginary being, painstakingly etched in fancy script and decorated with a border of vines and tiny flowers, should stir in him such a confusion of emotions. Nothing in his life's experience had prepared him for this. He was, consequently, speechless.

Meanwhile, having gotten no response to her query, Dixie had turned her head to look at him over her shoulder. Which, given their relative positions, put her face approximately a hand's width away from his. And there they stood, for what seemed a very long time. Rhett didn't move because he couldn't. He seemed to be in some sort of shock, frozen, except for a frantically racing heartbeat, like a wild creature pinioned by a car's headlights. What Dixie's problem was, he couldn't have begun to guess.

God, how he wanted to kiss her.

It would have been so easy, too, just a matter of giving in to natural laws—like gravity... the magnetic attraction of one body for another. So easy... and as disastrous in its own way, he knew, as gravity's effects could be.

He knew that. And still he found his field of focus narrowing until all he could see was her mouth, the full, generous curving wonder of it. Not only could he see every smallest detail of it, its shape and color and texture and the way it quivered slightly—with nervousness, perhaps—but he could actually *feel* it. Feel it opening under his, *taste* its mysterious essence on his tongue...

She made a small sound and moved away from him, looking so disturbed, he realized suddenly that he was scowling at her—a habit of his, when in deep emotional turmoil. Would it have disturbed her more or less, he wondered, had she known the true nature of his thoughts?

However, Dixie had drawn her own conclusions as to the reason for his black and uncompromising expression.

"Listen," she said—somewhat breathlessly, he noticed—holding up a defensive hand, "I know what you're probably going to say. Lolly told me y'all don't do this tooth fairy stuff. But I just want to say—''

"That's right, we don't." Profoundly relieved, Rhett set his scowl more firmly and folded his arms across his chest. "My wife—ah, hmm. That is, I don't think parents have any business lying to their kids about something as important as where money comes from."

"Or presents, either, right?" Dixie had her arms folded on her chest, now, too, in what even he recognized as a parody of himself. "I hear y'all don't even allow your kids to believe in Santa Claus."

"That's right," said Rhett staunchly. "Santa Claus is a myth—a pretty story, and frankly one that's become so commercialized, nowdays it's no more than a great big marketing ploy. Kids need to learn to face reality. The sooner the better."

"Poor little things," Dixie muttered.

"Now just a darn minute!" Rhett shouted, surprised to find his blood coursing hot through his veins, all his nerves and senses armed for battle. Surprised to find that he felt stimulated, fired up in a way he never did in court, even going up against the state's best and toughest prosecutors. "In this day and age—''

"In this day and age, more than *ever,* kids need to believe in goodness and . . . and giving, and happiness and *fun!*'' Dixie's voice was so soft and intense it was a moment or two before it occurred to Rhett that she suddenly seemed very close to crying. Her eyes . . . her lovely, brilliant, deep-set eyes were brimming with unshed tears, so that they seemed to shimmer with golden lights, like the eyes of a sorceress.

When she went on, he could almost see her vibrating with the tension of too much emotion under tenuous control. "Listen, real life is scary, dammit. There's ugliness and heartache and . . . and all sorts of disappointments. There's pain, and loss and betrayal and injustice—even for kids." She caught and held her breath. "For God's sake, don't you understand? Santa Claus *is* real. Just like stories and songs and imagination are real. And as long as we have those things then . . . we can have hope . . . and joy . . . too." Her voice faltered. She reached out and touched his arm where it lay across his chest like a barricade against her, and whispered, "Rhett . . . can't you remember . . . wasn't there *ever* a time when you believed in Santa Claus?"

He couldn't answer her. The fires within him died out, leaving him feeling futile and indefinably sad. Because the truth was, he *couldn't* remember.

Ah, hell, do what you want.'' He tossed her the victory—along with a half smile that tried to be superior and only succeeded in making him feel stiff and sardonic—as he turned back to his desk. "I said I'd trust your judgment. Dammit, I'm trying, but sometimes . . ."

He remembered something, suddenly, and reached for his wallet. Extracted a dollar bill and waved it at Dixie with an awkward little cough. "Guess you'll be needing this—for the, uh, Tooth Fairy."

She took the bill from him with a prim, uncomfortable "Thank you."

He watched without saying anything while she rolled it into a slender tube and wrapped her fairy-size letter around it. Watched her take something that he first thought was a piece of string from her pocket and, after several tries, finally succeed in getting it tied around the rolled up dollar.

He didn't try to help her. He knew he didn't dare risk getting so close to her again. Consequently, it was only after she'd finished and was holding the tiny package out to show him, balanced on a finger, that he recognized the slightly iridescent "string."

"Good Lord," he muttered, torn between laughter and awe, "that isn't . . ."

A smile was flirting with the corners of her mouth. She curled her fingers carefully around the Tooth Fairy's gift and gave him a wink before she answered, in her best West Texas drawl, "Well, now what else would you get from the Tooth Fairy?"

What it was, was dental floss.

But this time he didn't fail to notice the fact that neither Dixie's smile nor the wink brought the glint of laughter back to her eyes.

It was only after she'd said her good-nights and left him that he thought of all the things she'd said to him, about real life being so ugly. He remembered she'd used words like . . . *heartache. Pain.* And *betrayal.* What could have happened in her life, he wondered, that would make her eyes fill with tears when she spoke the word *injustice?*

He suddenly thought of Newt and Madeline and their investigation into Dixie's past. For the first time, he worried about what they might find.

That night she had The Dream again. It was the first time she'd done that in years. She'd almost forgotten the horror of it.

It always began so sweetly . . . so beautifully. So happily.

*She was walking in a garden with Peter, hand in hand . . . laughing, smelling the flowers. Peter picked one and handed it to her in that impulsive way he had that she loved so much. She buried her face in its petals, inhaling deeply, taking in its lovely fragrance.*

*Except that suddenly it wasn't lovely—it was the terrible stench of death. And when she lifted her head from the flower, the garden had disappeared, and all around them lay the bodies . . . the bodies . . . women, children, old people . . . babies. They were everywhere, all over the ground, and the stench was so overpowering she couldn't breathe.*

*She was choking, trying not to breathe. Peter was choking, too. She knew he was dying, and she couldn't help him. She reached out to him but she couldn't touch him. All she could do was stand helplessly, crying, choking, watching him die.*

*And then she was alone with the bodies, except that now she could hear a sound. Somewhere, a baby was crying. She ran frantically among the bodies, trying to find the living, crying baby. But no matter how hard she tried, she never could. And the crying went on . . . and on. . . .*

"Dixie! Dixie, wake up! Come *on*, Dixie . . . look what I found under my pillow! Look what the Tooth Fairy left for me— Dixie . . . "

An earthquake was shaking her bed. A very small, tow-headed earthquake. She clawed her way out of the nightmare, trembly and cold with shock, to discover Ethan on all fours on the double bed beside her, his face close to hers, so close she could feel his moist warmth, smell the sweet, clean smell of a child fresh from sleep.

"Hey, sugar . . . wha's up?" she croaked. Her throat felt stiff and dry and ached terribly.

"Dixie, *look*." Ethan gave an excited all-fours hop, then sat back on his heels and held out his hand. "I found this under my pillow. Right where I put the letter. I just ... stuck my hand under and felt around, and ... there it was. Do you think ..." He swallowed and finished in an awed whisper, "Do you think it's *real?*"

Dixie hitched herself up on her pillows, thankful that, in deference to the cooler temperatures, she'd worn a sleeveless tank top to bed. She raked a handful of hair back from her face, cleared her throat and murmured, "Let me see ... what you got there? Ah...hah." She took the tightly rolled tube tied with iridescent floss from the palm of Ethan's hand ... such a small hand, she thought, surprised at the hurt she still felt inside. "Well, my goodness, you know what this is?" Ethan excitedly shook his head. She went on in a musing tone. "You know, I think I got one almost like this once, when I was a real little girl?"

"You *did?*"

"Yeah, I did. You want me to open it for you?"

Ethan nodded, overcome. She could barely hear his whispered, "Yes, please."

Oh, how hard it was to endure the avid brilliance of those eyes as he watched her untie the floss and carefully roll out the dollar bill and the tiny paper that surrounded it.

"What is it?" How excited he was ... his voice so hushed.

"Just what I thought," muttered Dixie, bending over the paper in her hand, squinting at it. "It's a letter, sugar. From the Tooth Fairy." She handed it to him, beaming. "Wow, how 'bout that, huh?"

"A *letter?* For *me?* Oh boy!" The little boy caught his breath and thrust it back at her, as if it were simply too wonderful, too magical to dare touch. "Would you read it for me, please, Dixie?" His head tilted winsomely, his eyes took on that limpid glow. "I can't read handwriting yet."

Dixie cleared her throat. "Well, okay, I guess I can give it a try ... but it's been a long while since I read fairy writing." Before she'd finished, Ethan had bounced himself around so that he was snuggled up against her in the curve of her arm, with his silky head nestled right up under her chin.

The tears rose suddenly, unexpectedly, an itching, burning pressure in her nose and the backs of her eyes that reminded her of driving down a Texas back country road in springtime, when the air was alive with birdsong and thick with pollen and just a whiff of the wind could make your head fill up like a cloud of black pepper.

"Okay, sugar, lemme see," she mumbled thickly, closing her eyes briefly as she hitched the little boy into a more comfortable position. She took a deep breath so her voice wouldn't shake.

But before she could begin with the words, "Dear Ethan," the door to her room opened and there stood Rhett, wearing a plain white terry cloth bathrobe, a shadow of beard stubble and a fearsome scowl.

She stared at him in frozen panic, just...stared at him, with her mouth open, unable to speak, unable to move. It was worse than being caught naked—or, more accurately, it *was* being caught naked. Only this was a kind of nakedness so much more profound than simply having no clothes on...so much more. This was having her very soul exposed, her heart stripped bare, all her pain and most deeply buried fears laid open for him to see.

"What the hell's—oh..." Rhett had stopped himself just short of entering the room, one hand braced on the doorframe like an anchor, the other still holding the knob. "I'm sorry—I thought..."

"Dad!" Dimly, Dixie felt Ethan lift his head from its nest on her shoulder and peer eagerly around her. "Come and see what I got from the Tooth Fairy! It's a letter—a real one. In handwriting. Dixie's reading it for me—go 'head Dixie. Read it, *read it.*"

"Uh...okay..." Desperately, she stalled for time while she struggled to pull air into her lungs. Her throat was locked up tight—she felt as if she were choking. Almost, she thought, like the nightmare come true. "Let's see...it starts out, 'Dear Ethan,' of course."

"Really?" Ethan whispered, nudging her chin with his head as he looked up at her. "It really says my name?"

"Really," murmured Dixie. She felt Rhett's silence like another presence in the room. Felt his eyes like heavy weights. "Um...and then it says, 'I'm sorry you lost your tooth in the sink drain. I had a hard time finding it—'" Ethan's excited gasp interrupted her. She hugged him and finished it in a rush. "'Thank you for keeping it so nice and clean. Love...' and it's signed, 'Mary The Tooth Fairy.' How 'bout that? She's even got a name."

"Wow!" crowed Ethan, bouncing up in that little boy way he had, as if all his joints were springs. He reached across Dixie, proudly thrusting his dollar at his father. "Look what she gave me, Dad! A whole dollar—I can keep it, can't I? It's mine?"

"Sure, it's yours." Rhett's voice sounded oddly gritty, but he didn't try to clear it. "Why don't you go put it in your bank? And then jump in the shower, kiddo—time to get ready for school."

But of course Ethan had bounced his way to the foot of the bed, jumped off and was running full tilt for his own room before it was finished.

After his departure there was a sort of *settling*, a moment that reminded Dixie of the seconds following a whirlwind, during which things stirred up by its passage tumble back into their proper places.

Rhett cleared his throat and murmured, "Sorry—didn't mean to barge in on you. I heard Ethan yelling, and I thought...well, to tell you the truth, I don't know what I thought. He had, ah...some trouble with bad dreams right after his mother left, and I guess...well. Sorry..." But he let it trail off, looking as if he wasn't quite sure exactly what he should be sorry for.

"It's okay, I was getting up anyway," Dixie lied. Although with Ethan gone she felt less vulnerable; she could breathe again, even manage a smile. She paused, wondering if her defenses were strong enough, now, that she could risk looking at the man in her doorway.

And then, while she hesitated, she heard a husky chuckle and an incredulous, "*Mary?* Where do you come up with these things?"

She laughed—still a bit shakily—and lifted her eyes to his. Found them unexpectedly bright...a soft, warming brightness that dispelled the last of the nightmare's horror the way a rising sun drives away the morning chill. She murmured, "I think it was...'Bewitched.'"

"'*Bewitched?*'" He said it wonderingly, as if he might be himself, just a little.

"Yeah...it was a TV show, remember? About a witch who was a housewife—or maybe the other way around, I don't know. And she used to twitch her nose to make magic?"

Rhett was shaking his head in an I'm sorry but I don't know what you're talking about sort of way. It didn't diminish that warming brightness, though; she felt it now in her face, felt it spreading out from there, just as the heat from his handshake had seemed to pour from that one small point of contact into every part of her.

She cleared her throat with a touch of desperation. "Um...anyway, once I remember there was a show about a tooth fairy who was a real klutz—Imogene Coca played her, I think. And...her name was..."

"Mary." Rhett finished it for her, his voice soft, still clothed in that gentle, bemused smile...so different from the frown he usually favored her with.

But why did she feel so drawn to that smile? Its warmth cocooned her. She didn't want to leave it. As if, after the last several days of wandering cold and naked, her heart had found a sheltered place.

"So..." she said with a shrug and a smile of apology, unable to remember what it was she'd been explaining to him.

"So..." He coughed and continued with more normal briskness, "Well, anyway, congratulations."

"Congratulations? What for?"

"The letter—it seems to have worked." His smile became lopsided. "Apparently I now have a son who believes in fairies."

"Oh." Dixie gave a gulp of nervous laughter. "Is that so bad?"

Rhett snorted. "I'll let you know in a couple of years." He straightened suddenly, his frown back in place. "That reminds me. After I told you last night not to cook for me—would you mind terribly fixing something for a few guests tomorrow evening? Nothing fancy—just a meeting with my campaign committee, but it's apt to run late, and I thought..."

"Campaign?" said Dixie faintly.

"I plan to run for State Attorney General next year." He tossed the information at her casually, as if announcing he might be working late. "These are mostly planning meetings, at this stage—what's the matter?"

What was the matter? He'd taken his warmth away with his smile, and without it she felt chilled. She was all too aware of the cold kiss of air on her bare arms and throat, and the thinness of her tank top, and the way her nipples pushed against it. She folded her arms across her breasts and rubbed at the roughening of gooseflesh on her shoulders and mumbled, "Tomorrow's Saturday."

"Yeah?" And then, "*Oh*. Oh hell, I'm sorry, I guess we didn't talk about days off, did we? Listen, I'll make it up to you, I promise. I'll pay you overtime, or... whatever."

"It's not that." She found that she could even smile a little at his discomfiture. It did make him so much easier to deal with. "It's just that, to tell you the truth, I've about run out of clothes. I was thinking I'd better take my horse trailer back to your sister's this weekend and pick up some of my things, if that's okay with you?"

"Of course... of course..." Once again his gaze rested on her, the look in his eyes thoughtful, almost puzzled. But this time the effect wasn't warming; it gave her no sense of safety or shelter. It was disturbing in a way she'd almost forgotten. Nerve endings stirred in long-neglected places. She felt his eyes like a physical touch... lingering on her bare throat... sliding along her collarbone... picking up a long tendril of her hair and following it upward to her ear... her cheek... her temple...

"Maybe..." her voice was a gasp—too desperate sounding; she gulped to control it "... you could have your meeting one day next week? I'd be happy to fix y'all a big ol' dinner then, anything you want."

"What? Oh... yeah, that's fine. Fine..." His eyes alighted for an instant on her mouth, a butterfly's touch—barely felt before it was gone. He rubbed a hand over his frown, thought for a moment, then said, "Tuesday okay?"

"Tuesday's fine."

"Okay... okay. Well. I guess you'd probably like to... uh..." His smile came and went like a light with a loose connection. He started to back out of the room, pulling the door with him, then paused. "Listen, I really do apologize for the, uh, wake-up call. Ethan—"

"He's no bother," said Dixie softly. "Really."

For a long moment his eyes held hers, dark, brooding, puzzled. Then he nodded and closed the door with a faint but unequivocal click.

It was several more minutes before Dixie eased her stiff legs from under the blankets and crept, hunched over like an old, old person, to the bathroom. There she turned on the shower

as hot as she could stand it. She peeled off her tank top and
underpants and stood under it until she was red as a lobster,
trying to drive the cold from her body...and the ache from her
heart.

# Chapter 8

On Saturday morning Dixie hitched her horse trailer to her dusty blue Chevy and drove the two hundred or so miles to Lucy's farm near Sioux City. She left early—not early enough to avoid Ethan, who clung to her neck in the front entry hall and sobbed, "Don't go, Dixie, *please* don't go."

"I'll be back, sugar," she promised, in a voice that was thick and slurred. "I'll be back..."

Once on the interstate, heading due west with the rising sun burning like fire in her side view mirrors, she felt a giddy, almost panicky sense of flight and freedom, like a bird escaping from a cage. As she passed the I-35 interchange she thought wistfully how easy it would be to bear south instead of west. South...then drop down through Kansas City and Wichita and Oklahoma City, all the way to Fort Worth.

She wouldn't, though. She couldn't.

*I'll be back...I promise.*

She remembered that Peter had said that to her, the last time they were together. Neither of them had known it was a promise he wouldn't be able to keep.

She made it to Lucy's before noon, even with a stop for breakfast at a truck stop near Atlantic. She had time to un-

hitch her trailer and look in on the colt, Rocky, before joining
Lucy and her family in the farmhouse kitchen for lunch.

The family group for a change included Lucy's husband
Mike, who was home for the weekend after spending the work
week in Chicago writing his nationally syndicated column.
Dixie always enjoyed Lucy's Aunt Gwen and the children, five-
year-old Rose Ellen and the baby, Eric, but she wasn't quite sure
how she felt about Mike Lanagan being there. He was a terrific guy and she was glad to see him, but she was always just a
little uneasy around him, and had been ever since she'd discovered that his father was Sean Lanagan. The Pulitzer Prize
winning photojournalist, still officially MIA in Vietnam, had
been Peter's greatest role model and icon. Seeing Mike—talking with him—was always a painful reminder of the past, and
she'd had way too many of those, lately.

Besides, there were things she wanted to talk to Lucy about.
Alone.

So, it was with a double motive that, after a wonderful meal
of beef stew and Gwen's incomparable homemade apple pie,
Dixie asked Lucy about the pile of scrap lumber she'd spotted
out behind the chicken house.

"I was thinking of building the kids a tree house," she explained. "They have this great tree in the back yard—it's just
perfect for one. I haven't asked Rhett, yet, but I figured if I can
get the materials . . ."

"That old junk? It's mostly leftovers from when we rebuilt
the cottage," Lucy told her. "I don't know if there's anything
there you can use, but if there is, you're welcome to it." She
snorted. "Don't expect Rhett to help you, though. He doesn't
do tree houses—just ask Earl."

"Okay if I go pick through it right now?" Dixie asked, getting up from the table to carry her dishes to the sink, as was the
family's habit. It had been her family's way, too, and the well-
remembered, farm-style informality always made her just a
little homesick.

"Sure," said Lucy, right behind her. "I'll help you. Mike,
can you give us a hand?"

"Yeah, me too," Rosie chirped enthusiastically.

Dixie's heart sank. But she'd underestimated Mike Lanagan, she realized as she intercepted the brief but intense look
that passed between him and his wife while he was depositing
his own dishes on the countertop.

In response to it he reached for the backpack child carrier that was propped against the wall nearby, turning to rescue his daughter's dishes just as they were toppling over the edge of the counter into the sink. Dixie watched the maneuver—which was executed with the poise and athletic grace of a shortstop initiating a classic double play—with admiration, and a pang that felt like disloyalty. It was hard not to compare Mike's casual and easygoing way of handling the role of fatherhood with Rhett's, which seemed to her to alternate between rigidness and total distraction.

"Not so fast, kiddo," Mike said to his eagerly bouncing daughter. "You forget we have a date with the pumpkin patch?" He raised his eyebrows at Lucy, not *quite* winking. "Do you mind? I promised the kids we'd go see how our Halloween pumpkins are coming along. Maybe you could pick out what you want to take, and I can help load it after a bit—how'd that be?"

"Oh—uh...sure, that's fine," Lucy responded on cue, looking momentarily taken aback, then owlishly wise. "Okay, see you guys later, then. Oh—and *take your time.*" That was Lucy—subtle as a truck.

In any case, that was how, after Dixie had thanked Gwen for the delicious meal and accepted a pie to take home for "Rhett and the children," she and Lucy collected work gloves and headed out to the chicken yard—blessedly alone.

"So, how is it working out?" Lucy inquired with her customary bluntness as they were crossing the graveled driveway together. "You getting along okay with Rhett?"

"Yeah, fine," said Dixie, frowning intently at the glove she was putting on...fiddling with it until she'd got it adjusted to her satisfaction.

"And the kids?"

"Oh yeah, they're great. Ethan, especially. He's...just great."

"Uh-huh," said Lucy. Dixie could feel that hawklike stare without even looking at her. After a brief little silence, Lucy prodded harder. "No problems, then? The other night you said something about some 'personal stuff.'"

"Oh..." Dixie shrugged and gave a light, meaningless laugh "...that. Yeah, I guess it's still there."

"I haven't asked—"

"—which is why I still consider you such a good friend," Dixie said firmly, smiling to take the sting out of the rebuff. It was impossible to maintain, however, and as the smile fell apart, she sighed and said, "I wish, though..."

"What?" Lucy prompted eagerly.

"Oh..." Dixie shook her head, then took a breath and blurted it all in a rush. "I don't like to pry, but sometimes I think it would help a little bit if I could just understand—you know, about the divorce and all? I mean, what kind of a woman would do that—just go off and leave her kids? I can't *imagine* any mother doing such a thing. And then—well, I guess it must have been a pretty big shock, and I can see it in the kids, but...to tell the truth, Rhett doesn't seem to me like a man who's just had his heart broken up and stomped on."

"I should hope not," Lucy muttered angrily. They'd arrived at the pile of scrap lumber, and she spent several minutes picking up boards and throwing them around, working off steam before she was ready to continue.

Finally she paused, dusted her hands on her thighs and smiled a crooked little smile. "I suppose we—his family—were the ones who got our hearts broken, Mama especially. And that happened a long time ago, when Rhett first married that woman." She threw Dixie a quick look and bent to the pile once more. "Rhett wasn't always like he is now, you know. I mean, we never got along, but that was because he was always so full of himself—such a Mister Big Shot."

Dixie couldn't help but smile at that.

Lucy paused to finger a wing of hair back behind her ear. "And now, here he is, running for Attorney General. Well...I guess it's probably what he was born to do—be a politician. He's always been such a stuffed shirt." And then her face grew sad, a little wistful. "But...he did used to laugh. And he'd tell me stories. Wonderful stories—you know, when I couldn't go to sleep? And he and Mom were always real close—they had the music, for one thing. Did he tell you about that?"

Dixie nodded. "A little."

"They used to sing together—for church, weddings and things like that. They even wrote songs, can you believe it? Mom always said Rhett was her poet, her dreamer...." She worked in silence again, throwing boards around, stirring up dust. Then she shook her head and said, "But after he married Elaine, all that changed."

"Changed?" Dixie bent over to pick up the other end of the long board Lucy was manhandling out of the pile. "How?"

"He forgot how to laugh, for one thing." Lucy was scowling at the underside of the board, inspecting it for spiders. "And for another, he pretty much stopped coming home to visit. We almost never saw him. And then the thing I can't forgive him for, he didn't ever even call Mom and Dad—it was like he didn't want to be reminded of where he came from. That's what just about broke Mama's heart." But it was Lucy's voice that broke. She swiped furiously at a traitorous tear, leaving a dirty smear across one freckled, sunburned cheek.

"But *why?*" asked Dixie, her own voice growing gritty. "What would make him do that?"

"Oh, it was Elaine's doing," said Lucy sourly. "Mike says she was just really, really insecure, that she felt threatened by Rhett's family—especially Mom. Mike says she was probably jealous of Mom. I know she hated her—which, if you'd known my mother, you'd know how incomprehensible that is. I mean, everybody loved my mother. *Everybody*. She was just the most . . ."

She paused, and Dixie saw her swallow. Then she snorted. "If you ask me, Elaine's just a selfish, coldhearted witch—spell that with a *B*. She didn't want to share Rhett with anybody—even his family. And she was like that with the kids, too, when they came along."

"Then how," whispered Dixie, swallowing against a painful knot that had just formed in her own throat, "could she leave them the way she did?"

Lucy shrugged. "I don't know. Obviously she found something—or somebody—more important to her than they were. But," she added darkly, "I'll guarantee you, when it suits her, she'll be back for those kids."

Dixie pressed her gloved fingertips to her lips. She still had the knot in her throat, which she recognized now as fear. "Do you think she *can* do that? After the way she—"

Seeing Dixie's distressed expression, Lucy hastily added, "Well, Rhett doesn't think so. And whatever else he may or may not be, he's a damn good lawyer. I wouldn't worry about it too much."

Lucy dusted her gloved hands together with an air of finality, then surveyed the pile of lumber with her hands on her hips. "Well—I think that's about the best of what there is here. And look, here comes Mike to help us load it. He has great timing, huh? I think there might be some scraps of plywood in the barn. Do you want those too?''

Dixie could only nod and whisper, "Yes, thanks." Because the knot in her throat had slipped down into her chest, making it hard to talk at all.

"Well, are you satisfied?" Gwen said to Lucy. It was Sunday afternoon, and they were standing at the foot of the back steps, watching Dixie's blue pickup rattle and clatter down the lane in a cloud of dust.

Lucy didn't say anything while she gnawed at her lip and thought hard. "I don't understand it," she muttered, turning to climb the steps. "She keeps saying everything's fine, but..."

"She doesn't look like everything's fine."

"No." Lucy let out her breath, a small gust of exasperation.

She hated to admit it, but the truth was, Dixie looked terrible. She didn't even look like the same person who'd driven away less than a week ago with sunshine in her smile and a glow of health and well-being in her skin, her hair, her eyes. Now her eyes looked...sad, Lucy thought. They had dark smudges under them, as if she hadn't been sleeping enough, or well. And the smile had only a faint and tentative glimmer of the radiance she remembered.

"I hope you're not going to say 'I told you so,'" she said with a sigh.

Gwen's eyebrows arched high. "I wouldn't dream of it."

"She says she has some...'personal stuff,'" Lucy mused as she held the screen door open. "I wonder what that means."

"Lucy..."

"It couldn't have anything to do with Rhett—she only just met him. So it must be something that happened in the past. Funny—I never thought of Dixie as having a past." She'd seemed so open, so uncomplicated. So...happy.

"Everyone has a past," said Gwen softly.

Lucy glanced at her, uneasy already, and felt a jolting pang of sorrow and regret when she saw the filmy sadness in the old woman's eyes. Too late, she remembered Gwen's husband, killed in the Second World War, and her only child, who'd died of polio soon after. It seemed so long ago, and sometimes she forgot about it. But, she realized suddenly, *Gwen* never for-

got. Never for one minute. Lucy thought of Mike, and Rosie
and Eric . . . but her mind shied away from imagining what it
would be like to lose them.

She swallowed to ease the icy knot of fear those terrible
thoughts always brought with them. "I just thought she'd be
perfect for Rhett. *And* the kids—after that coldhearted prig of
a mother of theirs. Dixie's just . . . so full of life. And fun." She
snorted. "Elaine wouldn't know how to have fun if her life depended on it."

"And Dixie?" Gwen asked softly. "Did you think about
her?"

Maybe she hadn't. Not enough. She'd taken Dixie at face
value, never even dreaming there might be pain buried deep
beneath that sunny facade. But there had been. She knew it
now. Because it wasn't buried anymore.

"Maybe you were right," said Lucy with a sigh. "Maybe I
should have let well enough alone."

"Well," said Gwen gently, "It's too late now."

"Too late for what?" It was Mike, coming in from the barn
with Eric bouncing in the backpack and Rosie dancing at his
heels.

Lucy turned into her husband's arms without a word, seeking forgiveness and solace from the one place she knew she'd
always find it.

On Tuesday, Rhett came home from work late—just before
dusk—and in a terrible mood. No surprise—he'd been in a bad
mood for days. The cause of his bad mood was no surprise, either. He blamed it all on Dixie. Oh, nothing she'd done,
just . . . thinking about her. Or more accurately, trying *not* to
think about her.

Which was a little like trying not to read a sign that says, Do
Not Read This Sign!

Rhett didn't really blame Dixie. If he blamed anyone—and
he *needed* to blame someone—it was Newt and Madeline. If
they hadn't warned him off the woman, he probably wouldn't
have given her a second thought.

Sure. He'd never in a million years have noticed that cute
little fanny of hers. He wasn't even a particular fan of fan-
nies—more of a breast man, actually, which was probably one
thing that had attracted him to Elaine, since she'd been pretty

well endowed in that department. He sure as hell wouldn't be imagining what it would look like without those tight-fitting jeans she always wore...little twin dimples on either side of her spine...gentle indentations at the sides...nicely firm and rounded muscle in between....

And, God help him, he wouldn't be catching himself, in the middle of one of the state's attorney's long-winded arguments, imagining what those nice, firm rounds of muscle would feel like in his hands!

He didn't understand it. Self-discipline had never been a problem for him before. He'd been *born* self-disciplined. Never had to be told to do his chores before play, wouldn't even think about turning on the TV until his homework was done. In college, he'd been the one guy in the library cracking the books while all his friends were tossing back brewskies and picking up chicks at the local pub. Cheat on Elaine? The opportunities had been there, but he'd turned them all down without a qualm. Why? Because he'd known what was right and what was wrong—for him—and more important, where he was going, and what he had to do to get there. His way had always been broad and straight and very clear.

It still was. And he still knew what was right and what was wrong. He knew getting involved with Dixie would be wrong—and not only wrong, but dangerous. He knew that, because Newt and Madeline had told him it was so. The problem was, in his heart of hearts, he didn't believe it.

Maybe he didn't want to.

When Dixie wasn't around, his jaws ached with tension from concentrating so hard on not thinking about touching her. And whenever she *was* around, he walked around in a cold sweat for fear he *would* touch her. He spent most of his waking hours in the approximate frame of mind of a grizzly bear with a bellyache. He wanted to yell, or punch something, just to release that terrible tension.

And while he was much too considerate, well-bred and adult to ever take out his frustrations on innocent bystanders—such as his children, secretary, law clerks or colleagues—he had noticed himself lately hollering "Objection!" in court a lot more than was necessary, just to have an excuse to argue with *someone*.

As his mother might have put it long, long ago, he was spoilin' for a fight.

He didn't know it, of course; not then. It was only later, looking back, that he realized he should have seen it coming.

At the time, driving up to his front door, he was conscious mainly of mixed feelings. On the one hand, he was concentrating like crazy on not imagining what it would be like to come home to find Dixie waiting for him....

*She'd built a fire in his study, and put on his silk smoking jacket... nothing underneath, he could tell right away. She'd offer him a brandy. They'd share the same snifter, smiling into each other's eyes...and then he'd take the snifter from her and set it carefully aside, and reach for the tie of the smoking jacket...pull it slowly, until it came loose and fell away...open the jacket and slide his hands inside, touch her skin...so smooth, so silky...so perfect. Mold his hands to her waist...her hips... that fantastic little bottom... pull her to him and feel her body come against his...naked...hot...*

And while he wasn't imagining all that, he was also hoping to God she had the kids fed and the house spotless and some sort of fantastic dinner all prepared, so Newt and Madeline and the others would see how truly wholesome and indispensable she was.

He was also hoping that she was wearing something huge and shapeless, and no makeup at all—although she never did wear much, come to think of it, that he'd been able to notice. But maybe she'd at least put her hair up in a bun.... Okay, forget that—short of wearing a turban, he had to admit there wasn't much she could do to camouflage that hair. But anyway, please God, let her *somehow* look mousy and dull, not so damn full of energy and vitality and warmth and that mysterious attractiveness that had very little to do with being pretty.

Oh, God. What she was, he realized—his stomach lurched as he gave it a name for the first time—what she was, was *sexy*. Newt and Madeline must have picked up on it right away. How could he have missed it?

Or, deep down, had he known it all along?

He parked his car in the garage but, instead of going through the arch and along to the kitchen, went around to the front door. His guests would be coming along shortly, and he wanted to check that everything was in order.

The first thing he spotted that was wrong was the newspaper, still lying on the mat where the paperboy would have thrown it early this morning. He picked it up and tucked it un-

der his arm, trying not to let it irk him; she'd been too busy
cooking and cleaning and getting things ready, he told himself. She'd just forgotten to bring it in.

He opened the door to... silence. Coupled with the errant
newspaper, that struck him as ominous. Furthermore, the entry was dark, and there was no strip of light showing under the
kitchen door at the far end of the hallway. He found that
downright alarming.

He called out, "Dixie? Kids?" as he strode the length of the
hallway, his heartbeat accelerating with every step. Pushed open
the swinging door. More silence. More darkness.

*What the hell?* It was well past six—why weren't the kids at
the table eating dinner? Where was everyone? Where was
*Dixie?* He could feel a strange vibration in his chest, like a low-
voltage electrical current. At that point, he didn't yet know
whether it should be outrage, or alarm.

Then he heard voices. Children's voices, thin and chirpy as
squabbling sparrows. And Dixie's voice... and laughter.
Coming from the backyard.

Alarm bowed out of the picture, and not with grace. It was
put to rout by the outrage that expanded—mushroomed—to fill
all the space inside him. He couldn't remember ever being so
angry; he felt as if the top of his head were going to come off.
*What in the hell is she doing? How could she? How could she?*
He actually thought he might burst something. He could see it
now—the headline in tomorrow's paper: Prominent Local Attorney Succumbs To Stroke In Own Backyard—Brilliant Political Career Cut Short!

That thought, while melodramatic, calmed him down somewhat. He was, after all, almost forty; he probably ought to be
thinking about things like blood pressure... heart attacks.

He took a deep breath and held it for a slow ten count. Then
he set his briefcase and the newspaper on the table and opened
the door, stepped through it and closed it after him, all with
great precision. Good man, he said to himself, mentally
straightening his tie and shooting his cuffs while breathing
deeply, and audibly, through his nose. You're in control. That's
good... that's good.

Order and sanity restored, he went off in search of the owners of the voices.

He didn't see them, at first. The sun had gone down, and
objects were blurring into their own shadows, slowly dissolv-

ing into the blue-and-purple wash of dusk. It wasn't until he'd stepped off the patio and skirted the first bank of shrubbery that he caught the flashes of movement from the lowest branches of the big elm tree. The one Dixie'd asked him about. The one...oh, God, he remembered, now. The one she'd asked if it was okay to build a tree house in.

He halted a few yards from the tree. It was Ethan who announced his presence, singing out, "Dad!" in that way he had—joyous, unconditional welcome.

Rhett didn't reply. The scene before him had rendered him incapable of speech. There was his son, barely six years old, sitting on a huge limb a good eight feet off the ground. He was straddling it like a horse, so little he looked like a monkey on a Clydesdale, waving his arms and kicking his feet as if exhorting it to go faster. And even more incredibly, there was his daughter, Little Miss Lolly Proper, squatting awkwardly in the fork of two limbs, clutching a hammer and what looked—he'd swear to God—like a cottage cheese carton. And there was...wait, where in the hell *was* Dixie?

"Dad," Ethan yelled, "come see what we're doin'! We're buildin' a tree house. Look, isn't it *great?*"

There was a violent rustling in the branches above Lolly's head. The leaves parted suddenly and Dixie's face appeared, flushed and smiling, magically disembodied, like the Cheshire Cat's. If he'd been in a mood to think philosophically—which he wasn't—Rhett supposed he'd have had to be thankful that at least one of his wishes had been granted. Her hair was nice and tidy—hidden, most of it, by a Chicago Cubs baseball cap.

"Come on up, Dad, there's lots of room," Ethan invited, patting the limb he was sitting on. "Guess what? You can see the who-ole yard from up here. I get to have a lookout, and *everything.*"

Rhett carefully cleared his throat. He tested his voice by saying, "That's nice, son." Satisfied with the result, he raised it slightly, both in aim and in volume, and inquired politely, "Uh...Dixie, may I have a word with you, please?" So far, so good. He was proud of himself.

Dixie said cheerfully, "Sure, be right down. Lolly, honey, you want to scoot over just a little bit, please? That's the way..." The Cheshire Cat face vanished into the leaves. There was some more violent shaking, then one foot appeared, clad in a battered athletic shoe. It searched for, then wedged itself into the crotch of the limb just vacated by Lolly, and a moment later the other one swung into view, dangling, it seemed, in midair.

"Here you go, sugar, let me have those. . . ." One arm, clad in a sweatshirt sleeve shoved above the elbow, snaked down and took the hammer and the cottage cheese carton from Lolly's outstretched hands. The carton rattled—and the light bulb came on above Rhett's head. *Nails.* It was full of nails. His mother used to do that, he remembered—use old empty cottage cheese cartons for containers for all sorts of things. His dad used to tease her about it, too.

"Can you make it down by yourself, or you want me to give you a hand?" Dixie was saying to Lolly.

Rhett started a little and stepped forward belatedly to help, but Lolly gave him a self-conscious, sideways look and muttered, "No, I can do it." So he had to stand there with his heart in his mouth and watch his only daughter wriggle herself around onto her stomach, then drop from his sight down the other side of the tree trunk.

Rhett shifted his gaze back up to Dixie. He had to wait while she shouted instructions and encouragement down to Lolly, but when he could get a word in, he remarked, still politely, "I don't suppose the children have had dinner yet?"

"Now me, now me!" yelled Ethan.

"What?" Dixie shot Rhett a look over her shoulder. "Oh boy, I guess it is getting kinda late, isn't it? Here, big guy, give me your hand . . ." She'd turned away from him and was half squatting, half dangling by one hand as she guided Ethan along the limb with the other. Her laughter was low and melodious, as enchanting, if he'd been in a mood to appreciate it—and he certainly wasn't—as a note of birdsong at twilight. "Okay, hon—can you make it the rest of the way?"

This time Rhett wasn't about to stand there as if he'd taken root while his son vanished down the backside of that damn tree. He lunged forward, rounding the trunk in what he hoped and prayed would be in time to prevent disaster.

Instead he was just in time to watch Ethan come down the tree backward, hand over hand like a little towheaded monkey. And now he could see that Dixie had nailed lengths of two-by-fours to the tree trunk, all the way up to the first branching limbs, like the rungs on a ladder. He let his breath out in a shaken rush and stood listening to the pounding of his heart-beat until his son was safe on the ground.

"Did you see me up in the tree, Dad? I was really high, huh?" Ethan was bouncing in sheer excess of energy, like Tigger. Rhett just reached out and ruffled his hair, since he still wasn't sure he could trust his voice.

"Okay, now, y'all go on in and wash up," Dixie hollered down from the tree. "I'll be in in a little bit, okay? I'm gonna make you some grilled cheese sandwiches—how's that sound?"

"I want tomato soup and Cheerios," yelled Ethan. "Can we have tomato soup and Cheerios again, *please?*"

*Tomato soup and Cheerios?* Another jolt of memory... vivid with the colors and sounds and smells of his childhood. He hadn't thought of tomato soup and Cheerios in...probably thirty years.

But he didn't want to think about those things now—he was *angry,* dammit!

"Okay, tomato soup, then—but y'all wash up good, now, hear?" Dixie called as the children raced each other to the kitchen door, making a megaphone of her hands.

Now, Rhett thought. His heart had begun to pound again, with impatience and anger, and something oddly like excitement. He waited, expecting Dixie to climb down out of the tree the same way the kids had. But she didn't. She sat herself down on Ethan's limb and gazed up into the purpling foliage with a blissful sigh, as if she meant to stay there awhile.

"Oh, it is just so beautiful up here." She stretched her arms wide to encompass the tree and all its branches. "I wish..." She stopped and gave her head a little shake, and he knew he wasn't going to hear what it was she wished for.

Instead she said lightly, with a smile he couldn't see in the deepening dusk, "You ought to come up here sometime, you know that?" Rhett snorted, and she laughed out loud. "Sure, why not? Being in a tree gives a person a whole new perspective. Hey—maybe when the tree house is finished, you can come up for a visit. It's going to be a fantastic tree house." She patted the limb she was sitting on. "This is where the swing's gonna go. It's a perfect limb for it, isn't it?"

Rhett thought of the great old oak in his parents' front yard, and the rope swing that had hung there until the tree had blown down in a storm . . . five years or so ago now.

But he didn't want to think of swings now! He was *mad as hell*, dammit!

Something in his silence must have finally gotten through to Dixie, because she suddenly leaned over to peer down at him, clasping her hands between her knees. "Hey, look, I'm sorry about missing the kids' suppertime. I guess we just plain lost track of the time. But... they were having such a good time—I can't believe those kids hadn't ever been in a tree before. I thought—"

"No, you didn't," Rhett said coldly. "If you had, you might have remembered what day this is."

"What day?" She tilted her head, like a puppy contemplating a puzzlement. "It's Tuesday..." He heard her gasp before she clapped a hand over her mouth. "Tuesday—oh God, Rhett, I'm sorry. Your meeting—I forgot all about it. For heaven's sake... why didn't you call... and remind me?"

The last sentence was delivered in breathless segments as she was scrambling out of the tree—not in the least like a monkey; more catlike, with agile, double-jointed grace. He was so distracted, watching her, that it wasn't until she was standing with both feet firmly on the ground that the absurdity of her question sank in fully.

"*Call* you?" he barked, on a sharp note of incredulous laughter. "I *told* you, dammit! You said—"

"Last week, you told me!" She rounded on him, aroused and furious, which struck him as so unfair, he was sure it must be out of a sense of guilt. "A lot's happened since then. You should have called to make sure I remembered. If it was so all-fired important—"

"It was important," snapped Rhett, following Dixie as she skirted the tree trunk and started toward the house in that long-legged stride of hers, slapping her thigh with her baseball cap with each step she took. He almost had to run to catch up. "It *is* important. I shouldn't have to call. You should have..." He broke off, panting with fury. *Elaine would have remembered, dammit!*

For some reason, that thought was the last straw. *Elaine?* the woman had betrayed and abandoned him. That he could think of her wistfully, even for an instant—he felt somehow as though he'd betrayed himself. All the emotion that had been backing up behind the dam of his self-control for the last weeks—all the rage and grief and worry and bewilderment and fear—seemed to be pressing on the inside of his chest, on the backs of his eyelids, at the bottom of his throat.

"Where are you going?" he demanded as Dixie charged on past him, reaching out to grab her by the arm. "I'm not finished—"

"I'm going—" She never got to finish it.

One moment she was tugging in outrage against his grasp, and in the very next—he wasn't sure how it happened—she was smack up against him. Suddenly his arms were full of her, and his hands were full of her hair, and her gasping breath and his own pounding heartbeat were all that he could hear.

# Chapter 9

"What's he doing now?" Ethan asked in a worried voice, pressing forward, trying to see past Lolly's shoulder. "Is he still yelling at Dixie?"

Lolly muttered, "I don't think so...it's too dark, I can't see." She was on her knees on the window seat with her face pressed against the glass, both hands held up at the sides of her face like blinders. "No...they've stopped. Now he's..." She swallowed. A strange, cold little lump, like an ice cube, had stuck in the bottom of her throat. But no matter how hard she swallowed, she couldn't make it go away.

"He's what?" asked Ethan, bouncing in impatience. "Tell me, Lolly, I can't see!"

"He's kissing her." Lolly felt very calm, even though the lump in her throat was making her feel cold all over now.

"Kissing?" Ethan sounded puzzled. "Why is he kissing Dixie? What does it mean?"

Lolly gave him a glance she meant to be scornful. "What do you think it means, dummy?"

*She* knew very well what it meant. She knew all about kissing from movies and TV. Plus, she'd once kissed a boy named Christopher, who was in her class at school, at noon recess out behind the music room. But Christopher's lips had felt soft and mushy, and she hadn't wanted to do it again, even though he'd offered to pay her a whole dollar if she would. As far as she was concerned, there wasn't anything all that exciting about kissing.

"Does it mean they like each other?" Ethan asked.

Lolly shrugged. "I guess. Anyway, who cares?"

"I care," said Ethan stoutly. "I want Dad and Dixie to like each other. I want Dixie to stay with us—don't you?"

But Lolly could only shrug once more. And she went on staring out the window even though it was too dark now to see anything at all. Because she knew exactly what it meant, her dad kissing Dixie. It meant—and for the first time Lolly knew, deep down in her heart—that her mother really wasn't coming back.

Dixie wanted to push him away. She meant to. She didn't want to be held close against a man's broad chest, didn't want to feel strong arms around her, didn't want to feel another person's body heat melting into her own pores, or to breathe in the achingly familiar scent of Old Spice and warm man. Oh God... she didn't want to.

She certainly didn't want him to kiss her.

Didn't want to feel as if she'd touched a live electrical socket, or as if the elevator she was riding in had snapped a cable. She'd forgotten about feelings like that. As she'd forgotten the way her skin prickled all the way from her scalp down to her toes, so that it *yearned* for the relief of a lover's touch. Forgotten the way every ounce of strength drained out of her muscles and her bones turned liquid and soft...

Push him away? How could she, when she had to lean against that broad chest and depend on those strong arms just to keep from falling? Oh God, it had been so long since she'd felt those things. She hadn't thought—or wanted—to ever feel them again.

Too late... too late. There was one soft, shocked intake of breath—his or hers, she couldn't tell—a blazing intensity of eyes, and then... his mouth, tasting of peppermint Life Savers... his lips, firm and silky and so warm... so warm. And surprisingly gentle, considering the anger in him, the tension she could feel quivering in all his muscles. Anger, yes... but surprise, too. And strangeness and uncertainty...and then discovery. And wonder.

She felt...joy.

And it *hurt*. Oh, God, how it hurt. She could feel it swelling up inside her, aching in her throat, stinging her eyes, making her lips tremble. What would he think when he felt *that?* She wanted to cry and sob and laugh and be kissed and held and kissed some more, all at the same time. What would he think if he knew?

But maybe he did know. Because all at once his body stiffened; his hands untangled from her hair and came instead to rest on her shoulders, briefly, then to grasp her upper arms, as if he meant to hurl her from him.

And yet...his lips lingered, as if governed by a different control center entirely, one not monitored by logic and reason, so that it was Dixie who finally broke away, though every nerve and sense and sinew in her howled in anguished protest.

She took a step backward, her own arms coming almost reflexively to crisscross her body, taking the place of the ones that had just so cruelly abandoned her. Small comfort they were; already she'd begun to shiver.

The first thing Rhett did, of course, was drive his fingers into his hair. When he opened his mouth to speak, only a raspy sound came out. Dixie wanted to laugh, to make light of it all, but her smile muscles wouldn't obey her commands. So she just clamped a hand over her mouth and helplessly shook her head.

Who would have recovered first in the normal course of events they would never know. It was a splash of light from the headlamps of a car pulling into the driveway that restored speech and brain function, like a bucketful of cold water, or a slap in the face.

Dixie gasped, and heard Rhett do the same, and then begin to swear.

"Oh God—they're here. I've got to—"

"I'll go start dinner...make coffee..." Dixie cast wildly about, recovered her bearings at last and bolted for the kitchen door.

Rhett, heading in the opposite direction toward his study, had to dance and dodge around her for one tension-filled, almost comical moment. "I'll get everyone something to drink...we'll be meeting in my study." He paused suddenly, hurled her a black, distraught look and growled, "We have to talk about this."

She paused, too, with her hand on the kitchen doorknob, long enough to gasp, "Yes." Then she was inside, alone in that cold kitchen, trembling and scared.

She felt as if she'd been hit by a truck.

But the instant the thought registered, she rejected it with silent, ironic laughter. Because, of course, she knew being hit by a truck felt nothing at all like this. Being hit by a truck was blackness...oblivion...waking up in a strange place surrounded by strangers, and remembering nothing at all.

What this felt like was later, a long time after that, leaving the hospital to go to a home she no longer felt at home in, and moving slowly and painfully, like an old, old person, feeling weak and disoriented and lost....

They spoke simultaneously, facing each other across Rhett's desk.

"I expect you'll be wanting—"

"I guess you'd like me to—"

They both stopped. Neither one of them laughed. They regarded each other for a long, somber moment, then spoke again in a rush.

"You can't leave."

"I don't want to leave."

This time Dixie gave in to a short, painful sounding laugh. Rhett let his breath out audibly and turned away from her, punching his hands into his pockets. To keep from tearing his hair, he wondered? Or from touching her again ...

Because he wanted to—oh, how he wanted to. It was all he'd been able to think about. He was certain, too, that Newt and Madeline, at the very least, had noticed his distraction. And knowing them, probably already suspected the cause. God, they'd kill him if they knew what he'd done. How could he have been so stupid?

"The children," Dixie said in a constricted voice.

Rhett nodded without turning. "It would be hard on them if you left." *And on me! Especially me...*

He forced himself to face her, to look at her, and winced when he saw how pale she was, and the way her eyes seemed to have retreated deep into shadowed sockets. But then, of course, it was very late. All their conversations seemed to take place late at night, he reflected, right here in this room.

"This was entirely my fault," he said, knowing how stiff and formal he must sound. "I can't tell you how sorry I am. I can assure you..."

"Maybe," Dixie said with a little gulp, "it would be better if we just pretended like it never happened."

Rhett actually smiled—crookedly, but a smile nonetheless. "Can you do that?" *Because I sure as hell can't.*

"For the kids' sake I can." She'd gone very still, her gaze level and unwavering.

His gaze dropped to his blotter, where his hand was carefully rearranging his already perfectly aligned pen, appointment book and glasses. He felt his smile grow forced, and abandoned it. "All right, then. I guess...that's where we leave it." His eyes found hers again, somber this time. "All I can do is promise you it won't happen again."

She nodded, murmured something he couldn't hear and turned to go.

So. That was it. It was over. He should have felt relieved, but he didn't.

He said her name softly and she paused to look back at him, eyebrows raised in polite question.

"About tonight—thanks for dinner. I have to tell you— coming up with shishkabobs out of that leftover roast was truly inspired."

Without looking at him, Dixie mumbled, "Well, my mama always said there's nothing can't be salvaged with a little bit of barbeque sauce."

He couldn't help but smile. "Well, you really came through for me. I appreciate it."

She said, "You're welcome," and went out, closing the door behind her with a quiet *click*.

Without her in it his study suddenly seemed terribly empty, the house around him silent and cold. *Maybe I was wrong*, he thought. *Maybe I only imagined the way her body seemed to melt into me...the way her mouth trembled when I kissed her.*

He'd never known a woman to respond to his touch like that. Certainly Elaine never had, and before that...frankly, he hadn't cared enough about any of the women he'd dated in high school or college to really notice. In any case, he knew it had disturbed him profoundly, left him reeling, like a taste of forbidden fruit, or some potent and addictive drug. It had left him craving more.

And he'd just promised he'd never touch her again.

The thought left him feeling inexpressibly lonely.

It was easier than Dixie had thought it would be, avoiding Rhett. So easy that she suspected he must be dodging her as diligently as she was him. Together they seemed to slip into a carefully choreographed dance, stately and courteous as a minuet. She rose and dressed early, listened for the sound of his shower water running before dashing along the landing and down the stairs—as he no doubt listened for the clatter of breakfast dishes in the kitchen before daring to run the same gauntlet.

The unavoidable morning confrontation in the kitchen was a performance for the children's benefit—bright smiles and cheery good morning!'s and an exchange of questions and concerns of the day, carried out under two pairs of avid and watchful eyes. Lauren's were wary and calculating—how much had she seen, or surmised? Ethan's were worried and full of questions—how much did he sense with his six-year-old's radar?

But then Rhett would dash off to work and the children to school, and she was left to fill the day any way she could, in a house that wasn't hers.

It wasn't so hard, really. On the housekeeper's off days there was plenty to keep her mornings full, and when Luby was there the house rang with laughter and rock music played loud on a portable radio that followed the cleaning progress from room to room. Afternoons, Dixie did the laundry, or the grocery shopping, or worked on the tree house. One day it rained, and she spent a long cozy couple of hours in the stables, grooming Star and drinking in the smells of tack and warm animals and trying not to think of Texas...the ranch...home.

Then it was time for the afternoon taxi runs—to the stables for riding lessons, or to the piano teacher's or the orthodontist, to Ethan's soccer practice. There was homework to supervise and, if there was time before supper, more work on the tree house. Evenings there were squabbles to referee and clothes to be organized for school the next day, tears and hysterics over school projects forgotten until the last possible moment.

"But I *haff* to have twelve different leaves by tomorrow—Mrs. Tatum said!"

"Why on God's green earth didn't you tell me before it got dark?"

"Well . . . I forgot."

Sometime around seven, Rhett would come home, look in briefly on his offspring, fix himself a tray from the stores Dixie had prepared and left on the stove for him, and retire to his study for the balance of the evening. After the children were in bed, Dixie would tiptoe downstairs to tidy up the kitchen, always with one ear cocked for the sound of the butler's pantry door, and with her heart beating just a little too fast. Then she, too, would sequester herself in her room, passing the hour or two until bedtime with a book, the TV or her guitar.

Oh, yes, the days were easy; she could hold memory at bay by keeping her mind focused on simple tasks, a process with which she was all too familiar. But the nights . . . oh God, the nights.

He came to her in the night, no matter how hard she tried to barricade her mind's doors. In the dark and quiet of night, somehow he was *there* . . . she felt his warmth and smelled his Old Spice after-shave, heard the quick, aroused rasp of his breathing—or was it hers? She tasted his mouth, and it tasted so good she wanted to laugh and cry at the same time. Sometimes she did, her body shaking with silent helpless laughter while tears trickled cold and lonely into her hair. She felt his touch with every nerve in her body—and where had *that* memory come from? He'd never touched her *there*. And yet her breasts were tight and swollen, her nipples hard with yearning, and lower down, pulses throbbed with an urgency she'd all but forgotten.

She would lie in bed staring into the darkness with hot, angry eyes, with her hand resting in the soft concavity of her belly, fingers spread comfortingly over the empty place where her womb should have been, and with their tips trace back and forth over the smooth, hard ridges of scar tissue there.

Never, never did she let her fingers stray lower, though the tender, feminine places craved touching the way a starving child craves milk. It wasn't *her* touch they clamored for.

*Damn you, Rhett.*

Because it *hadn't* been just a kiss, not for her. For her it had been the key that opened Pandora's box, releasing all the fierce and tender yearnings, the primitive needs and womanly wants she'd locked away so carefully so long ago. And she knew, with a cold and lonely certainty, that she was never going to be able to force those feelings back into their hiding place again.

*Damn you Rhett. Damn you...*

"Dixie, have you got a minute?" The question, accompanied by a rusty sounding cough, came unexpectedly from the half-open butler's pantry door. Rhett had paused there on his way through the kitchen en route to his study, as if it were a spur of the moment impulse.

Dixie turned off the water and looked up at him, acutely aware of another presence there at the table behind her. It was a rainy October Saturday, and Lolly had a project going, cutting pictures out of Dixie's horse magazines for a collage she was making for her room. Except Dixie noticed that now the rustle of pages had ceased, and the crunch of scissors had gone silent.

"Sure," she said, brightly smiling, "what's up?"

"I'd like to talk to you, if you... uh, have the time."

He was scowling, as usual, looking rumpled and masculine in his jogging sweats. He'd just come back from his morning run and was sweaty and unshaven, his hair arcing down over his eyebrows in damp, dark commas. Energy and vitality seemed to rise from his body in visible waves, like heat.

Dixie's stomach clenched and her heart began to knock against her ribs. Oh Lord, she thought, here it comes. He's finally had enough of this farcical "trial" of ours. He's going to call it off.

She should have been relieved, she supposed; the last two weeks had been right up there with the worst she'd ever spent. But relief wasn't anywhere near to what she was feeling as she wiped her hands on a towel and turned to trail after Rhett into his study.

For some reason, though, he'd stayed where he was, blocking the doorway, and was still regarding her with that black and measuring frown. Then he said abruptly, "Have you got a dress?"

It was so far from what she'd prepared herself to hear that for a few moments it seemed like a foreign language to her. She could only bat the words back to him, reflexively and without comprehension. "A dress?"

His face twitched in a brief spasm of irritation—at himself, not her. "I didn't mean that the way it sounded. I'm sure you have dresses. What I meant to say was, do you have one *with* you?" And then he actually smiled, lopsidedly and only in apology, but a smile, nonetheless. "I'm sorry. I guess what I should be asking is whether you have any plans for tonight. Do you?"

Dixie's stomach relaxed a little, although her heart went right on pounding. On the edges of her field of vision she could see that Lolly had turned in her chair and was openly listening. Keeping her tone noncommittal, she said, "The answer to both questions is no. Why?"

"Okay, here's the deal," Rhett said briskly, still frowning from the pantry doorway, his arms folded across his chest now, as if he were getting ready to examine a difficult witness. "I'm supposed to attend a banquet tonight—big fund-raiser, political. All the party bigwigs will be there—Senator Parkinson, the Vice President. . . . It's kind of important."

"I *guess*," murmured Dixie, impressed in spite of herself.

"Anyway," Rhett went on, both his tone and manner brusque to the point of impatience, "it's important that I be there, under the circumstances. And," he added, switching to his most earnest and persuasive mode, "it shouldn't be a bad evening. There's entertainment—I think they've got that country singer, what's his name, with the white hair and beard? *You* know who I mean . . ."

"Yes," murmured Dixie with a wry little smile, "I know who you mean."

". . . and I'm sure there'll be dancing and . . . so forth. It's a big, formal affair. I really hate like he . . ." he glanced at Lolly and lowered his voice a notch " . . . I really don't want to show up alone. You understand? I need a . . . um . . ."

"A date?" Dixie supplied, with a giggle. She blamed it on nerves.

"An escort," Rhett corrected firmly. Then he paused, while his features registered a look of unanticipated self-doubt, and an ingenuousness she found unexpectedly appealing. "Is that the right word? Well . . . anyway, if you wouldn't mind, and . . . uh, have nothing better to do, I'd like you to go with me." He coughed and carefully added, "For appearances' sake."

"Well, of course," said Dixie, straight-faced.

"As a friend. Of the family." For just an instant she saw something in his eyes that looked almost comically like panic.

She shrugged, carefully indifferent. "Sure, why not? I don't mind. Be glad to help you out. Sounds like fun."

Then there was silence while they looked at each other—a dangerous enterprise, with Lolly sitting only a few feet away, watching their every move, missing absolutely nothing. Dixie could feel that steady blue gaze almost as a palpable thing.

Rhett must have felt it, too, because he suddenly glanced his daughter's way and harrumphed gruffly. "Well. Okay, then. That's...thanks. I really appreciate it. Uh...you'll need to get yourself a dress, then, I guess. Something...*you* know, dressy. Just put it on my account—I'll give you my Visa card. Oh—" He opened the pantry door wide. "And while you're at it . . ." he made a vague, circling motion with his hand in the vicinity of his ear "...maybe you could do something with your hair."

Dixie's mouth dropped open. "My hair..." But Rhett had already gone, closing the door after him. She turned to Lolly and exploded, "Do something with my *hair?* What am I *supposed* to do with my hair? What does he mean?"

"He means elegant," said Lolly as she swiveled back to her magazines and scissors, giving her head a little toss. Although her voice and expression were both carefully aloof when she added, "Mom always looked elegant when they went out together. Like a queen."

Dixie let her breath go in a snort of laughter. *Elegant?* But I don't *do* elegant, she thought in exasperation, giving in to just a moment of panic herself. It was a helluva lot to expect of someone whose style ran to jeans accessorized with cowboy boots and a Stetson—both well broken in—and whose preferred transportation bore a license plate that said Texas Truck.

The amazing thing was, she did give it her best shot, even though she'd always been strictly a take me as I am or leave me alone sort of person before.

She even rather enjoyed walking into Younkers, Des Moines' biggest downtown department store, finding her way into carpeted regions populated with fur coats chained to their racks and beaded and sequined cocktail dresses that in her opinion resembled nothing so much as suits of chain mail, and announcing, "Hi, y'all, I need somethin' *elegant*. D'you have anything in a size 8 Princess Grace?"

The sales force, though maybe a little snooty at first, had unbent pretty quickly after that.

She actually found something she liked, too—a white silk jumpsuit that would have set off her turquoise earrings very nicely. But she didn't buy it. Rhett had specifically said *dress*, and she did her best not to disappoint him.

She did, however, use her own Visa card.


"Son, have you lost your ever-lovin' *mind?*" Newt Hendricks's voice crackled across the telephone lines, making Rhett wince even though he'd been more or less expecting it. "This is just the kind of thing I've been warning you about. The kind of thing that starts the rumors flying. We don't need that kind of thing to get started, not so close to declaring—"

"What the hell did you expect me to do," Rhett snapped, cutting him off, "hire somebody from an escort service? This is the first social event since the—since Elaine left, and I didn't care much for the idea of showing up alone. Okay? That's all this is. Don't make a big deal out of it."

"Look, son." Newt's voice took on a soothing purr. "I know divorce is hard. And there's nothing screws up common sense like a bruised ego. You're lonely, and you're vulnerable. I just don't want you getting yourself mixed up with the first bimbo that comes along because—"

"Bimbo?" There was a steely edge in Rhett's voice that surprised him, a little; he hadn't known he was capable of that kind of hardheadedness. Evidently it surprised Newt, too, because he immediately began to make placating noises, which Rhett bulldozed right through, in a quiet but deadly tone. "That *bimbo* happens to be building my kids a tree house. She puts Cheerios in their tomato soup. Let me tell you something—that woman has more class in her little finger..." His voice trailed off.

"Rhett? Son? Say, listen..."

Rhett lowered the receiver slowly, managing to cradle it successfully on the second or third try. "*Dixie?*" It emerged as a wheezy croak. He cleared his throat, swallowed hard and tried again. "Dixie—come on in. I was just...you look..."

She moved from the doorway into his study with an endearing uncertainty, like a doe venturing into a clearing. "Is this all right? I wasn't sure...you did say dressy. Do you think it's too..."

"No, no, it's...just fine. You look..." He couldn't for the life of him think of a word. All of them seemed either inadequate, vaguely inaccurate, or somehow, in ways he couldn't explain, simply inappropriate. Finely he gulped and said "Fine," and left it at that.

The dress she'd chosen was deep blue—royal blue, he thought they called it—with a wide sweetheart neckline that enhanced rather than revealed her small, high breasts. It had full sleeves, gathered at the elbow, a dropped waistline that hugged her curves, and a full skirt cut higher in front than in back so that it dipped at the heels of her high-heeled sling-back sandals. She'd piled her hair high in a loose knot, with curls on her forehead and neck, in a style that made him think of another century, of Gibson girls and bustles, and flirting smiles modestly hidden behind lace-trimmed fans. The whole effect was as sexy and alluring as a naked ankle peeking out of a nest of ruffled petticoats.

"Is...something wrong?" He heard a breathy note of panic in her voice. Her hand fluttered nervously to her bare throat, and he realized he'd been staring, scowling fiercely, at the spot where the sun had colored her skin a deeper gold and dusted it with freckles, in contrast to the flawless cream farther down.

He pivoted abruptly, crossed to the small, fireproof safe that sat on top of the corner filing cabinet, opened it and took out a long, flat box. "It needs something," he said, holding it out to her. "Try this."

She took it but didn't open it, saying in a worried tone, "I know...all I had was my silver earrings, but they weren't...quite..."

"That was my mother's," he said brusquely, nodding at the box. "Elaine never cared to wear it. I've been saving it for Lolly. Go ahead—open it."

He meant it as an order, and after a moment's hesitation, she obeyed. He watched in stony silence as she fastened the necklace around her own neck, making no move whatsoever to help her, knowing that any such effort would be worthless as well as dangerous in the extreme. He narrowed his focus to just the stones themselves, and was fascinated by the way the single bloodred garnet in its circlet of tiny diamond chips seemed to set fire to the skin it touched...

"There—is it all right?"

He let go of a breath he didn't know he'd been holding. "It's fine—perfect." He forced himself to look at her—all of her, knowing he was scowling again. "Well—are we ready to go? Do you have a coat?"

Her smile flashed suddenly; her eyes reminded him of chips of Kansas sky showing through a break in the thunder clouds. "Sure do. I rented a fur."

A fur. All Rhett could think of what the animals' rights people were going to say if they ever got wind of it. He sighed inwardly. Newt was going to kill him. But all he said was, "All right, then." And he held the door for her, being oh, so careful not to touch her.


"Dixie looks pretty," said Ethan, jockeying for window position under Lolly's elbow, as usual. "Doesn't she?"

"I guess," said Lolly with a shrug, forgetting, for once, to push him aside. "Not as pretty as Mom, though."

Ethan started to say something, then stopped, looking uncertain. "I can't remember," he said in a small voice.

Lolly didn't say anything, just went on gazing out through the window in her parents' bedroom, down onto the brick-paved drive where her dad was holding the door of his car open for Dixie. He looked very handsome, she thought, in his tuxedo.

"Lolly, do you miss Mom?" Ethan's voice still sounded small and uncertain.

Lolly didn't look at him. "Not really." She shrugged again, and after a moment, even though she didn't want to, heard herself say, "Do you?"

Ethan thought about it, chewing on his lip. "Sometimes. Not as much. Not when Dixie's around." He slipped from under Lolly's elbow and went running out of the room as the house began to shudder to the beat of Kendra's favorite rap music.

Lolly stayed there looking out of the window for a long time after the lights of her father's car had disappeared. She kept taking deep breaths, but no matter how hard she tried she couldn't make the cold, hollow feeling inside her go away.


As far as Rhett was concerned, the evening began badly and went downhill from there.

For starters, Newt Hendricks was waiting for him in the foyer of the grand ballroom, pacing up and down like a worried daddy. It would have been enough to set Rhett's teeth on edge, being treated like an irresponsible adolescent, but when Newt, who'd never been known for his subtlety, parked himself between him and Dixie like an overzealous duenna, he began to feel like one. He felt stubborn and contrary and hostile and uncooperative, all the things he hadn't felt when he actually *was* an adolescent. He had to keep reminding himself who and where he was, and why—with the result that inside fifteen minutes his jaws had already begun to ache with the constant effort it took to keep his smile from turning into a scowl.

His chief campaign strategist, with reinforcements from party chairman Madeline Hite, had taken him firmly in tow and was making the rounds, making sure he got introduced to all the party bigshots—the important ones, anyway—while at the same time trying his best to see that Dixie got left in the background, if not out of the scene entirely.

Which made Rhett, in his contrary mood, all the more determined to keep her close to him. He found himself taking a firm grip on her arm as they moved through the crowd, and keeping a hand on her when he was exchanging pleasantries with various and sundry celebrities and politicians. All of which had the result, of which he was completely—and furiously—aware, of making them look very much like a couple.

It was while he was engaged in polite conversation with Senator Parkinson, whom he'd already met, that he heard a voice from somewhere in the crowd behind him sing out, "Dixiebelle! Hot damn, is that *you?* Come on over here, sugar, and hug m'neck!"

He turned, cutting off the senator in midsentence, just in time to see a big, bearlike man with gleaming white hair and a neatly trimmed beard scoop Dixie into a hug that lifted her feet clear off the floor—no small achievement, considering Dixie probably pushed six feet herself, in those high heels of hers.

She was laughing as the man swung her around, and gasping, "Come on, Poppy, put me down, now. Behave yourself!"

Which the bear did, finally, only to bestow a loud kiss smack on her lips, then hold her at arm's length while he crowed, "Lemme look at you, doggone it. Last time I saw you, you were barely outta pigtails. Where in the hell you been keepin' yourself, darlin'? Last I heard, you were off in the Peace Corps, weren't you? Someplace down in South America."

Dixie laughed. "That was a long, long time ago, Poppy." She hooked the man's arm and turned him to face Rhett and his fellow spectators. He could see that her cheeks and throat were glowing with a soft, rosy flush. Something stirred inside him, something dark and primitive.

"Rhett, Senator, I'd like y'all to meet—"

"I know who you are," Rhett growled, as his hand was all but swallowed up in the legendary country singer's huge paw. The other, he noted, with more of that visceral churning, was still around Dixie, planted firmly on her waist.

"—my *uncle*," Dixie finished demurely, her eyes dancing with unmistakable laughter.

"By marriage," the famous man jovially clarified, giving Dixie's waist a squeeze. "Hey, Dixie-belle, we got an extra guitar around someplace—you gonna come an' cut a few licks with us?"

Dixie's flush deepened. "Come on, Poppy, you know that's not my thing."

"Well, hell, it oughta be. Ya know," the singer said to the assembly at large, "this little ol' gal has a voice that'd make an angel cry. And she can make a guitar talk, too." He pronounced it *gee*-tar.

Dixie threw Rhett a look he couldn't decipher, but before he had time to even try, the singer had his arm wrapped around her shoulders and was saying in his famous, raspy bellow, "Hey, would y'all mind if I steal Dixie-belle, here, for just a little while? Come on, darlin', there's some people over here I want you to meet...."

And just like that she was gone, swallowed up in the glittering crowd like a pebble in a corncrib, leaving Rhett to seethe in helpless fury and frustration.

A moment later there was a stirring and shifting near the entrance, and the crowd was suddenly parted by a platoon of grim-faced men with watchful, restless eyes. The Vice President was arriving.

After that, Rhett tried to keep track of Dixie, telling himself he was only concerned about how she'd handle herself in such a sophisticated crowd. It was, after all, the kind of social scene that had been Elaine's special forte. But Dixie was...something else. She'd be out of her league. That's what he told himself. He was worried about her.

But he couldn't help but notice that, wherever Dixie was, he heard laughter. During dinner, her end of the table, which someone—Newt, no doubt—had made sure was at the opposite end from Rhett's, seemed constantly to be erupting with loud and unseemly gales of mirth. He found it extremely irritating and distracting. He told himself he was embarrassed by it. What he really felt was excluded. And envious.

Hell. What he was, was jealous.

After dinner there were the usual speeches and introductions. The Vice President made one, which the news cameras dutifully recorded. Rhett tried hard to look as if he was paying attention, and to applaud at the appropriate times, but all he could think about was how much he wanted to get Dixie, get the hell out of there and go home. This sort of thing was the part of politics he'd always hated the most—schmoozing and kissing up to people somebody thought might be able to help him somewhere down the road. He knew it was important and necessary if he was ever going to get into a position to be able to do some good in the world, but . . . damn. The truth was, he'd always depended on Elaine's natural poise and polish to help him carry these things off. What had possessed him to think Dixie . . .

But he couldn't think Dixie. That was the problem.

The speeches ended and the entertainment got underway. The music was loud and raucous, the lights, except for the flash and glitter on stage, went down, and people were on their feet clapping, some getting up to dance. And all Rhett could think was, *Now.* Finally. He could manage to sneak Dixie out of there and go home.

Except that, when he tried to catch Dixie's eye, he found her place at the table empty. Then he noticed that Mrs. Parkinson, who was seated directly across from him, seemed to be watching the dancing with unusual interest, and with a polite little smile fixed upon her plain, wholesome Midwestern face. He followed her gaze and sure enough, there was Dixie, two-stepping around the dance floor with Iowa's senior senator himself.

Well then, what could Rhett do? He did what protocol demanded, under the circumstances. He asked the senator's wife to dance.

So it went, for what seemed to him like eternity. An evening in Hell. If he'd tried, he couldn't have imagined a more lonely way to spend eternity than dancing with other men's wives, making polite and charming conversation while his stomach tied itself in knots and his eyes searched endlessly for glimpses of royal blue in a whirling, shifting kaleidoscope of dancers.

His breaking point came unexpectedly, during a rousing Western line dance. With nearly everybody out on the dance floor laughing and making fools of themselves anyway, he saw his chance and took it. Before he even realized he was going to, he'd broken into the line of stomping, kicking, stumbling dancers, right next to Dixie.

"You sure you know how to do this?" she asked him out of the side of her mouth as he slipped his arm around her waist.

"I can sure as hell fake it as well as anybody else can," he said, and was shocked when it came out sounding almost like a snarl. Her startled glance bounced off him like a tossed pebble, but he kept his eyes resolutely on the line of dancers in front of him and concentrated as hard as he could on imitating everything they were doing.

The music ended with lots of whoops and cowboy yells and applause and laughter, which died away quickly with the opening chords of the next song. It was one of the singer's biggest hits, a slow, sweet ballad now become a classic, familiar even to a host of Midwestern politicians. The introductory bars ended and the famous, rusty nail voice filled the room. Couples found each other. The unattached drifted back to their tables. Dixie turned to join the exodus, but Rhett caught her hand and pulled her roughly back.

"Where are you going?" he asked, and heard again that inexplicable growl he barely recognized as his own voice.

"I thought—"

"I haven't been able to get near you all evening. You've danced with pretty near every man in the place—don't you think it's about my turn?" It was unconscionable, and he knew it. So he was truly shocked when she giggled.

And then simpered, "Why, Rhett, Ah do declare . . ."

He snorted and tightened his arm around her waist.

# *Chapter 10*

She hesitated, then came softly against him.

He felt his heart pounding, sending his blood surging like surf through his veins . . . felt a fine vibration in all his muscles, as if he'd been plugged into a low-voltage electrical current. Felt his own skin wrap him in liquid fire.

What he didn't feel was the floor under his feet. Or any sense whatsoever of guilt or danger or wrongdoing.

He did feel fear. Because the things he was feeling were things he'd never felt before. Because in spite of that, he knew somehow that the pounding in his blood and the fire in his loins were powerful and primitive forces, the same forces that make men draw swords, and drive stags to lower their antlers and square off against each other across rocky mountain meadows. He wasn't all that sure he could control them.

It terrified him, how much he wanted her.

"You never told me you were in the Peace Corps," he snarled in her ear, as the singer's rusty voice groaned on about the perils of falling in love.

"You never asked me." Her voice was light, breathy. It excited him as if she'd whispered erotic invitations against his naked skin.

*"God..."* he groaned, and didn't answer when she asked him what was wrong.

But his hands had shifted, just a little and of their own accord, and she obeyed their gentle invitation without a moment's hesitation. Her hand climbed his shoulder to claim the back of his neck... his lips brushed the cool porcelain ridge of her ear. Her body softened and seemed to melt into him, all along his front from his chin to his knees. And then he wasn't aware of anything else in the world, not the music, the movements of the dance, the other people in the room, or even what he'd come there for in the first place.

But he did feel her tremble. He pulled away slightly, just enough to ask her what was wrong. Before he could, she uttered a sharp little sound and tore herself out of his arms. For an instant she stood there, looking like someone who's awakened in a strange and frightening place, and then she bolted for the foyer exit, for all the world, he thought, as if she were Cinderella hearing the clock strike midnight.

Rhett went after her, of course. He got as far as the foyer, where he was in time to catch a glimpse of royal blue satin disappearing through the door of the ladies' room, far down a carpeted and chandeliered corridor. He was heading that way— polite convention be damned!—when an arm hooked his and hauled him into an alcove behind a six-foot tree planted in a terra cotta pot.

"For God's sake, son," Newt Hendricks croaked, in what was meant to be a whisper but which more closely approximated the voices of the bullfrogs Rhett and his friends had once hunted through boggy river bottoms on hot summer nights. "Mind telling me what in the *hell* you think you're doing?"

The potted tree was bedecked with tiny lights. Rhett fixed his glare on one of them and muttered, "She's, uh... not feeling well. I thought I'd better..."

"The hell you did. You weren't thinking at all. And what in God's green earth was that all about in there just now?"

Rhett transferred the glare to his campaign manager, drawing himself up to his full six feet, which gave him half a head's advantage on the man, and at least the illusion of comparable maturity. "I don't know what you're talking about," he said loftily.

"The hell you don't." Newt snorted. "My furnace doesn't put out as much heat as the two of you were doing out there on that dance floor."

"Now wait just—"

"No. *You* wait—and listen, and listen good." Newt leaned closer, so some of the urgency in him couldn't help but get through to Rhett. "Son, you're a newcomer to this game, but I'm an old player, and I know the rules better than you do. You, you're all full of ideas for changing the world, and you might even manage to do that. Some day. But first you've got to get yourself into a position where you can get the chance. And in order to do that, you've got to sell yourself—you follow me?"

"I know all that," Rhett growled. "What do you think I am?"

Newt snorted. "Right at this particular moment, I don't think you want me to answer that." He paused to take a calming breath. "Look, politically, you're an unknown product. Your biggest selling point is that squeaky-clean, all-American family man image of yours. Now, this divorce thing is likely going to hurt a little, but as long as you retain custody of those kids of yours, the public is likely to give you the benefit of the doubt. But let me tell you, if either the public or your wife or her lawyers ever gets even a hint that you've got some sort of hanky-panky going on with that woman, right there in your own house, you can kiss those kids goodbye, and the family values vote along with 'em. It won't matter how tough you are on crime, son, you won't have a snowball's chance in Hades of getting elected. And that's a fact."

Rhett was glowering at the tiny lights again, and beyond them, at the ladies' room door. He nodded, although he hadn't really heard much after the word "custody." Lose his kids? *Over my dead body!* "Look—there hasn't been any hanky-panky," he said, after carefully clearing his throat. "And there isn't going to be. I can promise you that."

"Well, I'm glad to hear it, son, glad to hear it." Newt didn't sound entirely convinced.

Rhett frowned harder at the ladies' room door and forced the next words past stiff lips. "How's the, uh, investigation going? Turned up anything yet?"

"Not yet. Tell you what, though, I called in a favor from Bob, and he's—"

"Bob?"

"Senator Parkinson. He's promised to pull some strings down at the FBI—"

"The *FBI?* Jeez, Newt, is that really necessary?" Rhett's stomach felt queasy.

"Can't be too careful these days." Newt touched his elbow. "Here she comes—you take care of this situation, now, you hear?"

"Yeah," said Rhett, and added gloomily, "She served in the Peace Corps, by the way." He had no idea why saying those words should give him a sense of doom and betrayal. The Peace Corps? What could be more innocent than that?

Newt nodded approvingly. "I caught that, son. Already noted and passed along." Apparently reassured as to Rhett's basic sanity, he waved and went off in the direction of the ballroom.

Somewhat less certain of his own mental condition, Rhett took a deep breath and straightened his shoulders, preparing himself for the impending confrontation with Dixie as he might have for a whole battery of hostile witnesses. Nothing could have prepared him, however, as he watched her walk toward him down that long, glittery corridor, for the experience of having his heart lurch with gladness and his stomach knot up with dread, both at the same time.

Dixie had come to an unavoidable conclusion while she was crouched, quivering and weeping, in an empty ladies' room stall like a jilted teenager at her high school prom. There was just no way around it. She would have to leave Rhett's house.

It would be a little bit tough on the kids, sure, but, she told herself, not as bad as it would have been a couple of weeks ago. They'd come a long way toward accepting their mother's absence—Ethan hardly ever cried at night anymore. Lolly was still keeping everything inside, but with a little time, she'd be okay. They'd get along just fine without her.

She wasn't so sure how she'd get along without them.

Or without their father.

Oh God, she thought wretchedly, what will I say to him? Look at him standing there, starched and elegant as a glitzy magazine ad for champagne, or diamonds, or some hideously expensive brand of car. Looking, as her mama would have said, as if butter wouldn't melt in his mouth. Shoot, Dix, she scolded herself, how could you be so stupid as to let yourself fall in love with a man—*any* man, but especially one in the middle of a divorce?

In the end, as she often did in times of crisis, she fell back on Texas.

"Whoo-ee," she breathed as she approached Rhett, smiling brightly and fanning herself with her hand, "guess I got a little bit dizzy in there. Sorry 'bout that."

"Would you like to go home?" He was frowning, as usual, though his tone was politely concerned.

*Home?* Her heart twisted. She smiled even more brightly. "Well, you know, maybe I would. I do have just a little bit of a headache. Would you mind?"

"Not at all," said Rhett stiffly. "I'll have the car—"

"Oh, don't do that!" She put out her hand and just did manage to keep from touching his arm with it. "For heaven's sake, you ought to be in there schmoozing with the Vice President—he seems like a real nice guy, by the way. Not a bad dancer, either, not stiff at all, once he loosens up." Not unlike someone else I know, she thought, as her stomach turned a flip-flop at the sudden and stunning recollection of the way his body had moved in perfect union with hers... "Go on, don't fuss over me—I'll just take a cab, or something."

He jerked involuntarily. "Oh, I don't think—"

"Really, Rhett," Dixie said, her voice suddenly turning soft, almost pleading. "I think it's best. Don't you?"

They stood for a few long moments in silence, Rhett glowering at something just beyond Dixie's left ear, she avidly studying the lines and planes of the face that had, in such a short time, become so familiar to her. As if committing them to memory. As if she needed to.

A breeze from some far-off furnace or air conditioner stirred the loose curls on her neck, like a lover's gentle caress. She shivered as goose bumps rose all over her body.

Rhett's glance jerked unwillingly toward her as he murmured, "Are you cold?" And then, without waiting for her reply, "I'll get your coat and ask the doorman to get you a cab. If you're sure that's what you want to do."

"It is. You just go on back in there and enjoy yourself. You can tell people I wasn't feeling well, or there was a call from the baby-sitter—whatever you want to."

What a performance this is, she thought. A performance for an audience of two. Neither of whom were buying a word of it.

"I'll be fine," she murmured. "Don't worry about me."

He nodded, his profile as stony and remote as a monument to some long dead general.

"You'd better take this…" Her hands lifted somehow to the nape of her neck, stiff fingers fumbled with the clasp of her garnet necklace.

Rhett's mouth opened as if he meant to protest. He seemed to pale a little as he took it from her, and stuffed it into his pocket, but all he said was "Thanks."

After that, the only words spoken were to others—to the coatroom attendant, to the doorman, to the driver of the taxi-cab. Rhett was careful not to touch her as he settled her coat over her shoulders, held doors for her, handed her into the cab and shut the door firmly after her. She returned his wave, then turned her face deliberately from him.

As the cab pulled away from the brightly lit hotel, she pulled her rented fur coat around her for warmth and comfort and prayed the prayer of another Southern woman who'd had the misfortune to fall in love with a damn Yankee.

*Tomorrow… I'll tell him tomorrow.*


The next day was Sunday, but there was no such thing as sleeping in, and not much privacy, either. The children were up early, demanding their custom-shaped pancakes, which had become something of a Sunday morning ritual in the household since Dixie's first memorable morning there. She fixed them with all the usual flair and laughter she could muster, but inside she ached. Oh, how it hurt, knowing that this would be the last time she'd hear Ethan shriek, "Mickey Mouse!" as they watched the circles of batter slowly flow together on the hot griddle. The last time she'd make a pancake horse with a shredded wheat mane.

It was a chilly morning, but bright and sunny, so after breakfast Dixie sent the children out to rake the backyard—a job they now fought over, since Dixie had demonstrated how much fun could be derived from a mountain of piled up leaves.

She could hear them squealing with glee—Ethan—and yelling orders—Lolly—as she knocked on the door of Rhett's study.

"Yes—come in." He'd known who it was, of course; he wouldn't use that gruff, preemptive tone with anyone else.

Her heart was hammering desperately already. Catching a breath and holding it, she turned the knob and pushed the door open.

He was wearing a sweater this morning, not a shirt; even so, in Dixie's opinion, he did manage to stuff it very nicely. Other than that, he bore no resemblance at all to the self-important, pompous snob his sister believed him to be. He hadn't shaved, and his hair had suffered a considerable amount of attention from his restless hands, which, denied their favorite distraction, were now drumming fretfully on the desk blotter. Behind his glasses, his eyes were red rimmed, as if he hadn't slept much.

"You aren't going for your run this morning?" Dixie asked brightly as she stepped into the room.

He shook his head. She could see his jaws cramp with his efforts to suppress a yawn. Nerves, she thought sympathetically as her own throat muscles tightened in reflexive response. Too much tension.

*Tell him. What are you waiting for?*

She opened her mouth, but what came out wasn't what she'd expected. She said, "I'm sorry I didn't tell you about the Peace Corps."

"Doesn't matter." He waved it away, then smiled slightly. "You were right—I didn't ask." The smile vanished, leaving his features aloof once more. "Nor should I have. It's none of my business."

Dixie forced herself to move closer, pushing against the cold buffer of his unspoken rejection. "It's no secret," she said with a half shrug, shoving the sleeves of her sweatshirt up over her elbows, then leaving her arms folded across her middle. "I just don't talk about it much—it wasn't a...good time in my life." Her attempt at a smile failed miserably.

"No?" He was frowning, as usual. How she wished he wouldn't look at her that way—as if she were an irritant he didn't know quite what to do about.

"No." She caught a quick breath, forcing it past the expected constriction in her throat. "I lost my fiancé there. Or...actually, right after we got back."

Rhett's face and body both softened and relaxed, like a movie dissolve from a mannequin to a flesh-and-blood person. "I'm sorry," he said softly. And after a moment asked in the same gentle tone, "Where did you serve?"

She didn't trust herself to make contact with his eyes, so she looked down at her hand, which was toying with a stack of transcripts that was piled haphazardly on the corner of his desk. She remembered suddenly the way she'd moved that same pile aside and sat herself brazenly down in its place, that first evening, and how amused she'd been by his attempt to intimidate her with his postures and barricades.

Now, it wasn't he who intimidated her. It was her own self. And the barricades were her own emotions.

*Tell him now. Tell him you're leaving, before you change your mind!*

But instead she heard herself say, in a soft, thickened voice, "Nicaragua. It was ten years ago—I'd just got out of college, and I didn't know what I wanted to do, so it just seemed . . ."

"Well," a cool, beautifully modulated voice interrupted, "isn't *this* cozy?"

Rhett's chair rebounded with a loud squawk of protest, accompanied by the hiss of the swear words he was uttering in a steady stream under his breath. They ceased abruptly as he said in a voice that would etch glass, "Elaine. You don't bother to knock?"

Please God, thought Dixie, don't ever let him talk to me in that tone of voice. It chilled her to her very soul.

The woman whose graceful pose was framed by the doorway of Rhett's private sanctum seemed unimpressed by it, however. She made a soft sound that might have been meant as a laugh and glided into the room, taking off her gloves as she came. She walked, Dixie thought, the way women do when they've gone to school to learn how to do it right.

Except for her mouth, which was thin-lipped and turned down at the corners, she was probably one of the most beautiful women Dixie had ever seen—and she'd grown up around singers and entertainers, not exactly a homely bunch. She had Lolly's eyes. Her hair was skillfully cut and expensively styled, and perfectly groomed even on a Sunday morning. She was wearing heather gray slacks and a short, silvery fur coat that Dixie was willing to bet good money was *not* rented.

"It's still my house," Rhett's wife said in her light, cool voice as she looked Dixie up and down. In spite of the similarity in their heights, Dixie suddenly felt huge and ungainly—like a camel next to a purebred Arabian mare.

"Half," snarled Rhett, "and only until the hearing. Your attorney already forwarded your acceptance of my offer."

"Ah, yes... the hearing." Elaine's lips formed a tight, upward curve she obviously meant as a smile. She was still looking at Dixie, though apparently addressing Rhett when she added, "So, this must be the new... nanny."

The tone, even without that subtle hesitation, would have made it an insult. Still thinking in her camel mode, Dixie resisted an impulse to spit.

Looking exactly like a cat with a bird imprisoned between her paws, Elaine purred, "How nice that you were able to find someone to live in, Rhett. I'm sure that makes it so much more... convenient, doesn't it?"

Rhett uttered a low, wordless growl. Elaine's smile widened and became positively photogenic. She held out her hand and spoke to Dixie for the first time, in a voice she might have used to address the First Lady. "I'm *so* pleased to meet you. Let's see—it's *Dixie*, isn't it? What a charming name. I've heard so much about you. I understand you were quite a hit at the ball last night. How sweet of you, Rhett, to invite her. Oh—my." She winced delicately and extricated her hand from Dixie's grasp with a little ripple of laughter. "What strong hands you have! Where in the world did Rhett find you? I do trust his judgment, of course... but I must say, you don't look like someone who makes a career out of looking after other people's children."

"I break horses," said Dixie, squeezing the words between her teeth. She had to concentrate hard on not balling her hands up into fists.

"Oh—" another ripple of that chilly laughter "—well, I didn't think you looked much like a *nanny*." She turned back to Rhett, effectively dismissing Dixie, who instantly went from enormous to invisible. "Where *are* my children? I'm dying to see them. I've missed them so much."

In spite of the effective little catch in her voice, Dixie thought it was the first thing she'd said that sounded sincere. Rhett, however, didn't appear to buy it. He muttered something which Dixie, not being able to see his face, couldn't quite make out.

Apparently Elaine had no trouble doing so. As if she'd been struck there physically, she touched herself in the region of her heart and cried in a wounded tone, "do you think I *wanted* to leave them? I told you in my note I'd be back for them as soon

as I was settled. I came as quickly as I could!'' Her voice
abruptly hardened, became brisk and businesslike. ''And now
that I'm here, I intend to spend a great deal of time with them.
I'll be staying with Deirdre, by the way, until after the hearing.
Of course, I will be stopping by to pick up my things—I hope
you aren't going to be difficult about this, Rhett.''

She pivoted then, moving out of the way just enough to give
Dixie a good clear look at Rhett's face. What she saw there
frightened her. His eyes were black and deep as ancient caves.

''Where *are* my babies? Is that who I hear out here?'' Elaine
was advancing upon the French doors, all roused maternal
passion.

Dixie had never seen Rhett move so quickly. Suddenly he was
there in front of those doors, barring the way like a wolf
guarding the entrance to his den. ''From now on you call before you come here,'' he ground out between bared teeth, ''or
I'll slap a restraining order on you so fast it'll make your head
swim.''

Elaine had already halted; now she seemed to freeze where
she stood. For just an instant. Then her eyes flicked toward
Dixie. Dixie couldn't see the look she turned upon Rhett, but
her soft voice had venom in it when she said, ''Don't threaten
me, Rhett.''

His gaze didn't waver. ''Oh, it's not a threat.''

Dixie suddenly had to remind herself to take a breath. She'd
never been caught in a cross fire like this before, and she felt
buffeted, bludgeoned. She was trembling, light-headed with
tension. And I'm strong, and an adult, she thought. But the
children . . . dear God, the children. How on earth do children
survive this?

Rhett gave the door handle a yank, pushed it open and called
without turning his head, ''Lolly . . . Ethan—come here a minute, would you please?''

The yelling outside came to a sudden halt; footsteps slapped
on the flagstone patio. Breathless voices queried, ''What is it,
Dad? What's up?''

''You have a visitor,'' he said, and stood aside to let them in.

Dixie's heart was pounding so hard she could barely breathe.
From where she was standing, behind Elaine and a little to one
side, she could see the children clearly. She saw them as they
burst through the doors, flushed and rosy with exercise and
anticipation, bringing with them a gust of crisp, cold air and the

smell of damp earth and decaying leaves. She saw them both check—almost simultaneously, it seemed—and all the color and light go out of their faces, leaving them blank for the moment, like movie screens awaiting the projectionist.

What followed was almost too painful to watch—a heartrending montage of all the emotions they hadn't yet learned how to hide. Confusion and hope ... uncertainty and joy ... anger, accusation and love.

"Hello, darlings! Come give Mommy a hug!"

It was too much for Rhett. Dixie heard rather than saw him leave the room, heard the door softly close. A few minutes later she heard his car backing out of the garage.

After those first frozen moments, Ethan had gone into his mother's arms in a blind little rush. Through a strange haze, Dixie could see his small fists clenched tightly against the back of the fur coat. Lolly was more reserved. She waited for Elaine to pull her close before she, too, slipped her arms around her mother and held on tightly.

For a moment or two. Then she stepped back, self-consciously brushing bits of leaves and grass from her sweatshirt. Even with her strangely blurred vision, Dixie could see that Lolly was very pale.

"What on *earth* have you two been doing? How did you get so *dirty?*" Elaine's laughter was silvery as her coat as she reached out to pluck a leaf from her daughter's hair.

Lolly's hand flew reflexively to the spot. A look of resentment flashed across her delicate, little girl features and then was gone, leaving them remote and still, like a doll's.

"We've been rakin' up leaves," Ethan announced, excited and out of breath. "It's fun—you make a bi-ig mountain, like *this*—and then you jump in 'em." He demonstrated. His mother frowned and said quietly, "Darling, do we do that in the house?" Ethan gulped and covered a guilty giggle with his hand.

"I have a horse," said Lolly, her chin lifting slightly.

Her mother's mouth dropped open in mock horror. "Oh *no*—you *don't*. He didn't."

"He's really beautiful. His name is Star." There was color in Lolly's cheeks, now, twin patches of rose pink, like painted on blush.

"Guess what? We're buildin' a tree house. Well...Dixie is. But we're helpin'." Ethan clutched at his mother's hand and began to tug on it. "Wanna come and see?"

"Perhaps later, darling." Ethan's face fell. He stopped tugging at his mother's hand, hung his head, then turned upon her his most soulful look, the one Dixie could never seem to resist.

Elaine seemed to have no trouble at all. Ignoring Ethan, her eyes flicked at Dixie, twin points of cold steel. "I'd like to take the children to lunch, if you don't mind," she said pleasantly, overdoing the courtesy just enough so that the intended sarcasm would pass safely over the children's heads. "Since Rhett doesn't seem to be around, perhaps you'd be so good as to tell him for me?"

"Sure," said Dixie, her voice a croak, rusty with disuse. She cleared it hastily and mumbled, "I'll, uh...just get them cleaned up."

Elaine's tinkling laugh cut her off. "I think I can take care of my own children, thank you!" She didn't even glance at Dixie as she took Lolly's hand. "Darling, I can see we have some shopping to do. I think maybe we should stop at the mall after lunch, what do you think?"

"Can we stop at the stables? I really want you to see Star..."

"Mama, can I get a cowboy hat? I want a cowboy hat like Dixie's. Can I, Mama? Can I?"

"May I...?"

They went out together, Lolly clinging to one slender, graceful, immaculately groomed hand, Ethan to the other, bouncing up and down like a yo-yo on a string. No one looked back.

*That's as it should be.*

Dixie thought of Mary Poppins saying that, wistfully, while the Banks's children danced off with their parents to fly kites. And *she* didn't believe it, either.

To escape the noises coming from upstairs, she went out into the backyard. She picked up the rake one of the children had dropped at their father's unexpected summons and began scratching furiously at the grass with it, using that activity as percussion accompaniment to the litany she kept repeating to herself, over and over: *They're with their mother. That's the way it should be. That's the way it should be....*

But no matter how many times she said it, she couldn't make herself believe it. Things were *not* the way they should be. She didn't know how she knew that with such certainty, but she did.

She just *knew* it, dammit. She *felt* it, deep in her mother's soul....

She dropped the rake when she heard the front door slam, and tiptoed shamelessly down the side path just in time to catch a glimpse of the children as they climbed into the back seat of a Cadillac that had apparently been waiting in the driveway. Elaine got into the front passenger seat, and the car moved soundlessly off. As it turned down the far side of the half circle, Dixie caught a glimpse of the driver, a woman with hair an improbable shade of coral. Deirdre, presumably. Whoever that was.

She took a deep breath and went back to her raking, trying hard to ignore the cold emptiness in the pit of her stomach.

She was still at it when Rhett came home, she had no idea how much later. She'd raked all the leaves in the yard into small piles, then all the small piles into one gigantic mountain, right in the middle of the lawn. She was quite proud of it, actually. The kids were going to have a ball in that pile of leaves.

Although she heard Rhett's BMW pull into the garage, she didn't stop raking until she saw him out of the corner of her eye, coming toward her across the lawn. Then she paused and leaned on the rake and waited for him, not even trying to kid herself that the thumping of her heart was due to exertion.

"They're not back yet," she said when he was still a few feet away.

He nodded. His hands were in his pockets, jingling his keys.

"She took them to lunch and then shopping. She asked me to tell you. I didn't know..."

Rhett snorted. "It's okay—you couldn't have stopped her. She has every right. I shouldn't have left you to deal with her. I'm sorry."

"She was with someone—a woman. She had...pink hair."

Again Rhett nodded, smiling slightly. "That's her sister. I spoke to her when I left. Deirdre's okay. She'd never be a party to..." He let it trail off.

*To what?* she wanted to ask, as the cold emptiness yawned open inside her once more. But she didn't. In the silence, she followed Rhett's gaze, which was fixed on the mountain of leaves. She'd have sworn the look in his eyes was wistful. She had a sudden and most wonderfully vivid vision of him falling backward, spread-eagled, into the pile, and of herself, tumbling in after him....

She coughed and became very busy with the rake, industriously rounding up strays.

"The tree house seems to be coming along nicely." He'd wandered over that way and was standing staring up into the huge elm tree's golden canopy, thinning now, with patches of cobalt blue showing through.

She went to join him, using the rake as a staff. "Needs a roof, but it's getting there," she said modestly. She was pretty darn proud of that tree house. "Of course, the kids help a lot."

Rhett looked over at her, his lips quirked in a half smile. "I'll bet." His hand rested on the gnarled old trunk. He pushed on it a few times as though testing its strength.

"You want to have a look?" Dixie invited, indicating the boards nailed, ladderlike, to the trunk.

He shook his head, laughing softly, like someone convalescent and still in pain, and lifted his eyes once more to the structure that was perched like a giant crow's nest in the lowest branches. "I think I'll take a rain check." There was a pause before he added, "Maybe when it's all finished."

She couldn't see his face just then. But she could see the tension in his shoulders, feel the waiting in his silence, and hear the question he wouldn't allow himself to ask.

"It's a date," she said softly.

His eyes flicked at her, dark with unexpected appeal. Ethan's eyes. "You're sure about that?"

"Oh, yeah." The emptiness inside her had been replaced with a growing pressure that pushed against her throat and made her eyes sting. She smiled valiantly and fought to keep her voice steady. "My mama didn't raise any quitters. I believe in finishing what I start."

"Always?"

Her breath caught, so when she repeated his word in reply, it was only a whisper, all but lost in the crunch of tires on the brick driveway, and in Rhett's gravelly, relief filled, "They're home."

The children had been returned well before dark, in plenty of time to do their homework before supper. However, Ethan was too keyed up and restless to sit still for more than a minute, and burst into tears when Dixie tried to help him with his arithmetic work sheet. Lolly, looking even more aloof than usual, insisted she didn't have any homework, and even though Dixie knew very well the social studies project due on Friday hadn't even been started yet, she let it go without argument.

For supper she fixed dogs in blankets—hot dogs wrapped in pastry—which both of the children loved. But Ethan protested that he wasn't hungry, and when Dixie insisted he come have "just a tiny little bite" anyway, he promptly threw up on the shiny black-and-white checkerboard floor.

Feeling guilty as hell, and very much like the wicked stepmother, Dixie took him upstairs, washed his face and put him to bed. And tried very hard to ignore the little twist of pain she felt when he turned his face away and wouldn't let her kiss him good-night. Of course, she knew he was bound to be upset and confused after his mother's visit. She knew he was hurting inside. She wouldn't take it personally, she was an adult, she understood.

It hurt anyway.

When she went back downstairs, Lolly was nowhere to be found.

An unobtrusive search made it apparent that she wasn't in the house, unless she was deliberately hiding, which Dixie was pretty sure wasn't Lolly's style. Nor did she think it likely that the child would have sought her father out in his study, although she did poke her head in his door on the pretext of inquiring whether he wanted anything to eat, just to make sure. She really didn't want to alarm Rhett until it was absolutely necessary.

Where would I go, she thought, if I were a little girl, hurting inside, wanting to be alone...but maybe, just maybe, hoping deep down inside that somebody would care enough to come and find me...where would *I* go?

Of course.

Taking a flashlight from the drawer beside the refrigerator, Dixie went out into the backyard. She didn't need the light—the sky was still a soft lavender, tinged with the rusty remains of sunset. Over in the middle of the yard the mountain of leaves made a dark purple blob; off to one side the elm tree's trunk and branches stood out in stark silhouette, although its remaining leaves still shone dark gold in the dying light.

She went to stand at the base of the tree and called softly upward, "Hey, sugar, you in there?"

The briefest of scuffles reassured her. Tucking the flashlight into the waistband of her jeans, Dixie began to climb.

A sullen, "What are *you* doing here?" greeted her as she drew herself up onto the tree house's gently sloping floor-boards.

"Looking for you," said Dixie cheerfully.

"How did you know where I was?"

"Oh . . . well, it wasn't too hard. This is where I would have come, if I was in your shoes." She lay back on her elbows and looked up into the canopy overhead, lacy black and gold against a purpling sky. "Nice, isn't it?" she said with a sigh. "Chilly, though. Be cozier when we get a roof on."

In the opposite corner of the tree house, in one of the more level spots, she could just see Lolly sitting huddled with her knees drawn up close to her chest and her arms wrapped around them. "I guess so," she muttered.

After a moment of what she pretended was a companion-able silence, Dixie said casually, "You have a good time today with your mom?"

She felt and heard the rustle of Lolly's shrug. "Yeah. She bought me some new clothes."

"So I saw. Did you get to show her your horse?"

"Yeah." There was a pause, then a barely perceptible sigh. "Mom doesn't care much for horses. I think she's afraid of them. She says they smell bad."

"Well," said Dixie judiciously, "they do. Sort of. I never did mind it, though."

"Me, either," said Lolly staunchly. It got very quiet. Then, in a voice empty of all expression, almost like a whispering of the wind in the leaves, she said, "She wants Ethan and me to come and live with her."

Carefully matter-of-fact in spite of the contraction in her chest, Dixie replied, "I'm sure she does. I reckon she misses you guys a lot." She turned over on her side, propping herself on one elbow so she could look at Lolly. "What about you? Do you want to go and live with your mama?"

There was another shrug, and a muffled, "I don't care."

"Because if you really do want to be with your mom—"

"I don't!" Lolly's fists came down hard on the rough ply-wood floor, causing the whole structure to quiver unnervingly. "I wish she'd never come back! I hate her! *I hate her!*"

Dixie sat up and gathered her in. "No, sugar," she murmured huskily as she wrapped her arms around the little girl's thin shoulders and rested her cheek on her soft, silky head and rocked her gently back and forth. "You don't hate your mama. That's the whole trouble, isn't it? You wish you could, but you can't."

"I *do* hate her," Lolly insisted through her sobs. "I do!"

Dixie laughed softly. "No, baby... you don't hate her. You love her. And that's okay... that's okay. Because, you know, she loves you, too."

"No, she doesn't! If she did, she wouldn't have left us. She doesn't *care*."

"Oh, sugar..." Dixie closed her eyes, and felt the warmth of her own tears. She whispered, "Don't think that...don't you think that for a minute. Of *course* your mama loves you guys. How could she not love you?"

"Then how could she leave us? I don't understand...."

*I don't understand either! If I had a child...*

Somehow, Dixie found the strength—and the wisdom—to stay silent. She only sighed deeply and held Lolly more tightly, and rocked her and rocked her while she cried.

# Chapter 11

Rhett might have known Dixie would make a fuss over Halloween, if for no other reason than that Elaine never had. His wife, in fact, had disapproved of Halloween in its entirety, and had been pretty vocal about the fact—it didn't do to get her going on the subject of pagan superstitions, sugar ODs and sickos putting razor blades in apples. As in most things having to do with the raising of his children, Rhett hadn't seen any reason to argue with her.

Nor, for some reason, did he see any reason to put a stop to all the fuss and preparations Dixie had insisted on making for the big night. In fact, as he watched her decorate the driveway with pumpkins and cornstalks and hang lighted ghosts in the upstairs windows, he found himself recalling, for the first time in years, how much fun Halloween had been for him when he was a kid.

There was a sweetness about those memories, he found, but a kind of melancholy, too. He found himself wanting to tell someone about them. Maybe it was the season of the year, or it might have had something to do with being about to turn forty, but for the first time Rhett thought he understood why older people like to go on and on, telling stories about their youth. Sharing them, he thought, would make the memories less lonely.

The person he'd most like to have shared them with was Dixie; he had a feeling she'd truly understand. Time and time again he found himself just on the verge of telling her some little incident he remembered. The fact that he couldn't only increased his loneliness, and added an element of adolescent wistfulness to his melancholy.

By a mutual, if unspoken, agreement he and Dixie had been avoiding one another since the night of the fund-raising ball. Or, to be more precise, since the day after. They saw each other, to speak to, only in the morning in the full presence of both children. He was in court a lot, so it was easy to contrive reasons to stay late in his office, and to put in weekends catching up on other cases. When he was home, he skulked around behind closed doors, feeling uneasy and restless, like a stranger in his own home.

One of the reasons he felt that way was because, since Elaine's unexpected Sunday morning visit, he'd not only been avoiding Dixie, but his own children as well. It was, he knew, pure contrariness. He was terrified of being without them, so he couldn't bear to be with them—even see them. Did that make sense? He doubted it. Nevertheless, it was the way he felt. Whenever he looked at their faces, he looked into the yawning chasm of the unthinkable . . . every parent's worst nightmare. He lived with it day and night—the fear he'd never admit to. The fear that he could lose the custody fight. The fear that he could lose his children.

Because of Dixie.

*God.* And what a bitter little bit of irony *that* was. He'd hired her because he'd sensed she could bring joy and sunshine into his house—like a breath of fresh air, he remembered thinking. And she had, oh, she *had.* And now, through no fault of her own, it seemed she might cost him the only real joy he'd ever known.

So why didn't he just fire her, and be done with it?

He couldn't have counted the times he asked himself that question, sitting alone late at night in his study, staring at his reflection in the French doors. Why didn't he let Dixie go?

The choice between her and his children should have been easy. It wasn't. It was impossible. Because he was beginning to understand that to choose between Dixie and the children would be like choosing between sunlight and air. Both were vital to him. If he allowed Elaine to force him to make that choice, she would have succeeded in destroying him.

He could not let her do that to him. He would not.

So, as far as he was concerned, Dixie was there to stay. He wasn't sure, sometimes, how she felt about it. There'd been moments when he'd thought she might be on the verge of leaving—the night of the ball, the morning after. But then, that afternoon after Elaine's visit, if he'd read her right, she'd all but promised him she'd stay. If he'd read her right. He was beginning to realize that, with Dixie, sometimes it was hard to tell. She was good at hiding things behind her big, sunny smile and breezy Texas ways, but he suspected there was more to Dixie Parish than she normally let anybody get close enough to see.

Rhett had every intention of getting close enough, once the custody hearing was safely out of the way.

But until then, he had to keep his distance. Stay away from her. Stand back and watch like a visiting stranger while she turned his household upside down.

Sometimes he couldn't believe what had happened to his calm, quiet, ordered and immaculate home. In just a few short weeks he'd gotten used to homework spread out all over the kitchen table and cut up magazines and Monopoly games littering the living room rug. Now, when he came home from work he had to navigate around bales of hay and piles of pumpkins on his doorstep, dodge skeletons dangling from the archway, and endure a recording of a yowling cat every time he opened the front door. The kitchen reeked of pumpkin. Its usually gleaming surfaces were strewn with newspapers heaped with slippery piles of fat greenish seeds and stringy pumpkin innards. Jack-o'-lanterns grinned at him from every level surface.

"What are you going to *do* with all of these things?" Rhett asked Dixie on the morning before Halloween. She looked at him as if he'd just asked her what she intended to do about the federal deficit. It obviously wasn't something she'd ever thought about—or ever intended to.

To add to the confusion, Dixie had insisted on making the kids' costumes. From scratch. On a sewing machine she'd borrowed from Luby and installed in her bedroom. Which didn't keep the resultant chaos from spilling over into the children's rooms, the landing, and on down the stairs to the kitchen and living room.

Ethan had wanted to be a cowboy, which to Rhett's mind seemed a sensible plan. The outfit was, after all, basically already complete. Lolly, however, had other ideas. After considerable debate—and many mind changes—she decided she would be Alice in Wonderland. It was Rhett's opinion that the character's arrogance and contrary attitude must have struck a sympathetic chord. Anyway, somehow, whether with bullying or bribery her father preferred not to know, she'd convinced Ethan to be her White Rabbit.

What Dixie's part was in the decision-making process, he had no idea; the actual execution of the idea, in spite of all the fuss and mess, he had to admit was pretty darn cute.

Her pièce de résistance, however, was rigging a life-size witch dummy to come swooping down the stairway bannister on her broomstick at a tug on a well-hidden string. The children thought it was totally cool. Rhett was totally in awe of the contraption. He tried, in secret, to figure out exactly how she'd done it, but had to conclude, finally, that it was beyond his engineering capabilities.

*His* chief contribution to the whole circus, other than footing the bill, of course, was to come home early on the big night to take the children out trick-or-treating. Because of Elaine's objections, they'd never been before, and Rhett was sure they were more excited about it than if they had been going to a circus. They'd been invited to a party at Lolly's piano teacher's house, but it had been agreed that they could leave early for the party and trick-or-treat along the way, as long as they had a grown-up with them. Rhett was appointed the designated grown-up, while Dixie stayed behind to answer the doorbell—or cat squall, rather.

Secretly, Rhett was a little disappointed with this arrangement. He'd hoped to be the one to pass out goodies, thereby giving him a chance to work the witch gizmo. But paternal duty—and a stern inner reminder that almost-forty-year-old candidates for state attorney general ought to be above such nonsense—prevailed.

So it was that on Halloween night he found himself, for the first time in his life, strolling along a tree-canopied city street at dusk, hands jammed into the pockets of his topcoat and the collar turned up against a wicked little goblin wind, scuffling through leaves and listening to thin, reedy voices piping in the distance, "Trick or treat! Trick or treat!"

And having the time of his life. A sense of freedom, and of inexplicable well-being, had settled over him. He drew a great breath, filling his lungs with air that was sharp and cold and scented with toasted pumpkin and candle wax. He looked up at the stars. High overhead, away from the lights of the city, they looked amazingly clear and bright. Like something Dixie might have hung, he thought—too many, too gaudy... and somehow, just right.

This is *fun*, he thought in surprise. Lolly was... what, almost ten? Why hadn't he ever done this before? And what other simple pleasures had he missed out on, being married all those years to a woman who wouldn't know how to have fun if her life depended on it?

The walk he'd thought he hadn't wanted to take ended much too soon. After depositing Ethan and Lolly at the piano teacher's and promising, on his word of honor, *not* to return for them before eight o'clock, at the earliest, he turned around and started home alone.

He wasn't really alone, of course; the streets were still filled with trick-or-treaters, and he passed—and nodded greetings to—a good many chilled looking grown-ups standing huddled together in small groups at the foot of walkways while their little demons and angels and ballet dancers and action heroes scurried, giggling, up distant flights of steps. The darkness was alive with scufflings and whispers and the *ding* of doorbells and the chirp of children's voices. Flashlights bobbed, and footsteps slapped on pavement. Leaves rustled and dark shapes flitted across sloping lawns. The air crackled with excitement.

It must have been contagious—that was the only explanation Rhett could come up with. Or perhaps prankish spirits *were* abroad that night. It was, after all, All Hallows' Eve.

A group of children scuttled past him as he turned up his own driveway, pushing and shoving and laughing and calling to each other. Rhett laughed, too. Like them, he felt wicked and reckless and *young*.

For a moment, then, he paused, hands in his pockets, head back, looking up at his house, which was lit up like a ghoul's factory, with flickering bluish lights in all the upstairs windows. A grin broadened across his face. Damn, but that woman had really done a number on the place! He was still grinning as he pushed the doorbell, and laughed out loud as a hellish yowl rent the night. The door creaked open.

"Trick or treat," he said drolly.

A hideous crone stood in his doorway. Her face was a sickly green, and her hair stood out in snaky black strings, like Medusa. She had on black robes and a droopy black hat that looped down over one cavernous purple eye, in much the same way her nose drooped over her black, toothless gums. She was bent almost double, and leaning heavily on a crooked staff. Clutched in her outstretched hand, guarded by spiky black fingernails, was a huge, rosy red apple.

"Ooh, a nice big one," she quavered, not missing a beat. "Come in, my dear . . . have a bite of my apple . . ."

He couldn't, for the life of him, think of a witty response. He was laughing too hard. When he could speak again, he gasped, "My God, you must have scared the poor things half to death!"

Dixie straightened up, grinning horribly. "Oh, I only go whole hog for the big kids. For the little guys I tone it down some." She took a huge, crunching bite out of the apple.

"Some?" said Rhett, registering disbelief.

She fluttered her lashes winsomely and struck a Mae West pose. "Listen, sugar, I can be a real sweetheart, when I want to be. Come on in, big boy, and let me . . . demonstrate."

He threw back his head and guffawed. The prankish spirits had apparently taken her, too, but he was feeling reckless enough not to see the danger in that. It was a magical night, and it had been too long since he'd seen her full of fun and laughter, and too long since he'd felt like doing much of it himself.

He went through the door she held wide for him, looking around as if he'd never seen the place before. "Have you had quite a few?" He lifted an eyebrow and paused before adding rakishly, "Uh . . . trick-or-treaters, that is."

Dixie showed her appreciation with a hideous grin. "Oh, oodles. But I saved one or two for you—I'm dieting. Have to watch my ghoulish figure, you know."

Rhett winced; laughter—or something—was making him breathless. He paused at the foot of the stairs, gazing upward. "Did your, uh, colleague make a big hit?"

"Did it ever!" Dixie closed the front door and came toward him, adjusting her nose. "I felt really bad, though—I must have misjudged one little guy. I think he wet his pants. Maybe

I shouldn't..." She let it trail off, and he could see confusion in the deep purple shadows of her eyes.

He didn't know why; he was just looking at her, laughing and shaking his head and thinking about how he'd never in his life wanted so much to take a woman in his arms...green makeup and all. He wanted to hold her and laugh with her and tell her what he thought of her witches and yowling cats and flashing blue lights and pumpkins. He wanted to tell her he thought she was wonderful, and that he was probably falling madly in love with her. He wanted to peel off her nose so it wouldn't get in his way when he kissed her. And then he wanted to peel off other things...lots of other things.

So he didn't understand why she suddenly took a wary step backward and said, in a voice that sounded more like the crone than Dixie, "Are you hungry? There's some clam chowder on the stove, if you'd...uh, like something."

He *was* hungry. He didn't think he'd realized until that moment how hungry he was. But what he wanted wasn't in the kitchen.

"Thanks," he said, just as the doorbell yowled. He winced as if it had been he who'd trod on the wretched cat's tail, and waved her on with a smile and a shrug as she started toward the door, then hesitated. "It's okay—I'll get myself something. Go on..."

But he didn't leave, not right away. He stayed there in the shadow of the staircase and watched her do her witch act one more time, and laughed out loud when the dummy witch came swooping down the bannister, cackling horribly, black cape flying out behind her...

It was magnificent.

*No.* Dixie...*that's* who was magnificent.

Suddenly, all the memories and vague nostalgic yearnings he'd been having, the strange and reckless mood he was in, all of it seemed to come together like an image coming into focus...or like a fog clearing away, leaving the landscape in shimmering sunlight. His life, with Dixie in it, would be like this...full of laughter and surprises. It would never be orderly. Or quiet. Or predictable.

Strange...he'd always thought those things were important to him. He'd thought that the grace and structure Elaine had brought to his existence were just the environment he needed in order to thrive.

Now all at once he was remembering his father—Ed Brown, sober and hard working as they come, a no-nonsense kind of man if there ever was one. Rhett was like him in so many ways—he'd always known that. But now he was remembering things his mother had said to him, long, long ago. "Your father has poetry in his soul," she'd told him once. "He just doesn't let it show. That's why he needs me. I'm his music...."

He'd thought it a pretty ridiculous thing to say at the time. Everyone knew Ed Brown couldn't carry a tune in a bucket. Now, for the first time, he thought he understood.

"I think that's probably going to be about it," Dixie said as she closed the door behind yet another band of trick-or-treaters—older ones, this time, she noticed. That meant it was getting late. She turned toward Rhett, who was standing at the foot of the stairs with an elbow propped on the newel post, just standing there, as he had been for a while...watching her. She hadn't minded it, really. Not tonight. There was something different, something playful and magical and not quite real about tonight. It was a make-believe evening, with no bearing or effect on reality. And besides, she was wearing a rubber nose and green makeup. She was safe. *They* were safe.

She scooped a plastic-wrapped ball out of the treat basket and tossed it to him. "Here—have a popcorn ball. It's the last one."

He caught it one-handed and held it, a peculiar little smile playing around his lips. He's never laughed or smiled as much as he has tonight, she thought, her heart turning over, as it always did at the sight. *I wish he could always be this carefree.*

"Popcorn balls," he said in a musing tone. "That's what my mom used to make for Halloween."

"Oh, really?" she teased him. "I thought you didn't believe in Halloween."

"On the contrary. Back when I was a kid, we used to really get into the... spirit of the occasion."

"Oh, very good," murmured Dixie, baring her blackened teeth in appreciation.

"Thank you." Rhett paused, examining the popcorn minutely. "Of course, we didn't go trick-or-treating the way these kids do—hard to do, out in the country. Some kids' parents took them around in cars. My dad went one better."

"Yeah?" Dixie cradled the treat basket in both arms and leaned a shoulder against the wall. "How's that?"

"He made a hayride out of the occasion. A couple of days before Halloween, he'd hitch the hay wagon to the old John Deere tractor and pile on a thick layer of straw, then my friends and I would decorate it with cornstalks and pumpkins and black and orange crepe paper. And we'd add some unauthorized surprises, like water balloons—that only happened one year—Dad put his foot down."

Dixie laughed. "I'll bet."

Rhett grinned and tossed the popcorn ball up and caught it, in the considering manner of a small boy trying to decide whether or not to chuck it at his sister's head. "Another time we recorded these horrible screams and gurgles, like somebody being murdered—slowly—and played them on a portable tape player as we were pulling into people's yards. It was great."

"Oh, brother," said Dixie, smiling and shaking her head. It was like a dream, being with him like this... listening to him talk in that relaxed, carefree way. She loved hearing about his childhood. She loved being close to him ... the walls seemed friendly to her, like shielding wings. She shifted, seeking a more comfortable support from the one she was leaning against, and murmured, "Go on."

She'd forgotten about the string. The string that operated the lever that released the witch, allowing it to swing downward as though it were riding its broomstick right down the bannister. The string ran along the wall, from the top of the stairs to the bottom, then down the hallway to a spot near the table by the front door, so she could pull it at just the right moment . . .

"We'd get the chores done early," Rhett was saying. "Then, along about sunset, we'd get into our costumes—Lucy and I, and the friends we'd invited. We'd make up something from what we managed to find in Aunt Gwen's old trunks. Then we'd all climb onto the wagon and off we'd go, Dad driving the tractor, everybody singing and yell . . . what's wrong?"

Dixie's mouth had fallen open; even with that advance preparation, however, she had no time for a decent reply. Only an inarticulate squawk emerged from her throat, at approximately the same moment that Rhett was being enveloped in yards of billowing black polyester. The popcorn ball went flying, bouncing off a distant wall.

"Yow!" he yelled, leaping forward as the prow of the witch's broomstick skewered him in the small of his back. "What in the . . . holy *hell*—" That was only the beginning.

"Rhett, for heaven's sake!" Dixie gasped, laughing so hard she could hardly stand as she tried to untangle his flailing arms from the witch's determined embrace. "It's the eve of All Saints—if you don't stop that, you really will wake up the dead! Here, hold still . . . a minute . . ."

"You did that on purpose," was the first thing he said when she drew apart the folds of the witch's cape to reveal one baleful, glittering eye.

"I did not!" Dixie's denial was spoiled somewhat by a fresh fit of giggles. She couldn't help it; the effigy's head, nestled in the crook of Rhett's arm, appeared to be grinning coyly up at him.

He tossed the head away, the cape giving the gesture a batlike flourish, and advanced upon her. "You pulled the string!"

"I . . . didn't, it got caught . . . I must have nudged it with my elbow." The wall was against her back; she couldn't retreat any farther. She finished it in a breathless, laughing whisper. "I swear . . ."

It happened so quickly. He caught her and pulled her to him in a tangle of witch's robes. Her head fell back. She felt her hat slip from her head, heard it hit the floor. She heard him swear, felt his hand touch her face. His eyes were very close to hers, gleaming with reflected jack-o'-lantern light as he ruthlessly peeled off her drooping rubber nose. It made a sticky sound. She gasped, and would have burst into laughter all over again. But for some reason she didn't.

Her heart was pounding so hard it hurt. So hard he must feel it. Or . . . no—that was *his* heart she felt, pounding as hard as hers. She was so close to him, held so tightly against him, she couldn't tell the difference.

He groaned something she couldn't quite hear—invoking her name, or the Deity's perhaps—it didn't matter. Words no longer had any meaning. The only things that made sense to her were the heat of his body and the strength of his arms, and the warm, moist wash of his breath across her lips . . . like a sorcerer's potion. It must have been; it robbed her of judgment, and of will. She forgot the past; the future didn't matter. The only reality, the only certainty was that, in the next second or so, Rhett would kiss her.

And she wanted it, more than she wanted breath. She was
starving for it. Had been starving for it for a longer time than
she could remember. Since a time when she had forbidden herself to remember.

She would have lifted her arms around his neck, if she'd been
able to free them. Since she couldn't without struggling, and
possibly giving him a message she didn't want to convey, she
simply relaxed her body and leaned against him, and closed her
eyes with a soft, giving sigh. She felt his fingers stroke her
cheek, his thumb trace the outline of her lips, and then his
mouth was there, too . . . so gently, so lightly, so warm.

It felt so good . . . so good.

His lips brushed hers and then drew away . . . just slightly. She
tried not to move, or to breathe, afraid of shattering the fragile bubble of joy in which she found herself, knowing that the
instant he moved to separate himself from her further, it would
be gone. Afraid she might never find such joy again.

But of course, no moment lasts forever, especially one so
exquisite, so perfect . . . so rare. She *would* breathe, and he did
move. But not away. He uttered a soft sound, and his mouth
came down on hers again, with all the hunger and wanting
she'd felt, and more. It wasn't gentle this time. This time it
didn't matter if she struggled to free her arms; his hands were
on a quest of their own, and as frustrated as she that barriers
that seemed so flimsy should prove so impenetrable.

Then all at once, magically, her hands *were* free. With a glad
little moan she lifted them to his shoulders, pulling away the
remnants of the witch's robes so she could feel the warmth and
strength of his muscles, stroke the taut, smooth column of his
neck, burrow her fingers into his hair. How good it felt, just to
*touch* him.

They were too heated, too roused; they ran out of breath
quickly. This time, when Rhett tore his mouth away from hers,
he caught her to him and held her tightly, as if he thought she
might suddenly vanish in a puff of smoke. She hid her face in
the curve of his neck and shoulder and clung to him, breathing
in tiny gulps, laughing a little.

"I've never kissed a green person before," he whispered to
her temple, avoiding the stiffened coils of her hair.

"You know, of course, that there's a curse attached," she
whispered back, her breath misting his warm skin.

"Don't tell me . . ."

"Uh-huh. It turns you green, too..."

"Oh...hell." She laughed as she felt him rubbing at the makeup on his lips, then lifted her face in response to his nudging and gladly accepted the kiss he gave her to show he didn't really mind.

There was more, and it was sweet. Too sweet, almost, to bear. But Dixie knew the spell had already been broken. By words...not magic words, just words, as silly and inconsequential as theirs. Words require a degree of logic and reason, and those, of course, are the stepping stones back to reality. *Reality.* She knew it first in Rhett's sudden stillness, as if he were listening to something far off in the distance. And then in her own sense of shame.

"Dixie..."

"I know...I know." She pulled away from him, a hand covering her mouth, the other arm creeping across her waist, pushing against the emptiness she felt inside. "We have to stop meeting like this." It was a feeble attempt at humor. She tried hard to keep her teeth from chattering.

Apparently without success. Rhett lifted his hands as if he meant to touch her, then lowered them without doing so. His eyes were dark and troubled; they reminded her, not for the first time, of Ethan's. He said huskily, "Dixie, I'm sorry."

"It was my fault," she said, shaking her head rapidly. "I shouldn't have..." She'd flirted with him—blatantly. *Why?* Partly, perhaps, because of the magic of the night. And because she'd felt secure in the repulsiveness of her witch's disguise.

But he'd kissed her in spite of it. And—oh God—what did *that* mean?

"It wasn't anybody's fault," Rhett said in an angry and raspy voice. "We're fighting something here...."

"Don't say it!" She turned from him, childishly covering her ears. "Please don't say it. It'll only make it worse."

"All right, Dixie." His voice was very quiet, but she heard him anyway. "I won't say it—not now. But I'm going to...when all this...just as soon as that damn hearing is over. I—we—*somebody's* got to say it, dammit."

She didn't reply, didn't turn. After a long moment of almost unbearable silence, she lifted her head, cleared her throat and said, "The children..." They made a ready excuse, as good as any.

"Yes." It was flat and hard, his lawyer's voice. "The children. Right now, they're all that matters. Speaking of which..." She turned her head in time to see him glower at his wrist in the dim light. "Damn."

He swore again, under his breath. "Eight-thirty. I was supposed to pick them up half an hour ago. Why don't you give them a call? Tell them I'm on my way." He started for the door.

"Uh...Rhett." He turned to scowl at her, fiddling impatiently with his keys. She smiled crookedly and touched her own cheek. "You, uh, look a little green around the gills. Maybe you'd better..."

The look that crossed his face was one of the ones that helped to make up for his scowl. It was nonplussed, distracted, endearingly guilty. It made him look, for a moment or two, like a teenager caught in his dad's car with the windows all fogged up.

"Ah...hmm," he muttered, sidling past her, "maybe I'd better...wash up. You make that call—the number's by the phone." The last part came as he was loping up the stairs, two at a time.

When he came back down a few minutes later, she was waiting for him in the front hallway. She tried hard to keep the panic from showing in her face, but apparently he read it anyway, even through the green makeup. He must have seen it in her eyes.

"What's the matter?" he growled, before she could even speak.

"They're not there," she said in a tight, flat voice. "They left more than an hour ago—walking. Mrs.—the piano teacher's daughter went with them."

"It's a ten-minute walk. Maybe fifteen at the most."

Dixie swallowed a cold, hard lump of fear. "I know."

# Chapter 12

"I'm going with you," Dixie gasped. Rhett was yanking at the door, and didn't bother to answer. She dove into the coat closet and grabbed the first thing she touched—one of Rhett's overcoats, she realized as she pulled it on over her witch's robes. It smelled like him—like Old Spice and man, and faintly, of smoke-filled rooms.

He turned to her as she reached the bottom of the steps, shoulders hunched in the chilling wind. "Maybe you should stay—in case somebody calls."

She hesitated, then said firmly, "If they were going to call, they would have already. I'm coming with you." It was selfish, perhaps, but she couldn't have borne it, staying behind while he went off alone into the night.

She kept pace with him stride for stride as they went down the far side of the drive together, hurrying and tense, not running. Rhett's coat was open, slapping against his legs. She found herself thinking about what it had felt like, being held so tightly against his body, the folded back lapels of that coat cutting into her breasts, buttons poking her in the ribs... She was only wearing a bra under her witch's costume. Her nipples were hard and tight, now, chafing uncomfortably against the lacy nylon fabric. She knew it wasn't entirely from the cold.

"I'm sure they're all right," she said, panting a little. "They have someone with them—how old is the piano teacher's daughter?"

Rhett's steps didn't slow. "I don't know—college age, I think."

"If anything . . . had happened, we'd have heard."

He glanced at her quickly, then away. "Not necessarily." His voice sounded cold and bleak as the wind.

"What d-do you mean?" They were passing a driveway just then, and she could see his profile outlined in the light from a gatepost lamp. What she saw frightened her. She shivered involuntarily.

"I mean Elaine." He said it quietly, looking straight ahead. She caught at his arm, forcing him to stop, to turn toward her, at least.

"Rhett—you can't be serious. She wouldn't . . ."

His steely gaze was focused on the darkness just above her head. "You don't know Elaine. She's probably the most selfish person I've ever met. If she wants something, she doesn't let up until she gets it. She's decided she wants the kids, and she'll play dirty, if that's what it takes to get them." He let his breath go in an angry, helpless rush. "I just don't know *how* dirty."

"Oh God . . . Oh, Rhett." How she longed to touch him, to put her arms around him and offer what comfort she could.

He must have heard something of what she was feeling in her voice, because suddenly his eyes shifted downward to her face. His lips quirked stiffly into a smile, of sorts. "That's why . . ."

"Why . . . we can't . . ." her breath caught. She finished in a whisper. "I know."

"She'd use you," he murmured, the intimacy in his voice reaching out to her across the cold, dark distance between them, so that she felt closer to him than she ever had before, even in his arms. "She'd drag you through the mud, to get at me. To get the kids."

"I know," Dixie said dryly. "Believe me, I got that when she was here the other day."

"That's why I can't let myself touch you." He spoke slowly, tonelessly, his face hidden in shadow. "Not even in the privacy of my own house. Do you understand? I have to be able to tell the truth at that hearing." His laugh was soft with irony. "Not too many people would believe it, probably, given my profession, but I've never compromised my integrity. I don't intend to start now.''

Maybe he is a stuffed shirt, Dixie thought, gazing at him in a fog of tenderness. But, in his own way, a magnificent one. And God help me, I love him ...

"Dad! Dixie! Hey, what are *you* doin' here?''

Their heads had jerked in tandem toward the first glad cry. Dumbstruck with relief, they watched the small, white bunny shape trundle toward them down the grassy verge, long white ears flopping with every step, bulging belly in its red waistcoat wobbling from side to side. Dixie burst out with a high little bark of laughter, which she instantly stifled by clamping a hand across her mouth.

"Hey,'' said Rhett by way of a greeting, scowling in that way he had of doing, Dixie was beginning to realize, when beset by strong and conflicting emotions.

"We've been tricker-treatin'—look!'' Ethan proudly held out his bag for their inspection.

"Hmm,'' said Rhett. He cleared his throat. "And what do you think you're going to do with all that junk?''

"Eat it!''

"Like hell ...'' He muttered it under his breath, but Dixie jabbed him in the ribs with her elbow anyway, and scolded him in a whisper.

"Hi, Dad...hi, Dixie.'' Lolly had joined them, out of breath more from guilt, Dixie suspected, than from running. *She,* at least, was old enough to know when she was walking on shaky ground.

Close behind Lolly was a slender girl wearing jeans and a hooded sweatshirt with the Iowa State logo on the front, hugging herself against the cold. She said, "Mr. Brown...hi...'' in the tone of voice that says, "What in the world are you doing here?''

"Hello, Cindy. We called your house. Your mother said you'd left with the kids an hour ago.'' He said it lightly, smiling a little. "We thought maybe we should send out a search party...''

"Oh, gosh—I'm really sorry. They wanted to go trick-or-treating. I didn't think you'd mind.''

"That's all right, Cindy. Lauren knows better.'' Rhett's dark and forbidding gaze dropped for a moment to his daughter, who instantly shot Dixie a look of blatant appeal.

"Perhaps you should call and check with me next time, okay?" he suggested to Cindy, smiling pleasantly again.

"I will. I'm really sorry. Well ... gotta be getting back...."

"Thanks for seeing them home safely."

"No problem. Have a happy Halloween."

"Thank you. Bye, now."

"Bye." Cindy hurried off, head down, shoulders hunched.

Rhett turned to his offspring and growled, "Now, then ..." He looked over at Dixie.

She took it from there. "You guys are grounded. No TV and no tree house for a week."

Lolly's mouth popped open. This time the look she gave Dixie was one of betrayed innocence. She turned instead to her father. "Da-ad ..."

"If it were me, I'd have made it two weeks," said Rhett darkly. "You guys got off easy. And as for this stuff..." He confiscated the bulging treat bags, to predictable howls of protest.

"Da-ad!"

"Hey—that's *my* candy!"

"You guys didn't actually think you were going to eat all this, did you?"

"When I was a kid," said Dixie, stuffing her hands in the pockets of the borrowed overcoat, "my parents used to hide my trick-or-treat candy. Then every night, *after* dinner and *before* I brushed my teeth, I got to spread my loot out on the rug and pick out one thing to eat. It wasn't so bad, really. It lasted a long time that way—clear 'til Christmas." Her eyes sought Rhett's over the children's head, asking for confirmation.

He hefted the bags thoughtfully. "More like ... Easter." As the children began to whine and groan he shrugged and said in his best defense attorney's manner, "Take it or leave it—that's as good a deal as you're going to get." His eyes locked with Dixie's and held for a long moment of unspoken communion. Like parents, she thought, or two people who've been working together for so long they know each other's thoughts....

Oh God, she thought, do I dare hope for this?

Here they were, walking home together, Rhett on one side, Dixie on the other, the two children in the middle. She couldn't help but think how much they looked—and felt—like a family. *Could* they be ... someday? It was all—it was *everything*— she'd ever wanted.

Oh, but she knew how cruel hope could be. That happiness could be snatched away in a heartbeat...in the blink of an eye.

I couldn't bear it, she thought. I couldn't live through that again.

What frightened her the most, as Ethan's cold little hand crept into hers like a baby animal seeking shelter, was that she might not have the choice. Instinctively, her hand closed around the small one, warming it as a mother would. And she shivered as the wind freshened, bringing with it the smell of snow...the promise of winter.

The custody hearing was scheduled for the first week in November. In the end, to Rhett it seemed almost anticlimactic.

With Elaine in town, the weeks preceding the hearing had grown increasingly tense, culminating in that ridiculous panic attack of his on Halloween night. Well...all right, maybe he didn't really think it was so ridiculous, not down in the dark bottom of his soul. He still didn't know just how far Elaine might go in order to gain custody of the children.

He didn't like to think about it.

In the days following Halloween, he concentrated on getting himself prepared for the hearing, in every way he could think of. His lawyer—Jerry Cline was handling the case for him, since family law wasn't exactly his field—had told him to relax. His best weapon was the truth. It was in the best interests of the children to remain in the environment they were accustomed to, all else being equal. The judge would see that. He had nothing to worry about.

But he did worry. And he could see that the children were upset, too. He'd had to limit their visits with their mother to weekends, since inevitably afterward they were so wound up they couldn't get to sleep until all hours. Ethan had reverted to bursting into tears over every little thing, the way he'd been those first weeks, before Dixie came. And Lolly...he didn't know quite what to make of Lolly. She was more than usually quiet and withdrawn, but without the air of disdain that reminded him so unpleasantly of her mother. And unless he was mistaken, she and Dixie seemed to have grown closer, especially in the last couple of weeks.

Rhett thought long and hard about whether or not to include the children in the hearing. On the one hand, to be fair, they were probably old enough to have some say in where they wanted to live—especially Lolly. He had to ask himself the painful question: If his children truly did want to go and be with their mother...would he try to keep them from her? If he did, what kind of a father would that make him?

Finally, he'd decided to talk to Lolly about it, one evening as he was tucking her in for the night. If he lived to be a hundred, he would never forget the way her face had crumpled, all bunched and swollen with held back tears, or the words she'd spoken, in a voice that was high and tight with pain, like the sounds a hurt animal makes.

*Please, Daddy...oh please don't make me choose....*

His heart ached whenever he thought about it.

So he'd whispered, "All right, sweetheart, I won't. We'll do what's best for you—I promise." And he'd kissed her good-night, breaking apart inside.

He was absolutely certain *he* knew what was best for her—and for Ethan. He just had to believe the judge would agree with him.

Something else he thought long and hard about was Dixie. And whether or not to bring her to the hearing was only one of the reasons.

On that particular subject his lawyer had been neutral. "If you think it'll help your case..." Jerry had said when Rhett asked him. But Jerry had never met Dixie.

Rhett couldn't help but remember the way Newt and Madeline had reacted to Dixie the first time they'd met her. Hell, he thought, he could dress her in burlap and orthopedic shoes, and she'd still be sexy. She was sexy wearing a false nose and green makeup. He'd found that out the hard way.

He had a feeling that if he took Dixie to that hearing, he'd be playing right into Elaine's hands.

So in the end, it was just Elaine and her lawyer, Rhett and his, and the judge. They met in the judge's chambers, with the sunlight streaming through the windows, making checkered patterns on the judge's dark green Oriental rug.

Elaine presented her argument, and Rhett presented his. The judge asked questions, peering through his bifocals as he leafed through the documents in his hands.

"And you are currently living in...California?"

"That's right, your honor. Right near the beach. It's a wonderful environment for children...."

"And this, uh, man you're planning to marry—how does he feel about adding two young children to his household?"

"Oh he can't wait. He couldn't be more thrilled, your honor."

As Rhett had anticipated, the judge wanted to know more about his child care arrangements.

"You say you've got somebody living in? You believe this person to be reliable?"

"Yes, sir, I do," said Rhett firmly, and added, "The children are very fond of her." He'd have sworn he could hear Elaine's teeth grinding, but she didn't interrupt. He thought her lawyer must have her on a short leash.

"Uh-huh," said the judge. He was flipping through the pages of Rhett's petition. "Where did you find this person, if I might ask? Is she licensed? What sort of qualifications does she have? I don't see anything here . . ."

"I have a copy of her résumé right here, your honor," said Rhett, feeling a little smug. That had been one of his prehearing precautions, having Dixie draw one up for him. He handed the judge a copy. "She's a friend of the family, actually. My sister recommended her to me. She has no previous experience with children—professionally, that is. She's a, uh . . . horse trainer."

"Horses?" The judge chuckled and said dryly, "Having raised three kids of my own, I'd say that makes her eminently qualified."

He then removed his glasses, folded them and placed them on top of the small stack of papers before him, and made a brief statement saying essentially that since he could find no good reason why the children should be uprooted from their present environment, he was granting the father's petition for custody. The mother would, of course, have reasonable visiting privileges, to be determined . . .

Elaine's gasp of shock and outrage cut off the rest, but Rhett barely heard it anyway. His ears were ringing; he felt lightheaded. He couldn't believe it was over. He'd won. The children were safe in his—and Dixie's—care.

"This isn't over, Rhett," Elaine hissed at him as they were leaving the judge's chambers. "If you think I'm going to let you and that . . . woman take my children away from me . . ." Her lawyer ushered her hastily out of range.

Rhett didn't care—let her rant and rave all she wanted to. Later, when he thought about it, he'd probably feel sorry for her. Having won, he could afford the generosity of granting that his children's mother loved the kids as much as he did, in her own way. He knew how much it must hurt to lose them. He knew how much *he'd* hurt. But right now he didn't want to think about that. He didn't want to think about anything. All he wanted to do was go home. He wanted to see his children. He wanted to see Dixie.

He drove home in a weird sort of fog, as if he were suffering from shock. The last months...Elaine's leaving, the worry, the fear, coping with the children, Dixie's coming, having his world turned inside out...it seemed as if he'd been existing in some kind of twilight zone. Now, suddenly, he felt as if morning had come at last. Life was starting anew for him, right from this moment.

It seemed limitless...exhilarating. It seemed terrifying.

He felt shaky as a newborn calf. He needed someone to hold on to, someone strong enough, and with enough common sense to bring him down to earth. Someone to laugh with him, and who wouldn't be the least bit upset if he cried a little, too. He needed his music. He needed...Dixie.

When he got home, no one was there. Dixie's old pickup was there, parked in the garage, but the house was empty. So, where in the hell was she? His disappointment was profound. She'd known about the hearing. He'd have thought she'd be pacing up and down, waiting...wondering.

He went through the house, calling. But she was unmistakably not there—when Dixie was in a place, you *knew* it. Tense and panicky as a child coming home from school to an empty house, he opened the French doors and stepped out onto the patio.

"Dixie—you out here?"

"Hi—I'm up here." Her voice seemed to come floating in from far away, but he could see her now, waving at him, head and shoulders framed in the small, square-cut window of the tree house.

He started across the lawn toward her, his eyes clinging to her frozen, smiling face as if it were a beacon. He hadn't thought about how he'd tell her, but the way it turned out, he didn't have to. As he got closer to her, he could see her face soften, take on color and life, begin to glow. He could see her beautiful eyes grow liquid and shiny. And he knew that she knew, just by looking at him.

"Oh, Rhett . . ." She got that far before her voice broke.

He held his arms out, then let them drop to his sides. "It went . . . very well," he said huskily. And then he just stood there, looking up at her, needing her and not knowing how to ask.

But again, she seemed to know. "I'm coming down," she said breathlessly, and disappeared.

"No, wait—stay there. I'll come up."

Her face reappeared in the window, smiling as only Dixie could. She gasped, "You serious?" as her wrist-thick braid tumbled forward and over the windowsill.

"'Rapunzel, Rapunzel, let down your hair . . .'" he intoned, grinning foolishly, feeling at once reckless, and shy as a schoolboy.

She gave a shout of laughter and flipped the braid back over her shoulder. "Maybe you better use the stairs—be easier on both of us. Come on around and I'll give you a hand."

He put his hands over his heart, pretending insult. "Hey—I think I can still manage to climb a tree."

"Yeah?" She waited for him to prove it, watching his progress with dancing eyes, and her teeth planted firmly on her lower lip, catching back laughter. She gave him a hand to help him through the door and to his feet, then stood back, tucking her fingertips in the back pockets of her jeans in a moment of endearing uncertainty. "Well," she said, sounding as if she'd been the one doing the tree climbing, "what do you think?"

"Not bad." He looked around, nodding judiciously as he brushed splinters from his hands. He felt as if he were entering an enchanted place, one he might not ever return from. "Not bad at all. Cozy."

She lifted a shoulder modestly. "Well, it'll be cozier when we get the roof finished."

"I like it this way," said Rhett, gazing up into the tracery of branches, black and mostly leafless now, against the porcelain blue sky. It was warm for November—the cold front had moved through on All Saints' Day, and the high pressure system behind it seemed reluctant to leave. It felt like Indian summer. Or spring, he thought, watching the afternoon sunshine cast lacy shadows across the rough plywood walls . . . and across Dixie's face. He smiled crookedly. "At least I can stand up."

And then he just looked at her, not knowing what else to say. After a moment she put out her hand and shyly, tentatively touched his. He wrapped his hand around her strong, callused fingers and held on as if she'd thrown him a rope. God, how he needed her. It was a new thing for him, this vulnerability; he wasn't quite sure what to do with it.

"The children," he said at last, in a voice that rasped in his throat. "Shouldn't they be home from school by now?"

"Riding lessons," she murmured. "I have to pick them up in a hour or so."

"Ah..." He nodded.

He didn't know which of them moved first. They came together in a duet of sighs, acknowledged that with a little laughter, then settled softly into each other's arms as if it were something they'd done a thousand times before. Her arms came around him, inside his jacket; her head nestled on his shoulder. He wrapped her in his arms and buried his face in her sunwarmed curls, and found them soft and sweet and fragrant as new-mown hay.

"Ah...God," he whispered, "I've wanted to do this for so long." What an incredible luxury it was, just to hold her.

"Me, too..." Her head turned, nuzzling in the hollow below his collar. Her body moved subtly, fitting itself to his. He grew light-headed and oxygen starved as the blood in his nether regions suddenly left them to converge on the center of his body.

"Dixie..." His voice was thick and unrecognizable to his ears, but she seemed to know what he wanted; she lifted her head from his shoulder and he found her mouth with no trouble at all. And again there were mutual sighs...little murmurs of welcoming laughter, like old lovers finding each other again after a long separation.

How sweet it was, to take his time about it. Her lips were soft and full, and he gave them the attention they deserved, getting to know their shape and texture, sipping the sweet, warm flow of her breath like the finest and rarest of wines. He was fascinated by the way her lips changed shape in response to his caresses...quivering with laughter when he teased them, growing lush and swollen when he nursed them in his own warmth...parting sweetly when he finally asked her, without any words, to open to him. He felt, then, as if a whole new world had been opened to him, one in which he could easily get lost and not mind at all. He didn't want to leave it... he wanted to explore, to taste, to savor until... whatever came next. He was in no hurry at all.

But... even delightfully lost as he was, he felt it when she began to tremble. It occurred to him, then, that there were better places for what they were doing than standing upright in a tree.

With great reluctance he eased his arms from around her body, slid his hands upward to her shoulders and then to her face, tenderly framing the kiss while he brought it to its conclusion. She moaned and let her head drop to his shoulder, as if it were simply too heavy for her neck to support. When he laughed in sympathy, she looked up, then pulled back to gaze at him. Her eyes were slumberous... and troubled.

"What's wrong?" he murmured, cradling the side of her neck in his hand, stroking her glazed lips with his thumb.

She hadn't expected this. She'd expected to feel nervous, apprehensive... scared. It had been so long, and she was risking so much, letting herself fall in love again. But she hadn't expected to feel guilty. Making love with Rhett was something she'd thought about, certainly since the first time he'd kissed her, even though that had been more in anger than desire—at least on his part. Maybe even before that. Almost certainly before that.

She'd never once thought of it as something illicit. Now, suddenly, she was thinking about the children. In a way she couldn't explain, the children made it seem... wrong.

"Dixie?" He kissed her forehead, gently. "What is it?"

Eyes closed, she shook her head and gave a little laugh of irony. "Oh... it's kind of silly, I guess, but I feel..."

She couldn't tell him. Bad enough that she felt like a moral dinosaur; the worst of it was, she knew she was going to let it happen anyway. Because she wanted it. Because she was human, and her body ached and her heart had been lonely for way too long.

She opened her eyes and saw his brow furrow with concern. "If you're worried about Elaine, I told you—"

"Not Elaine. The children..."

"Ah." He went very still, as if he were listening to something faint and far away. After a moment he lowered his head, gently nudged her chin up with the knuckle of his first finger and kissed her. He kissed her slowly, sweetly, almost thoughtfully, and when he finally lifted his mouth from hers, her knees buckled. "We don't have to do this now," he whispered, "if you don't want to. We have all the time in the world."

Her breath caught; she touched his face almost fearfully. "I do want to. I do."

"Then . . . maybe we should . . ." He sandwiched her hand between his and smiled.

But before he could turn, she clutched at his arms and said breathlessly, "Let's stay here."

His eyebrows shot up, making her laugh; she'd never seen them do that before. "You're kidding—*here?*"

"Why not? It's warm enough."

"In a *tree house?* My God, woman—I'm forty years old!"

She waited for the look of incredulity on his face to broaden into a smile before she said, with as straight a face as she could manage, "and never made love in a tree before? Heavens—high time, don't you think?"

Tensely she watched, holding his hands and trembling inside, while his face slowly changed . . . softened . . . became younger, more carefree. While her heart swelled with so much love for him, it *hurt.* And when he finally cleared his throat and said wonderingly, "Well, I guess maybe it is," she felt as if it had burst, like an overheated jug, and was pouring warm whiskey through her veins.

High time? Maybe it is, Rhett thought as he took off his jacket and laid it with a flourish on the uneven plank floor. He'd been middle-aged for most of his life, maybe it was time he learned what it was like to feel young. Maybe . . . just maybe, he thought, that was why fate . . . or Lucy . . . had seen fit to send Dixie to him. To teach him how to be a child . . . . before it was too late.

"M'lady . . ." he growled, taking her hand.

But he could feel that she was tense, so instead of laying her down right away, he kissed her. He kissed her a long, slow time, first her mouth, then her neck, and her throat. . . . There was a natural progression to what he was doing. But when he slid his hands under her sweatshirt and would have lifted it up and then off over her head, her breath caught audibly and she put her hands over his, staying them where they were, pressed against the sides of her waist. He felt her back muscles go rigid as iron.

It surprised him. She'd always seemed to him to move with such unconscious grace, like someone who was completely at ease in her own body. He'd imagined her wanton and uninhibited in nakedness, not tense like this, and shy. He was surprised, and to be honest, a little bit disappointed.

He didn't ask her what was wrong, not this time. He let her loosen his tie and toss it aside, then go to work on his shirt buttons while he contented himself with nibbling her neck until he could feel her nipples harden, even through the thickness of her sweatshirt.

Only when his shirt and undershirt had joined his jacket on the floor did he lay them both down, stretching himself out as much as he could, in the space allowed. Then he lay back and drew Dixie over to lie full-length on top of him.

"Splinters," he explained as he wrapped her in his arms and brought her mouth back down to his, where it belonged.

He kissed her until he was drunk and dizzy from lack of oxygen. She must have been, too, because this time she didn't object when he slipped his hands under her shirt, unhooked the clasp of her bra and pushed both up to her chin. She moaned at the first sweet shock of skin touching skin... her nipples brushed his chest hair, then flattened warmly as she settled against him. Her back arched beneath his hands as he stroked her. He nearly groaned aloud at the pressure she was putting on the part of him that already had as much pressure as it could reasonably bear.

He swept his hands over her back, down into the gentle valley of her waist, then up again to cup the firm little swell of her bottom.

She was still wearing her jeans, and the harshness of the denim frustrated him. He'd wanted to take it slowly, this first time, but he was running out of patience. It was only her soft, warm, yielding body his hands—and other parts of him—wanted to feel now. He tried to ease his hands inside the waistband, but that didn't satisfy him. So he slid them under her and between them, searching for the buttons. She must have been of the same mind as he, because she whimpered a little and tightened her belly muscles, raising herself enough to give him the access he wanted.

The buttons parted easily... one, two, three... and that was enough. He lifted his head, deepened the kiss that had become unending while he pushed the rough fabric over her hips. *Now*... Once again he slipped his hands between their bodies. His fingers dipped inside the last nylon barrier and turned to fan across the smooth satin plane of her belly.

Instead, they touched...

His hand froze. At the same instant, he felt her flinch as if he'd hurt her. Her stomach muscles tightened as she jerked away from his touch.

"Dixie—what ... in God's name..."

She rolled off him, pulling at her sweatshirt with one hand and covering her face with the other. Her face was turned away from him as far as it would go, as if she couldn't bear to look at him.

"I'm sorry," she said in a small, breathless voice. "I should have told you."

She was lying on her side facing away from him. He pulled her toward him, forcing her onto her back. "Let me see it," he said. He didn't recognize the harsh, angry sound as his own voice.

Without a word she gathered the sweatshirt material into her fist, leaving her slender, supple body bare from her breasts to the tops of her thighs. Her eyes were closed. He could see the sheen of moisture at their corners, almost hidden beneath the thick, black lashes. But she didn't cry.

"They didn't have time to do it pretty," she said softly.

# Chapter 13

His stomach had rebelled; he couldn't help it. He waited until he was sure he had it under control, and then said with dreadful calm, "How did it happen?"

She hesitated, drew a breath. "An...accident. I was hit by a car. I know it's ugly..." She was nervously smoothing the sweatshirt over her breasts, pulling it down to cover the zigzagging scars that marred the beautiful symmetry of her torso. "If it bothers you..."

"It doesn't bother me." His voice was still so harsh...he tried to atone for it by laying his hand on her belly and gently stroking, tenderly smoothing the ridges of scar tissue, trying to get across with his touch what his emotions wouldn't allow him to say.

That the words he'd just spoken were a lie—that it did bother him. Terribly. But not in the way she thought. It bothered him—hell, it hurt him like fire!—because it was obviously still so painful for her. As if the wounds had happened just yesterday.

"Tell me about it."

She made a small gesture of denial. "There's not very much to tell, really. It was a hit-and-run. They never caught...the ones responsible." Her voice was toneless, utterly without expression, which, for Dixie, was like the Mormon Tabernacle Choir singing off-key.

Rhett squirmed restively, sweeping his hand once more across her belly. "But this . . . why?"

"Like I said—they were in a hurry. I was bleeding to death inside. Things were ruptured—among other things, my uterus." Her voice became even fainter. "I was . . . five months pregnant at the time."

"*God . . .*"

Her head swiveled toward him. "You probably should know," she said, her voice cracking with the strain of keeping it matter-of-fact, "I can't have children. They had to take . . . almost everything out."

"The baby?" He had to know, but it was all he could trust himself to say.

Her lashes dropped like a curtain over her eyes, which was a mercy, for him. "My son was too small. He couldn't live."

He reacted instinctively; except for his own parents' death, when he'd been too involved with his own grief to be aware of anyone else's needs, he'd had no experience with such things. Now he didn't offer platitudes or words of sympathy—he didn't say anything at all. He simply gathered Dixie into his arms and pulled her close and held her, cradling her head against his heart.

She wasn't crying, but he stroked and comforted her as if she were. He comforted her for now and for all the other times she must have wept inside, safely hidden away behind the blinding radiance of her smile. Never again, he vowed, would he ever take a smile for granted.

Strange, he thought as he lay staring up into the black-lace pattern of winter bare branches, listening to his own heartbeat and the soft, slightly irregular sound of Dixie's breathing. Only moments ago his body had been on fire and the most important thing—the driving force—in his life had been to make love to this woman he held in his arms. Now . . . to be honest, his body was still smoldering, but now it seemed much more important to simply *hold* her. He wondered if that meant what he thought it did.

Presently, Dixie stirred and sat up, pushed back her hair with both hands and said in a normal voice, "It must be time to pick up the kids. You want to come with me...you know, break the news?''

''Good idea.'' *His* voice was a croak. He sat up, too, stifling a groan—his bones weren't accustomed to hard board floors— and began gathering up his clothes. ''You know, maybe we should all go out somewhere this evening—celebrate.''

Dixie shook her head. ''Tonight's a school night.'' Then she clapped a hand across her mouth and exclaimed, ''Oh, God— I'm startin' to sound just like you!''

Rhett had to laugh—her horror was absolutely genuine. ''Since we disagree, I guess that must mean I'm starting to sound like you,'' he said lightly. He wondered if *that* meant what he thought it did.

As he was climbing down the ladder, it occurred to Rhett that he was still an almost-forty-year-old man who'd never made love in a tree house.

''What was that for?'' Dixie asked curiously as he licked his palm and gave the trunk of the old elm tree a slap.

''Someday...'' he growled, putting the promise of erotic mischief into his smile. It was a promise he meant to keep.

Later, as they were driving to the stables, with Dixie sitting beside him in the passenger seat of his BMW, Rhett thought about the first time they'd ridden together like that, the first night they'd met. He remembered how wrapped up he'd been in his own troubles, then, feeling distraught and helpless because he couldn't seem to handle his own kids. He felt chastened and ashamed of himself, now. And damned lucky.

He cleared his throat and said in a gentle, musing tone, ''I guess it doesn't matter when you lose a child, does it? Whether you have that child for five months or fifty years...I can't imagine anything worse. No parent can.''

She glanced at him quickly, then looked away, out the window. Her voice, when she spoke, was so quiet it seemed to come from a long way off, but at the same time, something about it wove a bond of intimacy between them, a bond as gossamer and strong as silk.

''People used to tell me it would get better with time. They say you never really heal, when you lose a child...But I was told that eventually you get to a point where you can find comfort and joy in the memories.'' There was silence, which he didn't interrupt. When he heard her take a breath, he knew it was to ease the aching in her throat so she could go on.

"The thing is, I don't *have* any memories. I have *nothing*. No photographs, no toys or baby clothes... I never got to hold my son. I never even got to *see* him. Just... one day I had a child that I loved, that I talked to, sang to... planned a future for. And the next day I woke up in intensive care... and he was gone. Everything... was gone."

This time, Rhett reached across the silence to cover her hand with his. "The baby's father," he said gently. "You said he'd died, too. Was it the hit-and-run—"

She shook her head. "He'd died a few days before... in a fire in his studio." For some reason her voice grated a little when she added, "It was an accident, too."

"My, God..." His hand tightened convulsively around hers. He cleared his throat and managed to say huskily, "You really did lose everything, didn't you?"

He felt her turn her head to look at him. After a moment she said, very softly, "I thought I had."

He didn't answer her, because suddenly he couldn't speak at all.

She came to him that night.

He'd wondered if she would. He'd been lying there in his king-size bed, wondering if he ought to go to her, thinking maybe she'd be feeling insecure because of her scars, thinking maybe she'd need the reassurance.

But on the other hand, he didn't want to put any pressure on her, after the battering her emotions had taken that afternoon. She was bound to be feeling especially vulnerable—he didn't want to take advantage of her. Didn't want her thinking he was only interested in her for one reason.

Which nothing could be farther from the truth. And it bothered him like hell to think of her lying there in her room, maybe hurting, and him not there to comfort her. Yes... he'd be content to do only that, if it was what she wanted. He'd gladly spend this or any other night just sleeping with her, holding her in his arms.

But on the *other* hand... this afternoon he'd gotten the impression it really did bother her, the idea of cohabiting with him, with the children in the house, even though the custody issue had been decided and it was now nobody's business but their own. Still, it was a delicate issue, and an easy one to rationalize. In the end, he supposed it came down to a matter of intentions.

Okay, so what *were* his intentions, where Dixie was concerned?

He was confronting that question head-on, with sweaty palms and pounding heart, when he heard a soft tapping on his bedroom door.

She didn't wait for a response, but slipped inside with a breathlessly whispered, "Are you awake?"

As an answer—and an invitation—he lifted up the edge of the covers. "Yeah," he growled, "I'm awake."

She came into his bed without a sound and crept close, shivering.

"Cold?" he asked tenderly as he cocooned her with the blankets and his arms.

Her head moved against his chest. "Just nervous."

"Don't be." He pressed his lips to the top of her head, breathing deeply, luxuriating in the sweet warmth of her scent. "I was thinking about doing this myself."

She snorted softly. "It's better I did—you've got a bigger bed." She lifted her head for a quick look around. "My Lord—it's huge, by the way. Was this your bed . . . with Elaine?"

He sighed. "Yes." He was trailing his fingers lightly up and down her back, under her T-shirt. His voice was just as light when he asked, after a brief pause, "Does that bother you?"

"Not really, no . . ." She listened to the playback of her own words and decided she believed them. Her breath caught. She murmured, "It's hard to think about anything . . . much less your ex-wife . . . when you're doing that . . ." His hands . . . his big, warm, wonderful hands . . . were moving into new territory, places they hadn't quite gotten to this afternoon.

It had been a long, long time since anyone had touched her there.

"I know what bothers you," he said, his voice thoughtful, and just a touch sly.

"Not *that*," she whispered, puffing warmth into the hollow of his neck while his hand wandered where it pleased. "That feels..."

He laughed, and gently squeezed the rounded part of her he'd been measuring. "That's not what I meant." He withdrew his hand from inside her panties and touched her shoulder, nudging her onto her back as he raised himself on one elbow. "This afternoon, in the tree house..." She started to interrupt, but he laid a finger on her lips, asking for silence. "I think... it bothers you... being here with me, like this, in this house... doesn't it? Because of the kids."

After a moment, she nodded. "It's not you," she whispered, reaching up in the darkness to touch his face, tracing the outline of his lips and almost losing her train of thought because it felt so good to do that. "I want to be with you... like this. It's the secrecy, I guess. It feels sneaky. It feels... dishonest."

His fingers brushed her cheek, swept past her ear and found a resting place in her hair. "Would it help," he said gravely, "if I told you I love you... and that as soon as everything is finalized, I would like very much to marry you?"

The words hit her like a thunderclap. They were followed by a moment of absolute silence, while the shock wave carried her breath away. She sat up abruptly, narrowly missing a collision of heads in the process. Her heart was pounding. She said hoarsely, "Rhett, don't say that—you don't owe me any promises."

His chuckle was dry and didn't quite disguise the vulnerability in his voice. "Well, that's not exactly the response I'd hoped for."

Again, her breath caught painfully. She wanted his arms around her, wanted him touching her again... wanted it so badly, the only thing she could do was turn away from him.

"It's too soon... too soon, don't you know that?" she said almost angrily. "You're going through a divorce, dammit. You're bound to be hurtin'... You have to give yourself time to heal first, before you even think..."

He caught her by the arms and pulled her around so that she faced him across the charcoal darkness. His hands weren't gentle, now; she could feel the tension in them. Almost...a trembling. *Trembling? Rhett?*

"Too soon?" He sounded strangely, on the verge of laughter. "Too soon? My God...I feel more like it was almost too late. When I think that I might have lived my whole life, and never found you."

He stopped there, and she could feel him trying to regain control of the emotions that had almost overwhelmed him. His grip on her arms eased, and he began to stroke them instead, as if he were asking her pardon. She heard a faint rustling, then his sigh, and she knew, just *knew*, as if she'd seen it, that he'd plunged his fingers into his hair.

"Ah, damn, I hate telling you this, because it's going to sound like a line. But the truth is..." He gave a frustrated laugh, paused, and began again. "Look, I'm not going to tell you I never loved my wife. I must have felt something for her at one time, or I wouldn't have gotten involved with her in the first place."

"She's very beautiful," said Dixie helpfully.

He let his breath out in another gust of laughter. "Oh, yes, she is that. But..." his voice became somber "...physical attraction fades. Everyone knows that. At least when ours went, we still had a pretty good thing going—at least I thought we did. We both wanted the same things, and we each thought the other was the best person to help us get what we wanted. It worked real well—she was good at her job, I was good at mine. I was happy...or at least, content. But things change, I guess. People change...goals change."

"*She* changed," Dixie whispered.

She thought he nodded. "In what she wanted, at least." His voice was dry. "Believe me, it came as a pretty big shock to find out it wasn't me. I was so angry, at first...I felt betrayed. I didn't even stop to ask myself how I could have missed the fact that she was so unhappy. Now, I think I must have had blinders on."

He was silent for a moment. When he went on, it was in a thoughtful, almost musing tone. "I think I was just so focused on my goals—I had been, all my life, you know. Even as a kid, there was only one thing I ever wanted, and that was to get into politics—well, not politics, really, I hate all that wheeling and dealing stuff. But I wanted to be a part of government, running things, so I could help people . . . fix things that were wrong. I think that, in Elaine, all I really saw was someone who could help me get where I wanted to go. I never saw her as a person at all, so I didn't notice that we were . . . basically incompatible. When she left, the way she left—well, of course it hurt. My pride, if nothing else. I suppose I *was* wounded. But. . ." His voice broke unexpectedly, as shocking to her as a branch breaking under her foot. She held her breath, holding back her own sob as he finished in a whisper, "The day I started to heal was the day I met you."

She whispered his name . . . touched his face. And the moisture she brought away on her fingers was like a healing balm to *her* wounded soul.

She felt so fragile. Hearts . . . feelings . . . emotions as exposed and raw as theirs frightened her; she'd kept hers wrapped up and hidden away for so long. She didn't want to cry. So instead, in a voice like ripping cloth, she said, "Rhett, make love to me. . . ."

It was, he thought later, in more than one sense, his very first time. The first time he'd made love with Dixie, of course. But also the first time he'd ever made *love*. He figured that out right away. And it was a whole new experience for him, making love to a woman, not just with his mind and body involved, but with his whole heart and soul.

There wasn't anything fancy about it. In fact, if he'd had to rate himself . . . but the whole point was, he didn't have to. He didn't think about himself at all. He didn't *think*. All he did was *feel*. There was so much feeling. And he didn't try to hold any of it back. He wanted her to have all of it, everything that was in him. He wanted her to *know*.

It was in his hands . . . in the way he touched her; it was in his arms, as he held her cradled against his heart. It was in his heart, in the way it shivered within him like something fragile and newly born. It was in his heated skin, in his tensed and quivering muscles, in his mouth when he kissed her. And yes, in his loins . . . although, for the first time in his memory, in those circumstances, that part of him seemed almost unimportant.

Afterward, he thought, with faint twinges of regret, of all the ways he wanted to make love to her...with his mouth, his hands, with all the masculine strength and power in his body. He thought about the ways he wanted to touch her, the ways he wanted her to touch him, all the parts of her he hadn't kissed yet. All the erotic possibilities there were yet to explore. But at the time, as he eased himself into her so gently, so sweetly...at the moment he felt her tender warmth enfold him, he was conscious only of the most incredible sense of joy...of completeness...of homecoming.

He hardly remembered moving, with her and within her; the ancient rhythms, which he knew from experience could sometimes be more like a struggle than a dance, seemed to come as naturally to them as breathing. He felt the pulses of her body as if they were his own. He knew exactly when the pressures inside her had reached the breaking point. His body knew. He knew just how long to hold her there...and when to let her go. And his body went with hers, as naturally as the water follows the river's course....

Afterward, they lay joined together, barely moving, for a long time—something else that was new to Rhett. He was a fastidious person, and had never cared much for the messier aspects of sex. Afterward he'd usually been eager to get himself washed up and back into his own personal space again. But Dixie's body didn't feel alien to him. It felt like an extension of his own body, like the missing half of himself he'd spent a lifetime searching for. To separate after so brief and sweet a time seemed almost frightening to him. Like the anticipation of pain. Like preparing to have a tooth pulled, or an adhesive bandage ripped off....

"What's funny?" Dixie murmured, her words warm and furry in his ear.

"Mmm...I was just thinking." He laughed soundlessly, holding her close, his lips pressed against her forehead. "I don't want to leave you."

Her chuckle was comfortable...tender. "You don't have to...not for a while, anyway."

"Hmm...I suppose not." He slipped onto his side and pulled her with him. "I'll just hold you like this..." He'd hold her, and they'd sleep for a little, and then he'd kiss her awake and make love to her again . . . and so on until morning.

But she was stirring, shaking her head. "I'd better go. Ethan might wake up...sometimes he has bad dreams. He won't know where I am."

Rhett groaned. "Oh, God—you mean to tell me . . . there's another man?"

She laughed. "'Fraid so, darlin'." There was a pause, and then she said somberly, "I fell in love with him first, you know."

He tightened his arms around her once more and raised himself and kissed the top of her head. Then he lay back on the pillows with a sigh and murmured huskily, "I guess I'll have to get used to sharing you, won't I?"

"Yeah, you will..." She propped herself on one elbow, leaned down and kissed him a long, lingering...intoxicating...mind-blowing time. When she finally lifted her head, her words were slurred, and full of Texas. "But ah'm a big girl . . . there's plenty of me to go around."

He groaned in heartfelt agreement and reached for her, but she'd already slipped away from him. He could feel and hear her searching in the darkness among the tumbled bedclothes for her underpants.

She was standing beside the bed pulling on her T-shirt when he turned on the lamp. For a moment she froze, half crouched there, her lovely eyes startled, like a doe caught in the beam of a car's headlights. Then she straightened and hastily tugged the shirt down so that it covered her to midthigh, smiling uncertainly. "That's okay, I think I found everything."

He swung his legs around and sat up on the edge of the bed. "Come 'ere," he said, beckoning to her.

She hesitated, half poised as if for flight, her hair, only loosely braided, tumbling around her face and over one shoulder, her eyes shadowed and wary. "What . . . I have to..."

"Come here," he said again, his voice gravelly. "There's something I want to do first." He held out his hand, and when she took it, still uncertain, guided her gently to him. "Something I've been wanting to do..."

He brought her close, positioned her between his knees and let go of her hand. She uttered one soft gasp when he lifted up her T-shirt, but didn't try to prevent what he did then, even though he could feel her tremble. He could feel it with his mouth as he kissed the smooth, hard ridges of her scars, feel it in his hands as they stroked the sides of her waist, her rib cage, her back, her hips. He felt it in his face when he buried it in the tensed hollow of her belly, and in her hands when she finally... tentatively, as if almost afraid to believe... let them come to rest on his head, and began to weave her fingers through his hair.

She didn't make a sound when he moved lower, not even when he hooked a finger in the elastic of her panties and pulled them down to the tops of her thighs and pressed his mouth to the thick warm nest of curls there, but only swayed toward him and held him more tightly, as if afraid she might fall.

And it was a long time after all before she left him to go back to her own bed.

Newt Hendricks fell into step beside Rhett as he was going down the courthouse steps the next afternoon. "Hey, hold on— got a minute? I need to talk to you."

Rhett glanced at his campaign manager and slowed but did not stop. "Can it wait? I'm late for an appointment."

"Son." Newt put a hand on his arm, giving him no choice. "This is important."

Rhett refused to be daunted by the look of gravity on the older man's face. Life was too damn good right now. Nothing was going to go wrong that he couldn't fix. And nothing needed fixing that couldn't wait until Monday. "Better be," he said in a warning tone. "I told Dixie and the kids I'd be home early. We're planning on taking them out—a little pizza, some thirty-one flavors, miniature golf—you know, to celebrate the custody thing? I don't want to keep them waiting. What's up?"

"Maybe we should go somewhere... sit down—"

"Haven't got time." He started down the steps and again Newt kept pace with him. "Talk to me while we're walking— I'm already late."

Newt took a thick manila envelope from under his arm and slapped him in the arm with it. He growled, "You might want to read this before you start celebrating."

Rhett paused long enough to take the envelope. As he glanced down at it, he could feel his face settling into stony, professional lines. It felt strange to him, after feeling so young and carefree all day. Keeping his tone light, he said, "Is this something that's going to screw up my weekend?"

"That was...messengered over from the senator's office...this morning." Newt was a smoker and overweight; he was beginning to pant. Rhett took pity on him and stopped walking. "It's the FBI file on that nanny of yours...what's her name...Parish."

"Ah...jeez." He had a sudden urge to chuck the damn envelope, just as far as he could throw it. "You can't be serious." He gave a bark of disbelieving laughter. "You're telling me the FBI has a file...on *Dixie?* That's ridiculous."

Newt shrugged. "Better take a look at it before you say that."

"Oh, for..." Rhett eyed his campaign manager with distaste. With the weather so warm, he was hatless, and his bushy white hair was stirring in the mild Indian summer breeze. With his rumpled suit jacket open, revealing his big, button-straining belly and his maroon suspenders, he looked like central casting's idea of an old-time Midwestern politician. Which was precisely what he was. Rhett wondered now why he'd ever hired the man, when he stood for everything about the system he hated. "The FBI investigated Bobby Kennedy, for God's sake," he said coldly.

Newt shook his head. "Trust me, this isn't like that. I think you'd better read it."

Rhett turned and started down the steps again; he didn't want to acknowledge the compassion in those shrewd blue eyes. But he couldn't escape Newt's next words.

"She was investigated as a suspected foreign agent, son."

*"What?"* He stopped, threw up his arms and burst out laughing. "You've gotta be kidding. Whose?"

Newt wasn't laughing. He was obviously dead serious. "Castro's—Cuba. Back in the early eighties. In Nicaragua. It's all there in the file."

"Newt," said Rhett cheerfully, "you're fired."

"Read the file, son." Newt's voice, like his eyes, was quiet and grave. "Then you tell me what you want to do."

Rhett never knew how he made it to his car. When he got there he slammed the envelope down on the hood of his BMW and kicked viciously at the tire. Then, with both hands braced on the fender, head down, he swore and swore and swore.

He didn't want to know what was in the damned envelope. He didn't want to look at the damned file. What he wanted to do was burn it. Throw it in the river on his way home.

But of course he couldn't do that. He couldn't do it because it wouldn't make whatever was in that envelope go away. So, whatever it was, he was going to have to know about it. Because sooner or later, everyone else in the world would.

He picked up the envelope and slowly, slowly eased his fingers under the self-adhesive flap. He felt as if the ground were opening up under his feet.

Dixie had never been so happy. She'd had an idyllic childhood, and then those lovely, golden months with Peter, but her happiness then had been a child's, naive and uncaring—considering such sunny days no more than her due, and certain they would last forever. *This* happiness was the sweeter, so much more intense and precious because now she knew it for the miracle it was, and how quickly it could be snatched away.

She floated through the day in a fog, hearing music where there wasn't any, even dancing and singing along to the rackety rock on Luby's stereo, until the cleaning lady had exclaimed suspiciously, "Good heavens, girl, you are higher than a kite! What in the world you been sniffin'?"

So Dixie told her about the custody hearing, which was explanation enough for Luby. In a festive spirit, Dixie had broken out the bottle of cognac and they'd raised a couple of shot glasses in celebration. After which, the music had seemed even better.

Now, for the first time all day, she was alone in the house. The children were at the stables—she'd taken them to their riding lessons as scheduled, even though she knew it would delay the evening out by an hour or so while she got the horse smell scrubbed off of them. She'd done it for purely selfish reasons. Because she wanted a few precious minutes alone with Rhett when he came home. Because she wanted the house to herself while she bathed and dressed and primped for him, like a bride on her wedding night.

*Silly*...

She blushed at her own reflection, in the privacy of her room. But she couldn't help it—she was in love.

And it had been so *hard*, sheer torture, seeing him this morning and trying not to blush under the children's ever-watchful eyes. Greeting him with the same casual cheeriness as always, pouring his coffee and catching a whiff of the fresh-from-the-shower smell of him...the familiar, cozy scents of Irish Spring and Old Spice...and not being able to so much as *touch* him, not even to lay a hand on his shoulder. Saying goodbye to him with her heart in her eyes, and seeing the joy and the promises in his.

So, silly or not, she washed her hair and blew-dry the frizz out of it, and soaked in a bubble bath and shaved her legs and even did what she could with her work-ravaged nails. She fixed her hair in a style that was impractical for everyday—pulled back loosely in an inside out ponytail that left it soft and wavy around her face. She'd decided on her best silk blouse and her silver belt and matching earrings, but with her usual jeans, rather than the skirt she briefly considered. That, she felt, was a little *too* obvious—Lolly was bound to notice.

Now she was pacing nervously in the entry, her best boots thumping on the parquet floor, looking at her watch every few seconds. Like a bride whose groom is late showing up at the chapel, she thought wryly. This being in love business was going to take some getting used to.

But I could be happy here, she thought, looking around at the empty house. It had changed a lot in the weeks since she'd been there. Of course, she'd added a few touches of her own, here and there. It seemed homier, now...warmer. More relaxed. She'd miss Texas, but if this was where Rhett was...well, then, this was where she wanted to be.

There was no longer any question or fear in her mind. Rhett...Ethan...Lolly. She loved them—all of them. It was as simple as that. She wanted to spend the rest of her life with Rhett. She wanted to raise his children, and rock his grandchildren to sleep in her lap, and sing them lullabies.

A smile broke like sunrise across her face when she heard the BMW roar into the driveway.

Thank you, God, for this miracle, she thought as she hurried to greet the man she adored. *Thank you . . . for giving me another chance.*

## Chapter 14

She knew instantly. She knew when he got out of his car and stood there looking at her across the top of it, with eyes that had no joy or promises in them at all, but instead were black and deep as caves. She'd seen that look on his face before, the day of Elaine's visit. And she'd prayed to God that it never, ever be turned on her.

Perhaps it was a mercy. The suddenness of it—the shock—numbed her.

She thought she spoke his name, making it a question, as he came up the steps; if she did, he didn't answer her. He handed her a large manila envelope and walked by her without a word. Walked by her and on down the hall and through the swinging door.

Left alone, Dixie moved like a sleepwalker to close the door, and then stared dumbly at the envelope he'd placed in her hands. She felt jerky, trembly inside, but amazingly, her hands were quite steady.

She followed slowly in Rhett's footsteps, frowning in puzzlement at the envelope. In the kitchen, she paused beside the table to open it...pulled out what was inside. She read the first page standing there in the waning light, and when she had finished, slipped the papers back into the envelope and closed it carefully. She felt very calm, and cold as death.

He couldn't think what in the world to say to her. He couldn't think, period. His brain—his whole *being*—felt shut down, as if the main circuit had been tripped. Sort of an emotional power surge, he thought. He was pleased with the analogy because it seemed to suggest that at least some part of his reason was still functioning.

He watched her come into his study and lay the envelope on his desk, then take a step back. She stood very straight, head high, arms folded across her waist, and waited—like Joan of Arc, he thought, awaiting sentencing. Her face was utterly still . . . remote and pale as death.

Someone had to say something. So he tried, without clearing his throat first. "Did you read it?"

By some miracle she understood the garbled sound he made. She replied, "Only the first page." Her voice was as distant as her expression.

Her calm infuriated him. He wanted to rant and rave, to pick up something heavy and hurl it through the French doors. Instead he said, with what he thought was admirable composure, "You want to tell me what this . . . crap is all about?" His throat felt as if he'd swallowed glass.

He could see her throat muscles move, and wondered if she felt the same. He searched her face for answers, and watched her lashes drop like a curtain across her eyes.

That was when his control finally deserted him. He brought his fists down on his blotter and in anguish whispered, "My God, Dixie, *talk to me*. Why didn't you tell me about this?"

"Because I couldn't." She said it flatly, without emotion. Which somehow gave the words all the more meaning. She meant it. He believed it.

Softly, scared to death, now, that it must be true, he said, "What do you mean . . . you couldn't?"

"I mean that I *couldn't*." Her lashes lifted and her eyes pierced him like twin swords, shockingly alive and angry in that pale, still face. "I did once—I tried to tell someone. A long, long time ago. It cost me everything I loved. *Everything*. Do you understand?" Her soft, tense voice faded to a whisper. "It still is . . . costing me . . . isn't it?"

He didn't want to hear her. Didn't trust himself to speak. He felt as if the universe had stopped, as if he existed with her now in a tiny, electrically charged space all their own. Through a peculiar humming in his ears he heard a voice—it must have been his—say, "Tell me now...please...you owe me that much."

She threw him a look of stark entreaty that seared his soul, then turned away. After a moment she dropped into a chair, the big, comfortable one he used for reading, and said in an exhausted voice, "God...I really thought it was over. I thought...they promised."

"Promised? Who promised? Who are *they?*"

Her laughter was bitter and ironic. "You're just about to get into it, Rhett—you sure you want to know?"

He frowned at her, not understanding. "Get into what?"

She shrugged. "Government...politics."

"Come on." He sat back in his chair, rejecting the inference with his whole body, it seemed, as well as he mind.

She turned her face from him, remote once more. "You asked..."

He didn't want to know, if the truth were told. He had a feeling what she was going to say might change his life in a lot of ways he wasn't ready for. But he found himself rising, almost like a sleepwalker, crossing the room and taking a seat on the footstool facing her. He leaned forward, clasped his hands between his knees, and dropped the words like bricks, one by one, into the deadly silence. *"Tell me. I want to know."*

She uttered a sound, half laugh, half whimper, and pressing her hands against the arms of the chair, squirmed back in it as far as she could go, almost as if it were him she was trying to get away from. For some reason, he found himself staring at the buttons of her white silk blouse, at the clasp of her Navajo silver belt, and thinking of the scars that lay hidden underneath.

And suddenly he was remembering what she'd told him of her fiancé, of his accident and hers. Remembering other things she'd said, here and there, especially the look in her eyes when she'd said the word *betrayal*. Hearing the echoes of her words: *It cost me everything I loved.*

He felt cold, deep, deep inside. He didn't want to hear it. But he knew he had to.

She began hesitantly, seeming almost embarrassed, like a shy, closet singer shoved onstage against her will. Laughing a little, her eyes hidden behind the hand that supported her bowed head. "God...I don't even know if I can. It's been so long...I tried so hard for so many years to forget...."

*And yet, it seemed like yesterday.*

It was surprisingly easy, at first. She told him about joining the Peace Corps, fresh out of college and so young and full of idealism and rebellion. She told him how excited she'd been to be going to *Nicaragua,* of all places, right in the middle of one of the world's hot spots.

"I didn't even know we had people in Nicaragua," Rhett interrupted her, frowning. "I thought they were officially pretty much in Castro's camp."

Dixie felt her smile grow tight and strained. "Oh, we were a select group. Personally invited by the government. See, at the time there was a big push by certain..." her mouth twisted— she couldn't help it "... factions in this country to get funding to aid the rebels through Congress. Naturally, the Nicaraguan government wasn't anxious to have that happen, so they were doing their best to be—or at least appear to be—cooperative with us. Of course, I didn't know or care much about the politics of the thing, at the time. I was just thrilled to be going to a place where I felt like I could really make a difference, you know?"

And it had been so wonderful, at first. Everything had been new and exciting—even the inconveniences had seemed no more than an adventure to her. And the people...their poverty and hardship had broken her heart at times, but that had only made her all the more certain of her purpose in being there. She really was helping people who needed it.

And then, to top it all off, she had met Peter Grant.

The telling began to get harder then. She couldn't look at Rhett and talk about Peter. But he listened, frowning with laserlike intensity, never interrupting, not trying to hurry her along, seeming to understand that she had to come to it in her own way and in her own time.

So she was able, finally, to tell him about the man she'd been so much in love with, all those years ago, when she'd still been young and innocent and full of optimism. Peter Grant had been a photojournalist—one of the best. He'd been at it a long time, covering wars and disasters all over the world, so when she met him he was already battle-scarred and cynical. No two people could possibly have been more different. She'd never understood how in the world they'd ever fallen in love. But they had. Incredibly, miraculously.

It was only when she began to tell Rhett about that terrible day that Dixie discovered that at some point—she didn't know when—he'd taken her hands, and was holding them tightly sandwiched in his warm, strengthening grasp.

"He'd heard about this place—sort of a mission, I guess." She was staring down at the two pairs of clasped hands as if they had no connection to her. "Just a school and a small infirmary, run by a Canadian priest and a handful of nuns, including a couple of Americans. It was in the mountains, a really remote area, right in the middle of rebel-controlled territory. He was determined to get up there and talk to them, find out exactly what was going on from the rebel point of view—that was the sort of thing he liked to do. He asked me to go along—said I might learn something." She laughed softly. "He was always doing that, too—trying to educate me. He couldn't stand it that I was so optimistic—he called it naive. . . .

"Anyway, I was delighted to go along. I remember that when we started out, it felt like an outing when I was a kid—like a picnic, you know? It was so beautiful up there . . . all the incredible birds, and the flowers. . . ." She stopped and swallowed. And swallowed again.

Rhett squeezed her hands and encouraged her in a soft-rough voice, "It's okay . . . just tell it. Come on."

And somehow she did, her eyes sliding past him and focused on nothing, her voice detached and almost matter-of-fact, as if, he thought, she were relating a dream she'd had.

"It was the birds we noticed first . . . they'd come for the bodies. It couldn't have happened long before—the mission was still smoldering. You could smell the smoke, and the . . . other . . . You could smell death. They were all dead—the priest and the nuns, the children in the school, the people in the infirmary—old people, mothers . . . babies. There were some other people there, from the neighboring villages, I guess. They were trying to do what they could. We tried ... we ... I helped to bury the bodies.''

Her hands were clammy. Rhett wanted to warm them with his, but she withdrew them gently, and sat back in the chair, closing her eyes, leaving him feeling curiously abandoned.

"Who did it?" he asked raggedly. "Did you find out who was responsible?"

She nodded. "The villagers said it was the government forces who'd committed the massacre. Someone had seen soldiers in the area—who else could it have been? But Peter ... he kept saying it didn't feel right. It didn't *smell* right. I thought he was just being his usual cynical self, at first, but then ... the thing was, it was all rebel-held territory, all around there. There hadn't been any battles, not even a skirmish, for weeks. How could a government force get in there and do such a terrible thing and then leave again, and not even be seen by any of the rebels? He was right—it didn't make sense.

"Anyway, the authorities came and we ... left. We were on our way home. It was just one of those things...pure luck, you know? We were looking for a place to camp—to rest. Thank God we heard the voices—we'd almost stumbled into the middle of them. There they were, sure enough—they had government vehicles, uniforms, everything. But the strange thing was, they were taking their uniforms *off*. And there were three men with them who weren't Nicaraguans. We heard them talking.'' Her voice rasped like metal filings. "They spoke English.''

"Dear God," Rhett whispered.

Dixie just smiled slightly, one of the bleakest smiles he'd ever seen. "Of course, Peter was going crazy with his cameras. He'd already shot rolls and rolls at the mission. So had I—with my little point-and-shoot. I don't really know why ...

"Anyway, I managed to get him away from there before we were discovered. By the time we got to the city, it was already all over the news—the massacre, I mean. The American press was blaming the government forces, the government was denying it.... Peter was convinced by this time that there was something really dirty going on. He had a lot of contacts—sources of information, you know? He had the pictures he'd taken of the three Americans. So he started making inquiries. And ... the next thing I knew ..." She spread her hands; her mouth twisted. "He was gone. Vanished. Without even saying goodbye."

"Gone?" Rhett was scowling furiously, feeling a little lost, as if he'd missed something. "What do you mean?"

She shrugged, remote again. "I was told he'd been called back to the States—I assumed by the paper he worked for. A couple of days later, I was told my mission there was being cancelled. I was to leave immediately. As soon as I got back to Texas, I called Peter's number. There was no answer. So...I called the paper he worked for. They told me..." Her voice broke at last. Her throat moved convulsively a few times, and then she drew a shaky breath and finished it. "They told me he'd been killed. That there'd been an explosion and fire at his home—which was also his studio—and that all his photographs had been destroyed."

"My God..." It seemed to be all he could think of to say. His mind was in a turmoil, full of images, thoughts, suspicions...all too terrible, too *unthinkable*, to give voice to.

He couldn't sit still any longer. He found himself on his feet, pacing, driving his fingers through his hair, and then heard himself saying the unspeakable, in that voice he hardly recognized. "You don't believe it was an accident, do you?"

She shook her head. That was all. But those eyes of hers held his, saying everything.

His breath burst from him in a futile attempt to reject it. "God—the hit-and-run—you don't think that was *deliberate?* That someone tried to..."

"Kill me," she whispered. "Yes."

*"Why?"*

She hadn't left her chair, so her voice came from behind him, cool and even, as if she'd been suggesting the menu for the evening meal. "Because I'd just called Peter's editor to tell him I had proof that would prove his suspicions. But I didn't tell him—" she broke through his startled exclamation "—because I was afraid I was being watched...listened to, so I told him I'd call him back. I was walking to a restaurant down the street—I thought it might be harder for the surveillance to pick up the call in a crowded place like that—when a van started keeping pace with me. I was crossing a driveway—some kind of fast-food place, I think—when I heard the motor roar, and

I saw the headlights coming straight at me. That's all ... I remember."

"But the proof?" He was bending over her by that time, his hands braced on the arms of her chair, his voice a horrified croak. "You said—"

She gazed up at him, her eyes like bruises. "It was a roll of film—the one I'd shot at the mission, and later. I had it in my pocket when I started for the restaurant. When I woke up in the hospital ... when they gave me my things ... it wasn't there. I asked, but no one knew what had become of it. The paramedics hadn't found a roll of film on me. It was just ... gone."

For what seemed like a long time he couldn't say a word, couldn't even move. He just stayed there, hanging over her like a great black cloud, pinioned by her eyes, paralyzed with horror, rage, disbelief—no, *wishing* he could disbelieve. And that almost made it worse.

Finally he pushed himself away from her with a hiss of anger and began pacing again, stabbing his fingers into his hair. "The FBI file," he growled, through jaws so tightly clenched they hurt. "You still haven't told me about that."

He heard her clear her throat. "You have to understand ... I was very young. I was angry ... probably in shock, not thinking very clearly. Also very stubborn. The first thing I did after the accident, as soon as I could function at all, was go to the press with my story. To the police. To congressmen, priests—everybody I could think of. I was determined not to let it rest.

"Well ..." she gave a light laugh that had no humor in it at all "... the next thing I knew, I was in a mental hospital. An emotional breakdown, they called it. A combination of trauma and shock ... grief over the loss of my child. I was diagnosed as delusional, with episodes of paranoia."

She laughed again, out of the chair and pacing too, now, restless with remembered anger. "Oh, don't worry, I wasn't there long. My family was very supportive and loving." She paused, rubbing at her arms as if she'd felt a sudden chill. "A couple of days after I got out, I found an envelope on my doorstep. That file—" she nodded her head toward his desk "—was in it. A little bit later the phone rang. The person on the other end told me the file would be closed . . . provided I let the unfortunate episode in Nicaragua stay closed as well.''

She slanted a look at him, her blue eyes glinting like liquid steel, her lips curving in a wicked smile—and suddenly there was the Dixie he'd first met, and been missing lately. Full of sass.

''Well, you know I wasn't about to let 'em get away with *that*. Like I said, I was young and still pretty idealistic, not to mention bullheaded as sin. I'd probably have gone on with it, and told 'em where they could shove that file. But . . .'' She walked slowly to the French doors. ''They finally came up with a surefire way to shut my mouth.''

Rhett was almost afraid to ask what that might be. He wasn't sure how much more of this incredible story he could take. Before he could ask, though, she turned her back to the dark glass and folded her arms across her waist—a familiar protective gesture he finally understood—and went on in a quiet, musical voice, as if she were relating an amusing story.

''One night—actually, about three in the morning—I got a phone call saying that my parents' tour bus had collided with a tractor-trailer rig in a dense fog, somewhere on I-40 between Knoxville and Nashville, Tennessee.''

Rhett exploded in a barrage of swearing, most of it low and under his breath. She shook her head, gently smiling.

''Hold on a minute. I called up my brother to tell him the news. Well, he thought I was headed back to the rubber room for sure. Told me Mom and Dad were in Saint Louis right that very minute, that he'd talked to them both after their concert, and they'd been about to go to bed for the night. I don't need to tell you, I called 'em up anyway, just to make sure.''

Rhett let his breath out, feeling bludgeoned. ''So it was just a hoax?''

Again, that gentle smile. ''Yeah, but I got the message. They just wanted me to know they could make it happen, if they wanted to. To anyone and everyone I loved.'' She shrugged, and the smile slipped away. ''So . . . I went back to Texas and took up horse raisin'. And that's where I've been. Just . . . tryin' real hard . . . to forget.''

He didn't know what to say to her. On the one hand he had so many questions. He wanted to ask her who "they" were. He wondered if she even knew.

But on the other hand, he wished that, for a while, at least, he could just forget it had ever come up. He felt strangely relaxed, all of a sudden...limp and drained...as if, he thought, they'd just had a terrible quarrel and were coming around to the making up. He wanted to have things go back to the the way they'd been last night. He wanted to hold her...make love to her...pretend that none of it mattered.

But it wasn't going to be that simple. He knew it, and so did she. And neither of them knew quite where to go from there.

*Please, Rhett...hold me.*

If he would just hold me, she thought, it might be all right. I might be able to survive this.

But she wouldn't ask him. She was *still* bullheaded as sin.

He was frowning at her, as usual...his mouth opened, as if he meant to speak...she saw his hand move, as if reaching toward her. Her heart leapt into her throat and began to pulse there, frantically.

A tiny, electronic beeping shattered the taut silence. Such a commonplace sound; no reason why it should have made them both jerk as if they'd been shot.

Rhett looked at his watch as if he'd never seen it before. Dixie clapped her hand to her mouth to smother a horrified gasp. "Oh Lord—the kids. I forgot. We were supposed to pick them up...what time is it? Oh...damn."

She was furious with herself, almost in tears. Some part of her knew it was the emotional wringer she'd just been through, making her react out of all proportion to the seriousness of the situation, but she couldn't seem to control herself. "How could I have forgotten?" she cried, storming out of Rhett's study in search of her jacket. "How could I? They were looking forward to us going out tonight—oh, God, they must feel so abandoned...."

"Take it easy," Rhett said calmly, "I'm sure they're fine."

He was right there behind her, his car keys in his hand, reaching past her to open the door, touching her elbow as they clattered down the steps together. He opened the car door for her, waited until she'd pulled out her seat belt before closing it and going around to his side. So gentle and solicitous she began to feel faint and convalescent, a feeling she despised.

On the way to the stables Rhett drove with quiet competence, frowning only slightly, as if his mind were on a mildly troublesome case. Dixie sat coiled and silent, her elbow on the windowsill, hand clamped across her mouth, glaring furiously at nothing.

Once, when they were stopped at a traffic light, she moved her fingers from her mouth long enough to murmur, "Rhett, I'm sorry. I don't know how I let this happen."

He glanced over at her briefly, long enough for her to see his crooked little smile. For some reason, it made the ache inside her worse. "It wasn't your fault," he said softly. "I dropped a bombshell in your lap."

Not a bombshell, she thought. A bomb. One that had just blown their lives . . . her happiness . . . all to smithereens. But, as she knew all too well, that's the way life was, sometimes.

"I don't mean just this—forgetting the kids," she said in a flat, dull voice. "I mean . . . everything."

This time the look he threw her was dark and frowning, but they were turning into the riding stable complex, and there wasn't time to ask, or to explain.

It was full dark, and the floodlights around the arena and practice track had been turned off. There was a light on in the stable office, however. Rhett was heading for it with a long, hurrying stride, car keys still in his hand, Dixie close behind, when the door opened and one of the riding instructors—Sarah, a slender, impossibly young girl with blond hair cut short, like a boy's—came out. She'd pulled the door shut and was turning, hitching her jacket on over her shoulders, when she saw them.

"Oh, hi," she piped in her teenager's voice. "I'm sorry, we're closing right now. Um . . . can I help you?" Then, as recognition came, "Oh—hi, Dixie. Did . . . one of the kids leave something? I didn't see anything when I was closing up, but . . ."

"They're not here?" Rhett interrupted in a hard, flat voice.

Dixie couldn't speak. She felt as though a giant hand had closed around her chest.

"Well . . . no." Sarah was looking from one of them to the other, a puzzled little frown accompanying her smile.

"They...left. I mean...I thought you knew. Their mom picked them up."

"*Oh God*..." The horrified whisper was Dixie's, and only she heard it. Rhett's voice rode over it, like the crack of a whip.

"*When?* How long ago did they leave?"

Sarah's smile had vanished. She seemed to shrink a little as she hugged her jacket around her. "I...I don't know—an hour ago, maybe. We'd just finished the lessons. That's why I thought—I mean, I made sure it was okay. The kids *said* she was their mom. I wouldn't just...let them go, you know, with *any*body." Her voice was rising, frightened.

"I know—it's okay." Rhett's throat was gravelly. He cleared it, paused a moment, then spoke very slowly, as if calming a child. "Can you tell me anything about where they might have gone? Did she...say anything? You know, to the children? Can you remember anything at all...the way she was dressed...?"

Sarah brightened. "She was pretty dressed up. Um...wearing a coat, you know, like she was going somewhere? And she seemed like she was sort of in a hurry. She like...kind of hassled the kids, you know?"

Rhett swore softly. After a moment's hesitation he said, "Yeah...listen, do you mind if I use your phone?"

Sarah looked very young and bewildered, almost dazed. "What? Oh, yeah...sure. I'll just—I'm really sorry. I thought...I mean, she was their *mom*."

"It's all right." Rhett gave the girl's arm a reassuring squeeze as he waited for her to unlock the office door. "You couldn't have known." His voice was calm...so low-pitched and even, only Dixie heard the desolation in it.


"Yeah...I understand. No, that's all right—you did the best you could. Uh-huh...okay, well...keep me posted. Yeah..." Rhett's chuckle was dry "...I'll be here."

He returned the phone to its place on his desktop, exhaled in a frustrated gust, then said to the heavyset cop in the rumpled overcoat who was occupying his chair, "Okay, that was the airport. Nothing. If they went that way, they're already long gone." He swore bitterly and resumed his pacing. "They had an hour, dammit. If they went straight to the airport...Hell, they could be anywhere by now."

The cop straightened up, making the chair creak. He coughed diffidently and rumbled, "Yeah, but it's more than likely they'd be headed for California. That's what her sister says. If they do..."

Rhett snorted. "They aren't going to go waltzing into LAX, that's for sure. Elaine's not *that* stupid. She'd take a round-about route. Say she took a shuttle to O'Hare..." He let it trail off, his mind simply too exhausted to confront the possibilities.

"Well..." The cop—Gervase, Rhett thought his name was—slapped the desktop and stood up. "We'll have the terminals covered—that's all we can do. If they slip through..."

Rhett came around in his pacing in time to catch Gervase's shrug. "What do you mean, *if they slip through?*" he demanded. "You're not going to let that happen, you understand me? You've got to stop her, dammit—she's got my kids!"

"Take it easy, Mr. Brown, we're doing everything we possibly can to get your kids back," Gervase said in his best calm-the-hysterical-victim voice. His eyes were sympathetic, though, and Rhett wondered if maybe the man had kids of his own. That thought, more than the words, helped him to get control of himself.

"Sorry," he muttered. "I know that." He pulled in a breath, steadying himself on the edge of the yawning void he'd been teetering on so precariously for the last several hours. He didn't want to ask, but he had to. His throat felt as if he'd swallowed cement. "Listen, tell me the truth, okay? What, uh..." He cleared his throat, to absolutely no effect. "What are the chances of finding my kids? I know this happens all the time. You must have some idea...."

Gervase coughed uneasily. "To tell you the truth, Mr. Brown, in cases of parental abduction like this, it pretty much depends on how far the abductor is willing to go to cover his tracks. If he—or she—is willing to give up everything—name, identity, even leave the country...well, they can be pretty hard to find. I don't know how well you know your wife..."

"*Ex*-wife," Rhett growled.

"Yeah ... right. Listen, Mr. Brown, my advice to you is, try to get some sleep, okay? There's not very much you can do right now, except stay by the phone and hope she calls. I'll have a uniformed officer bring that equipment over first thing in the morning, get you set up for a trace in case she does. Okay?''

''Yeah...okay.'' Rhett frowned, swallowed hard and added, ''Thanks. I appreciate it.''

''No problem,'' Gervase said gruffly, and touched his arm in a spontaneous gesture of sympathy. ''Meanwhile, try not to worry. We'll do everything humanly possible to get your kids back.''

Rhett just nodded. Gervase said, ''Stay with the phone—I'll show myself out. Hang in there....''

And he was left alone.

The house had never seemed so empty. It seemed to press against him like a great, suffocating weight, pushing him closer and closer to the edge of that void....

Where in the devil was Dixie?

# Chapter 15

It didn't take him long to find her. Even if he hadn't known already where she'd be, the rhythmic banging coming from the backyard would have led him straight to her, like the pinging of a homing beacon. Taking a flashlight out of a drawer in the kitchen, he crossed the lawn in the cold November darkness, stood at the base of the old elm tree and gazed up into its branches. They were shivering, now, against the pale light of a waning moon, shivering with each echoing *thump*.

In a state of jangled bemusement, he spoke her name softly, tucking it into one brief, silent interval. The banging stopped; the tree waited, suspenseful and still.

"Dixie," he said, with tenderness in his laughter, "how can you see to hammer in the dark?"

There was a pause, and then her voice came, accompanied by two more percussive thumps. "It doesn't *matter*... if it's dark, if you aren't too particular about what you...*hit.*"

"Well, don't hit me...I'm coming up."

She'd almost finished the roof, he saw as he hoisted himself through the trapdoor and onto the tree house's gently sloping floor. So he didn't try to stand up. Still in a half crouch, he thumbed on the flashlight.

"Turn that off," Dixie croaked. "Please..."

He did, but not before he'd seen her clearly, huddled in a corner with her face and forearms resting on her drawn up knees, the hammer dangling from one hand.

He let his breath out slowly and scrubbed a hand across his face. "Dixie..." His voice seemed too harsh in that soft, enfolding darkness. "In no way, shape or form are you to blame for this."

She didn't answer, and after a moment he said more gently, "Don't you think I know how you're feeling? I've tried pretty hard to blame myself. I keep thinking I should have seen this coming...should have taken more precautions...." His laugh was a contradiction, full of irony and sorrow. "I knew she'd play dirty, but I never thought... I thought she might try something before the hearing, but...my God, to do this—violate a court order...jeez, she could go to *jail*."

There was a faint rustling, a careful throat clearing. "I've been thinking," Dixie said, her voice still low and rusty. "I've tried real hard to hate her, but...the truth is, I don't know what I'd do, in her place. If I thought..."

"Yeah, well, she obviously *didn't* think," Rhett said roughly. He wasn't ready yet, himself, to give Elaine those allowances. "If she had, she'd have known she couldn't possibly get away with this!"

"Will she?" Dixie asked in a cracking voice. "Get away with it?"

Rhett was silent for a long time, forcing himself to look in to the yawning pit he'd been trying so hard to avoid. To his surprise, the edge of the precipice seemed to have retreated a little. The ground under his feet seemed more stable than it had since the moment he'd heard those terrible words: *Their mom picked them up....* Something the cop, Gervase, had said.

He took a deep breath. "I don't think she will, no." He couldn't imagine Elaine being willing to do what it would take to get away with it. To give up so much... She'd surprised him quite a few times, lately, it was true, but she was still basically the most selfish person he'd ever known.

He had to believe that. *He had to.*

"We're going to get those kids back," he said harshly. "And when we do..."

*"And then what?"* She didn't say it, but he heard it anyway, in the profoundness of her silence.

Rhett set the flashlight carefully aside and settled himself against the wall of the tree house, not touching Dixie, but close enough to do so. He put his head back with a sigh. It felt oddly comforting, being with her in that small, private space. For the first time in hours, he felt the rigid muscles in his neck and shoulders begin to relax. He felt the knot in his stomach begin to loosen, just a little.

"About that file," he said, his words slurring unexpectedly, "it's not true, is it? Any of it?" She didn't answer. After a moment he added softly, "If you tell me so, I'll believe you." He heard a note of pleading in it.

There was a faint, sticking sound, as if she'd tried to swallow. She whispered, "It isn't. But I can't prove it."

"I'd make it go away, if I could," he said, anguish thickening his voice. "I wish I could ... but I can't. You know that, don't you?"

There was no sound, but he knew she'd nodded.

After a long, cold, unbearably lonely time, he said huskily, "Dixie, I sure do need to hold you right now."

They found each other in the darkness, coming together, not in a blind rush, but unerringly, like magnets. They clung to each other tightly at first, trembling and tense with fear and relief. Then, gradually, little by little, their arms eased and their bodies melded ... They lowered themselves in subtle stages until they were lying, entwined together, on the rough plank floor.

So it was that Rhett Brown finally became one of the very few almost-forty-year-old candidates for State Attorney General ever to make love in a tree. It wasn't anything like the lighthearted, youthfully whimsical experience he'd imagined it would be.

There was no feverish urgency in their coupling, but rather a sweet and aching sadness ... an unconditional giving and receiving of each other's strength and care that reminded Rhett of the way people had held on to each other at his parents' funeral. So much grief ... so much heartache ... but so beautiful, too, that it seemed almost unbearable...like a requiem, he thought. A requiem for a lost love.

She cried when her release came. He wished to God he could have.

How would I survive it? he thought as he lay in the cold darkness with Dixie's warm body still enfolding him, feeling her quake and tremble. If I were to lose them—my children...Dixie...the people I love most in this world—how could I ever live through it?

But even as his aching heart asked the question, even as his mind rejected it, he knew that the answer was lying right there, in the woman he held so closely in his arms. Like her, like countless others before him, he *would* survive . . . find his purpose, and go on.

"Lolly?" Ethan said in a loud whisper. "Are you awake?"

For just a moment, Lolly thought about not answering. There had been a time, she knew, when she wouldn't have, or at the very least said something mean, like, "Well, I am *now*, pea-brain, thanks a lot!" But for some reason, this time she didn't mind.

She turned on her side and propped her head on her hand. It wasn't very dark—she'd noticed that it never really got dark, here—so she could see Ethan sitting up cross-legged in the other twin bed. She could see that he had his arms wrapped around his new Mickey Mouse, with his chin propped between its ears. She could even see that his eyes were big and round.

"Yeah, I'm awake," she whispered back. "What's the matter? Can't you sleep?" Ethan shook his head. "Well, why not? After all that walking around we did today, I should think you'd be exhausted." Exhausted...that was a word her mother used a lot. Lolly thought it sounded much more grown-up than "tired."

"I am 'sausted," said Ethan with a sigh. "I just can't go to sleep. Lolly, will you sing me a song? Like Dixie does? Please . . . ?"

"You know I can't sing," Lolly said irritably, but not unkindly. "Why don't you...just lie down and try to go to sleep? An inspired thought came to her. "Close your eyes and think about how much fun we had today at Disneyland. That ought to do it."

"I did that already." Ethan's voice sounded sulky. But after a while he heaved another big sigh and said, "Lolly? I wish Dixie was here, don't you?" And Lolly could tell he was about ready to cry.

She really didn't want Ethan to cry. The thought made her feel scared and lonely.

She said impatiently, "Mom's here, isn't she? You said how much you missed her."

"I know," Ethan sniffed, "but now I miss Dixie. And Dad. I want to go home."

Lolly wanted to go home, too. She missed Star, and her own bedroom with all her things in it and the window seat that looked out over the whole backyard. She missed Dad and Dixie. They hadn't even got to finish the tree house.

"Well," she snapped, "we can't go home. You heard what Mom said. The judge changed his mind, and we have to live with her and Bob, now. It's the law. I told you—that's the way it is when your parents get divorced. You have to live where the judge tells you to. Anyway—" she tossed her head, more to make herself feel better than anything—"it won't be so bad, when we move. Mom says the new house is almost ready, and then we're going to have our own rooms, and a pool and everything. Plus, we'll be close to the beach. You'll like that, won't you?" Her voice was almost pleading.

"I . . . g-guess . . . s-so," sobbed Ethan.

Lolly couldn't stand it. In another minute, she was going to cry, too. She was never going to forgive Ethan if that happened. She swallowed hard a couple of times then said, "Ethan? If you stop crying, I'll let you get in bed with me."

There was a pause, a sniffle, and then a really pitiful, "O . . . kay." Ethan bounced off of his bed and came scrambling into hers, Mickey Mouse and all.

"All right, now, for heaven's sakes, *be still,*" she ordered in a loud whisper, as he squirmed down into the pillows, taking up more than his share.

Lolly lay down, too, but she didn't close her eyes. She was thinking very, very hard. She thought about Star, and the unfinished tree house, and about the judge, and his stupid old law and how unfair it was. And she thought about her dad who was a lawyer, probably the best lawyer in the whole world, and she remembered one time she'd asked him exactly what it was that lawyers did, and he'd told her that lawyers help people who are having trouble with the law....

After a while she began to sing, very softly, "The farmer in the dell, the farmer in the dell...Hi-ho, the derry-oh, the farmer in the dell..."

When the phone rang, Rhett jerked and grabbed for it like a contestant on a quiz show. The uniformed cop sitting on the corner of his desk held up a warning finger; Rhett nodded grimly, his hand frozen on the still cradled receiver. The phone rang again. He silently counted seconds until the cop nodded, then, in perfect sync, picked up the receiver just as the cop punched a button on the console spread out in front of him.

"Hello?" he said, with a calm that belied the rapid thudding of his heard.

"Rhett?"

He closed his eyes, then quickly opened them again and shook his head at the cop. "Lucy... hi," he breathed.

"Yep, it's just me." His sister's voice sounded apologetic, which was something he didn't think he'd ever heard before. "You were hoping it was someone else, I know. Still no news, huh?"

Rhett sighed and said, "It's only been two days, Luce." But his heart sat like a lump of lead in his chest, and he avoided looking at the cop. They both knew that the chances of finding a missing child dwindled with every passing hour.

"Well, it's been all over the news—the children's pictures and everything. Mike's even got it in his column—I think it'll be out tomorrow. Rhett, somebody's got to know where they are. Maybe someone will see it...."

"I know... thanks, Luce. And tell Mike thanks, too."

"I will." Her voice seemed to catch before she added, "Gwen says to tell you we're all praying for you."

Rhett was rubbing methodically at his temples with the middle finger and thumb of one hand. He smiled and murmured, "Thanks... I guess I could use it."

"Rhett, how's Dixie?"

"She's fine." His voice softened as he glanced over at her, curled like a squirrel in his reading chair. "She's—" The phone

suddenly beeped in his ear. "Oops—hold on a minute, got another call." He punched the disconnect button, then said,
"Yes—hello?"

"Rhett?"

His heart dropped out of his chest. His eyebrows shot up; he
stabbed a look at the cop and made a frantic gesture with his
free hand, then fought for control while his pulse rate went
clear off the scale. "Elaine," he said, and his voice cracked
anyway. He felt light-headed, and cold as ice.

He frowned at the cop, who was holding a receiver to his ear
and making circling motions with his hand that meant, "Keep
her talking as long as you can." But suddenly he couldn't think
what to say to her...to the woman he'd been married to for
fifteen years, the woman who had borne his children. The
woman who had taken them away.

"Rhett..."

Something was wrong. His body knew it already; it had gone
absolutely still, suspended in a kind of nothingness that was like
death. His ears had picked up the unnaturally high pitch of her
voice...his mind had registered it as fear. *Elaine—afraid?*

He found that he was standing, with no recollection of having done so. And that Dixie was suddenly there, right beside
him. He groped for her hand as he growled, "Elaine, what is
it, dammit? *What have you done with my kids?*"

Her laugh was brittle, like glass breaking. "I guess that
means...they're not there with you?"

He couldn't control the sharp intake of his breath. "What
the hell do you—"

"Rhett, I'm sorry..." Elaine's voice was thin and airless as
a child's whimper. A terrified child. "I didn't think—Oh,
Rhett, I'm afraid..."

He was gripping Dixie's hand so hard he wondered that her
fingers didn't break; it was the only thing keeping him from
falling into the void. From somewhere outside himself he heard
a firm, commanding voice say, "Tell me what's happened.
*Now.*"

"Oh, Rhett..." He heard a quivering indrawn breath. "The
children...I think they've run away."

* * *

"That's funny," said Lucy as she hung up the phone in the middle of the recording that was saying, "If you'd like to make a call..."

Her husband placed a cup of coffee on the table in front of her and bent down to kiss the top of her head before pulling out a chair for himself. "What is?"

"I just got cut off. Oh God, Mike..." She dropped her face into her hands, ruthlessly holding back the slippery side wings of her hair. "I hope everything's okay."

"Lucy," Mike said severely, "quit blaming yourself."

"I'm not—"

"Yes, you are—I can see those little wheels going around and around in there, saying, 'If only I hadn't meddled, if I hadn't sent Dixie...'"

"Well," Lucy flared, "maybe it's true. Gwen told me nudging fate might be dangerous. Who knows? I might have set something in motion..."

"Hey," Mike said gently, reaching across the table to take her hand, "I think you're giving yourself too much credit. Aren't you forgetting? Sometimes fate—or Providence—works in mysterious ways."

He smiled, and his eyes took on a certain glow, and she knew he was thinking of the same thing she was... of a certain Chicago high rise still under construction, and of a fire—definitely arson—started with a little pile of clothing and an Oreo cookie wrapper....

"Yes," Lucy whispered, "sometimes it does." She closed her eyes, and still holding tightly to her husband's hand, began to pray.

"I have to go... God, I wish..."

"I know you do, I know..."

Their voices were whispers in the dark, urgent and breaking, breathless with pain.

"I have to be there—I can't stand it, being so far away."

"I know—I just wish I could go, too..."

"God, I wish you could come, but... you have to be here in case they... in case someone calls."

"I know... I know..."

He was holding her so tightly... so tightly, with a kind of desperation, she thought. She could feel their hearts bumping against each other, echoing each other's rhythms. She held on to him just as tightly, but with more poignancy than desperation. Soaking up his warmth and drinking in his tremendous strength and vitality as though she were about to embark on a lonely journey across an endless, trackless desert. That was what her life would be like, she knew, without him....

"I'll be back," he whispered raggedly in her ear. "I promise."

She couldn't hold back the sound she made, more like the cry of a wounded bird than a laugh. Rhett pulled back a little, just enough to ask her what was wrong.

"That's the last thing Peter ever said to me," she told him, trying to laugh it off even though her tears had started to fall.

He gathered her close and held her even more tightly than before, kissed her and then, bowing his head, buried his face in her hair. "It's not the same," he growled, his voice muffled by his own emotions. "*It's not the same, do you hear me?* You're not going to lose me. Me, *or* the kids. I'm coming back, and I'm bringing them with me. *You're not going to lose us—understand?*"

She nodded. He kissed her once—hard—and was gone.

Dixie was hammering nails into the last board on the roof of the tree house late the next morning when she heard the crunch of tires on the brick driveway. She let the hammer drop to the ground and scrambled after it, but checked when she reached the bottom of the tree trunk ladder and saw the stocky figure in the dark overcoat striding toward her across the frost-burned lawn.

"Mr. Hendricks... hi," she said as she pulled her sweatshirt hood over her hair and went to meet him, not even trying to keep the note of puzzlement out of her voice. "I'm sorry, but Rhett's not here right now. He had to leave for California late last night. The children..."

"I know that, Dixie... I know that. He called me before he went. Say, I'm just so darn sorry about what's happened. Can't imagine what Rhett must be going through. Actually, though, you're the one I came to see." His eyes were sparkling and his nose and cheeks rosy with the cold, so that he looked like a kindly uncle standing there, smiling at her and puffing out vapor.

"So . . . this is the tree house I've heard so much about." He strolled over to the elm tree and reached out to touch the trunk, leaning on it as if testing its strength, at the same time staring up into its branches, exactly the way Rhett had once . . . it seemed so long ago.

"He told you about it?" Dixie asked faintly.

He looked at her in surprise. "Oh, you bet he did. Talks about you a lot, as a matter of fact. From what he tells me, you've done one helluva lot for Rhett and those kids."

"Oh . . . well," she mumbled, uncomfortable and squirming, "I . . . they mean a lot to me. I'm . . . very fond of them."

"I know you are, Dixie . . . I know you are." Newt Hendricks dusted his hands carefully and buried them in the pockets of his overcoat. In a thoughtful, almost musing tone, still squinting up into the tree, he said, "They're pretty fond of you, too."

"Uh . . . Mr. Hendricks, would you like to come inside? Can I get you some . . . coffee, or something?" Dixie was beginning to feel very cold herself. Cold, and uncertain.

"No, thank you," said Newt, "I can't really stay . . ." He began walking slowly back toward the house. Dixie had to shorten her stride to keep pace with him.

"Mr. Hendricks," she blurted, when they were about halfway there, "you don't like me very much, do you?"

Newt gave a short bark of laughter and looked over at her. But his eyes were serious and his voice quiet when he said, "That's not true, Dixie, I like you fine." He looked down at his foot, watched it kick at a clump of frosty grass. "It's what you're doin' to my boy that I don't like."

"I don't know what you mean," Dixie said. Her lips felt numb.

He glanced at her again and said softly, "Oh, I think you do." They'd reached the flagstone patio. Through the French doors they could see Rhett's desk . . . the lamp Dixie had left burning there . . . the telephone, still hooked up to the police recording and tracing equipment.

Newt nodded toward the desk. He said almost conversationally, "I'm the one who gave Rhett your FBI file, you know that, don't you?"

Dixie nodded; she hadn't known, hadn't even thought about it. It hadn't mattered *who*. It didn't matter now. She said dully, "Of course."

Newt chuckled. "You know, he fired me when I gave that file to him. Ah, well ... That's okay—he'll get over it. He knows I've got his best interests at heart." He paused. "He'd like me to make it go away, but you and I both know I can't do that." There was another, longer pause, before he shook his head and looked up at her, squinting against the cold November sun. "Because, the fact is, if I could get my hands on that file, somebody else can, too. And believe me, they will."

Dixie didn't say anything. She jammed her clenched hands together in the front pocket of her sweatshirt and stared fixedly over Newt Hendricks' head. *Stubborn as sin ...*

Newt said quietly, "He means to marry you, you know."

Dixie jerked slightly and moved her lips, but no sound came out. She heard Newt sigh.

"Well, I don't guess he'd be the first man to give up a kingdom for a woman...."

She made herself look at him; he was gazing thoughtfully across the yard, looking at the tree house. She cleared her throat and this time was able to move words past her frozen lips. "I don't know what you mean."

Newt's shaggy head snapped back to her, his eyes glinting like the sun on frost. "Let me ask you something, Dixie. How well do you think you know Rhett Brown? How much do you *believe* in him? Because I'll tell you something—I've known Rhett Brown for fifteen years, ever since he first started practicing law in this town. And I know what *he* believes in. I know what his goals are. And I believe he can reach those goals. He's got what it takes. But, dammit, Dixie, the man's not made of stainless steel! No one is, nowadays. Things like this stick to a man. They can cost him. Maybe not a lot, but enough to make a difference between winning an election, and losing. And that would be a damn, cryin' shame."

There was a long pause. Then he touched her arm and moved past her. "You think about that, Dixie. Think about it long and hard. That's all I'm askin' you to do."

Dixie didn't answer. Didn't dare nod, or swallow, or breathe for fear of dislodging the tears that coated her eyes like a crystal veneer.

"You know, Dixie..." She dashed a hand across her eyes and turned to glare at the stocky, dark-coated figure framed in the brick archway. "That wife of Rhett's—she was a beautiful woman, too, but selfish. Very selfish." There was a pause. "I don't think you're like that."

And then he was gone.

The phone in Rhett's office had begun to ring. Dixie clamped a hand over her mouth to stifle a quivering sob, and ran to answer it.

"May I speak to Mr. Brown, please?" said a masculine voice, with the unmistakable ring of officialdom.

"Um...I'm sorry, he's not here. Can I—"

"Who am I speaking to, please?"

"I'm, uh...his children's nanny. Dixie Parish. Who is this?"

"Yes...this is the Laguna Beach Police Department, Ms. Parish. I'm trying to get in touch with Mr. Brown. I believe...we have something here that belongs to him...uh, Ms. Parish?"

But she had her hand clamped across her mouth again, and was shaking with laughter, and crying too hard to reply.

"Now, you listen to me, Lucy!" Rhett shouted into the phone, "I know she's there, dammit!" A quick glance out the French doors caused him to moderate his tone to a raspy growl. "Let me talk to her."

"You haven't changed a bit, have you, Rhett?" Lucy said waspishly. "You still think you can order me around. Look— she asked me not to, so I'm not going to. That's it. Leave me alone." Typically, his sister's voice was escalating, growing angry. "I don't even want to get into it. I don't know what you did to her, but—"

"I don't know, either, dammit! That's the whole point—I need—ah, hell." He was silent for a moment, watching his children outside on the patio pelting each other with the first meager snowfall of the season. Their shouts and squeals made him feel warm and syrupy inside…a kind of melting glow that spread outward from his heart, into his muscles and nerves and bones, and finally, into his voice, when he finally spoke again.

"Lucy…all I can say, is…I love her. I told her I wanted to marry her. Something must have happened while I was in California, to make her leave like that, without telling me why, without even saying goodbye to the kids. I have to know what it is—she owes me that much. Please, Lucy…"

He heard a sigh, and then his sister said in a voice suddenly gone small and shaky, "I don't think she can, Rhett. I don't know what to do. I've never seen anyone hurt so badly. I just don't think she *can* talk to you. I think she just wants to be left alone."

"If she wanted to be left alone," Rhett exploded, "why in hell didn't she just go back to Texas? I wouldn't even know where to look for her there! Why in the hell is she staying at your place? She must have known—"

"Oh, well…" Making a quick recovery, Lucy cleared her throat and said in a tone of self-righteous innocence he knew all too well, "She *wanted* to go back to Texas right away. She was just going to pick up her trailer and then leave. But Rosie's colt was…well, since Dixie left he'd picked up so many bad habits…. I don't know, maybe Rosie and I spoil him. But he *bites*, for God's sake! What can you do with a horse that bites? You can't have him around kids, that's for sure—can't even sell him, right? So, anyway, I asked Dixie, since she was supposed to train him, if she'd at least stay long enough…"

"Lucy," Rhett breathed, "thank you. I don't know whether you're a devil or an angel, sometimes, but…I love you. *Thank you.*"

"Maybe you have changed," Lucy said thoughtfully. "You've never said *that* to me before." And then, before he could respond, added in a voice that was soft, and suspiciously husky, "See you *soon*, Rhett. Don't take too long…"

Rhett was already dropping the receiver into its cradle. He crossed the room in two strides and threw open the French doors, letting in the sweet, cold November wind. "Ethan— Lolly! Come on, let's go!"

Their footsteps thumped across the flagstones, scuffing through the well-stirred and rapidly melting slush. They halted before him, red-cheeked and sparkly-eyed, clapping their snowy mittens in an excess of childish energy. Rhett's throat filled, just looking at them, thinking how close he'd come to... He couldn't bear to think about it.

"Where, Dad? Where are we going?"

"We're going to find Dixie," he growled, gathering them in, hugging them close, one against each side, "and bring her home."

"Try the barn," Lucy told him a few short—and much too long—hours later, tucked under his arm like a little brown hen as they walked together from his car to the back porch of the old white farmhouse. He'd forgotten how tiny she was. "My guess would be the loft—there's a new litter of kittens up there." She lowered her voice, chuckling in that rusty nail way he remembered. "If you ask me, I think she's hiding from Rosie. That child is just like a dog, you know? She always seems to know when you're feeling blue, and she sticks to you like a little cocklebur."

"Thanks, Lucy." Rhett's throat felt as if he might have swallowed some of those cockleburs. And his chest was tight...tight with what he knew was fear. He pulled his sister into a quick, hard hug, cleared his throat and said, "Uh...are you sure the kids are going to be all right? They can't get into any trouble?"

He could hear their voices down by the hog shelters—Ethan's excited shouts, at least, and Rose Ellen's bossy, scratchy voice that was so much like her mother's. Lolly would be quieter, of course—as the oldest, very conscious of her dignity. And the more so, recently, since her brief but hair-raising brush with the law. God...Rhett had to shake his head and smile, if a bit ruefully, whenever he thought about the way that little girl of his had taken matters into her own hands out there in California. It scared him to think about the years ahead of him...he was going to have his hands full with that child, he could tell. She did have a selfish streak that was too much like her mother's for comfort, but unless he was very much mistaken, the world hadn't heard the last of Lauren Elizabeth Brown!

"Of *course* they can get into trouble," Lucy said placidly. "That's what kids *do*. Go on, now—if they do, Rosie and Gwen and I will look after them. You go and take care of Dixie."

"I will," Rhett said huskily. "I mean to do just that." He started down the lane.

"Rhett?"

He turned. Lucy was still standing where he'd left her, her hands in the pockets of her overalls, the sun on her face and the wind lifting the wings of her hair. Something about her brought tears springing to his eyes, even before she spoke.

"By the way... welcome home."

He nodded and walked on, carrying the lump now in his throat. To ease it, he tried filling his lungs with the cold, clean air, but that brought its own poignancy, along with the memories. He'd forgotten how big the sky was out here in the western plains... forgotten how black the soil was, and how the winds always seemed to blow. Forgotten how good the sun could feel, on a day like this. Forgotten how much warmth it could carry to the sheltered places, out of the wind....

The loft was one such place. Dixie had found it, like the little calico mother cat before her. He found them both there, dozing in the sweet prairie hay, in the rectangle of sunlight cast by the open loft door. The mother cat stirred when he came silently over the top of the ladder, shot one paw and chirruped softly, then curled herself more closely around her tangle of sleeping kittens.

Dixie was lying on her side with her knees drawn up and her head pillowed on her arm. He couldn't tell if she was asleep or not.

Quietly, carefully, Rhett stretched himself out behind her... put his arm around her and buried his face in her thick, soft, sweet-smelling hair. She tensed, and turned in his arms, and he saw her eyes flare with recognition, with consternation, with hope... with joy. And then she closed them with a sigh, and kissed him.

He knew then, for the first time, that it was going to be all right.

There were no questions or exclamations or recriminations, no talking at all, not at first. He couldn't stop kissing her... never wanted to stop kissing her, ever again. He kissed her mouth, her eyes, her ears, her throat... pushed up her sweater—roughly, almost defiantly—and kissed her breasts, and her belly and then her breasts again. He'd wanted to, for so long.

It was, he thought later, a little like tossing a match into a haystack.

*Here* was all the passion, all the urgency they'd both held back before. Here was the joy and youthful abandon they'd dreamed of without even knowing it, longed for and denied themselves for so many barren years.

Dixie thought of those years as they undressed each other feverishly, kissing, nipping and nibbling at whatever part of the other they could reach. Then they were altogether naked, and she was lying on her back with Rhett's fingers laced in hers and his hard body pressing her down into the billowing hay, and her legs twining around him, and she heard them both panting... gasping... laughing... whispering words of love and promises... and she didn't think of anything at all.

For those moments, as she closed her eyes and wrapped her arms and legs around him and felt her body break... and cry... and joyfully welcome him... for those moments, at least, nothing of reason, and honor, and nobility and sacrifice mattered. Nothing mattered but this... her man, her love... with her at last.

"What if someone comes?" she asked feebly, a long time later, when her heartbeat and breathing had slowed enough to allow her to speak.

Rhett's chuckle was soft and thick. "A little late for that, isn't it?" He kissed her a long, sweetly lingering time, then murmured, "It's all right—no one will. Lucy will see to that."

"Rhett..." Her throat tightened; her words broke. "I can't let you do this."

"Too late for that, too," he said tenderly, moving inside her. "I've already done it."

"I mean... I can't let you give up... everything. For me."

"Who said I was going to?" His eyes were soft, amused.

"Newt—Mr. Hendricks. He said—"

"Ah," said Rhett, nodding sagely. He kissed her nose. "Don't worry about him. I fired him."

"He told me. But he's right, Rhett. It could cost you..."

"It could," he agreed, and thoughtfully kissed her again. "That's a gamble I'm willing to take."

"Rhett..." her voice broke "...are you sure I'm worth the risk?"

This time when he kissed her, it wasn't gentle, or thoughtful. It was fierce, passionate, almost, she thought... angry.

"You," he growled, when he finally lifted his mouth from hers, leaving it bruised and throbbing, "us... this... what we have together... is the only thing that *is* worth risking everything for. It *is* everything—do you understand? The only thing that's important. I know that now. And believe me, I mean never to forget it. Besides..." He rolled to his side, taking her with him, safely wrapped in his arms. "I'm not sure the risk is all that great."

"What do you mean?" She asked it in a whisper, hardly daring to hope.

Under her head, his shoulder moved in a shrug. "I mean, things have changed. Attitudes have changed. There's a demand for...call it accountability...today that wasn't there ten years ago. I mean..." he pressed a hard kiss to her forehead "...it's time you were exonerated. And Peter Grant, too. I intend to open up the can of worms you dropped in my lap, lady. And then... we'll see what happens." He laughed softly, confidently. "You've already got a great big ally in the press, you know."

She raised herself shakily on one elbow. "Really? Who?"

"Your soon-to-be-brother-in-law, of course. Mike Lanagan—ever hear of him? This kind of crusade is right up his alley." He wrapped her in his arms again and pulled her down to him with a gusty sigh. "Ah... Dixie. I don't know how you thought I'd ever let you go." There was a pause, and when he spoke again his voice sounded almost savage. "Listen—divorce is hell. I wouldn't wish it on my worst enemy—but if that's what I had to go through to have you in my life, then it was *right*. You understand? No one should go through life with the wrong person—*no one*."

"But," she protested in sudden, unreasoning panic, "I'm not perfect, Rhett. We're so different...."

"Hey, you tried that on me once before, remember?"

"But," she insisted, "I don't know how I'll fit into the life you live. Politics is compromise, and I don't do that very well. I'm stubborn and bullheaded as sin. I'm loud and brassy, and I hate wearing dresses, and..." She stopped suddenly. "Oh God, Rhett—I just thought of something."

"Mmm...what's that?" He sounded amused, tender.

She propped herself up on her elbow again, earnest and serious. "I mean, here you are, destined for greatness—are you sure you want to be saddled with a wife named *Dixie?*"

She'd wanted to see his face—and it was a study. She bit down on her lower lip as she watched the war that was being waged inside him played out there—the old Rhett doing battle with the new. The stuffed shirt versus the poet.

The poet won, hands down.

She felt her heart fill up with love and light as a smile broke slowly across his handsome but somewhat austere features, like a sunrise across a rugged and beautiful land.

"Dixie...absolutely. It's great! Perfect. Maybe even appropriate—you know...The South Shall Rise Again...."

He rolled her over in the hay, laughing.

It was only a little later, drowsy and satiated with sunshine and sex and happiness, that she heard him murmur, "And it's sure as hell no worse than Lady Bird...."

# Epilogue

An inch of snow had fallen by the time Lucy slipped through the big barn door and pulled it shut after her. New flakes brushed her cheeks with icy, wind-driven kisses as she stuffed her gloved hands deep into the pockets of her slicker and set off up the lane to where the farmhouse waited, like a little white hen, she often thought with affection, to welcome her into its shelter and warmth.

As she did so often on this same short journey, she found herself drinking deeply of the cold, winey air and feeling her throat swell and her eyes sting with the almost unbearable joy of *being*. Of being *here*, in the one place on earth she wanted to be, the place she'd always known she belonged.

Well...maybe not always. To be honest, there'd been a brief time in her youth when she'd thought the world might have something better to offer. But her parents had died and she'd come home to run the farm, and then she'd met Mike, and...it was true, as she'd told Aunt Gwen more than once, that Providence had known what was best for her, after all.

The snow squeaked beneath the soles of her rubber boots as she trudged along, a sound that always reminded her of her childhood, the thrill of that first snowfall. She liked winter—winter was the quiet time on a farm, a time when she could spend a morning in the cozy old barn teaching a steaming-wet new baby calf how to nurse, and not feel the least bit guilty about it.

Although she *did* feel a little guilty about leaving most of the work of preparing Thanksgiving dinner to Gwen—the more so because she much preferred the barn to the kitchen, and always had. But calving heifers and farrowing sows were famous for not respecting holidays—Lucy couldn't remember an uninterrupted Christmas or Easter morning. Besides, she told herself, Gwen had plenty of help from Chris and Dixie, and from Mike, too. Quite frankly, Lucy was glad her husband had had a good reason to stay out of the barn. Bless him, his intentions were good, but the fact was, just the mention of the word *childbirth* was enough to make him turn green.

On the other hand . . . She felt her insides go mushy and her cold lips curve with a smile as she thought how nice it had been to have both Earl and Rhett there to lend a hand with the calf-pulling. The sight of Rhett in an old pair of overalls, with his tie off and his sleeves rolled up . . . ah, that had almost been worth having a first-calf heifer with a backward delivery in a snowstorm on Thanksgiving Day!

It was only a little after two now, but with the storm settling in, twilight had come early; lights were already burning in the farmhouse windows. They would all be sitting down to Thanksgiving dinner, she thought, taking their places around the big oak kitchen table, which would be covered with Mama's good lace tablecloth—the long one—and all three leaves in for the first time since Mama and Daddy died. . . .

Oh boy, thought Lucy, and paused for a moment at the top of the steps to wait for the unexpected lump in her throat and the stinging in her nose and eyes to subside. Then she opened the screen door and went into the porch, stomping mud and snow off her boots, just the way Dad always used to do when he came in from chores.

She could hear them in there, in the warm, fragrant kitchen, all laughing and talking at once, arguing, as usual, over who should carve the turkey.

". . . Here—let Rhett do it. He's got seniority."

"Oh, ho . . . low blow!"

"Ouch! Watch it, little brother—your day is coming. . . ."

"Yeah, Wood, everybody's got to turn forty sooner or later."

"Gwen—leave that and come and *sit down!*"

"Hey, maybe Mike should do it . . ."

"Not me, I cooked the blasted thing. If you ask me—"

"Why does it have to be a man who carves the turkey?" That was Dixie, poor innocent. Lucy grinned to herself as she listened to Chris's cool reply.

"Shh—don't you know? It's like outdoor cooking—if we ever let on we know how, then we'll get stuck with it from now on."

"Ho, ho—*now* we know!"

"Oh, *brother!*"

There were more shouts of protest and laughter, and then Rhett's voice, taking charge, naturally.

"Here—Mike, you do the honors. It's only right, as head of the household . . ."

"Says who?" That was Mike, catching Lucy's eye and winking as she came through the door.

"Well, *somebody* carve the darn thing," she said tartly as she passed through the kitchen on her way to the washroom across the hall, "or maybe we should all just fall on it like a pack of wild dogs. . . ."

She hid a smile as she listened to the laughter and her brothers' hoots and groans.

But when she came back after washing up and running a quick comb through her hair, she found the kitchen unnaturally quiet. There was expectancy in the silence, and in the six pairs of eyes that watched her cross the room to take her place at the foot of the table.

"What?" she demanded suspiciously. And then, without waiting for an explanation, scolded, "You guys shouldn't have waited for me. Where are the kids? Did you feed them, at least?"

"They're at the little table in the parlor—already taken care of," said Mike quietly. Then he looked at Rhett. Everyone else did, too.

Rhett pushed back his chair and stood up. He held out the bone-handled carving knife and fork with both hands, as if it were a sword of honor, cleared his throat and said, "Uh . . . Lucy, we took a vote, and it's unanimous."

"What is? What vote?" Lucy asked uneasily, her eyes seeking Mike's as if they were on a homing beacon. She found them soft and reassuring, glowing with affection and love.

Then she looked back at Rhett—and to her absolute shock, found almost the same expression in his eyes, too. Her throat began to swell, and she knew a moment of utter panic. *Oh, please, God, don't let me cry!*

Rhett fiddled with the tablecloth, rearranged his water glass. Lucy saw him reach for Dixie's hand, saw her give his hand a squeeze, and then he took a deep breath and looked straight at Lucy, scowling, of course—same old Rhett. "Uh, see, Luce... the way we see it, if anybody can claim to be head of this household, it's you—now wait a minute... just shush, for a change. Okay?" He coughed, and when he went on, his voice wasn't quite steady. "You're the one who stepped into Dad's shoes when nobody else would. You're the one who made a go of this place... kept it here... for us to come back to." He paused.

Lucy snapped, "Well, I knew you would—sooner or later."

Everyone laughed, the kind of relieved laughter that eases aching throats and postpones the threat of tears. Rhett ahem'd loudly and said, "So, anyway, it's Thanksgiving, and we all want to say thank you. So... here you are, little sister. You do the honors."

He solemnly placed the bone-handled carving set in her hands. Earl—she was never going to be able to call him Wood—got up from his chair and picked up the turkey on its heavy serving platter and set it in the place that had been hastily cleared in front of her. Panic-stricken, Lucy looked over at Gwen. The old lady's eyes, crinkled as if with imminent laughter, were shining with a film of tears. She slowly nodded. Lucy took a deep breath and stared down at the glistening honey brown turkey, which was shimmering and blurring alarmingly.

"We should say grace," she said in a cracking voice. "Dad always said grace."

There was a murmur of agreement. Hands not already joined, reached... found one another and held tight.

Lucy took a deep breath. "Father, we thank you..."

*Daddy...Mama...we're all here. All of your chil-
dren...together again. But it's not the same without you....*

There were murmurs of "Amen." Feet shuffling, throats
clearing. Then once again Rhett spoke softly. "How 'bout a
song? That one we always used to sing...Dixie?"

She nodded and pushed back her chair. Everyone else stood
up, too. Dixie ducked out into the hall and a moment later was
back with a guitar cradled against her chest. She drew her fingers across the strings, then looked at Rhett and nodded.

And then, holding Dixie's eyes with his, smiling the way he
used to smile, Rhett began to sing in the beautiful baritone
voice Lucy hadn't heard in more than thirteen years—her parents' funeral had been the last time. After the first few notes,
Earl joined him, taking the harmony, and then Dixie, and even
Chris. Gwen watched, nodding and smiling. The children came
to stand in the doorway and listen: Ethan and Rosie jostling for
position, Lolly holding the baby, Eric.

*"We gather together..."*

Lucy was glad to have an excuse not to sing. But, as everybody knew, she couldn't carry a tune in a bucket.

As she watched them all through a rainbow shimmer of
happy tears...Gwen and Mike, Earl and his beautiful, pregnant Chris, Rhett and Dixie, both looking so happy...for a
moment, just a moment, she was sure she saw two more gathered there. *A slender woman with soft brown curls, also cradling a guitar...and a big, quiet man in overalls, proudly
smiling, but not singing. Everyone knew Ed Brown couldn't
carry a tune in a bucket, either.*

And all at once Lucy was laughing, not caring if the tears *did*
fall. She wanted to shout with joy and thanksgiving.

*Mama, Daddy, we made it. All of your children are finally
home....*

Then, as she looked at Gwen and saw her laughter reflected
there in those wise old eyes, she silently amended her prayer:

*"...with a little help from Providence."*

\* \* \* \* \*

# INTIMATE MOMENTS®
## Silhouette®

# COMING NEXT MONTH

### #679 HIDE IN PLAIN SIGHT—Sara Orwig
*Heartbreakers*

Safeguarding single mom Rebecca Bolen and her two cuddly kids from a crazed killer was tying Detective Jake Delancy into some serious knots. He'd had worse assignments, more crafty adversaries, but he'd *never* before taken his work to heart—or fallen in love....

### #680 FIVE KIDS, ONE CHRISTMAS—Terese Ramin

They'd married for the sake of the children, but Helen wanted more. She *needed* Nat Crockett as surely as any love-struck bride. Only problem was, Nat didn't seem to share her newlywed notions. But with mistletoe and five darling matchmakers, Helen vowed to change his mind.

### #681 A MAN TO DIE FOR—Suzanne Brockmann

One minute her life was normal, the next Carrie Brooks was on the run with a man she hardly knew. Felipe Salazar *was* dangerous, but he'd somehow captured her trust. And while she knew in her heart to stand by him, only the face of death revealed the extent of her devotion.

### #682 TOGETHER AGAIN—Laura Parker
*Rogues' Gallery*

*How dare he?* Meryl Wallis knew James Brant for the power-hungry tycoon he was. She'd loved him once, only to be betrayed. Now he *needed* her to save his reputation. Well, she had control this time around—of everything but herself....

### #683 THE MOM WHO CAME TO STAY—Nancy Morse

Native American Trace McCall had done his best, but there were some things he simply couldn't teach his preteen daughter. So when Jenna Ward took an interest in his parenting dilemma, he figured there was no harm in letting her "play" a maternal role. Then he found he wanted her—for real.

### #684 THE LAST REAL COWBOY—Becky Barker

Jillian Brandt knew there was no place safer than Trey Langden's remote ranchland—and rugged embrace. Her enemies were getting closer, and her life depended on staying out of sight. But hiding away with her former love posed problems of a very different sort....

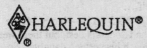

**Silhouette**

**SPECIAL EDITION**

is proud to announce the latest
miniseries by SHERRYL WOODS

AND BABY MAKES THREE

Discover how the Adams men of Texas all find
love—and fatherhood—in most unexpected ways!

Watch for the very first book in this series, coming in December:

**A CHRISTMAS BLESSING** (Special Edition #1001)

Luke Adams didn't know anything about delivering babies. But when
his widowed sister-in-law showed up on his doorstep about to give
birth, he knew he'd better learn fast!

And don't miss the rest of the exciting stories in this series:

**NATURAL BORN DADDY**
(Special Edition #1007), coming in January 1996

**THE COWBOY AND HIS BABY**
(Special Edition #1009), coming in February 1996

**THE RANCHER AND HIS UNEXPECTED DAUGHTER**
(Special Edition #1016), coming in March 1996

**HEARTBREAKERS**

We've got more of the men you love to love in the Heartbreakers lineup this winter. Among them are Linda Howard's Zane Mackenzie, a member of her immensely popular Mackenzie family, and Jack Ramsey, an *Extra*-special hero.

In December—HIDE IN PLAIN SIGHT, by Sara Orwig: Detective Jake Delancy was used to dissecting the criminal mind, not analyzing his own troubled heart. But Rebecca Bolen and her two cuddly kids had become so much more than a routine assignment....

In January—TIME AND AGAIN, by Kathryn Jensen, *Intimate Moments Extra:* Jack Ramsey had broken the boundaries of time to seek Kate Fenwick's help. Only this woman could change the course of their destinies—and enable them both to love.

In February—MACKENZIE'S PLEASURE, by Linda Howard: Barrie Lovejoy needed a savior, and out of the darkness Zane Mackenzie emerged. He'd brought her to safety, loved her desperately, yet danger was never more than a heartbeat away— even as Barrie felt the stirrings of new life growing within her....

INTIMATE MOMENTS®
*Silhouette*

HRTBRK4

*Silhouette*

SPECIAL EDITION™

CELEBRATION 1000

# Nora Roberts

## THE PRIDE OF JARED MACKADE
### (December 1995)

The MacKade Brothers are back! This month,
Jared MacKade's pride is on the line when he
sets his heart on a woman with a past.

If you liked THE RETURN OF RAFE MACKADE (Silhouette
Intimate Moments #631), you'll love Jared's story. Be on
the lookout for the next book in the series, THE HEART OF
DEVIN MACKADE (Silhouette Intimate Moments #697)
in March 1996—with the last MacKade brother's story,
THE FALL OF SHANE MACKADE, coming in April 1996
from Silhouette Special Edition.

These sexy, trouble-loving men
will be heading out to you in
alternating books from Silhouette
Intimate Moments and Silhouette Special Edition.

## HE'S NOT JUST A MAN, HE'S ONE OF OUR

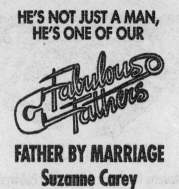

## FATHER BY MARRIAGE
### Suzanne Carey

Investigator Jake McKenzie knew there was more to widowed mom Holly Yarborough than met the eye. And he was right—she and her little girl were *hiding* on her ranch. Jake had a job to do, but how could he be Mr. Scrooge when this family was all he wanted for Christmas?

### Fall in love with our **Fabulous Fathers!**

Coming in December, only from

ROMANCE™

# HAPPY HOLIDAYS!

Silhouette Romance celebrates the holidays with
six heartwarming stories of the greatest gift of all—
love that lasts a lifetime!

**#1120 *Father by Marriage***
**by Suzanne Carey**

**#1121 *The Merry Matchmakers***
**by Helen R. Myers**

**#1122 *It Must Have Been the Mistletoe***
**by Moyra Tarling**

**#1123 *Jingle Bell Bride***
**by Kate Thomas**

**#1124 *Cody's Christmas Wish***
**by Sally Carleen**

**#1125 *The Cowboy and the Christmas Tree***
**by DeAnna Talcott**

## COMING IN DECEMBER FROM

### ▼ *Silhouette* ROMANCE™